Adèle Geras was born in Jerusalem. She was an actress, singer and teacher of French in a girls' school in Manchester before becoming a full-time writer in 1976. Since then she has published more than ninety books for children and young adults, as well as five novels for adults. Adèle lives in Cambridge and has two grown-up daughters and four grandchildren.

Also by Adèle Geras

Facing the Light
A Hidden Life
Hester's Story
Made in Heaven
Cover Your Eyes
Out of the Dark

Love, or Nearest Offer

Adèle GERAS

Quercus

First published in Great Britain in 2016 by Quercus
This paperback edition published in 2016 by

Quercus Editions Ltd
Carmelite House
50 Victoria Embankment
London EC4Y 0DZ

An Hachette UK company

A CIP catalogue record for this book is available
from the British Library

PB ISBN 978 1 78206 609 5
EBOOK ISBN 978 1 78429 540 0

10 9 8 7 6 5 4 3

Typeset by Jouve (UK), Milton Keynes

Printed and bound in Great Britain by Clays Ltd, St Ives plc

For Wendy Cope

Spring

IRIS

There were times when Iris Atkins felt old. Holly and Dom, who worked with her at Robinson & Tyler, estate agents, looked a great deal younger. Holly was twenty-four, a techno whizz, who rode a motorbike and emphasized the teenage look by gelling her hair into forbidding spikes – though they tended to flop by the end of the day. Dom resembled someone from a boy band, which went down well with female customers of a certain age, and even though many people thought he was nineteen, he was, in fact, twenty-nine. I'm only three years older, Iris thought, but I look like his mother. That wasn't quite true, but she certainly qualified as a very much older sister. On good days, she liked to think of herself as a slightly dishevelled Emilia Fox, but today she felt like a small blonde person who hadn't had time to wash her hair before work because she'd been busy having a row with the man who used to be her boyfriend.

There was also this: when her friends started talking about their children, their mortgages or their husbands, Iris realized that being totally unencumbered by such things at the age of thirty-two was much more common than it used to be, but still a little odd. To hear them talk, she thought, anyone would think I was on the shelf, past it, doomed to a single life for ever.

That wasn't strictly true. She'd been living with Neil for more than six months but as of this morning, that was over.

She sighed, gritted her teeth and thought: I'm not going to cry now. She'd kept it together since coming into the office rather late, at half past nine. This morning, almost before they were both properly awake, she and Neil had quarrelled bitterly. She'd thrown as many of her things as she could manage into a suitcase and flung it into the back of her car. 'I missed my shower and you've made me late for work as well,' she'd shouted, as she left the flat. 'Thanks a bunch.'

On the way to Robinson & Tyler, she'd calmed down a bit. Still, today had been awful. She'd sleepwalked through the morning. Fortunately, her only house showing was in an hour, at half past two. Holly and Dom were absorbed in something or other, which was quite unusual for lunchtime on Friday, when work normally began to wind down a little. Bruce was on the phone – Iris could hear him from the other side of the room.

'Ah, well, the chickens are coming home to roost with a vengeance, aren't they?' he said, and chuckled. Clichés were scattered through Bruce's speech, like currants in a bun, but he had a kind heart and a jolly outlook on life. He looked like James Corden but that chummy exterior belied a rather shrewd mind.

Robinson & Tyler was a London-wide firm and their office in Barnet was tiny. Other branches had electronic displays in the window, showing off the best and newest properties, but theirs was still what Bruce liked to call 'reassuringly traditional', which meant a bit grotty. There was a wooden ladder arrangement in the window and it was Holly's job to print out photos of the new houses, and put them up for prospective buyers to see. One of Iris's tasks was to go over the text to make sure it wasn't full of spelling mistakes; Holly had a bit of a blind spot with some words.

Iris's desk was nearest the window. She had a good view of

the coroner's court, St John's Church and a bit of the high street. The office was conveniently situated: Carluccio had just opened a restaurant in the Spires, Barnet's own little shopping mall, which also had branches of Waterstone's, Costa, Starbucks, and even Waitrose. At the back of the Spires, there was a big library. A person hardly needed to go into London at all, and many Londoners were trying to move into this area, which was good news for Robinson & Tyler.

Iris looked at her diary. She was meeting someone called Patrick Taylor at two thirty. There was time to ring her mother, which she ought to do if she was intending to turn up on her doorstep after work. She took a deep breath. June would cut up rough. She loved Neil. She was impressed by him. Well, why wouldn't she be?

Iris had been dumbstruck when she met him. It was at a party to celebrate the new Robinson & Tyler website, which he'd designed. He was handsome, charming and clever. He had his own flat. He designed websites for some very rich customers as well as for estate agents and the like. This meant lots of perks for both of them. Iris had fancied him from the moment she met him. The day he asked her to move in with him had been one of the happiest of her life. They'd got on well. Or, at least, they'd got on well as long as she did what he wanted.

That had been fine for a month or two, but lately she'd become irritated by his control-freakery, as she saw it, but not enough to leave him. The benefits (great sex, fun times, lovely home, exciting travel opportunities) had outweighed the disadvantages, so she'd gone on living with Neil and shrugging off, as best she could, the stuff that annoyed or irritated her. All her friends were at pains to point out that no man was perfect and that there was always, always something to put up with.

What had happened last night and had come to a head this morning was simply Neil being unreasonable. The problem was, he couldn't take no for an answer. Perhaps she was the one at fault. He'd asked her to marry him. He'd produced his mother's engagement ring, and Iris had felt like running out of the flat. What's the matter with me? she wondered. Maybe I'm mad. June will certainly think so. She'll do everything in her power to get me to apologize, change my mind, move back in with him.

But Iris had no intention of changing her mind. She was determined to stand her ground. She dialled her mother's number, feeling more than a little nervous. June would probably still be at work, although Iris was never sure how the shifts operated at the Orchard Hotel, where her mother was one of the receptionists.

'Hello, darling,' said June, answering almost at once. Iris had joked that her iPhone was grafted to her hand. 'What a nice surprise! How's things?'

'Hi, Ma,' Iris said. 'I'm ringing to ask you a favour, actually. Would it be okay if I came to yours after work?'

'Yes, fine, no problem. Where's Neil? Aren't you going out on the town?'

This was it. No going back now. 'Neil and I have had a row. I've left him.'

The silence at the other end went on and on. At last June said, 'Well, I'm sure you'll patch it up, darling. Are you miserable? Of course you can stay.'

'We won't patch it up, Ma. I've left him. I've got a suitcase in the back of my car. I'll ask Neil to bring the other stuff round to yours when I'm out or something.'

June sighed. 'What happened? What was the row about? I'm sure it can be sorted. I'll help, you know.'

'Thanks, but no thanks. He . . . well, he asked me to marry him.'

Her mother's gasp didn't come as a shock. Iris had known that June would react like that. 'Why, for Heaven's sake? When will you ever find anyone half as nice as Neil? What's the matter with you?'

'That's three questions, Ma. I can't go into it now. I'm still at work. I'll tell you everything tonight, okay?'

'I suppose so . . .' June sighed. 'I'll see you later. We can get a takeaway.'

'Fine,' Iris said. 'I'll be there about six.'

What, Iris wondered when she ended the call, am I going to say to her? What are the answers to those questions? She stood up and began to get ready for the viewing with Patrick Taylor.

'You go on home after you've dealt with Mr Taylor, Iris my dear,' said Bruce, as he passed her desk on the way out somewhere. 'You look tired.'

'Thank you,' Iris said, telling herself, not for the first time, that Bruce was kind as well as slightly comical. She was lucky to have him. 'I don't feel all that brilliant, actually.'

'Well, have a good weekend and I hope you're bright-eyed and bushy-tailed on Monday.'

Patrick Taylor turned out to be a tall, dark man in his forties. He didn't say that he was married, but Iris thought he must be because the house they were looking at was a four-bedroom semi. It wasn't half as nice as the details (which she'd written) made out and Iris knew even before she'd got out of the car that it was probably a no-no. Still, people were odd and here he was, this Mr Taylor, so she had to try to sell it.

The windows were ugly and made the place look like someone

with a cross face. The house was too small and too near the main road. And so on. The viewing was probably a complete waste of time, Iris was sure, but she couldn't say so. She knew, from experience, that 'poky' was always a no-no. 'Shabby' was different. If you threw a lot of money and love at a house that had been neglected but was basically beautiful, you could often end up with something amazing. But there was no cure for low ceilings, horrible windows and a view from the front of cars going past. She'd made things sound much better than they were when compiling the details, as she very often had to. She'd called it 'a delightful, conveniently situated 1950s semi-detached dwelling'. Now, she was pretty sure Mr Taylor agreed with her that there was nothing for him here.

Iris went upstairs with him anyway. They were in the back bedroom and there was no hiding the fact that he was looking less than enthusiastic. 'I'm afraid,' he began, and Iris interrupted him.

'I know,' she said. 'It's not great. No worries. I'm sure there are lots of other properties we can show you.'

'Okay.' Patrick Taylor smiled. 'I'm sorry to have wasted your time. I suppose we can call a halt to looking at this place. I need walls.'

Iris laughed. 'I see walls. I see four of them. They're in every room, what's more. They're almost the only good thing about this house.'

He explained: 'I want spaces to hang my pictures. I'm a painter.'

'Really? Do you have time to do much?'

'I'm a professional.'

'You mean painting is your job?'

'That's right. Haven't you met any artists before?'

7

Iris said, 'No, Mr Taylor. You're the first. I'm impressed. If I can find a couple of places to look at, are you free to do that next week? I'll get on to it on Monday.'

'Actually, I'm off to the States for a couple of months. I've got an exhibition coming up. But do email me with any details of likely places. And it's Patrick, by the way, not Mr Taylor.'

'I'm Iris. I'll keep my eyes open for houses with extra good walls.'

They walked down the stairs. Patrick Taylor left first, waving goodbye to Iris as he went. She locked up and followed him outside. They drove, one after the other, into the traffic but Mr Taylor – Patrick – turned off within moments, and Iris made for her mother's house, still trying to work out the answers to June's questions before she had to confront her determined pro-Neil position.

'Right,' said June, as they sat down at the kitchen table with a cup of tea. 'Those questions. I want to know everything.'

Iris took a sip and looked at her mother. She was good about things like this, always had been. She hadn't hassled Iris the minute she came through the door. They'd discussed the takeaway and June was ringing them up as Iris took her suitcase up to her old bedroom. Only once she'd settled in did June sit down, facing her daughter across the table, and a slight feeling of being in a police interview room came over Iris. This was nonsense, of course. June looked like the personification of deep sympathy, as though about to hear news of a bereavement.

'Where to begin?' Iris said, playing for time. 'Well, I've been feeling a bit . . . I don't know . . . for a while.'

'A bit what? What do you mean?'

'Neil's bossy. He likes his own way.'

'Is that all? Lots of men are bossy. You can work round that, surely. What about agreeing and then doing what you wanted to do in the first place? I believe they often don't notice.'

June was at a disadvantage where men were concerned, never having lived with one. Iris hadn't known her father. June had her baby without telling him about her pregnancy, and even though she'd never said 'one-night stand', that was clearly what had happened. June always maintained she had never regretted it. There had been a few men over the years, but none had been serious husband material. Once, when Iris asked her about marrying, June said she didn't see the point. When Iris went to school, the story had been that her dad was dead. So it was a bit odd that June was now so keen on Iris marrying. Should she mention it? Iris decided not to.

'That may be true, but I didn't want to marry him.'

'Why not? What's wrong with him?'

'Nothing, really. But he's . . . overbearing. He didn't understand why I didn't want to marry him. Not now. Not ever.'

'I also don't understand.' June poured herself another cup of tea. 'He's handsome, he's fun, he's not poor, he loves you. What more do you want?'

'I want *less*,' Iris said. 'I don't want to be someone's wife. And, most importantly, I don't want to have children.'

'Then you don't have to,' June said. 'Although—'

'I know! Don't say it. I'm not getting any younger. My biological clock is ticking. That's what you're thinking, isn't it?'

'I don't see that as a deal-breaker. If you wanted to marry him and not have children, why can't you do that? Lots of people don't have children.'

'He really wants them. It wouldn't be fair to him, would it?'

9

'Presumably you said that?'

Iris said, 'Yes, I did. But he said he wanted children with *me*. And I really don't want any.'

'Why ever not?'

Iris didn't answer. It was almost impossible to explain her views on this matter. In many ways she was ashamed of her feelings. They were unnatural. Everything she saw around her, from ads to television programmes to the pronouncements of every single woman she'd ever met led to the same conclusion: women were supposed to be mothers. If you didn't want, ever, to be a mother, there was something wrong with you. Well, Iris thought, maybe I'm peculiar, but that doesn't make any difference. I don't want to spend any time whatsoever looking after a baby, then a child. Now she said, 'I don't know. Selfish, I suppose. That's what all my friends say.'

'But you're glad I didn't think like that, right? I've loved having you. You've been nothing but a pleasure to me your whole life. Don't you want something like that?'

Iris took her mother's hand and squeezed it. 'Of course I'm grateful, and maybe I *will* change my mind one day, but at the moment, I'm afraid the whole prospect is a massive turn-off. I'm not keen on kids. Sorry, Ma. You won't be a granny any time soon.'

'I wasn't keen on kids before I had you. The keenness comes with the child you bear. Not liking children in general makes no difference. Also, you don't have that much time. It gets harder as you get older. I don't just mean having the baby but having the energy to look after a demanding child. That's hard after you're thirty-five or so.'

'Well, I've got some time then, haven't I?' Iris wanted to change the subject. There was more to leaving Neil than just the baby thing.

June tried another tack. 'I don't think this needs to be final, you know,' she said. 'What have you told Neil? Does he think you've left him for ever?'

'I don't know,' Iris answered. 'But he'll get the picture soon enough. I really am not going back to him. There's all sorts of things . . . He tries to control me. We always have to do what *he* feels like doing. He arranges the flat according to *his* taste. He won't let me read in bed after he wants to turn the light off. And on and on. I can't ever eat rubbish. Certain perfumes he can't stand . . .' Her voice trailed away.

June was unconvinced. 'That's small stuff. You can change that. I'm sure you can. Once you're married.'

'You've never been married, though. You don't know how *interfering* a bloke can be. You have no idea what it's like to live with someone who sulks when you don't do what he wants you to do.'

June stood up. 'Okay,' she said. 'I give up. For now. But I won't stop trying to persuade you . . . I really like Neil and I think you're letting a chance of happiness disappear. Anyway, I'm off to bed now. Night-night, darling. Try to sleep well.'

The posters from her teenage days had gone, but otherwise the bedroom was exactly as it had been when she'd left it to go to college. Iris hadn't expected to be back again, lying in a bed that was narrower than she was used to, staring at the three-sided mirror and the dressing-table decorated with a ridiculous flouncy skirt thing. When she was fourteen, Iris had thought it the height of glamour and had nagged June to buy it. Now here it still was, reminding her of how mad teenage taste could be.

What had she dreamed of becoming when she was fourteen? An estate agent wasn't it. She probably hadn't known what one of those was at that age. 'I'd like to be an estate agent when I grow up' wasn't a sentence much heard in school careers offices, Iris was quite sure. Not because it was an unrealistic ambition (*I want to be a ballet dancer. I want to be an astronaut* . . . you heard those the whole time – in primary school) but because it was desperately unglamorous.

The fact that she was happy in her work, Iris knew, was almost odder than not wanting children. She would have been equally tongue-tied if she'd ever had to explain why she loved the job. As she lay in bed, trying not to think about Neil and the row and her mother, and whether there was any point in trying to patch things up with a sort of renegotiated set of assumptions, Iris deliberately turned her attention to Monday's meetings and viewings.

Thinking about her work soothed her. She thought of how important houses were. How the right one could make dreams come true and how the wrong one could wreck someone's entire life. Also – and this was the main thing she couldn't explain to others – she felt she had the power, like the fairy godmother Bruce jokingly said she was, to prevent mistakes and guide her clients towards what would suit them best. Many people thought they knew what they wanted, but very few understood which of the houses they were looking at was the right one for them. They had only a dim idea of what would suit them best, and sometimes they were seriously misguided. But I know, Iris thought. I always know.

AIDAN

It wasn't exactly striding over the fells, or walking around Lake Windermere, but Aidan Church still needed to walk. In the two years since Grace's death, walking to the cemetery and back was something he did often, to visit the grave, tidy it up a bit, and also to keep up some proper walking. Two miles each way, through suburban streets mostly, but towards the end of the journey there were fields on either side of the road, and he always approached the cemetery through them, enjoying the things he had enjoyed all his life: the state of the trees at different seasons; the birdsong, the grass under his feet, covering the dark earth, which was solid and reliable and *there*.

Grace was no longer there. He had loved her for thirty years and now there was nowhere for the love to go, except backwards, examining the life they'd had together, regretting some things, of course. Sins of omission, most of them, like allowing Grace, simply because she was good at such stuff, to run their finances and the day-to-day business of the household. He should have made sure he was, as they said nowadays, up to speed.

He found Grace's grave and stood in front of it, as he did every time, wondering what was expected of him. Prayer was out of the question: even though they'd been married in church, and Grace had had a religious burial, neither of them was a believer. Going to church was a social thing for Grace, but he went because the hymns and prayers had been part of his childhood and he couldn't help loving the language, the ceremony. I'm a historian, he told himself. I love the history, the tradition, even though I'm convinced of the non-existence of a deity, benevolent or otherwise.

He spoke to Grace in his head, as though she were standing beside him. It wasn't exactly speaking because no real words were involved, only a general feeling that what he was thinking was directed at her while he was in front of her headstone. He'd brought some cloths and a small spade in his rucksack and did his best to tidy the plot, marvelling at the tenacity and vigour of weeds and also at the way just being there, standing around in weather of every kind, made the headstone dirty.

Always, on the way home, his thoughts turned to his life without Grace. The rhythm of his steps was soothing to him. In the first few weeks after Grace died, there'd been days when he'd walked for miles because that was the best way to feel even a little normal. It also had the added benefit of tiring him out so that sleep was possible for a few hours at least. He imagined her beside him, as she'd been so often, pointing out things to him he'd never have noticed.

'You're the map person,' she used to say. 'You can tell us where we're going and what route we'll take, but I'm the one for details.'

She was right. Everything he knew now about trees, birds and clouds (it had become quite a lot, over the years) was down to Grace, with her sharp eyes and love of nature.

Once he was back at home, he made himself a cup of tea and took it up to his study.

I'm ready, Aidan thought. I can do it now. For two years, he'd been circling round the subject of moving house. At first, he'd wanted only to hide, had spent months in a state of unhappy hibernation, but now, without making a conscious effort, as far as he could tell, he was beginning to feel something inside him changing. When he tried to analyse it, the only image that came to mind was Arctic ice breaking up in spring. Grief had been icy cold. You had to brace yourself against it. These days, he felt warmer. He could go for hours now without checking his state of mind. He could think about his life with some degree of calm. He even admitted, though he felt treacherous doing so, a measure of satisfaction, if not exactly happiness, in being able to choose something, in getting ready to take action off his own bat. The question was, where did he want to live? Grace had been very emphatic about his options and, typically, had set about organizing his life as a widower.

'You don't want to rattle around here,' she'd announced. 'You must sell and move to somewhere more manageable. Farnley Estates are building lovely houses. High spec. Very near Barnet, but also near the countryside. One of those would be perfect for you.' He'd nodded. You couldn't, he'd thought, argue with the terminally ill, so he'd said nothing. Grace was only thinking of his welfare. She'd been looking after him for more than thirty years, so there was no reason for her to stop just because she was dying. There were times when Aidan was bemused at everything Grace knew about such matters. How had she discovered all that stuff? True, she was great peruser of the local paper. He'd never understood what she found to read in it, but it was full of property news and Grace had clearly been taking notice.

The last twenty-six months had dragged unbearably but also

flown by. Maybe both at the same time: how did that work? He looked around his study and wondered what his late wife would say if she walked into it now. The desk chair was one of those that leaned back and he hardly ever tilted it into a reclining position, preferring to be sitting forward, bent over the laptop, peering into the glow of the screen. Now, though, he leaned back and stared at the ceiling, which, if he was honest, could have done with a coat of paint.

He'd never given a thought to the decorative state of the house while Grace was alive. She was in charge of that side of things. To tell the truth (and he *had* been telling himself the truth much more often lately), what he mostly did was attend to his own work, which involved nothing more than reading, writing, moving bits of paper from one surface to another and emailing colleagues. He did a great deal of thinking, of course. He went for long walks, thinking. He sat in front of a blank screen, trying to write but doing very little of it, compared to the hours and hours he spent staring into space. Also, there was the time he spent online, reading the latest research.

Sometimes he gave himself a treat and went into London to the Imperial War Museum or the British Film Institute. Grace used to meet him there. It was one of the things they'd always loved to do together. Before they were married, they used to walk over Hungerford Bridge, their footsteps making a racket on the metal. Going by himself wasn't the same. He'd arranged once or twice to meet a friend, but hadn't enjoyed those outings. His thoughts had kept straying to home, where he knew that Grace was dealing with pain, weakness and his own absence, so he'd simply stopped going. There were plenty of good films on TV.

I could go again now, he thought. There was much he could

do, now that he was on his own. At first, the idea had terrified him. In the weeks following Grace's death, he had been almost too busy to grieve. Her younger sister, Peggy, came to stay with him, leaving her family in Aberdeen, and had sorted through what she called 'the difficult things'. Aidan was grateful to her for attending to the clothes and personal effects. He wouldn't have been capable of doing that. Every garment kept Grace's fragrance. Every scarf smelt of her favourite perfume, whose name he didn't know but would have been able to identify anywhere.

Peggy had arranged the funeral. She'd seen to everything. Aidan smiled to himself when he remembered it now. Clearly the organizational gene was very strong in that family. After a couple of weeks his sister-in-law went back to Scotland, and then the staff at the school where Grace had been secretary for twenty years had come into their own, bringing round casseroles and inviting him to their homes from time to time. He was grateful to them – on one level, he couldn't have coped without them – but whenever he did go out, he was always glad to come home, to settle into the space he'd grown used to. The marital bed.

Was it wrong still to be sleeping in that bed? Grace had died in hospital after a stroke, so there was nothing morbid about it but, still, the memories Aidan had of lying in it were filled with pain: Grace's pain before she was taken to hospital, and his own at being completely powerless to make it better. The happy memories, of sex, laughter and reading in bed together (Grace on her Kindle, him with an ancient second-hand copy of some hardback), had disappeared.

After the funeral, there had been letters to answer, financial stuff to sort out. If I'd died, Aidan reflected, she'd have dealt with everything without any fuss, and the house would be spick and span. She might already have started to go out, see people and get on with her life.

'You had a chance to grieve together,' his friends told him, 'to sort things out and see what needed to be done.' Aidan had nodded and agreed. The time they'd had together, the months between the terminal diagnosis and the day of Grace's death, had indeed been both precious and useful. He doubted he'd have had any idea of what to do if she hadn't taken him through it in her thorough way and revealed to him the secrets of her filing cabinet. Throughout the years they were married, that piece of furniture had been a source of mystery and power . . . They used to laugh about it. It was known as the Black Tower and it contained what Grace called 'My Systems': banking details, building-society bumph, tax returns, house specifications, guarantees for all the white goods and electrical appliances – the thousands of bits of paper that had come through the door over more than three decades.

But now he was lonely. It had taken him till now to admit it to himself. Or, at least, to use the word 'lonely' in relation to himself. He'd experienced what it was like to be entirely alone in the world but shied away from giving it a label. But, yes, he told himself. I am lonely. How did that happen? Aidan prided himself on being interested in many things. He liked people. He'd got on well with his colleagues while he was still teaching and he had friends, but they'd all dispersed to different parts of the country or to the far reaches of London, and somehow it was hard to meet up. At the age we are, Aidan reflected, all people's spare time is taken up with visiting their children and grandchildren.

It was supposed to be women who regretted not having

children, but Grace had never made a huge fuss about it. Nowadays they might have considered IVF, and even back then there was adoption, but Grace hadn't been keen, and she'd had enough contact with the children at school for her infertility somehow not to matter to her. Perhaps she'd never wanted children as much as he had. The way things were now, he was conscious of the gap where their children should have been.

Aidan returned his chair to its normal position and looked at the mess on his desk. Grace had systems and he had chaos. She'd found his mess rather endearing and hadn't often nagged him to tidy up, get his head together, get himself sorted. Instead, it had been clear that she'd enjoyed being in total command of everything. And I colluded, Aidan thought now. I'm lazy, and I liked her being in charge. I liked being able to leave everything practical to her and lose myself in looking at things that happened long ago to other people. History.

Before his early retirement, three years ago, he'd taught history in a local college. There were things about his job that annoyed him (the admin, some of his colleagues, some of his students) but, on the whole, he was happy passing on what he'd learned about the past. He had started a research project of his own, not imagining for one second that it would take over his whole working life. The anniversary of the First World War was looming. On a visit to his home village in Cambridgeshire, he'd stood in front of the war memorial at the junction of two main roads and looked at the fading wreaths gathered at its base. He'd read the names and imagined the young men: they would have been just like the young men who were at that moment sitting outside the pub, laughing, drinking pints. It came to him in a flash of what he'd described to Grace at the time as inspiration. He'd look into those names. He'd find out, or try to find out, about those particular people. He'd write an account of the war dead from this one place. And from that day to this, being able to go back to thinking about those soldiers gave him comfort. While Grace had grown thinner and paler and weaker, while the morphine doses had become stronger and stronger, going back in his mind to the mud of the trenches had helped him. *If it's happening to them, it's not happening to me . . . or to my darling wife.*

He picked up the phone – which people now called the landline. Apparently, landlines were going to disappear. Aidan had a mobile but he often left it in another room, or lost it between the sofa cushions. It had a habit of sliding out of his trouser pocket. The landline was good for times when he needed to have his wits about him, like now. On the face of it, it wasn't a difficult call to make but, still, Aidan felt a sort of shyness about making it.

Grace had left a hardback A5 notebook full of useful things. Just after her death, her handwriting had caused him physical pain, but he could read it nowadays with only a slight catch of the breath. He found 'ESTATE AGENT'S NUMBER FOR FARN-LEY ESTATES HOUSES'.

Then he hesitated. What on earth was he doing? What was wrong with this house? They'd lived in it for more than twenty years. It was set in beautiful Hertfordshire countryside. There was a small orchard at the bottom of the garden. Could you call six trees an orchard? There was a shed, currently full of Grace's gardening stuff, which he should have made some effort to use by now, but hadn't. You don't garden, he told himself. The garden is neglected. The house is neglected. There was no reason he couldn't take it all on and get someone in to fix things. To decorate. To tidy the garden. He could replace the old furniture. Still, as Grace hadn't failed to point out to him, he would rattle around in such a big place. How many rooms did he go into now? The study, the kitchen, his bedroom, the sitting room, but only when he wanted to watch television, which wasn't all that often. He felt a fool, sitting in front of the box (and it was a box, an antique in telly terms) by himself, with his hands folded on his lap. A man in a room, with his eyes on a screen emitting a bluish light. Nowadays, he watched most programmes on his Mac, either lying in bed or sitting on his comfortable chair in the study.

Nothing for it. 'Hello? Is that Robinson & Tyler?'

'Yes. My name's Iris Atkins. How can I help you, sir?'

'Um. I want . . . that is, I'm thinking of moving . . . of selling my house.'

The young woman laughed. 'Well, you've come to exactly the right place. Do you know what sort of property you're looking for?'

Aidan liked the sound of Iris Atkins. No doubt she was trained to be the same to all prospective customers, but he felt as though she was properly interested in knowing what he wanted. So he told her, at far greater length than necessary. His speech – it felt like a speech – was full of references to Grace. 'My wife . . . my late wife . . .' He could hear himself saying it far too frequently.

'Don't worry, Mr Church,' said Ms Atkins. 'I've taken some notes of what you've told me, but would it be possible for you to come in and talk to me here? I think we ought to sort out the paperwork and then, of course, I'll visit you. And the house, of course, because we'll need to take some good photographs.'

They made an appointment for the next day. Aidan was relieved that he wasn't going to have to spend hours right now tidying up the house for a visitor. But it hadn't occurred to him that he'd need to make the place attractive for photographs. He decided to cross that bridge when he came to it. Tomorrow afternoon he would go in and meet Iris Atkins. He was quite looking forward to it, but acknowledged that he was nervous about her coming to him. He chided himself for being ridiculous. She won't be visiting you, he told himself. She's going to look at the house. She's going to take photographs. His home of the last twenty-odd years would soon be on one of those sheets of paper stuck in an estate agent's window. Aidan didn't know how he felt about that, but he was quite sure that Grace, if she was somehow looking at him from an afterlife, which he didn't for one moment believe, would be smiling with satisfaction.

VINA

'Vina? Is this a good time?'

'Not really, Geoff, no,' she said. She was standing in the garden wishing, as she'd started to wish more and more often, that the mobile phone had never been invented. She'd come outside on the first day of sunshine for ages to look at how things were in the garden. The first snowdrops were out. Tiny green spikes of what would be the most gorgeous tulips ('Big Eartha', 'Going Baroque', 'Flaming Spring Greens', 'Angélique') had appeared in the pots she'd grouped together on the flagstones at the back of the house. Vina doggedly refused to refer to this part of her garden, even in her head, as a 'patio'.

'Where are you?'

'It's none of your business. We're divorced, Geoff,' she added wearily.

'I know, I know . . . but I just thought I'd ring for a chat.'

'What's the matter?' It was not like her ex to ring for a chat. What did they have to chat about? He'd left her ten years ago for a woman he'd met while he was checking in at Heathrow.

'I thought we might have a meal together. How are you fixed?'

'I'm busy,' said Vina, despairingly. He was fishing for an invitation to dinner. He missed her cooking. She never asked about what was happening in his life but suspected that his second wife, whose name was Gloria, might have left him. 'Has Gloria left you?' she asked. The days when she thought about sparing his feelings had long gone.

'I'm not sure . . . Can I come and have dinner with you sometime? I'll tell you all about it. What happened.'

'I'm not that interested, Geoff. But, yes, I suppose you can come and eat. Next Monday. How's that?'

It gave her almost a week before she had to sit down with him.

'Can't you do any other night? How about tomorrow?'

'No, Geoff. I'm busy. It's Monday or nothing. Take it or leave it.' She wanted to add: *No skin off my nose if you do leave it.*

Grumbling and muttering, Geoff rang off at last. Vina sighed and sat down at the wrought-iron garden table. This afternoon she was going into Barnet to have a chat with Iris Atkins. She and a colleague, whose name she hadn't caught, had been to the house last week and taken photographs for the website and the leaflets that Robinson & Tyler were going to produce. She'd been sent the photos by email already and had given the go-ahead. Perhaps they'd be ready by three o'clock this afternoon . . .

Would she miss the garden? When Geoff walked out on her, ten years ago, and started divorce proceedings, he'd put the property in her name and paid off the rest of the mortgage. That generous gesture had made him feel less guilty, she supposed, and at the time she'd been grateful. The house was too big now. She wanted somewhere that didn't take hours to clean. Somewhere modern, perhaps a new-build, but she did want a garden. I'll miss this when I go, she thought, especially the pond.

Geoff had been scathing about that, she remembered. He'd

been scathing about a lot of things. He'd infected their children with his scathingness, if that was a word. Robert and Libby both smiled whenever the pond was mentioned, indulging their mother. *Mum's mad idea* . . . That was how Rob had described it back when she was still planning it. Her son was grown-up now, married to Janice; they both worked as solicitors for a firm in Guildford. Rob was thirty-two, which made Vina feel ancient. She liked Janice and got on with her perfectly well, but felt, probably with no justification, that the younger woman had judged and found her inadequate in some way.

Libby was only twenty-five and lived in Cornwall in a tiny cottage, which was picturesque and uncomfortable in every possible way: cold, dark, perhaps even damp. Low ceilings. Crooked doorways. A staircase that Vina took ages to negotiate because she was so terrified of losing her footing on the uneven treads. It was straight out of the gloomier bits of Thomas Hardy, she thought, but didn't say. You didn't object to things that Libby did. She'd learned that the hard way. From early childhood, Libby had been an Olympic-standard tantrum-thrower.

I should have been tougher, she thought, and Geoff should have been tougher, but it was too late now: their cowardice (anything for a quiet life) had turned their daughter into a charming-if-she-felt-like-making-the-effort but completely spoilt jeweller who lived by herself in a hovel almost as far as it was possible to be from both her parents. She was not only spoilt, but also irritating in other ways. She had very little energy when it came to things like publicizing her work, and trying to sell it to shops. This meant that she was not nearly as successful as she should have been. *Feeble* was the word Vina would have used to describe her. Dynamism was missing from her character. Vina could manage a telephone relationship with her daughter reasonably well and it was only when she was being particularly honest with herself that she admitted how relieved she was, in her heart of hearts, that Libby didn't live round the corner.

Well, she thought, they can be as scornful as they like. The pond was the best thing she'd done in the garden. It was small, true, but she'd managed to get waterlilies to grow there. There were three fish, too. Golden ones that came to the surface when they heard her coming and waited for their food. She'd given them names, Nemo, Tiddler and Dora, and regarded them as her pets, though she'd never said so to Rob and Libby. They would laugh at her. She had a reputation in the family for being soft-hearted and sentimental. Well, that wasn't untrue but what was wrong with loving your fish, with wanting to care for flowers and plants? What was wrong with waiting for the roses to come out every year, and rejoicing when they did? Nothing, Vina thought now. There's nothing wrong with it but I stopped telling Geoff and the children long ago what the garden means to me.

She got up and went inside. The kitchen could do with a makeover, she could see, but what was the point of modernizing it if she wanted to move? Even Iris Atkins thought it would be sensible to see if the house sold before resorting to renovations that might not be to the taste of a prospective buyer.

Vina had spent ages before the photographic session cleaning the place from top to bottom and tidying it in a way that it had never been tidied before. It was an Edwardian semi-detached. Two big reception rooms, big kitchen, utility room, four bedrooms (three doubles), attic, cellar and a beautiful garden. The ceilings were high and the rooms perfectly proportioned. The house had been built in 1910 and the original stained glass was still in every room, as a decoration at the top of the long windows and in all the internal doors as well as the front door. When the sun shone during the afternoon, pools of coloured light filled the hall.

There were times when Vina wondered why she was trying to sell it, and then she remembered: it was too big for one person. It cost too much to heat. The insulation dated from the early twentieth century and Geoff used to say they were heating the garden, which wasn't far from the truth. Also, it seemed to Vina sometimes that every speck of dust she moved simply wafted through the air and settled again on the same surface. The memories in this house, she told herself, are not entirely happy, either. She could admit that now.

She went upstairs to get ready to go into Robinson & Tyler. Vina neither liked nor disliked her looks. She peered into the mirror as she put on her lipstick. There she was: dark, with a scattering of grey in her hair. A good haircut. Good skin. Hazel eyes. Her own teeth. Not bad for fifty-seven. She spent money on expensive makeup, too, and liked clothes. She loved jewellery: she often wore Libby's creations and was happy to do that. Her daughter could be a pain, and sometimes even worse than a mere pain, but the earrings and necklaces Vina wore made not one but two statements. The first was *I have marvellous taste and, what's more, can afford designer jewellery* and the second, even more important, *I am proud of my daughter.*

IRIS

Whenever Iris met her friends for a meal, she was always the first person to arrive at the restaurant. She was punctual by nature, but working for Robinson & Tyler had made her even more anxious not to keep anyone waiting. Bruce had been clear on that part of her job: 'You've got to be there before the client,' he'd told her on her first day at work. 'If you're late, even by a minute or two, you risk them running away, getting fed up or just not forming the best impression of you.'

Iris's friends, Penny, Marilynne and Anne – the four had been a gang ever since their schooldays – would have cut her some slack but she was still punctual and still able to watch them come in one by one. Marilynne was the first to join her. She was tall, redheaded and quite bossy, and since they were fourteen had behaved as though she were the leader of the group. And we fell in with that, Iris thought, as she got up to greet her. Anne and Penny arrived a few moments later. Anne was dark, with very pale skin and blue eyes. She was, by common agreement, the sensible one, and Penny was small and fair, like Iris but prettier. She was the one they all regarded as completely incapable of malice; the good one. Iris was the dreamer, the creative one, on the basis of some talent in domestic science and sewing lessons. No one had ever allocated them these descriptions, but Iris knew that the invisible labels were there.

She was ready for tonight. It had been a couple of weeks since she and Neil had split up and her single state, announced to the others by email, would be the main topic of conversation. The four of them used to meet all the time: in bars and restaurants after work. They went to the seaside together on weekends; donkey's years ago they'd done Ibiza together. They'd known one another so long that they never had to watch what they said when they were together.

Lately, though, things had changed. The other three had married and had children, and though they came out for a curry from time to time and invited Iris to their houses constantly, she was aware of not being in the married/maternal/primary school loop. They tried to include her and, of course, she took an interest. She had been a bridesmaid three times. She'd bought presents for babies. She'd cooed and admired. But she noticed that the occasions when they did get together, just the four of them without husbands and babies, were fewer and further between, and not only that, but while they were eating or drinking, there were always texts going back and forth to the person left holding the baby at home. Their phones were on the table next to their plates and they couldn't resist glancing at them occasionally. Checking.

For quite a while, though, on this occasion, Iris noticed that all three of her friends were concentrating on her.

'You can't have left Neil,' said Marilynne. 'I don't believe it.'

'It's true, though,' Iris said, breaking a poppadom in a gesture she hoped would demonstrate how decisive and tough she was. 'I told you in the email. I've split up with Neil. More than split up. I've moved out.'

'Moved out? Of that flat?' Penny was easily impressed, and Neil had made a fuss of her when she'd come round to visit them. She'd been star-struck ever since. It had crossed Iris's mind that Neil fancied her. They were the same type, and men were very stuck in their ways, most of them. She could still recall every detail of the row she and Neil had had when she'd left and which Iris had never mentioned to Penny.

'Yup!' she said, in answer to Penny's question. 'No more lovely flat. Are we ready to order?'

A waiter was standing quietly beside them with a pad in his hand. No sooner had they ordered than Anne said, 'So, where are you living?'

'With my mum.'

They all gasped. Iris could see where they were coming from. To them, leaving home in the first place had been an achievement. To go back would represent total abject failure.

Marilynne, typically, had the cheek to say so. Not in so many words, but as good as. 'Back in your mum's house? Really?' she asked. 'Can't you find somewhere of your own? Don't tell me you can't afford it.' The subtext of this was: *You've no one to take care of but yourself, whereas I, and anyone else with kids, have many more calls on my income.*

'I probably could afford it but I can't spare the time to look and choose and so on right now. Don't look so shocked. June's taken down the eighties posters. And she's a good cook. I'll find a place of my own, don't worry. Eventually.'

'But Neil . . . He's so . . .' Penny began.

'He's overbearing and controlling. He proposed to me.'

This provoked general squeaks. 'I said no,' Iris added. More squeaks, this time with a few sighs mixed in.

'Honestly, Iris, you're mad. He'd be a perfect husband. Why on earth did you say no? We thought you were real lovebirds.'

Penny glanced left and right at Anne and Marilynne. 'Didn't we say that?'

Iris wasn't in the least annoyed that they'd discussed her and her life. She knew very well that when only three of them were together, the fourth was always the main topic of discussion.

'I'm sure you did say that. Many times. But you didn't know him like I did. He wanted me to get married and have children. At once. He said my biological clock was ticking. Can you credit it?' No one said anything. 'Oh, God. You agree with him. I can see you do.'

The others had the grace to look shamefaced. The food came then, which was fortunate because the faffing with who was having what and distributing the rice and condiments gave everyone time to regroup.

Eventually, they started eating and Marilynne spoke for the other two. 'Face it, Iris. Neil is right. You're over thirty . . . and, okay, I know loads of women leave having their first baby till they're forty but it's not ideal.' She looked at Penny and Anne for support. 'You need stamina for small babies, and by the time you're forty, well, you just don't have the energy you had as a very young woman, right?'

'I don't need energy,' Iris said. 'Having babies is not part of my plan at the moment. Not with Neil and not with anyone else.'

Three mouths literally dropped open. Prawn bhutan and chicken balti became much too visible and Iris turned her attention to an onion bhaji, which she began dissecting with the forensic skills of a police pathologist.

'But why?' Anne dared to ask.

Iris had to answer this without hurting anyone's feelings. She would have to be diplomatic. She took a deep breath. 'Well,' she said at last, 'I want to be able to do what I like. I suppose you'd say I'm being selfish.' This was to pre-empt them: they were sure to say that. 'I want to travel,' she went on. 'I want to be able to get up and move to some totally different part of the world on a whim. I want to be—'

Typically, Marilynne didn't wait to hear the rest of Iris's arguments. She waded in with exactly what Iris was expecting: the loneliness argument. 'Who's going to look after you when you're old?'

That was always the clincher. As an only child who actually loved her mother, Iris felt she could speak with some authority. 'It may be true that a child would make my last years more . . . well, not more pleasant but maybe less difficult. But . . . not everyone likes their mother, do they? To some children, being burdened with an ancient parent would be hell. I mean, I'd look after June, of course I would, because I love her, but I can't pretend I'm looking forward to it. What about the three of you? Are you gagging to have your mums move into your houses? Or to spend every waking hour traipsing back and forth to look after them in their own? Or in a care home?'

This was problematic stuff and Iris noticed that all three of her dearest friends moved the terrain of the discussion. Again, Marilynne spoke for the others. 'But it's not just about the end of life. Children are wonderful. We couldn't live without them. You do not know . . . You just *do not know* . . .' here she paused for effect and turned to the other two mothers at the table to support her . . . 'what love is till you've had a baby. You just have no idea.' She looked down at her phone, which was buzzing – thankfully she'd managed to eat quite a lot of her beef dhansak. 'Oh, God, sorry, I've got to go. Mickey's woken up and he's crying for me. Be in touch, Iris. Bye, you lot!' She took a twenty-pound note out of her purse and put it on the table. 'Tell me if it's more, eh? Iris, I'll phone you, okay?'

'Okay!' Iris said, relieved that she didn't have to respond to what Marilynne had said. Once she'd gone, they dropped the subject of Iris and her childlessness, turning instead to a detailed examination of Marilynne's mothering style. The others found quite a lot to object to, and Iris just listened. In her opinion (and she didn't breathe a word of this), every one of their children had nightmarish elements in their different ways, even while being (of course!) sweet and lovely and brilliant and small miracles, all three of them.

'Who've you got this afternoon, Iris?'

Iris could see that Bruce had a whole load of things for her to do, out of the office.

'I'm seeing this chap at two thirty. He rang me . . . His name is . . .' she turned her desk calendar round '. . . Aidan Church. Looking for one of the new-builds on Farnley Estate, I think. He's a widower. Wants to move from a biggish place near—'

'Okay, as you were, then. As you were. And don't forget you've got Mrs Brownrigg at three o'clock. She's going to be asking what we're doing to get her house looked at by more people. And make an appointment with Mr Church for photos. We need to get all pics up on the website sharpish.'

'*We* means *me*, right?' Iris smiled at Bruce to show that she wasn't in the least resentful but, on the contrary, very happy to oblige.

'Copy that,' he said, and made for his own desk. He watched, in Iris's opinion, far too many boxed sets about dangerous people in America.

She'd come into the office early and was therefore on top of all her admin. There was a great deal of admin, too, every day. There were houses, plus clients trying to buy and to sell, lots of them and some with unrealistic desires and hopes of money from the sale that would never be fulfilled. Iris tried to be even-handed and give everyone the same amount of attention, but at any time, there were always some customers she became involved with to a far greater extent. There were also some properties that spoke to her, and when it came to these, she was passionate about seeing the right people inhabiting them. Sometimes a horrible family would move into a really wonderful house and that always made her feel a bit of a failure. Of course, there were many instances of people making avoidable mistakes but Iris did her best.

She'd mentioned this once to her friends and was surprised by how interested they were.

'What do you mean, mistakes?' Anne had asked.

'You know,' said Iris, 'someone retires from a job in the City, say, and decides that a cottage by the sea is his heart's desire, not realizing how much he'll miss the people, the bustle and the crowds of London, which he's probably been moaning about for years. Or young married couples, who don't understand that the house they've set their heart on will be a nightmare when kids are born. Or a woman who thinks she'll feel better if she moves away from where her three sisters and elderly mother live round the corner – they've been driving her mad – doesn't reckon with how much she's going to have to spend on travel when her mother falls ill and she has to cope because her siblings have high-powered jobs. I could go on.'

Marilynne had chipped in: 'Isn't that what all estate agents are meant to do? I mean, isn't that part of the job description?'

Iris had smiled brightly to hide her annoyance. Marilynne had been making her achievements seem petty since they were girls but Iris always tried to assume she meant it affectionately. Maybe she did, but Iris's opinion of her was lower than it had been before that remark.

'Well,' she'd said, 'perhaps they should, but lots of them don't. I, on the other hand, have the gift to an almost supernatural degree.' And she had grinned to show that she'd been joking, though she hadn't. Not really. Bruce had given her the Fairy Godmother nickname because, as he put it, 'Iris finds the houses that make people's dreams come true. Their dream houses.'

Now she went back to dealing with today's work. But, sure enough, no sooner had she turned on her laptop than Holly was gesticulating from her desk, clutching the phone and indicating that Iris needed to take the call. There were several people she hoped it wasn't but it turned out to be Josie Forster. Iris remembered Josie's red-gold curls, and the freckles on her nose. She was small and friendly, and they had liked one another. Iris was pleased she'd rung back. She, her husband and small son Zak (very lively, but cute) lived in a most desirable-sounding property: a third-floor riverside flat near London Bridge with views Iris could only imagine but was longing to see. Josie had been visiting a friend in Barnet and had come into the office a few days ago (purely on impulse it seemed, as she was passing the branch) and poured out her heart. She wanted to move to somewhere less glamorous but more suitable for children. Somewhere with a garden. She wanted more children. She wasn't sure if her husband did. Zak wanted a dog. He'd played with Dominic while he was in Iris's office with his mother, but Dom was almost as much of a boy as Zak and they'd had a good time whizzing the paper aeroplanes Dom made around the room. Bruce had been out at the time.

35

'Hello, Mrs Forster,' Iris said.

'Josie, please,' she said. 'I feel like my mother-in-law if I'm called Mrs Forster.'

'Josie,' Iris said. 'How can I help you? Have you discussed things with your husband?'

'Not yet. But I will . . . I was just wondering whether you could come and look at the flat. Value it, you know. So that I have some real facts to show Will.'

'Have you thought about asking an estate agent nearer where you live?' Iris said, frowning.

'But could you do it? I think this area is lovely and some of the houses in your window are . . . well, could you do it?'

'Certainly. There's no reason why not, especially if you are thinking of buying up here. When would suit you?'

They arranged a date and time a couple of days hence and Iris hung up. She decided to get Bruce to come with her, then made a note to go on to the property websites later and see how much a top-n▬▬▬▬▬de flat would fetch. Well over two million, she thought. Josie had made it sound like something an oligarch or prince might live in. Selling such a property would be a bit of a triumph for their little branch of R & T. Maybe Bruce would raise her salary. She needed to save now, more than ever, and buy her own place.

Iris liked living with June and she liked not having to worry about cooking. Also, Neil had stopped nagging her.

June was still trying to persuade her daughter that she'd made a terrible mistake, and Iris had tried several times to make her see that she was not going back to him.

While the two of them were talking, June managed to agree with Iris, but then, a few days later, she'd be back on the subject, pointing out this or that advantage to be had in Iris marrying Neil. Iris was clear that that was never going to happen. He could send messages and texts and even roll up to June's house unexpectedly but she was determined not to soften. It irritated her more than she could politely express every time she saw Neil's car in front of the gate but she was powerless to prevent it.

'He's come to see me,' June said. 'Come in and have a cuppa, Neil dear.'

Iris could cheerfully have throttled her mother at such times. As it was, she herself said nothing inflammatory, but smiled at Neil and either went straight out of the front door to drive somewhere – anywhere – or made her excuses, went upstairs and shut her bedroom door behind her.

And June complained every single time. At first she used to say, 'Well, it doesn't matter that you've broken up, you might at least be polite and exchange a few words. He's not exactly throwing you over his horse and riding off with you into the sunset, is he? It's just a cup of tea, wh— another t and done.'

'But I don't want to see him,' Iris said. 'He's putting pressure on me. It's not just a cup of tea to him. If I sat down with the two of you, nattering away, he'd think there was hope. And there isn't. Not a jot.'

June sucked her teeth, which annoyed Iris even more. She knew before the words were spoken what her mother was going to say and, sure enough, she said it: 'You're not getting any younger, you know.'

'How many times are you going to say that? I've heard it before, Ma. I am *not* going back to Neil. Turn your attention to something else, okay? Please get used to it. Neil's a fool, thinking he can reach me through you. He'll get the message eventually.'

June gave a sigh that Iris felt would have broken the heart of any normal daughter so she changed the subject. 'What have you done with the remote?' she asked, and turned on the TV to watch the latest episode of *Mad Men*. Don Draper seemed able always to lull June into a starry-eyed silence.

More recently, after about three weeks of to-ing and fro-ing with June and Neil and too many phone calls, Iris and Neil had reached a state that she thought of as *cool friendship*. Which was fine. She was now able to answer the occasional email from him without feeling as though she had lost a war she'd been fighting. We are, Iris told herself, like neutral acquaintances, though he still fancied her. And if she was being completely honest with herself, there were ways in which Iris missed him too.

'Hello, Miss Atkins?'

Iris shook herself into the present and looked up to see a tall, grey-haired man standing at her desk. 'That's me. You must be Mr Church. Do take a seat.'

He looked quite nervous. He sat down and coughed. Iris had seen this before: people much older than she was looking quite apprehensive about talking to her. She had no idea why this should be. She wasn't intimidating. Once she'd asked Bruce about it, and he'd said, 'Well, they think you're in charge. They're putting their lives in your hands, if you look at it in a certain way. This is probably the most important thing they've ever done, bought a house or looked to sell a house. You can make a huge difference to them, so no wonder they're a bit scared. They don't know what you've got up your sleeve. You're holding their future in your hands.'

Now she said to Mr Church, 'Let me take down the details, address and so forth.'

Going over the facts, getting them down on paper, often

relaxed the client. By the time they had finished, and Iris had explained what R & T were going to do for their fee, she and Mr Church were practically best friends. They arranged a time for her to go and take photographs of his house.

'Thank you, Miss Atkins,' he said, and smiled. 'I feel much easier in my mind now. I'll look forward to seeing you soon.'

He stood up and shook Iris's hand. She liked him. He was a good-looking man of about sixty, with a resemblance to Clint Eastwood, but milder, more English and wearing glasses. His jacket was tweedy, his handshake firm and when he smiled, his teeth were good. His wife had died two years ago and they were childless. He didn't say so in so many words, but Iris suspected that he was lonely and resolved to do her very best for him. As Bruce would have put it: she'd *go the extra mile*.

As he left the office, Davina Brownrigg was coming in. Mr Church held the door open for her. Iris smiled to herself. He was clearly a real old-fashioned gentleman. Mrs Brownrigg thanked him. Then she came over to Iris's desk and sat down. Over her shoulder, Iris could see Mr Church looking through the window at both of them and couldn't help smiling.

JOSIE

Josie picked up her wine glass from the spotless marble counter and went to look at Zak. His door was open, just enough to let her see him: his adorable curly head, his perfect skin, his pink mouth . . . She didn't have the words to describe what she felt. Love wasn't enough. Love didn't quite fit the melting, terrified, protective, enslaved feeling she had when she looked at her sleeping son. She wanted to pick him up and kiss him and hug him and fold him into her . . . Oh, God, it was definitely time to have another baby. No child should have the burden of this much love lavished on him. It was too much. *Keep him safe*, she wished fervently. *Let him be okay*. She wasn't a believer in any God but that didn't stop her pleading with *something* to guard her beloved child from all possible harm.

She and Zak had made friends before bed. You always had to make up any arguments or fights or disagreements before you went to sleep. Josie believed this and would never let the sun go down on her wrath. She put it in those terms because that was what her mother used to tell her.

And tonight had been worse than usual. She'd actually lost it. Yelled and screamed like a fishwife (again, her mother's phrase).

She sat down on Zak's bed, smoothing the fluffy mohair blanket, loving the different colours of the squares. She remembered buying it with Will just before their son was born, enchanted by the muted colours, too many to count. She also remembered the eye-watering price tag and the way Will hadn't even glanced at it before handing over his credit card. It was at that moment she had understood that her husband earned what he called *serious money*.

After their row, she'd taken Zak's hand and said, 'I'm sorry I shouted at you, darling. I was frightened.'

'And angry.'

'Yes, Zak, I was very angry. But I was angry because I was frightened.'

'Why?' Zak wanted to know.

'Because you *know* you're not allowed on the balcony on your own without me or Daddy being there. Isn't that the rule?'

Zak had nodded. 'Sorry,' he said, and Josie threw her arms round him and pulled him close. She was finding it hard to hold back the tears. She ought never to have lost her temper. She'd run to the balcony, grabbed him by the arm, quite roughly, and almost dragged him into the flat. Her heart was thudding so loudly that she hardly heard Zak's rage. He'd shouted and thrown himself on the floor and writhed about like a soul in torment but eventually they'd both calmed down. And now, after a soothing bath and some macaroni cheese, he was in bed and asleep. Which was when he was easiest to love.

Josie returned to the kitchen and worried about what she was going to say to Will. How he'd react. She had to tell him. Not just about Zak and what had happened today on the balcony but also about going to see Robinson & Tyler. About how determined she was to move out of this place. It was a deathtrap.

'How can you say that? You weren't even bloody here. You're never here . . .'

'Oh, so that's what this is about!' Will Forster sat down heavily on the long leather sofa that divided the dining part of the room from the sitting area. 'Me. How seldom I'm here.'

'Well, that's true, too, but it's not what I mean. How dare you put the blame on me?'

'Well, it certainly wasn't me who left the door to the balcony unlocked,' Will said.

Josie was at the far end of the room, the kitchen, slamming plates into the dishwasher as though they were unbreakable. She shouted, 'You're fucking impossible, do you know that?' She threw a fork into the machine and strode over to where her husband was lying. 'Get up. Just sit up and talk to me properly for a change. I want to talk to you seriously.'

'What are we going to talk about? Now that you've finished yelling at me.'

'You have *no idea* – just *no idea* – what it's like for me. I'm here all day long—'

'No, you're not. You take Zak to playgroup. You have coffee with your friends. You natter and go to the playground. I wish I could do things like that. You're the one who has no idea. How hard I work. What it's like for me, staring into a screen all day long. Pressure. Work more. Buy more. Go here. Go there. This meeting. That meeting. Targets—'

'Shut up! You think I have it easy, do you? Try it, that's all. Just bloody try it before you lecture me about my wonderful life of idleness and leisure. Zak is a nightmare sometimes, a nightmare, and it's the kind of nightmare I could deal with if it wasn't life-threatening.' Josie was on the point of tears. 'He could have died, Will. He could have fallen over the edge. I can't bear it . . .'

Will sat up at once and put his arms around her. 'He didn't, though, did he? He's fine. You'd never let him be in danger, I know that. Really I do. I didn't mean to say that, about the door being unlocked. Maybe it *was* me who left it open.'

'No, it was probably me . . . But he's getting big now, Will. He's going to want to go out there more and more, and it'll become harder and harder to stop him. I've been thinking. Really. We need to move. I don't want to live here any longer.'

'But—'

'I know. It's near your work. It's convenient for you. You couldn't face a commute. But this is the kind of thing that hap-pens . . . One mistake, and your four-year-old finds his way out to a balcony three storeys above the river . . . I can't even bear to think about it. He was leaning over . . .' Josie started to cry.

'Don't cry, Josie. Come on, we'll sort it somehow. Don't cry – please.'

'I'm not crying. I'm just . . .' Josie sniffed and got up. She pulled a tissue out of her jeans pocket and wiped her eyes and nose.'

'Doesn't matter . . . come here and let me cheer you up.'

'No. I don't want to cheer up. I want to move. Say you'll come and see some places with me. Just to look. You never know. We might find something amazing.'

'This flat is amazing. You said so yourself, remember?' Will was proud of the flat, with good reason. He'd changed it, almost single-handed, from a long, long room into a place where every single element was designed to be harmonious with everything else. Josie had always known that Will could spend hours deco-rating and painting but she'd had no idea of what an excellent carpenter he was, and how he could transform a set of shelves into a thing of beauty. When it came to fitting the kitchen, Josie had suggested a professional firm but he'd been quite offended.

'We can afford the best, Will. Why don't we go for that?'

'I reckon,' he said, 'that I can do as well as any firm. If I don't, I'll pay to get it done over.'

They hadn't needed to change a single thing and, after that, Josie hadn't said a word about any improvements to the flat he'd wanted to make. Sometimes she thought he should have been an architect or something similar, instead of being a . . . What was he? A maker of money in an office, buying and selling imaginary *stuff*. That was how she explained his job to herself. Now she said, 'It *is* amazing – I'm not saying anything against the flat – but it's not suitable for kids and that's all there is to it.'

'Zak is four, and he'll be at school soon. He'll grow up. He'll become more responsible. We won't always have to watch him.'

'What about another baby?' Will said nothing. Josie continued, 'That's it, isn't it? You don't want to leave this bloody place, and a second child certainly doesn't come into your calculations, does it?'

Will stood up and went to the fridge. He took out a bottle of beer and began to drink.

'Stop drinking so aggressively!' Josie's face was red. 'You're not saying anything. That's just typical. Say what's on your mind, Will, why don't you?'

'Okay. I don't want to move. I'm not sure whether I want another child just at this particular moment. All hell is going on at work, and when I'm there I don't know whether I'm on my arse or my elbow. Now you're hitting me with all this.'

'I'm sorry . . . Listen, Will. Sit down. I want to tell you something. First things first. I don't want us to fight the whole time, okay?'

He sat down wearily at the long table and drank his beer.

'Okay. I hate fighting, too. And I hate to see you miserable, Josie. Please tell me we don't have to have the same argument over and over . . .'

'I've got a confession to make, Will. I've been to see an estate agent.'

'You what?'

'I was in Barnet the other day, having lunch with Pam—'

'Who's Pam?'

'Doesn't matter.' Josie decided that now was not the time to have a go at him for not remembering the names of her friends or which compartment of her life they fitted into. Pam was an old school friend. And, true, Josie hadn't seen her for a while and never mentioned her but, still, she thought, I manage to keep up with all *his* office politics and who was who in James & Shields. But there were more important battles to be fought. 'I was passing an estate agent's window, and there were some lovely-looking houses in the window, so I went in. On impulse.'

'And?'

Josie remembered how nice Miss Atkins had been to her and how nice that young man there, Dominic, had been to Zak. He'd made paper aeroplanes for him. Miss Atkins had been kind, too, after Dominic was called away on some errand. She'd told Zak her name (*I'm called Iris. What's your name?*), set him up on a chair at her desk and given him lots of paper and coloured pencils to draw with. She even explained to him what the estate agency was: *It's like a shop for houses*, she'd said. *I sell houses to people. They come here and I take them to see nice houses that they think they might like to live in.* She'd got him designing his perfect house. The first thing he'd drawn was a dog.

'I want a puppy,' he'd told Iris. 'A brown and white one. Or black and white, maybe.'

45

To Will, she said, 'I met a very nice estate agent called Iris Atkins and I told her my problem.'

'Did you tell her that you were living in what's probably the best bit of real estate in central London? That the flat was architect-designed? That you're the best interior designer I know, even though you've never done it professionally? That this place is quite beautiful. On the river? Not near the river but actually *on* it? That you can look out of your windows and see St Paul's and the Thames and the lights of the City? Did you tell her that?'

Josie nodded. She noticed that he'd left out his own contribution to the desirability of the property. 'She said that we'd be able to get a very good price for it and could pretty well pick where we wanted to live.'

'I don't want to live anywhere else. If I have to commute on top of doing that bloody job, which has me by the balls, it would be the last straw, I think.'

'Why do you do it if you think it's a bloody job?'

'Because it pays ridiculously well, as you know.'

Josie didn't say: *What about me? Why do I have to always do what's good for you and your job? What about what I want to do with my life?* Perhaps it was her fault for being so willing to push her own ambitions to one side. She'd been to art school, specializing in fabric design and interior decoration, and had always imagined she would use her skills professionally, but that hadn't happened. She'd met Will and fallen so much in love that every dream she'd ever had had dissolved and vanished. And now she had what she wanted, didn't she? Didn't she want to live with Will and love him and have his children? Of course she did but, suddenly, the love and the money and the desirable flat on the river in London were not as important as having . . . What, exactly? A husband who spent more time at home. A place where her son could have a dog. And another child . . . Josie wanted that more than anything, but if the flat was unsuitable for one child, it would be sheer hell for a family with two children. She wondered how it was possible for Will not to grasp all this without her having to point it out.

'Maybe just come with me to look at some places, when Miss Atkins finds some.'

'What have you told her we want? What *do* you want?'

'Somewhere we could have more children. And a dog. A dog for Zak.'

Will laughed. 'You mean a dog for you!'

'And for you. You love dogs.'

Will said nothing, then sighed. 'Okay. I'll look. Just to stop you nagging.'

'Thank you!' Josie said, settling herself in Will's arms. She'd known he would give in. The truth was, he hated the quarrels even more than she did, and however much money he was making, he wasn't happy. If I can show him other ways to live, she thought, maybe he'd see things differently. They sat in silence for a while, watching the lights across the dark stream of the Thames.

Then Will said, 'This Iris, when's she coming?'

'On Wednesday to have a look and value it, but even just from what I told her about it, she reckoned everyone would be fighting over it.'

'I'm not saying I'm moving, mind,' Will said, kissing his wife. Josie kissed him back. She didn't say a word about the photographs Iris would be taking on her visit to go on the property websites. She would make a nice meal and tell him about those tomorrow, maybe. And she wouldn't dream of pointing out that she'd won the first round.

47

AIDAN

'Please call me Iris,' said Ms Atkins. 'We're probably going to be meeting quite a lot.'

'Thank you,' said Aidan. 'But you must call me Aidan.' Until she'd arrived to take the photographs that would go on the leaflet, Aidan thought he'd made quite a good fist of clearing up the house to a satisfactory standard. But he could see, as soon as he looked at everything through her eyes, that it was going to need a bit more sprucing up before it passed muster. Iris (that would take some getting used to: he'd been thinking of her as Ms Atkins, which was what it said on the little plastic nameplate on her desk) went through every room, asking his permission to hide things behind other things, to put books more tidily on the shelves, to pull the curtains back as far as they would go, to arrange cushions from the spare room on his bed in the master bedroom . . . On and on the small adjustments went. Iris kept talking throughout and he was sure she was only doing it to soothe him. 'This will look much better,' she said. And 'This will brighten the kitchen up' or 'Do you mind if I just move these books away from the windowsill? I'll put everything back later just as it was.'

He followed her from room to room, wincing slightly as she nonchalantly moved things that hadn't been moved for months. He'd given instructions to Raina, his cleaner, and she'd done her best, but with so many books and papers, there was always dust. He said, 'I suppose we ought to have moved years ago, but Grace, my late wife, loved this house and it was only when she got ill that she . . .' Aidan's voice faded to nothing.

'I'm ready for a cup of tea, if you are,' said Iris.

'Of course,' said Aidan, and went into the kitchen. That had been tactful of her. He'd had tears in his eyes and she must have noticed. Her words had turned him back from an emotional outburst that would have been embarrassing.

Iris was in the kitchen now. 'A mug and a teabag will be fine for me,' she said, and he smiled to himself as he obeyed her. He didn't confess that that was what he'd been going to provide all along. 'May I sit here?' she continued, pulling a chair out from the kitchen table.

'Yes, of course,' Aidan replied. 'And there are some biscuits somewhere . . .'

'Not for me, thanks,' said Iris.

He took his cup and sat down in the chair opposite her.

'I've got some leaflets here for you to look at,' Iris said. 'Give me a ring when you've looked at them, and if there are any properties you'd like to see, just tell me and I'll come and look round them with you.'

'Really? That's very kind of you. Grace would have made the decisions about matters like this, you know. I don't want to seem useless but I'm not that great when it comes to practical things. Grace used to do all that. She dealt with our finances, the shopping, the cooking, and she had a full-time job too. I have no idea how she managed it. I'm finding it hard to stay on top of what there is to do in the house and continue with my own work.'

'Didn't you tell me you'd retired?'

'Yes, when Grace became ill . . . about three years ago now. But I'm trying to write a book and get on with my research.'

'Gosh, I'm impressed!'

Aidan smiled. 'Can't think why. It's what I've done my whole life, in one way or another. Writing things. Nothing to be impressed about, I assure you.'

When Iris left, promising to send leaflets and to show him the details of his own house when they were ready, Aidan felt more alone than ever. He realized he could count every single occasion since Grace's death that he'd had visitors. Iris had altered the atmosphere in every room while she was there. The sound of voices that weren't on the radio or the television, voices in real life, seemed to stir the air, and he listened to the silence with a growing sense of panic. He turned on the radio, and tuned it to Radio 3 where a Bach cantata was playing. For a while longer he wanted to preserve the memory of his voice and Iris's speaking together in a house that had been silent for too long.

I could invite people, he thought. My friends . . . Grace had been in charge of inviting friends as she had been of everything else, but he could easily ask them round. And then what? I would have to cook. I'd have to send emails and arrange dates and times and make sure the house was tidy. He felt tired even thinking about it. For the last couple of years, he'd been the one invited to other people's houses, and when it came to reciprocating, he'd always suggested a convenient restaurant. That was easier. Or he would get in touch with a friend or two, and arrange a good long walk, somewhere convenient, with a pub lunch to break it up.

As he washed up the two mugs, he looked out of the window at the garden. Iris had tactfully suggested it could do with a tidy-up and he made a mental note to phone Declan, the gardener and odd-job man. When they'd bought Mansfield Cottage, only a year after they'd married, both he and Grace had imagined that the garden would be loud with the shouts of their children. Well, that had never happened. Should they have got rid of the house then? It had always been too big. Who else had a dedicated sewing room? There was a guest bedroom, which had hardly ever been used, and his attic study. There were two reception rooms, both very large, and a kitchen/morning room, his centre of operations when he was downstairs.

He sighed and sat down on the kitchen sofa. A family with children. Pets. People who would run up and down the stairs and shout from room to room, as he and Grace never had. They'd gone to find one another if they wanted to say something. We could have texted, Aidan thought, but by the time texting had become second nature, he was with Grace most of the time anyway. Sitting beside her and watching her get weaker and thinner, paler and closer to death.

He stood up. Pull yourself together, man. The image of Grace's bedside at the hospital was in his head. The strange light. The shiny greenish lino. The kind nurses, whose faces he would recall till his dying day though their names had already gone. There, in his mind, was the bedside table where Grace's books stood in a tidy pile. He saw her box of tissues, and the little lime green portable radio he'd bought her, which didn't work terribly well. There were no pills, because those came round on a trolley, but often there were tubes he couldn't bear to look at, stuck into the back of her hand, and drips whose contents he was never completely sure about. Liquid squeezing into her through her veins.

Thinking about veins nauseated him, and he'd kept his gaze away from Grace's hands when she was attached to a drip. Round the bed there were blue curtains made of a funny kind of paper doing its best to be mistaken for fabric: disposable curtains because, presumably, it was cheaper to throw them away than to wash them. Aidan could transport himself to that ward in the blink of an eye and tried to do so as seldom as possible. Sometimes, however, it was hard to dislodge those thoughts and then, if the weather was fine, he left the house and started walking, deliberately thinking of the times he'd walked for miles with Grace beside him. She'd liked finding out about the history of the ground they were walking over. Who had lived there? What kind of lives had they led? He and Grace had been happy, he thought, and wondered why he'd never stopped to acknowledge it while he was in the middle of living his life, their lives, his and Grace's.

IRIS

As she left Aidan's house, Iris made herself a promise. She was determined to find him a home he really loved and was intending to make that one of her priorities. She was able to tell, both from what he'd said and what he hadn't, that his late wife had turned him into someone who thought he couldn't do anything by himself. Iris regarded that as part of the help she could give him: she would make him see that he, too, could make a decision, arrange to move, get things sorted out in a much more appropriate way. He wasn't incompetent. He was just lazy, probably, not helped by having had a wife who had done everything. He hadn't been curious about their financial situation so he was now in the dark.

'Grace did all that,' he had told Iris over the tea as they'd sat in the pleasant morning room, which looked out on to the patio and a fence covered with what she thought was honeysuckle. 'I can't say money interests me at all. I welcomed not having to think about such things, to be perfectly honest. I suppose I should have been more involved. And now I'm quite surprised by how much Grace managed to squirrel away.'

It turned out that Grace had inherited quite a lot of money when her parents died. Iris had asked him about his situation, even though that wasn't strictly professional, but she wanted to know because it would help her to fix the price range they'd be dealing with. When he told her roughly how much was in various savings accounts, the tea she was swallowing nearly went down the wrong way.

'Don't you,' Iris said, once she'd recovered, 'have any expenses? Holidays?' It was the only thing she could think of. Home improvements clearly hadn't been at the top of any agenda.

'No, not really,' he said. 'We went walking a great deal, mostly in this country.' Mr Church (it was very hard to think of him as Aidan) thought a bit about other expenses. 'I buy things like books and DVDs. A few clothes. That sort of thing. We didn't travel abroad much, and now that Grace is . . . Well, I suppose I'm a bit of a stick in the mud!'

He smiled sweetly as he said it, and Iris didn't have the nerve to say: *You took the words out of my mouth.*

Instead, she told him that he'd have no problem finding a nice house. As she left, she promised to set up appointments to take him to a couple of properties on the Farnley Estate that Grace had been so keen on.

Mansfield Cottage, Aidan's house, had surprised her. She hadn't been prepared for how beautiful it was. The garden was overgrown and needed tidying but it had a few fruit trees at the far end and an outbuilding that could easily be turned into a studio or playroom. The whole place had a very cottagey feel. Iris had begun to compose the text for the details in her head as she drove back to the office. *A desirable rustic cottage very close to town.* Did that make it sound small? It wasn't small. Could she get away with *rustic paradise*? Probably not. But it wasn't hard to imagine a dog romping in the garden, and a cat sleeping on a cushion on a rocking chair by the rather wonderful fireplace. The chimney was still working, though it was clear that no fire had been lit there for years. Iris was sure that selling it wouldn't be a problem.

A text came through just as she was sitting down at her desk to upload the photos. It was from Josie Forster: *Husband okay with idea of moving! See you Wednesday 10.30.*

Iris texted her back at once: *Thanks! See you then. Iris.*

Bruce was in the office, for a change. Iris waved her phone at him. 'Going to see that flat on the river I told you about.'

'Superdoops,' said Bruce, beaming at her until his attention was snagged by something on his screen.

Two can play at that game, Iris thought, and opened her email.

There he was again. Neil. She sighed. He'd begun to send her messages. Nothing heavy, just newsy little paragraphs from time to time. *Look*, he was saying, *I'm not a stalker. Not at all. I have no ulterior motive. I'm just being friendly.*

She bit a biro rather too hard and left toothmarks on the plastic. June had been mounting a none-too-subtle propaganda campaign on Neil's behalf, and in the end, Iris had given in because it was exhausting fighting all the time. And, if she was going to be completely honest with herself, many things about Neil were fine and she couldn't think of any real objection to them being friends. Lots of separated lovers became friends, didn't they? Well, maybe they didn't but there was no reason why they shouldn't. There were parts of their relationship Iris missed. The sex, of course, but also the chatting. The shared laughter. The meals ready for her when she got home. June was a good cook but a bit haphazard. Her shift pattern at the Orchard Hotel was all over the place so she often ate at work before coming home, and on those nights, Iris could have cooked herself a nice meal, but generally fell back on something quick and tasty that she put into the microwave for a few minutes.

Also, Iris missed having someone to go about with – to see movies with, for instance. Dates with her child-oriented girl-friends needed to be set up in advance and were as complicated to arrange as a G8 summit. Neil was clever, too. He knew he had to do a bit of disarming and grovelling before Iris would agree to see him. So that was what the emails were: a softening-up campaign. Today's message was: *How about dinner tonight? Lovely new Lebanese opened in Crouch End. My treat. Would love to catch up. Neil.*

There was nothing good on telly tonight. It might be fun. Also, the meal was tempting. What the hell? Iris thought. We're grown up, right? I could walk out any time if I felt like it. I'll be taking my car. He isn't going to tie me up and keep me as a prisoner. Okay, she decided. She began to type. *Love Lebanese food. Time and place? Ta!* That, she reckoned, sounded suitably nonchalant. Neil couldn't find any tenderness in there, could he? No, he couldn't, Iris thought, because there wasn't any. She had not one single regret about leaving him, but she liked him, he was funny and he was offering to buy her a meal. That was fine.

She pressed send, and his answer came back at once. That threw her. Had he been crouching over his machine? She knew, from having lived with him, that the answer was probably *yes*. He was as glued to his screen as any teenager and an email never waited more than five minutes before it was answered. Talk about return of post! His message didn't say, *Hooray!* or similar but Iris hadn't expected that. He gave her a time and a place and she responded, *Okay! Iris.* Then she went on to open her other emails. Iris put Neil out of her mind and turned to look at the photographs of Aidan Church's house that she'd taken earlier.

VINA

'So . . .' Geoff wiped his mouth with the paper napkin and leaned back in his chair in a way that made Vina want to hit him. Anyone walking in now and seeing them would think he lived there. He was comfortable, relaxed. His jacket was hanging on the back of his chair, his feet were on the rungs of the chair opposite him, and his shirt was becoming untucked at the back. Vina cringed inwardly. This is not Geoff's house, she told herself. He's not my husband. He doesn't live here. I want nothing to do with him.

She interrupted him mid-flow. The tone of his voice alerted her to the fact that he was getting ready to embark on some kind of inquisition or scolding. That was the trouble with marriage. You got to know someone far too well for comfort. He was going to be pompous, and Vina determined to head him off at the pass.

'Have a bit more lasagne,' she said, holding a spoon in the air.

'Why not?' Geoff beamed.

Why did I make lasagne? I could have done a salad. Lasagne said 'work in the kitchen'. Especially Vina's lasagne, which was, in Geoff's word, *legendary*. Was a part of her still trying to please him? That was what a psychologist would say and it would be quite wrong. Geoff had seized on it, when he saw what she was bringing to the table.

'Aaah!' he said. 'How lovely of you to make my favourite! Thank you!'

'Don't kid yourself. This was all I had in the freezer. '

It was the truth, too. That was the annoying thing. Vina could cheerfully have strangled him when he tapped his finger to the side of his nose and said, 'Aye-aye . . . That's your story and you're sticking to it!' He then pulled out the chair he always used to sit in and plonked himself onto it so forcefully that the house shook. The lasagne was almost gone now but she felt more annoyed than was strictly necessary that Geoff genuinely believed she was covering up an afternoon devoted to making his favourite dish.

Why am I grinding my teeth? she asked herself. It's a whole decade since we divorced. And now that his second wife had had enough, here he was back at her table. Vina felt a little sorry for him. Geoff was so useless at being on his own. He was at a loose end and feeling sorry for himself. Vina would have hated him dropping in. Being kind was one thing and burdening herself all over again quite another. Today at least he was here at her invitation. If she hadn't invited him when he'd phoned the other day, he would have said, *Come and eat with me. I'll take you out*, and she couldn't have borne that. At least here he was on her territory and she was the boss.

Vina took a mouthful of what was on her plate. Geoff was tucking into his seconds, talking and talking. She didn't listen. She was back to how it used to be, with Rob and Libby sniping at one another, Geoff busy telling her every detail of his immensely boring work day, and she was thinking now, as she used to think then: *If I don't leave this room, I'll take a knife and stab someone*. Most of the time she meant Geoff but there were meals when one of the children behaved in a way that made her want to lie down with a duvet over her head. At such times, she had a formula. She went to do something in the garden. She planted out seedlings. She pruned. She weeded. She talked to the fish. She swept up leaves. She planted shrubs. She sprayed roses with something she hoped wasn't chemical. She pursued slugs with fanatical zeal. And when she felt really murderous, she mowed the lawn. She regarded the mower as a kind of silver trophy awarded for years of frustration. It didn't make up for constantly being belittled, or overlooked, or ignored, or talked over, but it was *something*: something she'd fought for. Her defiance over the mower was one of the few times in her marriage when she'd stood up for herself.

'How dare you say it's too expensive, when you buy all those fucking golf clubs and fishing rods you've hardly used? How dare you? I'm buying it, and if you don't like it, you can bloody well lump it! I'm going to the garden centre right now and I won't be cooking your supper tonight. Fend for yourself.' She'd slammed the living-room door so hard that the windowpanes rattled. Then she'd slammed the front door. She'd driven to the garden centre in a fury and bought the most expensive mower they had. Then she went to the cinema and cried and cried in the dark.

By the time she got home, it was late and Geoff was contrite. He didn't apologize – apologizing wasn't his style – but he was more subdued than usual, and when the mower arrived he admired it, and said something about having a good lawn from now on.

The lawn *was* beautiful. Every time Vina was annoyed with Geoff, she mowed it. Up and down, up and down, she went, as wide green stripes appeared under the blades. It was a form of exercise she really enjoyed.

'Are you listening, Vina?'

'Sorry, I was miles away. What did you say?'

'That if I did, you wouldn't have to sell the house. Why are you selling the house? I can't understand it.'

'If you did what?' This is what happens if you don't listen, Vina thought. What had Geoff been saying?

'You haven't heard a word, have you?'

There was a time when she'd have denied it, but now she genuinely didn't care about offending him, or making him feel bad, or working him into a temper. 'No, I haven't. As I said, I was thinking . . .'

Geoff sighed. 'What I said was, if I moved back here, you wouldn't need to sell the house.'

It took Vina a few moments to absorb the enormity of what her ex-husband of ten years had just said. She felt as though her blood had turned to ice. *Moved back here* . . . Her eyes misted and she found that her first impulse – to get up and move away from the table – was impossible. *Breathe*, she told herself. *Just breathe and say nothing for a bit.*

'You're not saying anything,' Geoff said.

'Well spotted.'

'Say something.'

'Okay. I will. No. That's what I'm saying. It's the only thing I'm saying. *No.*'

'What on earth do you mean? Why? Why are you saying no? It's sensible. We're both getting on. We might as well pool our resources and live here. I could save a fortune in rent. It was me who made sure you didn't have a mortgage to pay when we divorced. You can't say that I didn't do the right thing by you.'

'I'm not saying that.' Vina sighed. She would be careful, not lose her temper and simply explain. Nicely. Kindly. Sweetly, even.

'When we divorced, because of your adultery and your long-ing to live with someone else, you very kindly paid off the mortgage and put the house in my name. I was very grateful to you at the time and I still am. It meant that I didn't have to worry about such things as where I would live while my mar-riage was being dismantled. You might say that this house was the price you were willing to pay to get away from me.'

Vina paused. At the time, she'd been devastated. Now, and very soon after Geoff moved out, she regarded the divorce as the best thing that had ever happened to her. It was easy to look back at her marriage and recognize that it had been a mis-take, but ten years ago, Vina would have said she loved Geoff in spite of everything. She recalled the nights and nights of sob-bing after the divorce came through.

I was crying from fear, she thought now. I was scared of being on my own, of having to deal with the children by myself. Of having no one to turn to if things went wrong. Well, that didn't last. It hadn't taken Vina long to see that she was fine. She said, 'I was sad at first when we divorced, of course, but I'm happy now being on my own and I don't want to change that. I'm selling the house because it's too big to heat, clean and maintain for one person on her own. That's it. Nothing you can do about it. And I should say that there is no way on earth I will ever go back to living with you, so forget about that entirely. If you want to maintain some kind of civilized relationship, for the children's sake, don't mention it again. Ever.'

Geoff opened his mouth and closed it again. He bore more than a passing resemblance to Nemo. Or maybe it was Dora. In any case, one of the fish. Vina nearly laughed but stopped her-self in time.

'If you say so . . .' Geoff pushed his chair away from the table and picked up his jacket. 'In that case, there's no point in my hanging around, is there?'

Smile sweetly. Say nothing, Vina told herself. She did that, and stood up to show Geoff to the door.

'Anyone come round to view the place yet? Have you found anything? Bet you haven't!'

She took his camel-hair coat from the hall cupboard and handed it to him. It had a velvet collar, and if there was one thing she couldn't abide in a man's coat, that was it: velvet collars.

'None of your business,' she said, smiling to soften the words. 'And, yes, I've seen a few possibilities. I'll send you my new address when I have one. Bye, Geoff.'

He hesitated in the door. 'What about the kids?'

'What about them?'

'What do they think about this moving lark?'

'I have no idea. It's none of their business.'

Geoff frowned and sniffed loudly. Vina remembered all over again how much she'd detested that habit. She stared at him, marvelling that she'd had sex with such an unappealing man more times than she could possibly count. She shuddered. Geoff didn't notice. He noticed nothing about her, still. He said, 'You'll regret selling it when grandchildren come along.'

'Why?'

'Because you'll probably have a lot less space in anywhere else you buy, won't you?'

'Not necessarily,' said Vina. 'You're assuming I'm looking for a one-bedroom flat. You're assuming all sorts of things, as a matter of fact. Bye, Geoff.'

Once he'd gone, Vina leaned against the front door. The quicker she got out of the house the better. I must get on to Iris, she thought. I'll ring her first thing tomorrow.

AIDAN

Walking was the best cure for almost everything. Following the river from London Bridge to Tate Modern was one of Aidan's favourite routes. He'd done it so often that the spectacle was familiar, but the miraculous thing was that every time he was there, the light seemed different: the sky behind the buildings, especially St Paul's Cathedral, might be grey and pearly, or a blue so pale that it was hardly blue at all. There might be clouds. The water was brown or dark green, and the traffic on the Thames was always interesting. The poetry that had lodged in his head from years ago when he was at school came back to him when he was walking by the river: *Sweet Thames, run softly till I end my song*, and *Earth hath not anything to show more fair* . . . The last one was from Wordsworth's sonnet 'Composed upon Westminster Bridge' and Aidan loved the bridges best of all.

Today, though, he barely noticed where he was going. His head was filled with houses he'd been to see in the last couple of weeks. He was going to meet Iris this afternoon to look at another. She'd insisted that they'd hardly seen any of what was available, but Aidan was worried because he liked the house he was leaving more than anything he'd seen so far. The printed details of Mansfield Cottage made it seem very appealing: *A desirable and beautifully located property within easy reach of all amenities, but with a rural feel, this house has a large garden and several fruit trees. There is an outbuilding, which would be suitable for a studio or workroom. Three good-sized bedrooms. Three reception rooms. Modern kitchen/morning room. Attic study, easily converted to a well-proportioned fourth bedroom.*

How had Iris made the place look so good in the photos? He'd scarcely recognized it. There was no sign of him in it: that was the thing. He changed Mansfield Cottage from a rather lovely house into a mess. Why did he want to sell it? He had to remind himself of the reasons. Were they Grace's reasons or did he agree with her that he couldn't keep the place up? He did, when he was being sensible and not avoiding reality (*living in your own dream world*, Grace used to call it). He could see that a smaller house would be more sensible. A new-build would be easier to keep clean. An estate would give him neighbours to talk to, and so on.

A group of young women passed him, walking towards London Bridge, chattering and laughing in clothes he couldn't have described but which gave an impression of colour, patterns and dizzying brightness. His own clothes were mostly grey and navy. I could walk the whole length of this river, he reflected, and no one would notice me. This rather sad thought was followed by another: I don't think I'd want to be noticed, would I? Aidan concluded that he probably wouldn't but, still . . . He looked at his watch. He'd go to Waterloo and get on the Tube to meet Iris. Whatever the house was like that they were going to view, he always looked forward to seeing her. She cheered him up, whatever kind of mood he was in.

'The garden faces south,' Iris said. 'And the owners will take less than the asking price. Also, it's very convenient for the Tube. And there's a garage.'

Aidan looked around him. There was nothing he could put his finger on that was wrong with the house. It was so new that he could almost smell the paint. The kitchen was what he imagined a kitchen on a space ship would look like. It was quite small. Grace's dresser wouldn't fit in here. Did he care? He'd never much liked it, though it had been something of a fetish with her. The walls throughout were white.

'Aren't the ceilings a bit low?' he asked.

Iris glanced up. 'They're not bad, actually. I've seen much worse. They're lower for you because you're tall.'

They'd gone on looking, but Aidan had made up his mind. This was not where he was going to end his days. No bookshelves . . . He'd have to put in a great many, even if he did get rid of some of his books.

'Let me give you a lift back to our office,' said Iris, evidently seeing that the house was failing many kinds of test. 'I've got a whole lot of other leaflets you can look at.'

That was kind of her. He usually drove to R & T but Iris knew that there was a good bus from outside her office to very near Mansfield Cottage, and she was finding a tactful way, with her offer of leaflets, to help him get home. I'll reach an age, he thought, when young estate agents will offer me a lift all the way to my door. He would have been perfectly happy to walk home, but there would come a day when he wouldn't be able to do that. *I'll become infirm.* He had a sudden vision of himself bent over a walking frame and shuddered.

'Thank you, Iris, that's kind,' he said, and they got into the car and drove to Barnet.

Aidan took the sheets of house details from Iris and held them awkwardly.

'There's a few there that look interesting,' Iris said, and then her phone rang. 'Do sit down, please. I just have to take this call and I'll be with you . . .'

He sat down and pretended to look at one of the houses, but listened to Iris instead. Was that being nosy? He supposed it was, but anyone who called an estate agent could hardly be said to be making a private call, so he didn't feel too bad about eavesdropping.

'Hello, Josie . . . Yes . . . Yes. Absolutely. I'll have the photos to show you and Will. Is he okay about it all now?'

A pause. Josie was obviously telling Iris whether Will was okay. Aidan wondered briefly what he had to be okay about, then Iris said, 'You won't have a problem, honestly. That flat will have people queuing round the block. See you tomorrow, then.'

'Thanks for these,' Aidan said, when Iris turned her attention to him. 'I'll give you a ring when I know which ones I'm interested in. And . . .' He didn't know how to say the next bit. He didn't want to imply that Iris wasn't doing her job properly, that he was dissatisfied with the services of R & T. He took a deep breath. 'I'm a bit concerned about the level of viewings for Mansfield Cottage. Is it normal? I think we've only had about six enquiries, haven't we? And no one who's been round has asked to come again.'

'Don't let it worry you. The house hasn't been on the website very long and things will pick up, I promise. I . . .' She hesitated and seemed to stare into space for a moment. Then she smiled. 'Actually, I've just had an idea. I'll get back to you soon, Mr Church, I promise.'

'Aidan,' Aidan said. He knew why Iris called him Mr Church. It was his grey hair. He looked like someone who ought to be given the respect due to age. He got up. 'I should go now. Thanks so much for all your trouble. I'm very grateful to you.'

He was looking down at one of the sheets of paper Iris had given him as he pushed through the door to reach the street. Someone else was coming in at the same time, and when Aidan glanced up, he had the impression of a woman in a red coat staggering slightly, almost falling but just managing to keep her balance.

'Oh, goodness, I'm so sorry,' Aidan said. 'Are you all right? I didn't mean . . . I'm really terribly sorry. I ought to have been looking where I was going. Awful of me.'

He was babbling. He could hear the woman saying something but was too embarrassed to take in her words. For a few seconds, they were both speaking at the same time. Then the woman said, quite firmly, 'Honestly. It's okay. I'm fine. Really. I'm not hurt.'

Aidan took a deep breath and tried to salvage a bit of dignity from the situation. 'That's very kind of you. Very kind indeed. I hope I haven't held you up too much.'

The woman smiled. 'No, not at all. Thank you for your concern.'

Aidan held the door open and she walked in and right up to Iris's desk. She sat down in the chair he'd just left. He closed the door and walked towards the bus stop. *Clumsy fool*, he told himself. *Look where you're going.*

The woman he'd nearly pushed over was very attractive, which made the whole thing much worse. He recognized her, too. She'd been coming in when he was going out last time he was at R & T's. That was quite a coincidence – or maybe it wasn't. But why did bumping into an attractive person make him feel worse? Would it have been okay to push into an ugly person?

Would he have felt less of an oaf? He supposed he was preju-
diced in favour of beauty. I'm a beautist, he thought, and
smiled.

When he got off the bus, he realized that, for the first time
since his teens, he'd spent several minutes thinking about a
woman who was not Grace. He tried to conjure up the details of
the woman's face and voice and found that he couldn't. I want
to see her again, he thought. To see if she's really as attractive
as I think she is. Iris would know her name. I'll write to her,
apologize again, and ask her to have a drink with me. Or maybe
not a drink. Maybe coffee.

IRIS

Neil was wrinkling his nose in a way Iris recognized. He was bored. They were at the Lebanese restaurant and, so far, everything was going well. Or, at least, everything *had* been going well till Iris started telling him about Vina and Aidan. As she told the story, which she'd thought was quite sweet, about them bumping into one another in the door of R & T and how Aidan was covered in confusion and clearly struck dumb by Vina, and how she, for her part, had wanted to know more about him, she could see that his attention was straying so she stopped in mid-account.

'How's things with you?' she said. Then she sat back and waited for his good humour to return, which it did, because there was nothing Neil liked better than talking about himself. They chomped their way through all kinds of delicious things, and when they got to the baklava, he stopped talking about himself and began to talk about the two of them as a couple, him and Iris. To give him credit, he was quite up front about it. He put his hand over hers and stared into her eyes and said, 'Iris, how about giving me another chance? Come back. Come back to our flat.'

'No, thanks, Neil. Thank you for asking me, but I don't want to do that.'

'But why? Don't we get on well?'

'We do,' Iris answered, thinking, *Over a meal, and for an hour.* She'd start to feel differently if she had to sit there for very much longer.

'I miss you,' Neil said. 'Don't you miss me even a little bit?'

'No, Neil, I don't.' This wasn't entirely true. Iris did miss the good sex they used to have but she had no intention of admitting it.

'Well, never mind,' he said. 'I'll keep on asking you to have nice meals with me and maybe go to a movie. That'd be okay, wouldn't it?'

'Fine,' Iris said. 'Love going to the movies.' And, she recalled, *I don't have that many people who might go with me on impulse, now that my friends are all child-bound.*

'I'll be in touch,' Neil said, when he dropped her back at June's. 'May I kiss you?'

Iris let him. Or, rather, they kissed and she was reminded all over again how lovely it was kissing Neil. She'd meant to kiss him politely and kindly but that didn't work out as she'd intended and they ended up having what Iris thought of as a mini-snog.

'Stop, Neil. Please . . .'

'Or what?' His hands were starting to feel under her coat.

'Or nothing. Thanks for a lovely evening. Must go now.'

She got out of the car and let herself in, feeling as if she'd had a narrow squeak of some kind.

June was still up.

'Hello, Iris,' she said. 'I've just made myself some tea. D'you want some?'

'Yes, please.'

June did stuff with cups and saucers and pointedly didn't ask her daughter how her evening had gone. Iris put her out of her misery, knowing that her mother was practically bursting to hear any titbit of gossip. She said, 'We had a lovely meal and he kissed me a moment ago and that was that. I'm not going back to him.'

'Oh, right,' June said nonchalantly, as if she didn't give a damn. 'Well, I'm glad you had a good time. Here's your tea. I'm going up now. I'm on the early shift tomorrow. Don't forget to switch off the hall light. Night-night, darling.'

After she'd gone, Iris sat down at the kitchen table. She liked the house at night when everything was quiet. She liked thinking about things that had happened during the day: working out what she might have done differently, checking that all the things she'd set herself to do when she'd got up had been done.

Iris knew she had made her mother happy by going out with Neil, and now the little pilot-light of hope that June kept somewhere in her heart was being fed by dreams that maybe everything would be different now. She reckons I might still marry him, Iris thought. Give her grandchildren and be the daughter she'd love me to be.

And, Iris told herself, I didn't succumb to Neil's kiss, though it had been touch and go for a bit. He'd assumed she would go back to his flat, and she'd been tempted. She felt quite proud that she'd held out.

She took her tea upstairs to her bedroom and opened her laptop. It looked strange on the desk where she'd written essays about the Plantagenets and drawn pictures of glaciated valleys. Of course there was a message from Neil: *Missing you! Missing me? Nx.*

He prided himself on his economical style but it made Iris grit her teeth with irritation. She felt as though he grudged every word, but he'd explained to her once that short, snappy emails were a kind of art form, a bit like haiku. While she was living with him, Iris had retorted that she didn't think much of haiku either. She had no intention of answering his question. She responded, just as shortly: *Smashing meal. Ta. I x.* She thought about that x for ages before deciding that it would be odd to leave it off when she'd just spent about ten minutes kissing him properly.

Then an email from someone she didn't recognize appeared in her inbox. She wondered who CHURCHA was, but as soon as she opened it she realized that it was Aidan Church. He must have consulted the card Iris had given him when she'd first gone to his house. All the other email communications had gone to the office but her card had her personal account on it too. She smiled as she read his message: *Dear Iris, if I may . . .* How many times was she going to have to tell him that she liked being called by her first name?

You may have noticed the rather clumsy way I left your office today. I felt mortified about bumping into the lady who was on her way to consult you and I'd like to write to her and apologize, but do not know either her name or her address. I wonder if you can help me with this information?

Thank you in advance,

Best,
Aidan

If there was anything Iris liked better than finding the right house for someone, it was getting two people together. She thought about Aidan and Vina and decided that it would be wonderful for both of them if they could meet. He was clearly keen. She didn't know very much about Vina, but from what she'd learned of her ex, a real gentleman like Aidan would make a nice change. Of course she couldn't pass on her details, though.

Dear Aidan,

I certainly did see it and I'm sure Mrs Brownrigg would have understood perfectly that you didn't mean to bump into her on your way out of the office.

I can't, of course, give you any of her details but if you email a message to me, I will forward it to her. I hope that's all right.

Best wishes,
Iris

Leaving her laptop open on the desk, Iris got up, undressed, brushed her teeth and took off her makeup. She slathered on industrial quantities of moisturizer, brushed her hair, then went back to the desk, ready to close the laptop. She checked the email before lowering the lid and, yes, there was another message from Aidan. She wasn't a bit surprised. Iris was pretty sure that Aidan didn't sleep much and that he was pedantic about answering emails at once. Also, his speed showed how keen he was. In the subject line were the words: *Dear Mrs Brownrigg* . . .

Iris read what he had said to Vina before forwarding it to her. Of course she did. Aidan must have known she would and that it was okay to do that, because there was nothing private about his message.

Miss Atkins at Robinson & Tyler has said she will forward this message to you. My name is Aidan Church and I'm the person who bumped into you today on your way into the office. I apologized at the time, I know, but I would really like to make amends in a less perfunctory way. If you answer this email, I will invite you to have coffee with me, perhaps in Barnet next time you have occasion to be there. I am retired and therefore my time is my own, for the most part. I do look forward to meeting you properly.

Yours sincerely,
Aidan Church

Once Iris was in bed, her thoughts turned to Vina and Aidan. She decided that he really fancied her. He seemed to be so absorbed, still, in memories of his late wife, but perhaps his last sentence was saying a lot more than it conveyed at first glance. *I do look forward . . .* Iris was willing to bet that translated as *I can't wait.* But Vina . . . what would she think of Aidan? Would she see him as a Clint Eastwood lookalike or just a grey-haired bloke who didn't know how to manage a swing door? *Perfunctory . . .* There weren't very many clients of R & T who'd use a word like that in an email. Or, indeed, anywhere.

She was finding it hard to fall asleep and blamed Neil for that. The mini-snog had been nice but probably a mistake. It might have given him the wrong impression. He was sure to ask her out again but Iris decided to make him wait a bit before she agreed to meet him for a second time.

She turned over and stared at the ceiling. She'd developed a method of getting to sleep that often worked. She went over in her mind all the houses on the R & T list: which ones had sold recently, which had just gone up on the website. She ran through the viewings she'd lined up for the next week. Dominic and Holly sometimes did showings. Sometimes, and usually when he could sniff out a good price for a house, Bruce took charge. But Iris did most of the running around and viewing houses with various clients, because she enjoyed it. At the moment, Aidan, Vina and Josie were taking up most of her headspace, but there were plenty of others who also needed attention.

Iris knew that she saw possibilities in houses where other people often couldn't, and she knew she could be quite persuasive when she put her mind to it. And I love houses, she thought. I always have. When she was about six, she'd had a doll's house. It might still be in the attic. June had a bit of a hoarding habit. Iris made up her mind to explore sometime and see what it looked like now.

When she was a girl, she had spent hours rearranging the furniture, putting the dolls where she could see they would be happiest, and getting quite stroppy when June tried to put her right about the rules of her miniature world.

'Who's this?' she'd said, on one memorable occasion.

Iris had put a man-doll in the kitchen. 'The daddy is making a cake,' she'd answered. Even after all these years, she thought, I can remember wishing that she'd go away and leave me alone.

'Daddies don't make cakes. Mummies do.'

Why had her mother, a card-carrying feminist, said such a thing? Iris had no idea, though it was true that *The Great British Bake Off* and men in every cookery show on the telly were almost unknown back then.

Iris had watched as June picked up the poor little boy doll that Iris had decided was the daddy and moved him to an armchair in the sitting room of the doll's house. It was wrong, wrong, wrong. That daddy wanted to be in the kitchen, baking. Iris *knew* he did. As soon as her mother had wandered off to another room, she had picked him up and restored him to the kitchen. As soon as she'd done that, Iris was convinced he felt much happier. She could tell that that was exactly the right place for him.

Now she turned her mind back to Josie and Will Forster's flat. She'd been to see it three days ago, and made sure all the details were on the website almost at once. Of all the properties she had ever dealt with, it had to be the most . . . Iris couldn't think of the right word. The most upmarket. The most desirable. The most likely to sell for shedloads of money. The one Iris thought she would find a buyer for as soon as it appeared online.

She'd arranged to go down to London Bridge by car to view it for the first time. Josie had assured her that there was parking available nearby for visitors. When she'd got there, she did as Josie had instructed: she rang the bell on the intercom and was buzzed in. Then she'd taken the lift to the third floor and Josie was waiting for her as its door opened.

Iris had seen hundreds of properties, maybe thousands, but that one silenced her for a good few minutes. The hall, the bit outside the lift, led into a long room – maybe a hundred feet long – about thirty feet wide. More or less. Iris wasn't interested in the exact measurements, though they would have to be written up. What took her breath away was the property's sheer beauty. The long room had been divided into four sections, which flowed into one another: study, living room, a long dining table, then the kitchen. Two bedrooms were on the other side of the hall on that floor. A flight of stairs led up to another level and two more bedrooms. The bedrooms were not enormous but they were beautifully proportioned. There were lots of bookshelves. The bathroom was also small but the master bedroom had an en-suite. There was a balcony, which seemed to hang over the river. It was wide enough to accommodate a few pots with plants and a couple of small chairs. Iris knew as soon as she saw it that it would be perfect for the right person. Whoever it was would need to be rich . . .

She could hardly wait to tell Bruce about her find and had rung up the office from the balcony, looking across the river. 'Bruce, I'm ringing you from this amazing flat. I'll send you a quick pic of the view on my phone in a mo, but I need someone to come and measure up ASAP. It's just . . . I can't believe how beautiful it is.'

As soon as she'd ended the call, she sent two photos to the office: a view of St Paul's and a shot of the main room, with the adorable Zak curled up on the sofa.

Now, lying in bed, she knew that anyone who viewed it would be impressed. They couldn't fail to be. Aidan Church, on the other hand, wasn't a bit impressed by what Iris had shown him so far. She closed her eyes and tried to imagine where he'd be happiest. Where he'd be surrounded by things he liked and able to enjoy life much more than he'd done for the last few years. He'd clearly been knocked back by his wife's death, but now Iris knew he had a fair degree of freedom, financially, with the houses she could show him. Then a thought struck her. Was it even possible? She decided to think about it for a bit longer, then act on it if it still seemed a good idea in the clear light of day.

Then she thought about Vina. What would she do when she got Aidan's email? Would she go for coffee with him? Did she have a man in her life? Iris liked the idea of playing Cupid.

JOSIE

I wouldn't have to do this if we had a garden, Josie thought. I could send Zak outside. She found herself imagining her son racing around on lovely green grass, a dog bounding along beside him. She imagined birds singing so loudly that she could hear them from the kitchen. She envisaged herself making bread, planting herbs, sewing clothes for them all, at which point in her daydream she returned swiftly to the real world. There was no way she would be planting herbs or sewing clothes, no matter where she lived. Never mind, she told herself. It's the principle of the thing. We need space. Zak needs space.

He was okay for the moment in front of the telly. She could use the time to do . . . What, exactly? Hoovering the flat, tidying what needed tidying didn't take long. I need a job. A proper job, something I'd enjoy doing. The phone rang and she scrabbled in her bag to answer it.

'Oh, hello, Iris. I hope you've got some viewings for me.'

'I have, as a matter of fact. I've got three couples, and Bruce is in touch with someone I think might be a Russian oligarch.'

'Seriously? An oligarch?'

'Well, a Russian-sounding surname anyway.'

'That's great, Iris. I'm getting my diary out . . .'

They made appointments for the potential buyers to view

the flat, then Josie said, 'But what about a house for us? I have to say, I'm not impressed with what I've seen so far. I know it's not your fault, Iris, but I haven't been anywhere I felt I could show Will.'

'I think that might be about to change,' Iris said, and Josie could tell, even on the phone, that she sounded much more optimistic.

'Where are these places?'

'One of them is here in Barnet. The other's a bit further out.'

'Oh, he won't go and see that,' Josie said. 'He's determined not to commute too far and he's even moaning about Putney, which is next door. Sort of.'

'Then I'll take you on your own,' Iris said. 'I do want you to see it before it gets sold. And it will be sold soon, I'm sure.'

Zak had wandered over to her and started to pull on her sweatshirt. The programme he was watching must have finished. 'Gotta go,' Josie said into the phone. 'Email me the details of these places.'

She ended the call and turned to her son. What was she supposed to do for the rest of the day? It was too early for lunch. Should she ring one of her friends and arrange a playdate? Did she have the energy to go to the park after lunch? The months between her child needing a nap in the middle of the day and when he was ready to go to school stretched out before her as a featureless desert, which she somehow had to fill with interesting things for them both to do. So why do I want another baby? But she did. She didn't want her son grow up as an only child, however inconvenient the early days would be for her. And he won't, she vowed. We'd be fine if only we could have a garden. And if I could work.

'We'll go to the shops after lunch,' she told him. 'Come and help me get lunch ready.'

'Don't want to. I want to paint.'

'Really?' Sometimes Zak could spend a long time painting. There wasn't any reason why he shouldn't do that and so she said, 'Okay. You go and fetch some paper from the paper box and I'll get the water.'

'And my apron.'

'Yes, apron too.'

'What shall I paint?'

Josie thought for a bit. 'What about our dog? The dog we're going to get when we find a new house.'

'A puppy,' Zak said. 'I want a puppy.'

'Well, a puppy grows into a dog. A big dog.'

'I don't want a big dog. I want a small dog.'

'Okay. Let's draw all kinds of dogs. Big ones and small ones and long skinny ones and funny fat ones.'

'Spotty ones and stripy ones,' said Zak, laughing.

'Flowery ones and zigzag ones,' said Josie.

She covered the long table with an oilcloth, gathered the equipment together and sat down next to Zak. He began sloshing the paint around, but Josie found herself painting a detailed picture, with one of Zak's smaller brushes, of a black and white dog with a long nose, triangular ears and a bushy sort of tail.

'Hello, you two. You look happy!'

'Daddy! Daddy!' Zak jumped off his seat and ran towards Will, paintbrush held out in front of him.

'Watch Dad's work suit!' Josie called out.

'Doesn't matter. Come here, kid!' Will bent down, gathered Zak into his arms and lifted him into the air. 'Doesn't matter a scrap if my suit gets paint on it. Won't be needing it from now on.'

Josie blinked. What did he mean? Had he been sacked? He must have been. There was no way otherwise he'd say such a thing. Of course it mattered if one of his work suits got paint on it. She stood up slowly and went over to her husband in the middle of the room, still holding Zak up and carrying him in the way he used to like when he was much smaller. She was nervous about approaching him. He was not the same Will who had left the flat earlier that morning. He was somehow changed. What was it?

'Will? What's happened?' *Why are you at home at eleven forty-five in the morning,* was what she was thinking. 'Are you feeling okay? Come and sit down. Zak and I were about to start making lunch.'

Will put Zak down and when the little boy protested, he said: 'Come on, let's make lunch together.'

'Mummy makes lunch,' said Zak. Josie heard a sulky note in his voice.

'Not today,' Will said. 'I'm making lunch today. I'm making fish fingers. They're in the freezer. You open the freezer and see if you can find the packet. Do you know what it looks like?'

Zak ran off to search the freezer and Josie lowered her voice. 'Why have you come home, Will? Something bad must have happened.'

'No, something good's happened. Don't worry. I'll tell you over lunch.'

'Will I think it's good?' Josie couldn't imagine it but maybe . . .

'You'll think it's even better than I do! Wait and see. Come and butter some bread if you want to make yourself useful.'

'I thought you were doing lunch. Buttering things counts as making lunch.'

'I can have an assistant, right?'

'Okay,' said Josie. 'I guess I can clear the table too.'

'Exactly. While I'm doing the grilling.'

Lunch was over. Zak had gone to his box of cars and was busy setting up a race with elaborate rules that only he could understand.

Josie sat on the sofa, shell-shocked. 'Okay,' she said. 'Tell me in detail.'

'I've left J & S. Effective as of now. That was their way of showing that they didn't mind losing me. They could do without me very well, thank you.'

'But what happened? I thought you were their golden boy.'

'I was, but no longer. I told them I was unwilling to work at such a pace and with such pressure for the rest of my career with very little thanks. And that I was leaving. I told them I had plans of my own, which, of course, I don't, but I wasn't about to admit that.'

'But what will we do? What about money? And your pension.'

'That's the best bit. They were so anxious to get me when I joined five years ago that they agreed to very good terms. It's true that I forfeit some severance pay but what I do get amounts to a year's salary, so I'll be fine. We'll be fine. And I have a pension. Again, not as much as I'd have had if I'd stayed till I was sixty but good enough. I'm not intending to sit on my arse for years, though.'

Josie waited for Zak to notice that his dad had said 'arse'. Normally, he was very quick to tell anyone off who dared to swear or utter anything he thought of as a rude word. But he was still whooshing his cars up and down the floorboards. Clearly this race was more exciting than it looked. 'But word will get round, won't it?' she said. 'J & S will spread the news and no one will want to take you on. Will they?'

'They might, actually, just to spite J & S, but I don't want to swap this job for another just like it. I'm going to work for myself. Be my own boss. I've worked for other people for far too long. '

'But,' said Josie, 'what sort of thing will you do?'

'Haven't the faintest idea,' Will answered. 'But I've got time to think of that. A whole year's salary, don't forget. Come over here and give us a cuddle. We'll think of something.'

VINA

Most people hated driving in London and avoided doing so, if at all possible. Vina loved it. If you weren't in a hurry, if you could avoid the rush-hours, there was a great deal of pleasure to be had from looking at the buildings, shops and cars and even, when things slowed down a lot, at the people walking past you on the pavement. When she was younger, she sometimes dared to venture out on the Tube carrying two huge bags filled with the knitwear she'd made over the last month. She called them Refugee Bags, because you saw them in footage of war zones on the telly and whenever people were fleeing from some atrocity. They were made of crackling plastic in hideous colours, and could hold about six new jumpers apiece. Vina had become very skilful at folding up her handiwork, so that it wasn't crushed.

She negotiated her dark blue Ka along Regent Street and reflected that it was always good to come along here, however long it took. If the traffic was slow, you could practically window-shop. She made the journey only once a month, seldom enough for her to regard it as a treat rather than a chore.

Vina always felt she'd found the perfect job. Geoff, when she was still married to him, couldn't figure out who would pay such a huge sum for a jumper. Still less could he understand why anyone in their right mind might want to spend hours knitting only to give up the fruit of their labour at the end.

'The pay's nothing special, I agree,' Vina had tried more than once to explain. 'But I'd be knitting anyway, in all probability. Might as well turn a profit.' She used that term, though she hated it, because she thought Geoff would sympathize with the desire to make money. He merely sniffed and muttered, 'Must be easier ways to do it.'

Vina said nothing, and bent her head to her needles. *And who'd be the first to have fifty fits if I had a job that took me out of the house?* she thought. Knitting was a comfort and an escape, like the garden. The way the wool turned into fabric soothed her. If the pattern was complicated, it got her out of conversation with her husband for hours. It often occupied the whole of her mind. She could watch TV while she knitted when the pattern allowed. And once a month, there was the drive to Georgiana's studio, the pleasant chats they had together and, of course, the money.

She was always paid the price that Georgiana paid for the wool, but the sums mounted up. Only the very best and most expensive wools were used. Georgiana put a mark-up on the price, and then the shop added another huge percentage. So the customer got something that was *reassuringly expensive*, as the Stella Artois ads used to say, and also beautifully knitted. Georgiana's piece workers were craftspeople (two were men) of great skill.

Vina kept a ledger of her earnings but had never made enough in one year to be taxed. Still, George was a good employer and encouraged the people who worked for her to consult accountants.

It wasn't only Geoff's disapproval that had kept Vina out of the job market. She'd trained as a teacher of what used to be called domestic science, and when they were first married, before Rob was born, she'd taught at a local school. She'd hated it so much that she'd vowed never to go back to teaching. Every day was a battle with a very determined enemy. The classes she taught had nice children in them, of course, but that was as individuals. As a cohort of twenty or so people determined to ignore every word she said, they were terrifying, and she was very grateful to leave school for ever. Once her children were old enough, once she could begin to consider maybe going back to work, she found that merely thinking about domestic science made her feel as though a heavy stone had lodged itself in her stomach.

She'd found the knitting work entirely by accident: she'd read an article about Georgiana in a magazine and written to her, volunteering to do piece work. She'd been doing it now for years and it was a part of her life that was entirely hers. The money, even though it wasn't very much, especially at first, was also entirely hers. She opened an account in her own name in a bank that was not the one that held their day-to-day accounts. She had managed to resist Geoff's blandishments about the advantages of a joint account and was very glad she had. All the money in the account he set up for both of them when they married came from him. To be fair, he wasn't mean, and over the years she was with him, he'd given her more than enough. She'd even managed to move a lot of the housekeeping money into what was known as the Knitting Account.

Her parents had died after the divorce, and she hadn't bothered to tell Geoff how much she now had at her disposal. It was none of his business. Her parents' three-bedroom semi was sold, and the money it fetched surprised her. She was an only child and their sole beneficiary, so she had inherited everything. She found it hard to think of herself as wealthy and

likely to be even wealthier if she could sell the big house she'd
lived in for the last twenty years.

I suppose, she thought, I don't need to knit for Georgiana
now, but I like it. I'm used to it. Most months, on the drive from
Barnet to Lambeth, Vina thought about what she'd be given to
do next. Georgiana was always coming up with surprising
things. There was never a dull month, though some were more
interesting than others. Georgiana's designs were made in very
limited numbers: each pattern was only knitted half a dozen
times at most. Vina was one of only a dozen workers employed
by the studio and a cardigan made by her or another member
of the team would sell for almost a thousand pounds.

Today, though, she was thinking about an email she'd read
when she woke up this morning. *I do look forward to meeting you
properly*. That was how he'd signed off, Aidan Church. She
remembered that a man had bumped into her as she was going
into R & T and he was coming out, but what else did she recall?
Grey hair. He was tall and skinny. What did his face look like,
though? She had no idea. She was much more interested in
women's clothes and faces than men's, and if a woman had
bumped into her, she'd have noticed her shoes and, in all probability, recognized her perfume. The man . . . Well, he hadn't
smelt bad. That was one thing in his favour.

He might be horrible. He might be boring. Vina was quite
close to George's flat now and was starting to watch out for a
parking space. It won't hurt me to have a coffee with him, will
it? she asked herself. Nothing much can happen to me over
coffee.

'It's me, George,' she said, to the intercom, and pushed the door
open when the buzzing began. The flat was on the first floor.

'Darling Vina,' said George, opening her arms and making

her mouth into a kissing shape even before Vina was through the door.

'Hello, George,' said Vina. They embraced. Vina was briefly blanketed in cashmere and a strong whiff of Arpège.

'Darling, come and sit down. Let's have a cup of tea before we do the boring stuff. What's new and funny?'

The boring stuff was the work. Vina loved discussing it, but George was eager for gossip, news, anything. She listened, and seemed to be interested no matter what the subject was. And today Vina was glad to have a titbit of news. She told George about Aidan Church, his email and the reason for it.

George's eyes lit up. She was plump and small, and wore her bright scarlet hair in a messy chignon at the nape of her neck. Vina had looked her up on Wikipedia and been surprised to find how old she was – very nearly eighty-four. She had been, in her younger days, what she called *a proper redhead*, but when grey had appeared, she was having none of it. She leaned forward now and her necklaces (she wore about six at the same time, which rattled and clanked as she walked. *A necklace as a statement?* she used to say. *You must be kidding. I wear whole* paragraphs *of necklaces!*) made their usual noises. 'Right,' said George. 'That sounds very promising. You are going to go, aren't you?'

'Should I? Mightn't it be risky?'

'Why? He's an old guy, you said. He's hardly going to sell you into white slavery, is he?'

'No, of course not.'

'Well,' said George, 'that's that, then. I'll expect a full report next time.'

On the way home, Vina thought about Geoff. I should have known from the beginning, should have worked out from the very first party we went to as a married couple, that he was the sort of man who was practically programmed to be unfaithful. She remembered standing in a crowded room, full of people dancing ('writhing' would have been a more accurate description) in the gloom, which was partly down to dim lighting and partly to smoke. In those days, everyone smoked and the place must have reeked, but no one noticed or cared. She'd glanced over to where she'd thought Geoff should be but he wasn't there. She went to look for him and found him in a room on a completely different floor, leaning over a woman so tiny she might almost have been a child. She had her back against the wall and Geoff was looming over her, his arm making an arch above her head.

What should I have done? Vina asked herself now, as she settled down to a much slower journey home through the rush-hour. Ought I to have walked out then and there? We'd only just unpacked into our first home. It was tiny and not very desirable but Vina had loved it and vowed to make it happy for ever. She'd made up her mind to avoid rows, and not fall into the trap that a lot of her friends seemed to be stuck in: the furious quarrels and passionate making-up sex afterwards. I wanted a quiet life too much, she thought. I always have. It's my fault. I ought to have turned round when I saw Geoff's hand stuck to the wall above that woman's head, gone home, packed and started all over again.

Vina had thought a great deal about adultery while she was married to Geoff and just after their divorce. She'd come to the conclusion that the truly hurtful thing, the thing that was worse than imagining the physical sight of her husband with another woman, worse than the disloyalty, worse than any other aspect, was the deceit. The lying, the setting out of a narrative that had nothing to do with the truth. When Geoff had finally confessed and after she'd got over the initial shock and disgust, what really rankled – and still felt like a piece of grit in her shoe when she thought about it – was that their whole history together was in fact two different histories. Two realities they did not share. He was, in the well-known phrase, living a lie, and that lie spread over the life he was leading with Vina, tainting everything, spoiling their shared memories, and even affecting his attitude to his children. That was what she hadn't been able to stomach: being lied to.

But if I'd divorced him at the beginning of our marriage, I wouldn't have the children, she thought. And, in any case, I'm divorced now. I'm happy. *You could have been happy years ago*, said a voice inside her head. *You're scared of too many things.*

As soon as the front door closed behind her, Vina took the bags of wool and the new pattern George had given her into the Knitting Room. She used to think of it as Geoff's Hellhole. It was described as a study in the house details that had come from R & T a few weeks ago, but from the moment Geoff had left the house, it had been hers: a beautiful, sunny room, full of baskets overflowing with wool and a huge cork board pinned with patterns and postcards. Her desk was there too, and her Mac Airbook. She opened this at once, clicked on her email and reread Aidan Church's message. Here goes, she thought, and clicked reply.

*

From: bruce60@R&T. com
To: client mailing list; staff mailing list
Subject: Bruce's Barnet Bulletin, number 401

Hello all,

Well, it's been a brilliant week for our office, with Iris Atkins (who's known to some of you out there) achieving offers on three properties, two of which were homes for first-time buyers, which always gives us a lift here in the office in these days when buying a house is such a challenge for so many. Customers of R & T know that they will be helped in every possible way, and that means you, First-time buyers, too!

Check the details of all our properties on the website. We've taken on some beauties recently, and here is an outstanding highlight to get you all fired up!

5, Riverside Court, Barket Street, London

This is a flat but not as you know it! A penthouse at the top of a converted warehouse, facing the River Thames just opposite St Paul's Cathedral, it needs to be seen to be appreciated. Apart from the spectacular views, this architect-designed duplex flat has one long reception room (95 feet long x 20 feet wide) with two bedrooms and a bathroom on one floor. The upper floor houses two more study/bedrooms. There is also a rooftop terrace with possibilities for a small garden. Ring our office for the chance to see this amazing property.

IRIS

June sighed heavily. Iris deliberately took no notice, but that didn't stop her mother commenting.

'At breakfast? Really? Can't we have civilized conversation instead? You'll be in the office soon. Surely this can wait.'

This was Iris on her phone checking emails as she ate a bowl of granola and gulped her coffee. June was already dressed and made up and would, Iris knew, be leaving the house in about thirty seconds for work. She'd probably been doing her own emails before leaving her bedroom. At least, Iris thought, I waited till I'd had most of my breakfast before firing up my device.

'Bye, dear Ma,' she said. 'Have a good day and I'll see you tonight.'

'I give up! Have a nice day yourself.'

'I'll put all the breakfast things in the dishy . . .' Iris called after her. Then she returned to her emails. She recognized most of the senders and mentally consigned them to office hours. Nothing from Neil, thank goodness, but who on earth was TaylorP70?

She opened the message and remembered at once. He was the artist who lived in New York and was keen on walls. Patrick Taylor. He didn't say much, but had attached some photos: *This is what I mean by walls! Any luck finding such things on your side of the Pond?*

Iris turned off her phone and took her plate and mug to the dishwasher. She didn't think much of him calling the Atlantic *the Pond*. He'd be asleep at this time of day anyway so there was no hurry to answer him. It could wait till tonight. There were more urgent things to be dealt with first.

She rang Josie, then Aidan. She had a feeling that the powers that dealt with whether things worked out or not were on her side today.

'You're looking very happy,' Iris said to Aidan, as they drove through the traffic rather more slowly than she'd been hoping.

'It's not every day I get invited to go on a mysterious expedition. It sounds most exciting. I have no idea where we're going, though I'm deducing it's south of the river.'

'Very clever,' Iris said. They were crossing the river at this point. Aidan was good company. He knew her a bit better now and was more relaxed than he had been. Did she dare to ask him? She glanced at him as he looked out of the window and thought, Well, he doesn't have to answer if he doesn't want to. Nothing ventured.

'I forwarded your email to Mrs Brownrigg,' she said.

He turned to her at once. 'Oh, my goodness, I'm so sorry. I should have told you I'd received an answer. I do apologize. It was very kind of you to pass my message on.'

'That's fine – really.'

Is he, Iris wondered, going to tell me what she said? Or do I have to ask another question?

He spoke before Iris could. 'We're meeting, actually,' he said, and gave an embarrassed laugh. 'For coffee on Saturday morning. At Prestwick's.'

'Lovely!' Iris said. Prestwick's was posher than Costa and much less likely to be filled with noisy children and their mothers than many of the other cafes near the office.

'Davina . . . Mrs Brownrigg suggested it. She said the cakes were homemade.'

Iris nodded. Cakes. Davina. There must have been a real flurry of emails. She smiled. 'That sounds brilliant. Right, we're here.'

'The adventure is about to begin, is it?'

'You're going to be pleasantly surprised, I think.'

Aidan's reaction to the flat was more than Iris had hoped for. He said hello to Will. Josie and Zak were at the shops and would be back shortly.

'Do have a look around,' Will said.

'Thank you,' said Aidan, and went over to the window to look at the river, at St Paul's, at the white clouds and dark water and London Bridge. Iris heard the sigh he gave and interpreted it as one of longing.

'Let me show you upstairs,' said Will, and they disappeared to look at the bedrooms.

'What did you think of it?' she asked Aidan, on the way back to Barnet.

'I'm trying to work out why you took me there,' he said. 'I mean . . . I don't mean I'm not grateful to have seen such a property but I can't imagine why you thought it might be of interest to me. It's not the sort of place I've been thinking about moving to. Not at all. And it's rather out of my price range, isn't it?'

'Well, a little pricey I know. But I wanted you to see it. I thought . . . I'm not sure what I thought exactly, but I did feel that you were spreading your net too narrowly. You're looking at the kind of house you think you want. But maybe you could consider a flat. Even if it's not *this* flat. You might find something similar. Or just . . .'

'I know. I'm very glad to have seen it, really. But it's so far out of my reach . . .'

'Never mind. You have to have a dream. Something to aim for. That's what I think, anyway.'

He nodded. 'I suppose so.'

They drove along in silence for a bit. Then he said: 'Are the details available online? Or do you have them on paper?'

'Both,' Iris answered. 'I'll put the hard copy in the post but, yes, it's online and there's a whole video tour.'

'Thank you,' he said.

Iris smiled to herself. She was ready to bet good money that Aidan would be on the website the minute he got home, printing out the details on that ancient printer of his.

AIDAN

Ridiculous. I'm ridiculous. Aidan looked at himself more carefully than usual in the bathroom mirror and spent a few minutes making quite sure there weren't any stray grey hairs poking out anywhere. Grace had drummed into him that men with unwanted facial hair were an eyesore that should not be inflicted on the world, and he'd always taken trouble to trim his eyebrows and any other outcrops that happened to sprout on his face. And sprout they did. Who would have thought the human body was capable of so much unnecessary growth?

After a particularly close scrutiny, and a very thorough session with the scissors, Aidan was satisfied. He went into the bedroom and looked at the clock beside his bed. Not even eight. He didn't have to leave the house for at least three hours. What was he going to do till then? He didn't feel at all like working. He had no desire to sit at his desk in his comfortable chair. Then what? What the hell *do* you want to do between now and when you have to go and meet Davina? Well, for one thing he'd have to decide what to wear. He couldn't recall ever worrying before about this aspect of his life, and in truth there wasn't much choice. He had blue shirts. He had white shirts. He had the odd striped shirt. He had grey jumpers and navy cardigans. He hardly ever wore ties, these days. He had trousers in the usual trouser colours. He had jackets in the usual jacket colours and fabrics: tweed, corduroy, and linen for the summer. He liked good shoes and every pair in his cupboard was expensive and well polished, but where style was concerned, they were all traditional. Classic, if you were being kind. After breakfast, he decided, he'd work out what to wear.

At the table in the morning room part of the kitchen – *Is it good or bad to have the same breakfast every day of my life?* he wondered briefly – he tried to organize his thoughts. They had been all over the place for the last day or two. Since he'd written the email to Davina, his life had taken on a different colour. Things didn't look the same as they had before he'd clicked send.

First, he'd gone through a sleepless night, wondering if he'd done the right thing. It doesn't matter if she doesn't answer, he'd told himself over and over again, but it was no good. He couldn't settle and eventually got up, made himself a cup of tea and read for an hour before dropping off at about three.

She'd answered. The feeling he'd had when he'd opened her email and seen that she was *happy to meet you for coffee*, her words, was like nothing he'd experienced in years. Over the hours that followed, he'd tried to analyse it. To give it a name. To describe it. In the end, he decided it wouldn't be too strong to call the feeling *euphoria*. He couldn't remember when he'd last felt such a soaring upward lift. *Euphoria*.

And then there were the emails making the arrangements. He studied each one as if it might yield secret knowledge about her feelings. He took the same trouble when he answered her, considering every word, wondering whether she would be able to discern his feelings in utterances as banal as *Prestwick's sounds lovely. I do like homemade cake.* Would she think he was greedy? Would she understand that *Prestwick's sounds lovely* actually meant *Prestwick's with you sounds lovely but in fact I don't care about the venue. You are the important thing about this meeting.*

He kept all her emails and his to her in a specially created folder, which he named 'DB' after toying with various other options.

He was dressed by nine o'clock. What was he going to do now? He went up to the study and opened his computer. The video tour of that flat: could he find his way to it? Well, trying would use up some time. And he found himself wanting to see those rooms again. He still couldn't quite understand Iris's reasoning. Why would she take him to see the place? She surely couldn't think he'd be able to buy it, even assuming he wanted to. Did he want to? In his wildest dreams? Perhaps. But even if he sold Mansfield Cottage and used up all the savings Grace had accumulated for them both, he didn't think he'd come anywhere near the price of the riverside flat. Still, it wouldn't hurt just to go on the video tour.

Looking at it, Aidan remembered how much he'd liked it. There was the view, the way the downstairs room seamlessly turned from study to living room to dining room to kitchen, all in the space of ninety or so feet. He imagined himself looking out of the balcony and watching the river change through the seasons. The sky behind the dome of St Paul's was pink in the video . . . It must have been taken at sunset. That's never going to be my view, he thought, so I might as well forget about it. He left the R & T website and turned instead to one about transport in 1915, which he'd found the other day. That will take my mind off Davina and the dratted flat. What on earth was Iris up to? He'd have a word with her, set up another viewing for a house that was at least within his means.

Ten a.m. Only another hour. He'd leave early, and get there

before Davina. It would be dreadful to be late today. He'd allow a lot of extra time. It was a lovely day. He'd walk a good part of the way. He would have set out earlier and walked all the way but didn't want to wear trainers and arrive red in the face. By the time he left the house, thoughts of the riverside flat had left his mind entirely.

As he made his way across the small park towards the bus stop (two bus stops along from the one he usually went to) he thought of Grace with something like guilt. She'd not come into his mind at all for the last couple of days, and Aidan wondered whether this was a kind of betrayal. Was he starting to forget her? Of course not, he told himself. It's just that for once I've got something else preoccupying me. Someone else.

He thought back to the first time he'd asked Grace out. They'd gone to see a film. He could remember being nervous. He could still bring to mind, with some effort, what Grace looked like in those days. But the years of a shared life had blurred into an undifferentiated mass in which occasional moments sometimes surfaced. For the most part, still, when he thought of his wife, the memories that were most vivid were recent: the long months of illness, pain and grief. When he deliberately tried to recall better times, it was harder and harder to reach the days when they were carefree, happy and well suited. The days when they'd had fun together, when they were in love.

I'm not going to think about Grace now, he thought, as he stepped onto the bus. It's not a betrayal. Grace would be pleased for me. She'd probably be pleasantly surprised that I've managed to do something as dynamic as asking someone to have a cup of coffee with me.

⁑

JOSIE

'Where's Iris? I want Iris!' Zak was pulling at Josie's skirt.

'Zak!' Will pulled his son away as Josie tried to pretend he hadn't spoken. She smiled at the person she'd vaguely noticed on the other side of the room a couple of times when she'd been into R & T. He'd probably have described himself as 'stout' or 'portly' but 'obese' was nearer the mark. Still, he was beaming and friendly, and he had with him someone small, dark and thin. A man in a beige raincoat.

'Ha, ha!' he said. 'My name's Bruce Fletcher. I see your little boy has fallen under our Iris's spell. And quite right too. She's a treasure. I sometimes call her that. A proper treasure.'

'I'm sorry. Iris was very nice to him last time we were in the office, that's all. He likes her.'

'As do we all. As do we all.' He did more beaming and turned to the silent man at his side. 'This is Mr Raskoff. He's from Russia and he's very interested in your beautiful home. As well he might be. As well he might be.'

'Lovely!' said Josie. Did Bruce Fletcher always say everything twice? If anyone close to her did that, she'd have gone bananas. Was Mr Raskoff an oligarch? If he was seriously considering the flat, he couldn't be short of a bob or two. 'Would you like me to show you round?' she said, smiling at the silent Russian. She was rewarded by a slight lifting of the lips.

'I go alone,' he said, and set out round the flat, examining everything in detail. He peered into corners. He stood for a long time on the balcony. He avoided the kitchen, where Zak had set up a farm that spread over the floor and most of the surfaces. He simply peered over the counter to look at that part of the room, then moved away upstairs. While he was up there, Bruce chatted about markets, house prices, the weather and what a wonderful property this was. He lowered his voice to say, 'I think Mr Raskoff is really keen. Really keen.'

'Is he? Did he say something to you?' Josie couldn't help but ask. She'd seen no sign of enthusiasm.

'He didn't have to. Didn't have to. He flew over yesterday and he's flying back this afternoon. In his private jet. That says *enthusiasm* to me. It does. It says *enthusiasm*.'

'How did he know about this flat, though? If he's in Russia?'

'We advertise all over the world, of course,' Bruce assured her. 'But you'd be amazed at how many foreigners go through the property websites in London. They're on the internet day and night, scouring this city for desirable homes like yours. That's what they're after: desirable homes.'

Josie bit back a remark along the lines of *Aren't we all?* as Zak and Will created a diversion by deciding to go out.

'Where will we go?' Zak wanted to know. Will was wrestling his son's feet into his shoes and his arms into a coat and didn't answer. 'Where, Dad?' Zak persisted.

'We'll see once we're out,' said Will, and then: 'Say goodbye to everyone.'

'Goodbye, everyone!' said Zak, and at last they were gone. Silence settled over the flat.

Mr Raskoff came downstairs then and said, 'My thanks,

madam,' to Josie. A brief flurry of chat, mostly from Bruce, followed and then they were gone.

Josie went to the kitchen to clear up the farm before Zak came back. Where would they have gone? Along the riverbank? Or would they have walked to the nearest playground, which wasn't near at all? Will would probably take him to a cafe and buy him an ice cream to keep him quiet while he sat on his phone, read newspapers from all over the world and answered emails from his ex-colleagues. She imagined a scenario in which her son could simply be let out into a lovely garden. She imagined a dog, which was something she was doing more and more.

'You're keener on a dog than Zak,' Will had said the other night. 'You spend half your life on breeders' websites.'

'Not half my life,' said Josie. 'Only a bit of it.'

'Well, all I know is, I'm always having to open links you've sent me. Or get up when I'm sitting down and come and peer over your shoulder at some flea-bitten mutt.'

'No mutt of ours is going to be flea-bitten, I promise you.'

So far, Josie hadn't seen a house she liked or wanted to move to. Up to now, it hadn't been urgent, but she had a feeling that everything was about to speed up. Everyone else who'd come to view had been awestruck but no one had looked like the sort of person who'd have the right money. Mr Church, whom Iris had brought round the other day . . . He was nice and loved the flat but he looked like the retired teacher he was and they weren't known for being rich. But Mr Raskoff seemed serious. He'd flown over, for God's sake. But maybe he had other flats he was also considering . . .

The kitchen was tidy. Josie had no idea of how long Will and

Zak would be. She opened her laptop and there was an email from Iris:

Hello, Josie. Just a thought: Mr Church, who came to see your flat the other day, has a very desirable property to sell. Are you free to view it with me? I think you might like it. I could show you round one day next week. And do feel free to bring Zak if you like. Here's the link to the website details.

Cheers,
Iris

Josie clicked on the link. The photograph showed something that looked like a very large country cottage. There were even roses round the door. She read the details. Could this be it? No, of course it couldn't. Look where it was. Fifteen minutes' drive from High Barnet. *In the wilds*: that was what Will would say. Or *In the boondocks*. What on earth would either of them do, stuck out there in the middle of nowhere? It was practically the depths of the countryside. She read on: *Delightfully situated between Potters Bar and High Barnet, this property is within easy reach of shops, schools, a good railway line and all modern amenities.*

Hmm, she thought. Cinema? Library? Cafes? Will wouldn't think this place was convenient. But as she clicked through the video tour, Josie's heart beat faster. It was a bit like falling in love.

IRIS

Iris felt there should probably be a special circle of Hell reserved for children's birthday parties. She had high hopes for later on, when her friends' children were a little older and she might be invited to bowling alleys, movies, pizza parlours, theme parks and other such treats. Now, though, she was on her way to a couple of hours' free-range mayhem in a suburban semi. Little kids of two and three didn't know much about birthday parties, and Iris was clear that if their parents decided to have one at home, it was the adults who were celebrating. After having been to a couple of these events, she had concluded that it was a combination of showing off (*Look at my nice life and my lovely child, and admire my homemade cake in the shape of a Very Hungry Caterpillar*) and creating a good setting for photo opportunities: getting super pics to put on Facebook.

Perhaps, she thought, I'm being a bit unkind. But she also knew that if she confessed these feelings to anyone, they'd immediately answer that it was her jealous body clock speaking. If she'd been prodded sufficiently by a competent psychiatrist, she'd no doubt discover that her dislike of children's parties stemmed from a deeply hidden but very strong desire to host such a party herself for her very own child. As people said on Twitter: *Whevs* . . .

So, here she was, walking to Marilynne's house when she'd

have much preferred to stay at home wearing jeans and a sweat-shirt and watching back-to-back episodes of *Sons of Anarchy*. What she had on now was smart-casual, more smart than cas-ual because she was wearing heels. She didn't have a child to compete with Marilynne's, so her shoes and bag had to be really classy. Iris smiled as she made her way carefully along the pave-ment. She and Marilynne had been in competition for years.

When she reached the house, she found five sets of adults, which meant about twelve kids, who were too young for organ-ized games. That, of course, didn't prevent Marilynne from having a good try at getting them to obey orders.

Mickey's party turned out to have a theme. The cake was in the shape of Thomas the Tank Engine, and very impressive. Iris noticed that she was the only person there who didn't take a photo of it. She helped herself to a glass of prosecco and went to sit out-side. Late March wasn't exactly barbecue season, but the sun was shining and a few of the dads had already made a getaway to the terrace. She looked at the carefully maintained garden and the top-of-the-range Jungle Gym. Marilynne and her husband, Ted, she thought, would have no trouble selling this place.

Her phone pinged and Iris took it out of her bag.

A text from Neil: *Are you there yet? I'm on my way xx*

Iris stood up. Bloody Marilynne had invited Neil to the party. She knew nothing about the meal and the kiss after it, because Iris hadn't mentioned it to anyone, so there was no reason on earth for him to be there, but she had invited him, the interfer-ing cow. She clearly believed that Neil and Iris ought never to have split up and had taken the law, as ever, into her own hands. *How could she do that and not tell me? If she'd said anything, I could legitimately have refused the invitation to this terminally bor-ing party.* She made up her mind to leave, right this minute. She turned off her phone and went to say goodbye, determined to get out before Neil arrived.

Marilynne was sailing towards her as she came back into the house, a vision in lime-green linen. 'Ah, Iris, so sorry I haven't had a chance to chat to you. You can see what it's like.'

Iris found it hard to smile but did so nonetheless. She said, 'Lovely party, Marilynne, but I've got to go. So sorry.'

'But you've only just got here and I've got a surprise for you . . .'

Iris opened her mouth to say, *I know, and that's why I'm out of here*, when she spotted Neil coming towards her, a huge grin on his face. She was holding a half-drunk glass of prosecco in one hand and the stupid handbag that was more pretty than practical was sliding off her silky shoulder. For a split second Iris considered throwing the rest of her drink into Neil's face. She pulled herself together and sense prevailed. Happiness is the best revenge, she told herself. That was what people said. Even worse than the prospect of dealing with Neil was the thought of Marilynne and the Girls discussing her *overreaction* (that was what they would call it, for sure) to his appearance at the party. So Iris smiled winningly. 'Neil, how lovely to see you! Didn't know you knew Mickey!'

'Course I know Mickey, Iris,' he said, leaning forward to kiss her on the cheek. 'Wouldn't miss a party of Mickey's for the world.'

'Iris, can you get Neil a drink? I have to go and settle the kids round the table. It's almost time for cake.'

There was nothing for it. Iris turned and made her way to the drinks table and Neil, of course, was right behind her. He cornered her before she started pouring and asked for fruit punch.

'Not prosecco?' Iris said, trying for nonchalant but realizing that she was probably coming across as pissed off.

'I'm driving. Thought you might drive with me, Iris. We could take in a movie. Or I've got Netflix at home.' He frowned meaningfully. 'It's still your home too, you know. I thought that maybe after the other night . . .'

'I got a bit carried away, Neil. I'm sorry. I don't think of it as my home, I really don't. I'm not sure what I've got to do to convince you.'

He put out his hand in a conciliatory gesture. 'No worries. Honestly, Iris, I'm not pressuring you.'

Not half. 'Great,' she said. 'Now, here's your drink and the nibbles are over there or you can wait for the cutting of the Thomas the Tank cake, which I'm told is chocolate. I've got to go home.'

'Why? I've just got here.'

That's why. 'Tons of work. I only came to give my present, then scoot. I'm up to my ears.'

'On Saturday?' Neil looked rightly sceptical but Iris was determined to escape.

'Yup! The great estate agents roundabout doesn't stop on Saturday. Emails to write. Houses to go and look at. Telephone calls to make. I'll see you another time, okay?'

She made a perfunctory kissing face in his direction and pushed her way to the front door through a scrum of small bodies, shrieking laughter and the soundtrack of some kids' movie.

'Bye, all,' she called loudly, and opened the front door. She could see Marilynne watching her from the next room unable to head her off at the pass because the maelstrom of bodies and legs and arms and flying toys was between them. Her mouth was open in a horrified O. Iris knew that she hated her plans to go wrong and this one, Operation Getting Iris Back with Neil, had clearly been a total failure. Tee-hee, Iris thought, as she walked home. I've got out of there. Back to *Sons of Anarchy*. What bliss.

She'd spoken too soon. There she was, congratulating herself and walking along happily in the early-spring sunshine, when a car horn tooted right next to her. Iris turned to see who it was.

'Neil?' she shouted into the open window, as the car drew up alongside her. 'What on earth are you doing?'

'Following you. I want to speak to you. Why on earth did you run away?'

Should she be honest? 'To get away from you, Neil.'

He laughed, as though that notion was entirely ridiculous. 'You can't be serious, Iris. It must have been that ghastly party. I don't blame you.' He leaned over and opened the door for her. 'Hop in. I'll give you a lift. Maybe we could go and have a drink or something.'

Iris was surprised to find herself tempted. She was a little ashamed of herself because she'd decided after the last time they'd met that she would not be tempted again, but Neil *did* look handsome and a wave of what she had felt for him until quite recently came over her. Nostalgia mixed with desire, she thought. Was that a thing? Was there a name for it? Retro-randiness, perhaps.

'Thanks, Neil, okay,' she said, and before common sense got the better of her, Iris stepped into the car. They drove off at once. 'Where are we going?' she asked.

'Wherever you like. Your treat. Maybe we could find a nice country pub somewhere. But I do have to go home first, I'm afraid. There's something I have to pick up, but I won't be long? Okay?'

'Fine,' Iris said. 'Drive on.' She looked out of the window as they travelled, concentrating on not stroking Neil's leg. I've only had half a glass of prosecco, so why do I feel so strange, she thought.

VINA

Who on earth was that? Someone was leaning on the doorbell in a way that reminded Vina forcefully that she'd always hated that ring tone. Now that she was selling the house, changing it would be a pointless expense, but on her way to the front door, with her coat on, her handbag over her shoulder and the keys in her hand, she wished she'd done it years ago. Why was someone ringing her bell as if their life depended on it? She'd have to put them off. She was on her way to have coffee with Mr Church. She'd enjoyed picking the right outfit and was pleased with what she'd chosen: something elegant but not too dressed up – black trousers and a silk shirt in a shade of green that she knew suited her. Over that, she wore one of her own intricately patterned hand-designed and -knitted Aran cardigans.

When she opened the door, Libby was standing in the porch with two suitcases at her feet.

'Libby! Darling . . . What on earth? Is everything all right?'

'Hello, Mum,' said Libby. 'I've come to stay for a bit, if that's okay. There's a jewellery and craft fair I want to go to. I need to make some contacts . . . you know.'

Vina didn't know. She didn't want to. There was no time now to ask for further details. She was furious that Libby thought she could just swan into the house as though it were her home, even though it *was* her home, in a way. But why no notice? Why hadn't it occurred to Libby to pick up the phone and warn her about this visit? Thinking such things made her feel bad, so she hugged her daughter and said, in a voice that she hoped didn't betray what she really thought, 'Well, darling, that's lovely. Do go in. You know where everything is. I'll see you later. I'm off now, as you can see. Can't stop.'

'Can't you put off whoever it is?' Libby had a great gift for looking petulant.

'No, actually, I can't. You'll be fine. I'll see you later. You'll find the spare keys in the usual place – and your room just needs the bed making up. Help yourself to anything you like. I'll be back later.'

She stepped out of the front door, smiling widely and waving as she made her way to the car. Am I overdoing it? Libby was staring after her, clearly bemused. I don't give a damn, Vina thought. Let her get on with settling in. She doesn't need me there to hold her hand. How long would she be staying? How long can I bear to have her mooching around my kitchen and moaning about everything? She remembered vividly how her daughter's moods had affected their family life. Discontent was Libby's default position. She had a real gift for making any situation harder and less fun.

Once she'd calmed down, Vina felt pleased that at least she hadn't let Libby divert her from this morning's meeting with Mr Church. Aidan. She'd been writing *Dear Aidan* in emails. He'd managed to push her house-moving worries (why had all the properties she'd seen been so underwhelming? Why had the viewings of her house not brought the offers she'd hoped for? What was the matter with everyone?) to the back of her mind. For the last couple of days she'd been anticipating this morning.

As she approached the cafe she could see Aidan sitting at the exact table she would have chosen: the one by the window. He had a newspaper open in front of him, but kept looking up to see who was coming in. He spotted her and stood up as she approached the table.

'Hello,' she said. 'Have you been waiting long? I would have been here earlier but my daughter . . . Well, it's a long story.'

'Hello!' Aidan smiled at her as they both sat down, facing one another. Vina thought of prison visits and police interrogations she'd seen on the telly and immediately felt bad. This was nothing like that. He went on: 'It's very good of you to come. I've been looking forward to meeting you properly.'

'Me too,' said Vina.

A traditional waitress in a traditional black dress and white apron came to take their order. Prestwick's made a point of being old-fashioned.

'You must try their cake. It's very good,' said Vina.

Aidan chose coffee and walnut, Vina lemon drizzle, even though she'd officially given up cakes for ever only a year ago. This counted as a special occasion.

Small-talk. That was what it was called, the to-and-fro of the formalities. Where do you live? What do you do? I'm a widower. I'm divorced. Houses. They'd met at R & T so house moves seemed the obvious topic of conversation. Years of saying nothing of any consequence to her husband had made Vina very good at small-talk. She could do it in her sleep, so she ate her lemon drizzle and spoke, and all the time she was looking at Aidan, working out what she thought of him.

He was handsome. And, better than that, he seemed not to know it. One of the things that had most annoyed her about Geoff, who was good-looking in a beefy way, at least when they'd first met, was that he used to glance into every mirror he passed and give a sort of self-satisfied smirk as if to say, *Who's a pretty boy, then?* It used to drive her mad.

Aidan could have done with a haircut. His thick grey hair fell over his forehead and he pushed it back from time to time. He had a nice smile. And a lovely voice. He was chatting now about his wife. They were moving away from small-talk.

'I have to confess that I was quite nervous about meeting you. It took me a long time to compose that email. I'm not used to . . . Well, Grace and I had been married for thirty years.'

'You must miss her,' Vina said. 'It must be hard living on your own if you're used to being with someone. Have you got children?'

Aidan shook his head and stirred what was left of his coffee. 'No, I'm afraid not. I always wanted kids but it never happened, and we were too old for IVF when that became available and so on . . .' He took a deep breath and Vina turned the conversation to herself.

I met him half an hour ago, she thought, and I know this about him already: he's uncomfortable at being the centre of attention. 'I've got two children . . . Rob is thirty-two. He's a solicitor and I hardly ever see him. He's married to Janice, who's also a lawyer. They live in Guildford. And then there's Libby, my daughter. She's twenty-five. '

'The one who's a long story?'

'Yes. She's a bit of a . . . I'm not sure what to call her. Not exactly a problem but not an easy person either. She lives in Cornwall by herself in a tiny cottage and makes jewellery. She doesn't earn much so her dad helps her out, and so do I. She's prickly and I know she's unpredictable, too, but I was a bit taken aback, to be honest, when she appeared on the doorstep just before I left to come and meet you.' Vina smiled. 'I didn't wait to see what she wanted, really. I just told her to make herself at home and left the house. I felt a bit bad about leaving her standing there with two suitcases but not bad enough to phone you and cancel.'

'I'm very relieved you didn't,' Aidan said, and smiled the smile that Vina was surprised to find she'd been waiting for. 'Let's have another cup of coffee.'

'Lovely, thanks,' said Vina. 'That would be great, only no more cake.'

There seemed to be no good reason not to go on talking.

'Are you busy?' Aidan said, as they stood on the pavement outside Prestwick's. 'Do you have to get home at any particular time? Only it's such a lovely day.'

'It is,' Vina agreed. 'I'm not busy at all.'

They walked round the park. They paused by the duck pond and watched the birds making small waves in the satiny water.

'It's a school day. Nice and quiet,' Aidan said. 'I often come here.'

'I used to go to the playground a lot when the children were small,' Vina said. 'I'm not keen on walking here by myself, to tell you the truth. Not having a dog as an excuse. I feel . . . I'm not sure what I feel, but strange.'

Aidan stopped on the path and looked straight at her. 'Are you okay walking round with me? '

'Oh, yes,' said Vina. 'That feels perfectly normal.'

'Good,' Aidan said. 'We must do it again. Maybe even bigger and better parks, if you like. We could be ambitious. Lots of lovely places to walk round in London.'

She smiled at him and wondered how to answer but he spoke

before she could work it out. 'I hope,' he said, frowning a little, 'that you don't think I'm being presumptuous. You may not want to go walking around London parks with me. I'm sorry.'

'Don't be,' Vina said quickly. 'I think your walking plan sounds marvellous and I'd love to join you.'

'Excellent,' Aidan said. 'That makes me very happy.'

They set off along the path that skirted the flowerbeds, which were filled with budding tulips.

Thank God for freezers, Vina thought. How lucky that I'm so used to making double quantities and putting half away. It meant that she could feed Libby with no problem beyond deciding what to heat. In the end, she opted for a bolognese sauce to make one of Libby's childhood favourites.

Vina would have preferred to eat by herself and process what she thought about Aidan and the time they'd spent together but, no, she had to chat to Libby about Libby's concerns. As ever. She supposed there must be mothers somewhere whose children were interested in their parents' news, opinions, problems and so forth, but Vina knew that her daughter wasn't one of them.

My fault entirely, she told herself. Years and years of asking how Libby was, how she felt, what was happening in her life meant that Vina had fallen out of the habit of talking about herself, and her daughter wasn't about to do anything to alter that. She looked at Libby, sitting in the chair she always used to sit in. Who did she look like? Not me, Vina thought, and she's far too skinny to be like Geoff. Her hair was blonde and long and fell over her shoulders. She wore no makeup. Her eyes were blue, like Geoff's. Her clothes were very much regulation-hippie style: a long blue and white patterned skirt and a thin, floaty kind of blouse. She always wore multiple necklaces, with too many bangles, and made a soft clinking noise when she walked.

'So,' Vina said, sitting down and picking up her fork. 'How are things with you, darling?'

'I didn't know you'd already put the house on the market,' Libby muttered.

'I'm sure we discussed it on the phone.'

'Maybe. I can't remember, but you might have consulted me about it.'

'Why?' Vina didn't mean to sound curt but the word came out too quickly and too unadorned. And she hadn't been smiling when she'd said it, either. She added, in a slightly kinder tone, 'You don't live here any more, Libby.'

'Well, but still.' Libby ate a few forkfuls of spaghetti bolognese. Fleetingly, Vina noticed that she hadn't said one word about whether it was tasty. Too much to expect. Libby went on, 'I might still want to come back, you know. Like now. And what about after you're dead?'

Vina nearly choked. Had Libby been sitting in the Cornish hovel waiting for her mother to die so that she could move in? Really? Calm, she told herself. Don't shout. Go easy. Find out first of all if it's as bad as you think or if Libby simply didn't express herself well. Until now, her daughter, always a bit abstracted and never really present in the world around her, hadn't shown the slightest interest in the terms of Vina's will. She knew nothing, for example, of the money Vina had inherited from her own parents. Or did she? Had Geoff mentioned it? Probably not, or she would have said something in this conversation. Vina took a deep breath. 'Okay, let me get this straight,' she said at last. 'You want me to rattle around in a house that's not exactly filled with happy memories till I drop dead when you and Rob can sell it for tons of money and divide it between you. Is that the idea? Please don't tell me you're thinking *the sooner the better*. I'm not even sixty.'

'That is so *typical* of you, Mum! You always think everyone's out to get you. That everything is about *you*. Of course I don't want you to die, of course not. I'm a bit hurt you even said that, to tell you the truth. But when you *do* die, it would obviously be better for Rob and me if this house became ours. Rather than a much smaller place, I mean. Even a flat.'

'Well, I can see that, but I'm not thinking of you and Rob in making this decision. I'm going to find a place I like and can envisage living in for the rest of my life, however long it may be, and I intend to spend the difference on holidays in posh hotels. I may even buy a new car and a few designer clothes. You never know. I'm not going to stint myself, that's for sure.' She smiled.

Libby looked horrorstruck. 'Well, okay,' she said at last. 'If that's how you feel, I can't force you to change your mind, but I think you're mad. Property in London is now worth so much more than it used to be. This place must be worth a small fortune.'

'I know,' said Vina. 'It is. I'm asking a million. I'm hoping to make a good sum from the sale and be able to buy something really rather special.'

'Have you seen anything yet? Do you want me to come round some houses with you?'

Vina's soul shrank from this prospect. Libby examining everything with an eye to her own inheritance was something she had to avoid at all costs. 'No, thanks,' she said. 'I'm afraid this is the kind of decision I must make on my own.'

'Suit yourself,' said Libby, sounding huffy again and getting up from the table. 'I'm going to bed now. Good night.'

It wasn't even nine o'clock. No watching box sets with Libby. She'd been like that since she was twelve, so it was probably a vain hope that growing up might have changed that aspect of her character. Vina said, 'Goodnight, dear,' and stood up to load the dishwasher. She could count on the fingers of one hand the number of times her children had offered to help her wash up or clear the table. My fault, she thought. Children do what they're brought up to do, and when they were small, I used to long for everyone to be out of the kitchen so that I could retreat into a world of radio and my own thoughts.

Vina felt too perturbed to start knitting. She wasn't in the habit of checking her phone, but tonight, as she sat drinking a cup of coffee at the kitchen table, she clicked through to her email to see if there was anything from Iris. It had been some days since R & T had brought a new property to her attention. What she found was two emails from Aidan. She opened the second first because it appeared at the top of her inbox: *Dear Vina, I apologize if my last email was a bit over the top, but I did want you to know how much I enjoyed meeting you today. Aidan*

AIDAN

Why wasn't she answering? Aidan kept going back to his inbox to see if things had changed since he'd last looked, but there was no answer. Maybe he'd offended her. He sighed. You're being a fool, he told himself. There are millions of reasons why she might not want to answer at once. Her daughter – maybe they'd had a row. Maybe they'd gone out. Or maybe she needed to think before replying to him, though on past form she was a speedy answerer of emails. Hadn't they got on brilliantly? She'd seemed to like him.

He thought back to when they'd said goodbye, with her standing near her car. He'd told a lie and said he had to go into the West End to meet an old friend because he didn't want to accept her offer of a lift. And why didn't he want to do that? If she'd been happy to prolong her time with him, why had he hesitated? He had no idea, really, but some of it was a desire to go home and write to her. He wanted to take out the memories of the last few hours and look at them, like a miser going over his hoard.

Now he clicked through to his own email and he read it again for what must have been the thousandth time. It had taken him at least an hour to write and now she wasn't answering. What was wrong with it?

Dear Vina,

I hope you don't mind my writing to you almost at once. I feel that, if I hesitate, I will lose courage and not say what I really want to say, which is this: I enjoyed our time together today more than I have enjoyed anything for many years. I am finding it hard to think of anything except you. You probably think that this is an exaggeration but it truly isn't. My thoughts return all the time to what you said, and what I said, and I find myself going over the conversation we had, which seems to be the first honest talk I've had with anyone for some time.

I am taking a risk in writing this email. You may feel quite differently, I know, but I would like to see you again. Would you like to visit Kew Gardens with me? I am very fond of it and at this time of year, it will be looking splendid.

Yours, with my very best wishes,
Aidan

Bloody hell, he thought. It's a bit much, but it didn't convey the ferment he'd been in since he'd left her. Standing by her car, opening the door for her, he'd fleetingly thought about leaning over and kissing her on the cheek, but thought that would be too daring. He'd allowed himself to take both her hands in his and squeeze them. He was not quite prepared for the shock of touching her: at the time, he'd felt as if a small earthquake was shaking him. Even now, remembering it, he felt a bit faint. Vina had smelt wonderful. He thought of what it would be like to lean into the curve of her neck and kiss it. The idea made him feel weak.

A tiny figure 1 appeared in his email inbox and he clicked

on it, holding his breath. Only Iris, he thought, and went to read her message.

How are you? I would like to bring the Forsters, who own River-side Court, to come and view Mansfield Cottage sometime. Can you give me a ring and we'll discuss a suitable day?

Aidan got up from his desk and walked around the study. He peered out of the high window at the view. There was a good tree visible from here, a sycamore, and the cloudscape was always a treat. How many hours had he spent looking at the passing clouds and not working? He was going to miss this place, unless he could come up with somewhere suitable to go to. Iris's email was good news. He and Vina had spent quite a while talking about Iris, R & T and the whole business of selling houses. She hadn't exactly told him her address but had mentioned the road, so the very first thing he did when he got home after their walk in the park was go to the R & T website and search for it.

When he found the house, he spent rather too long going over the pictures and the video tour, trying to imagine Vina in the rooms. It was a lovely-looking house, though Vina had confessed that it was much shabbier than it appeared on the video. 'They're good at making the most of a place,' she'd said, and he agreed that, yes, they'd even made his home look quite presentable. He'd mentioned its name and where it was, but it was too much to hope that she would be similarly going over the details to discover more about him.

I mustn't hope, he thought. That leads to huge disappointment. I'll go and make lunch, now, right now. As soon as I've just checked the email one more time. He went over to his laptop, clicked on the email and there it was: she called herself VinaB.

He stopped for a moment and looked again, in case his longing for a message had blurred his vision. It hadn't. She'd replied.

If I click on it and it's some kind of put-down or rebuff, what will I do? he asked himself. The despair that came over him slightly worried him. Pull yourself together, he told himself. You're acting like a teenager. You've only met her once. It's no skin off your nose if she cuts the friendship off now. Nothing hinges on it at all. You can put it down to experience and move on. He read the email.

Dear Aidan,

Thank you so much for your message. It was good of you to write at once and I'm so glad you did. I, too, had a lovely time and of course I'd like to see you again. I love Kew Gardens! I'm not as good at writing things as you are, but I did enjoy our time together so much.

Very best,
Vina

Aidan smiled and read the message four more times before closing the laptop. He would make lunch, then go for a long walk, and all the way, he knew, he'd be thinking about what Vina had written and how to answer it. He intended to wait till the evening to reply: if he stayed in the house, the temptation to write at once would be too strong, and he'd start pouring his heart out. Until this evening, he was going to enjoy every minute of analysing every single word she'd written, but the bottom line was: she wanted to see him again. *Of course*, she'd said. *Of course I want to see you again.*

*

From: bruce60@R&T. com
To: client mailing list; staff mailing list
Subject: Bruce's Barnet Bulletin, number 402

Hello all,

Well, things are warming up here as the weather improves. We have several very desirable properties that have recently come onto the books, but because they tend to be snapped up, we're recommending an early viewing for any prospective buyers!

Check the details of all our properties on the website.

Flat 4, 28 Bishop's Court, Barnet.

A compact, well-designed apartment suitable for a young couple's first home. One large reception and one spacious bedroom. A beautiful shower room and a galley kitchen make up a really tempting dwelling!

In an up-and-coming area with all facilities nearby. Two-minute walk to the Underground and served by many buses. Within easy reach of the beautiful Hertfordshire countryside.

Do ring the office to arrange a visit. The house of your dreams is only a phone call away.

IRIS

Iris recognized what she was feeling from novels she'd read, in which people woke up and didn't know where they were. It happened in real life too. She'd heard people say things, like *I woke up and for a bit I didn't know where I was.* She used to think that was mad, and that you'd always know the minute you opened your eyes exactly where you were, but she hadn't taken into account the effect that even a small amount of prosecco drunk out of desperate boredom at a kid's birthday party might have.

So, at first when Iris opened her eyes, she had no idea whatsoever where she was but, of course, she came to her senses almost at once. She was in Neil's flat. She was in Neil's bed. Neil was right next to her, still asleep. What had happened? Iris tried to recall the sequence of events and they did become a bit blurred after he'd picked her up in the car on the road leading away from Marilynne's house.

Iris didn't move. She took a few deep breaths. She was dying to go to the loo. Neil was out for the count and didn't look as if he was about to surface. She needed to get out of the bedroom and regroup. Rethink. Weigh up the events of last night.

She started to take Neil's dressing-gown from the hook behind the door of the en-suite, then paused. Wasn't that a bit intimate? Didn't wearing someone's dressing-gown prove that the two of you were still an item? We're not an item, Iris told herself. It's just that I've spent the last few hours catching up on all the sex I've been doing without. That's it. No strings. Surely, she thought, if you've been tangling limbs with someone for a good long time, in his bed, his hands all over you and yours all over him, borrowing a dressing-gown to stop yourself freezing to death was okay. She put it on. She'd deal with the fallout later, if there was any.

Iris made a cup of coffee and sat at the table looking out of the window. What on earth had she done? Whatever it was, one thing was certain: she'd set the Freedom and Autonomy for Iris cause back a bit, that was for sure.

The moment they'd shut the door behind them at about three-thirty yesterday afternoon, it was as though the two of them couldn't wait to get into bed together. Iris hadn't put up a token iota of resistance. She hadn't even spoken a single word, as far as she could remember. Both of us, she reflected, had been carried away. They were both naked before they'd even got upstairs. Since then, about seventeen hours ago, Iris hadn't left the bedroom. Neil had made several excursions downstairs to get food and tea to stop them starving to death but after each makeshift picnic in the bed, back they went, under the duvet. They'd fallen asleep eventually. And now here she was, back in the flat she'd walked out of so bravely such a short time ago.

It makes no difference, Iris told herself. I still don't live here. I am *not* weakening. She'd had no objection to shagging Neil. If she was being strictly honest, Iris would have admitted she'd loved it, but nothing else had changed. She did not want to get married. She did not want any children, and she had no desire to leave her mother's house. Maybe, she thought, I can try to negotiate a different kind of relationship altogether.

Iris sipped her coffee and opened her phone to look at the emails. She deleted Bruce's Bulletin, after a quick glance, and moved on to another message from Patrick Taylor.

What news of walls in your part of the world? Have any good ones caught your eye lately? I'm coming back to England at the beginning of June and look forward to seeing a few, if you've got any you think suitable. I'll be in touch with you when I'm back. Looking forward to seeing you again.

Regards,
Patrick

Iris smiled, and was thinking about her answer when Neil made her jump. She'd been sitting with her back to the door and hadn't heard him come in.

'Hello, beloved,' he said.

Beloved . . . That was new. He'd never said that to her before. She decided to take no notice and certainly not to reciprocate. He was dressed in tracksuit bottoms and sweatshirt. Iris kept her voice as even as she could. 'Oh, hi.' Dead casual. She didn't even look at him, but he came round the table and took the seat directly opposite her. 'Would you like a cup of coffee? Or tea?'

'I'll make another pot of coffee,' he said. 'Don't trust you to do it properly.'

He said it in a jokey voice but Iris knew it was exactly what he thought. It served as a small reminder to her of why she couldn't live with him. He was a control freak. He couldn't even let someone else make his coffee without overseeing the whole thing. Pah, Iris said to herself. I was quite right to get out when I did.

'What's your plan for the rest of the day?' Neil said, with his back to her. 'We could go for a walk or something.'

'Think I won't, ta,' Iris said. 'I'm supposed to be at work. I have stuff to do. I didn't mean to be . . . sidetracked yesterday.'

He turned to face her, while doing funny things with various machines that whirred and spluttered in a scary way. 'It was fun, though, wasn't it? I've never heard it described as *being sidetracked* before.' He smiled. 'Actually, I've got stuff to do too, but I want to talk to you, Iris. About something serious. Specific.'

'Neil—'

He interrupted her. 'Don't worry. I'm not putting pressure on you, Iris. Honestly. It's just that there's something I want to run past you.'

'Go on, then,' she said. 'What's this about? I'm not moving back. I really am not.'

'No, that's fine. I understand completely. This is something different. It's about . . . Well, have you made any holiday plans?'

'No,' Iris said. 'I haven't.' Her thoughts were racing. What was he going to suggest? She'd have to think of an excuse. She'd refuse. She *would* refuse, wouldn't she? She couldn't possibly go on holiday with him. That was practically married.

'Well, I'm inviting you to come on holiday with me. I've been redesigning a website for a chain that has hotels in various places and some of them are really beautiful. Scotland. Devon . . . And they're offering me three days free at one of their hotels. Part of my fee. All in for me and a partner. Wouldn't you call that an offer you can't refuse?'

Iris was silent because, actually, he was right. It did look as near to an unrefusable offer as she'd ever seen.

'You're saying you want me to come on holiday with you? For a free holiday?' It was as well, she thought, to establish the financial side of things at the very beginning.

'That's right. We'd have a good time, you know?'

Iris could hear the question mark in his voice. She didn't answer at once and he chipped in again: 'What's worrying you, Iris? I won't go on and on at you, I promise. Really I won't. And the hotels are beautiful. Very luxurious, though in good taste. Boutique, I'd guess. We'd just be two chums having a ball. And going to bed nice and early too.' Was he waggling his eyebrows? No, but she'd heard the innuendo.

'Do you get to choose your hotel? And can you specify the dates?'

'Yes and yes,' said Neil. He drank some of his coffee.

Iris took a deep breath and tried to arrange what she was thinking into some kind of order. Yes, she wanted to go on holiday to a boutique hotel. They'd be *chums* – very Enid Blyton, but with lashings of sex, instead of ginger beer. All very wonderful but still Iris hesitated. If she agreed to go with him, especially if they *did* have a good time, wouldn't that give him ammunition for his argument that they'd be mad not to be together for ever, yadda-yadda? *You don't have to listen to those arguments if you're really determined not to be pushed into anything permanent:* that was what the voice in her head was saying. Iris had visions of crisp white sheets, blue seas, delicious food and lots of sex. 'Right,' she said. 'I'll come with you, but at the end of the holiday, we'll be just like we are now, right? I am *not* going to live with you, Neil. Not ever. Okay?'

'Okay!' He stood up and came over to kiss her. The kiss went on for a bit too long and Iris could feel herself on the brink of getting sidetracked all over again. She pushed him away as gently as she could. 'I have to go, Neil, I really do. We'll be in touch to fix details. I fancy Devon, by the way.'

'Oh, wow, me too. The Devon hotel is fantastic. On the shores of the River Dart, very near Dartmouth. I'll look into what dates suit them and us. Maybe email me your best times, right?'

'I will. I've got a busy week ahead but I'll be in touch soon with dates. I'm going to shower now, okay?'

'Fine. Help yourself to everything. You look very good in my dressing-gown by the way. '

In the shower, Iris tried to think more clearly. She let the water run over her as she went through the implications of what she'd done. Was it a terrible mistake? Would Neil assume they were back together? *Were* they back together? Iris really didn't want to be. She'd been seduced by an offer of a few nights of good sex in a nice place. Was she being shallow? And, if she was, did it matter? She certainly liked Neil enough to consider a free, short and luxurious holiday not exactly a turn-off. What precisely *did* she want from a long-term relationship if it wasn't just good times in nice places?

She turned the shower off and sighed. As she was dressing, the answer came to her. I want love, she told herself. Real love. Completely overwhelming, can't-live-without-you love. *You're the only thing I see for ever* love, just like Tony and Maria in *West Side Story*. Whatever this was with Neil, Iris was perfectly certain of what it wasn't. It wasn't love.

JOSIE

'Dog shop,' said Zak.

'Park, Zak,' said Josie. It was a beautiful day and the idea of walking the streets of south London didn't appeal. Green space: that was what she wanted. 'We'd have to go on the Tube,' she added. Zak loved going on the Tube and was one of those children who behaved better in public than at home, especially on public transport.

'Don't want to,' said Zak. 'Dog shop.'

Josie wondered about the merits of making a stand, asserting her authority, and decided, as she very often did, against it. It wouldn't hurt to walk the streets for a bit. They could wander through Borough Market, look at the flowers and all the wonderful-smelling food stalls. She could see if there were any houses around that she'd missed. Just because she wanted to move to a place from which she could at least visit the countryside, she still kept an eye open in this area as well because, as someone once said, you just never knew when your dream house was going to appear.

'Dog shop it is,' she said, and Zak jumped up and down. 'Put your shoes on and don't wriggle while you put your anorak on. It makes everything much harder. Then wait for me till we're ready to go. Okay?'

Zak nodded seriously and got to work on the shoes. Josie

wondered briefly, as she gathered together a water bottle, a couple of little boxes of raisins and filled a Tupperware container with cream crackers, whether kids nowadays ever learned to do up shoelaces in the old-fashioned way. Did you learn how to tie bows at school? Was it part of the curriculum? Did it matter if it wasn't? Velcro had changed the universe.

She made her way down in the lift with Zak hanging on to her hand. He'd stopped jumping but Josie could feel through his fingers the jumping he was gamely repressing. As soon as they came out onto the street, he began to tug on her hand, eager to get to the Dog Shop.

'Hang on a mo, Zak. We don't need to run.'

'Yes, we do! We need to run. I want to see the dogs.'

Josie quickened her pace a little. If I'm honest, she thought, I'm quite happy to do the Dog Shop walk.

'There it is!' Zak shouted, and pointed.

And there it was, in all its glory. The first time Josie had seen it, she'd thought it was either a sweet shop or a nail bar. Gretta's Grooming had a pink-and-blue-striped awning and poodle shapes stuck all over the glass frontage.

Zak had been attracted by the dogs on the window. The first time they'd seen the grooming parlour, she and Zak had stood outside, peering through the glass that wasn't obscured by stickers. Josie had read the slogans on the back wall: *Dog grooming and pampering*, and *Turn your pooch into a pedigree*.

Now a woman went in and, before long, a dog was brought out of the back room.

'Look, Mum, a dog!' Zak cried.

It was cute, no doubt about it. 'It's a terrier,' said Josie.

'I want one,' said Zak. 'That lady's got one. You can buy dogs here.'

'No, Zak, you can't, darling. It's a dog hairdresser, that's all. Really.'

Zak sighed. His lip began to tremble dangerously. 'Why do dogs have hairdressers? Dogs don't need hairdressers. They haven't got hair. They've got fur.'

'I expect their fur needs trimming.'

As if to emphasize her point, at that moment an Old English Sheepdog came by with such a long fringe that he must have been negotiating his progress along the pavement by some kind of doggy instinct. His owner was a woman who looked far too skinny and feeble to control him, but she was hanging on to the lead for dear life and managed to manoeuvre him into the shop. Josie said, 'What about that dog, then? He couldn't see a thing. He really does need a haircut, doesn't he?'

Zak nodded. The next dog to turn up was a Cavalier King Charles Spaniel. The owner was chattier than most and stopped to let Zak stroke his pet.

'What's his name?' Zak asked.

'Monty,' said the man. 'Do you like dogs?'

Zak nodded and went on stroking. Josie felt she ought to explain why she, as a mother, was depriving her child in this cruel way. 'We live in a flat,' she said. 'Can't have a dog there, but we're hoping to move.'

'We're getting a dog,' said Zak. 'When we move.'

Josie smiled. She wondered where Zak's certainty came from. So far she and Will had presented it to him as a possibility but clearly he'd decided it was a done deal.

After a good long stroking session, Monty and his owner went into the shop. She and Zak stood outside the grooming parlour for a while longer, watching dogs go in for their grooming or come out afterwards. There weren't crowds of them queuing up to get in, but they saw three going in and two coming out. Their owners looked so happy when they got outside, and Josie could hear their delight: 'Don't you look a lovely boy, then?' and 'Aren't you a smart doggie? Yes, you *are*. You are!' or 'Who's a beautiful chap? You are!'

Josie decided that when they did get a dog she would speak to it in a sensible way. Then she reflected that she'd promised herself not to use baby-talk to Zak but that went straight out of the window as soon as she saw him for the first time.

While they were standing around outside the Dog Shop, Josie took the opportunity to ring Iris. The oligarch, as she and Will called him, had made an offer. All they needed now was to find a house they liked and they'd be set. They had drunk champagne last night to celebrate, then gone to bed and made love, and Zak had not woken up in the middle, which was a real plus and was happening more and more often, these days, thank goodness.

Maybe I'm already pregnant, she thought. Maybe last night was the night. She realized that this was wishful thinking and that it would be better to wait a bit, at least until they were safely in their new house.

Of course, Iris already knew about the oligarch.

'I'm *so* excited,' Josie said. 'All we have to do now is find somewhere to move to.' Iris, she knew, was doing her best, but Josie wanted to hurry her up without being too impatient. Surely there were more properties they could look at. All the houses she and Will had seen so far were wrong in some way. Tiny gardens. Horrid small rooms. No proper hall. Landings where you'd have to squeeze round somebody.

She didn't want to complain, but Iris seemed to understand that she was getting impatient. 'Josie, I know it's awful waiting.

I know how keen you are. And I've already mentioned a couple of properties I really do want you to see. One particular one. It's not exactly in the area you specified but one of them is really special. Both of them are nice so, could we do viewings of both in the same day? Maybe later in the week?'

'I'd have to bring Zak. Is that okay?' Josie was bending the truth a bit. She could easily leave him with Will, now that he wasn't at S & J, but she wanted to see her son's reaction to any house she looked at. They arranged a day and a time and, once more, Iris congratulated her on the offer from the oligarch.

'Time for lunch,' she said firmly, after she'd put her phone back into her bag. 'Let's go and find a nice cafe.'

If there was one thing that could distract Zak it was the prospect of a cafe. He was muttering something under his breath as they walked and it took Josie some moments to work out that he was saying 'Bye, Monty, bye, doggies, bye Dog Shop,' over and over again. If ever a boy needed a dog, Zak was that boy, and Josie was determined to get him one. As soon as they moved.

Will wasn't as interested in hearing about her morning at the Dog Shop as he should have been, in Josie's opinion. He was a smashing husband in many ways and she loved him to bits and wouldn't have changed him for the world, but there were certain things wrong with him. For instance, he wasn't very good at paying attention. Josie often had to check that he had heard what she'd been saying. He hadn't this time. She told him the whole story over supper.

'You haven't been listening, have you?' she added.

'I'm sorry,' he said. 'I got the main picture. You met a nice man with a dog. Outside Gretta's Grooming. Zak loved the dog. Got it.'

'You've missed the main point I was making,' Josie said, 'which was that lots and lots of people are taking their dogs to the grooming parlour. It's like a canine Vidal Sassoon.'

Will laughed. 'That's mad,' he said. 'Surely only poodles belonging to celebs go in for that?'

'You're wrong. Normal people take their normal dogs to be clipped and neatened up. I saw them.' He'd clearly missed the bit about the Old English Sheepdog.

'Well, we haven't got a dog.' Will leaned over and helped himself to more salad.

'I just thought it was interesting.' She took some more salad too. 'It stopped me thinking about houses for a bit. Whether we'd ever find somewhere to live. Though I am seeing two places next week. Iris seems quite excited about them.'

'There you are, then. Don't worry,' said Will. 'Now that the oligarch wants this place, we can step up the search.'

Josie nodded. Will was right, of course, but still, it was a job sometimes not to get disheartened. She made up her mind to be as cheerful and positive as Iris.

AIDAN

The last month, Aidan reflected, had been extraordinary. Or perhaps this was the way most people lived and he had simply been out of the loop since Grace's death. He was driving to Vina's house for dinner, and although they'd seen one another a few times since that first coffee at Prestwick's, this invitation was more significant.

They'd met so far in public places. Aidan ran through them in his head. First, a long day at Kew Gardens, with lunch in the cafe. They had walked the paths and gone into the glasshouses and she'd seemed impressed with his knowledge of the botanical names.

'That's thanks to Grace,' he told her. 'She knew all that sort of thing, and over the years, I caught quite a lot of them.'

'I love plants and flowers,' she said. And then she'd told him about her garden. 'You must come and see it one day,' she'd added, and his heart had lifted at the way she'd smiled when she said it. He was going to see it now, and was filled with excitement. He'd looked at Vina's house on the R & T website but seeing it in real life would be different.

The traffic lights were red as his car passed the cinema. He'd taken Vina there about three weeks ago. She liked going to the movies as much as he did and that had pleased him.

'Grace and I,' he'd told her, as they chatted before the lights went down, 'used to go to the cinema a lot, but I haven't been nearly as much in the last few years.'

'I go to everything I see that looks interesting,' Vina said. 'I can please myself. I sometimes go in the morning, which still feels somehow forbidden. Like bunking off.'

What would happen, he'd wondered, as they sat there in the dark, if I took her hand? Should I? What would she do? He'd debated with himself so hard that he scarcely noticed the film at all. In the end, he didn't dare to touch her, but as they made their way to the car park, he reached out, found her hand and squeezed it.

'That was great,' he said, though most of the action had passed him by.

'Yes,' she said. 'Lovely. We must go again.'

'Of course,' he said, and made up his mind to email her with another invitation as soon as he got home. They'd taken to emailing quite often. Somehow, the absence of a person in front of him made Aidan feel more relaxed and he had told Vina, quite frankly, how happy he was when he was with her. They always kissed (two kisses, one on each cheek in the French manner) when they parted, but lately Aidan had wanted to take things further, though how much further and how he would do it was still a bit of a problem. When he was on his own, he thought about her endlessly, like some callow seventeen-year-old, and chided himself for it. You're sixty, he told himself. Why on earth can't you do what you've wanted to do for ages? Tell her how you feel. Take her in your arms, for Heaven's sake. In the end, Vina had acted first and invited him to dinner.

Now, some hours later, he was in her house for the first time. 'I can't imagine,' he said, 'why you want to leave it. It's beautiful. And I don't understand why everyone isn't queuing up to buy it.'

He and Vina had just finished eating. He'd been worried that his excitement at being invited to dinner with her meant he wouldn't appreciate the meal, but it had been delicious. The evening was so warm that they'd eaten outside, on the part of the house that Vina never called the patio, though that was probably what it was. He had met Libby briefly on her way out (she'd come up to London again, to go to a friend's party, apparently, but this was a planned visit) and they'd exchanged a few words. Aidan had had time to register only that she looked nothing like her mother. She would be back very late, apparently. Vina had probably asked him for that evening because she'd known Libby would be at a party. He was surprised by how relieved he felt about this.

Aidan didn't know much about food but he could tell that Vina had taken pains to make a special meal. They'd had smoked salmon to start with, and a pretty salad too. Salad to Aidan meant lettuce, cucumber and tomato, possibly a radish or two, but this was full of strange and wonderful things he couldn't identify. Vina had told him the ingredients. Pomegranate seeds, toasted pine kernels, feta cheese, something called quinoa, which he'd never previously heard of.

'It's in all the supermarkets,' said Vina, refilling his glass. The wine was good too.

'I never look,' Aidan confessed. 'I just take the stuff I'm used to off the shelves.'

He recognized the main course. It was a chicken casserole, but not like the casseroles Grace used to make, and not like the ones he associated with the first weeks after her death. This one tasted totally different. He didn't bother asking why.

Vina lit a couple of scented candles as dusk fell. Plates with the remains of lemon and raspberry tart and cream were still on the table. When Aidan said, 'I'm happy,' part of him was surprised.

Vina said, 'Me, too,' at once, and he realized, with something of a shock, that he'd spoken aloud.

'I thought I was thinking that,' he explained. 'I didn't know I'd actually said it. I must be more drunk than I thought. But I'm glad I did. The last few weeks have been . . .' What had they been? He couldn't sum it up. The discovery that Vina was someone to whom he could talk freely and honestly made him happy. It wasn't until they'd started talking, about many different things, that he saw how very little speaking he'd done since Grace died. Most of his interactions were with people in shops, or strangers who struck up conversation. Of course he met up for meals with old friends but not nearly often enough. He and Vina had fun together whenever they met, and fun wasn't something that had been constantly present in his life. Grace and I, he thought, loved one another very much but our relationship was a quiet one. In his four dates with Vina, they had laughed at things that wouldn't have struck most people as funny, and chatted about art and history, his research and her knitting – which, to his great astonishment, turned out to be quite interesting in its way. They hadn't really spoken at length about their spouses, or anything too personal, though she had told him about her children and her friends.

Then, of course, there was the desire. He'd fancied Vina from the very first moment he'd seen her sitting across the desk from Iris in the R & T offices. Discovering this had shocked him a little. He'd been distracted by Grace's illness and had regretfully concluded that sexual feelings were now nothing more than a memory. He'd assumed that he was too old for them. But then he'd met Vina, and as he got to know her, he fancied her even more. That made him happy, as though he'd regained the use of a limb he'd thought was no longer functional. He thought about her all the time when they were apart, and when they were together, everything about her made him feel like a teenager again. He wanted to touch her. He wanted to kiss her. When he was in her presence, his mind swerved away from the rest, though when he was alone, he let his thoughts run and run and was shaken by how much he wanted her. He found it hard to gauge how she felt about him, though she'd not objected to a friendly goodbye kiss.

'More wine?' Vina raised the bottle.

Aidan accepted another glass. 'I've got a couple with a kid coming to see my house on Saturday. Iris said they were ready to buy. Apparently a Russian oligarch has offered for that flat I told you about.'

'Lovely,' said Vina. 'It's such a business, isn't it? I despair of ever selling this house. Everyone finds something about it that they don't like.'

'Can't think why,' said Aidan. 'It's a great house.'

'I know. But it's full of memories I don't enjoy revisiting.'

Behind her, the garden stretched out for nearly a hundred feet. That random fact had come from the website to which he'd returned so often that he knew every detail of this house as well as he knew his own.

Vina was still speaking. 'I should have left Geoff ages before I did. He was unfaithful to me almost as soon as we were married. Why didn't I leave him?' She took a sip of wine, and before Aidan could say anything, she went on, 'Because I was pregnant. Afraid of being on my own. And, yes, in love with him. It's hard to bring back those feelings from so long ago, now that I feel so differently about him, but, yes, I was in love. And . . .' she looked at him across the table and smiled '. . . part of me thought it was my fault. If you can't keep your man devoted to you just months after marrying him, well, there must be something wrong with you, right?'

The thought of Vina suffering in this way and for so long filled Aidan with rage. 'No! There's nothing wrong with you. I wish I could . . .'

'What?'

'I wish I could hit him. I wish I'd been there and could have rescued you. I wish you hadn't had to go through that.'

'You're very sweet. I wish you'd been there too. If you had been, I wouldn't have stayed with Geoff.'

Had she really said that? Was it the wine? Did she mean what he thought she did? Aidan, conscious that this might be the moment to speak, to tell her how he felt, was poleaxed by the emotions he was feeling and found the words had dried up in his mouth. At last he managed to say something. Not what he wanted to say, but something. 'Go on. Tell me,' he muttered.

'Oh, you can probably guess. It's such a boring, banal story. I just . . . Over the years I distanced myself. Rob was born, Geoff's business did well and he was out of the house a lot. Then Libby came along. And I made the garden. I lived in my garden, a lot of the time. Gardens are excellent places to escape to. D'you think that the love Englishwomen have for their gardens can be a reflection of how unsatisfactory their indoor lives are?'

Vina didn't wait to hear his answer, but went on speaking. The shadows grew and spread, and the garden was now a place of darkness, apart from the small circle of candlelight they were sitting in. She looked so beautiful that Aidan was hardly aware of what she was saying. Something was melting inside him.

'Vina,' he said, interrupting her.

'Yes?' She looked startled.

'I have to tell you something. I've wanted to tell you this since we first met, but I haven't dared. But now I must.'

'That sounds . . .'

'I want to kiss you. I've wanted to kiss you for ages. I haven't dared say so before, but I can't stop myself now because I've drunk too much, and if I don't say it now, maybe I never will and then I'll always regret it. Please. Forgive me if it's not what you want to hear.'

'I do,' Vina said. 'I do want to hear it.'

She stood up, pushing her chair back on the patio. The metal legs made a scraping sound on the flagstones. Aidan stood up, too. He took her hand and, without saying a word, they moved out of the circle of candlelight and walked to where the pond was, at the back of the garden, down a path between crowded, fragrant borders, her hand in his. Can I really hear my heart beating? he thought. Or is it in my head?

They stood beside the pond and looked at the black water. Aidan put out his other hand, the one Vina wasn't holding, and turned her to face him. He bent his head and put his lips on hers. How did you do this? When was the last time he'd done it? Her mouth was the softest thing . . . softer than anything else in the world, so sweet, so beautiful. He was shaking with longing and knew that he was holding on to her shoulders too hard, almost to steady himself. Oh, God, would he be able to remain upright? What now? What next? He couldn't think. He felt her arms around his waist and they tightened and pulled him

towards her and her lips were open now and Aidan felt himself
falling and falling into a trance of pure pleasure.

Much later, he woke up and stared at the ceiling. I am in Vina's
bed, he thought. I am naked. She is naked. This has happened.
He turned his head and saw her still asleep on the pillow beside
him. One strand of her dark hair was lying across her cheek
and under her nose, moving slightly as she breathed. With one
finger, he very carefully took hold of it and moved it away from
her face. Tears came to his eyes and he blinked. Did he deserve
such happiness? Why was he feeling guilty? As though he'd
been unfaithful. Grace . . .

The fact that his wife was no longer in the world overwhelmed him again, and for the first time since her death, he
found himself more aware of the possibilities in the future
than the sadness of the past. He tried, out of a kind of loyalty,
to remember how it used to be with Grace, sex, the aftermath
of sex, the tenderness, the pleasure, and discovered with some
sorrow that the details had faded into a kind of dim recollec-
tion, which he was unable to bring to mind in any vivid way.
Their shared history was just that: history. It resembled a series
of photographs in his head, photographs that brought things to
his mind but just to look at, not to feel. This, though, what had
happened to him, to them both, last night – *this* was real. It was
now and real and Vina was beside him. He touched her shoulder gently, and she murmured and put her arms around him,
and he buried his face in her neck. Oh, Vina.

VINA

'Libby? You're up early,' Vina said, taken aback at the sight of her daughter, already dressed and sitting at the table in the kitchen drinking what she liked to call an infusion. Camomile, if the smell was anything to go by. She hadn't thought of this. It had never occurred to her that she and Aidan . . . that he might stay the night. She took a deep breath and filled the kettle to make coffee. She couldn't help smiling, though she had no idea how she was going to manage the situation. It was like something from a French farce. Aidan was still in bed. She'd said she was going to bring him a cup of coffee.

Vina's mouth was dry. They'd both had too much to drink last night. Coffee was now an important priority. She bustled about with cups and a tray and wondered what to say. Could she get away with not mentioning Aidan? Was Libby on her way out? It was none of Libby's business, really, what she did in her own bed, but when she remembered what she *had* done last night, what they had both done, she blushed and had to turn towards the window so that Libby couldn't see. I'd totally forgotten what it could be like, she thought, lost in the kind of daydream she hadn't had for decades. I've wasted my life. I've been denying myself such joy . . .

Libby was reading the paper. She obviously felt no need to make conversation, for which Vina was grateful. She made a decision. She would take Aidan's coffee up to him and return to speak seriously to Libby. She would have to at some point.

'I'll be back in a minute, Libby,' she said. 'I want to talk to you, so please wait for me.'

Libby looked up from the paper and stared at her mother. 'Are you okay? You look funny.'

'Never better,' said Vina, and left the room.

'You took your time,' said Libby.

Vina couldn't stop herself blushing. Aidan had kissed her and kissed her, as if he hadn't seen her for hours, days, hungrily and eagerly, and she'd had to make a real effort to stop herself taking off her dressing-gown, getting into bed next to him and allowing him to . . . She gulped. 'Yes, well, that's what I want to talk to you about.'

'You're not ill, are you, Mum?' Libby actually looked anxious, and Vina was fleetingly pleased to see it. 'You don't look ill.'

'I'm not ill. I'm in love.' She hadn't meant to say it and hadn't even permitted herself to think it. The word *love* had not been mentioned last night, by either of them, but she knew that she had named her feelings correctly. Accurately. I love him, she thought. Whatever happens. If I couldn't see him again, I wouldn't be able to bear it. She'd told Libby so now it was out in the open, and she supposed she'd have to tell Aidan. What would his reaction be? She had silenced Libby, who was gawping at her.

'What did you say?' she said at last.

'I'm in love. With Aidan Church. You met him, remember? And saw him as he arrived last night, too. He stayed the night with me. He's upstairs in the shower.'

'Oh, my God!' said Libby, and her face was like a version of

Munch's painting *The Scream*. She actually put her hands on either side of her face and her mouth dropped open. 'How did that happen? How long have you known him? What . . .' Words failed her and she stared at Vina as though her mother had taken leave of her senses.

'I was on my way to meet him for coffee last time you were here. Remember? I met you on the doorstep as you arrived. Anyway, he came to dinner last night and we got, well, we got carried away. But I really like him and I hope you get on with him too. He'll be down soon.'

'Jesus, Mum, it's – it's not right. I have to go. I don't want to speak to him. Not now. I'm not ready. I have to take it all in.'

'Well,' said Vina, 'if that's what you want to do, that's fine, of course, but you'll have to meet him sometime.'

'Why?'

'Because he's going to be part of my life from now on,' said Vina, crossing her fingers under the table because, really, did she know that this wasn't just a fling? Was she quite certain that he felt the same as she did? She remembered the previous night and was sure of it; as sure as she could be of anything.

'It's a good thing I'm going home tomorrow,' said Libby. 'I wouldn't want to stay longer, if he's going to be here all the time.'

'He won't be here all the time,' said Vina. 'He has his own house. He's selling it. That's how we met, through our estate agent. I bumped into him as we went through the revolving doors.'

'Are you sure,' said Libby, seriously, 'that he's not just after you for your money? You're going to be selling this house—'

'Oh, bloody hell, Libby, grow up! Give me credit for a bit of sense, too. That's a dreadful thing to say and untrue. You're mad. He's selling his house. He's got plenty of money. How is it that you always find the one thing that's going to hurt me and then say it?'

'Shit. I'm sorry, Mum, honestly. I didn't mean it. Or, at least, I didn't mean it like you think I did. I don't think you haven't got sense. It's just that . . .'

'You can't imagine anyone wanting to go to bed with me. Is that it? I'm too old. Too ugly. Too fat. Past it.'

'No, no, of course you aren't. Of course not . . .' Libby was looking desperate now.

Vina sighed. She stood up and went to hug her daughter. 'Don't look so stricken. It's hard, I know, for you to take in. You'll get used to it.'

Libby gave Vina a brief hug back and slid out of her arms. She's been sliding out of my arms since she was tiny, Vina reflected. No one ever changes. She's never much liked anyone hugging her.

Libby said, 'I'm going out now. I won't be back till tonight. Will he be here for supper?'

'No, not tonight. Neither will I. We're going to the movies.'

'Okay. I'll see you later, then.'

'You should be pleased for me, Libby. You shouldn't be so disapproving.'

'I'm not disapproving. It's just I wasn't expecting it, that's all. Like you say, I have to get used to it.'

After she'd gone (straight out, without going up to her bedroom, just grabbing her handbag from the cupboard under the stairs, probably scared of running into a naked Aidan on the landing), Vina poured herself another cup of coffee and tried to think clearly.

Last night had been a revelation. What had she been

expecting? It wasn't as though she had any kind of yardstick by which to measure sexual performance. Was she the last person in the world only to have slept with two people before last night? She'd always been embarrassed about how unadventurous she'd been. She and her first boyfriend, Matt, had had a two-year love affair at college. What could she recall about that? Very little. Only – and this was important – that she liked sex and was good at it and had an appetite for it.

Then there were the Geoff years. Sex with him had been one reason, perhaps the main reason, for her continued presence in the marriage. He was energetic and enthusiastic and the very fact that their lovemaking was so good made it even more inexplicable and hurtful that he wasn't satisfied with her. To say that the break-up of their marriage had dented her confidence was putting it mildly. She hadn't even tried to find a man since her divorce. On the odd occasion, at parties, and once on holiday in Greece with some women friends about five years ago, she'd snogged someone and felt a stirring, then something would happen to put a dampener on things. One bloke who had kissed her turned out to be married. On another occasion, even though she'd very much wanted the man to make love to her, she knew she couldn't face the idea of talking to him afterwards because he was so boring. A third had lost her when he whispered obscenities in her ear as he put his hand under her jumper and caressed her breast. Something had always got in the way.

Aidan. She thought about how gentle he was last night. How tentative . . . more like a very young man than someone of sixty. He was shy, hesitant. He apologized. 'I haven't done this for so long . . . I'm sorry.' She had helped him, talked to him in words she'd never used before, touched him, moved in ways she had thought she had forgotten, held him, stroked him, kissed him and then, finally, blissfully, let him find himself, lose himself in her, crying out with him as they came to a climax together, clinging to one another, slick with sweat and trembling afterwards, as they lay for a long time against the pillows. That would have been the moment when they might have said, *I love you*, but neither of them did. They said nothing.

They'd held hands as they slept and then, in the early hours, Aidan had woken her and made love to her again. She woke from a deep sleep to find him kissing her and she drew him to her and their lovemaking this time was slow and loving and the aftershocks of her orgasm were still with her.

Vina sat in the sunshine in her kitchen and wondered when, if ever, she had felt happier. She closed her eyes. *Please*, she said, to a God she didn't believe in. *Please let him love me. Let him love me as much as I love him. Please.*

IRIS

Not every day of being an estate agent was as exciting as every other. There were mornings when Iris woke up and thought, *Oh, God, do I really want to sit at a desk and try to convince the people sitting in front of me that the two-bedroom terrace we're looking at is going to be their ideal home?* But today was different, she knew. Today was going to be really exciting. She'd been working towards it for ages and now it was happening. She'd arranged for Will, Josie and Zak to meet her at Aidan's house. Every time Iris thought of her plan, it made better sense. At first, she hadn't regarded it as a plan, but the more she thought about Aidan's house and what Will and Josie – well, Josie anyway – really wanted, the more convinced Iris became that Mansfield Cottage would be ideal for them. They might have had other ideas, but Iris could just see Zak running around among the trees in the orchard, even climbing them. Were you allowed to climb trees in an orchard? She had no idea. In any case, she had the strongest feeling that today was going to be a good day. She sang Dolly Parton songs in the shower. That was how good it was.

June, of course, didn't fail to notice. 'You were singing in the shower,' she said, as Iris, leaning against the sink, poured herself a cup of coffee and spread some marmalade on the toast she'd made. 'I hope you're going to sit down to eat that.'

It would have been pointless to argue with her and Iris knew what *I hope* really meant. It meant, almost always, *you'd better.* She sat down.

'You seem happy, Iris,' June continued. There was a questioning note in her voice, which meant she wanted details. Iris didn't mind. She told her mother about Will and Josie, and the visit to Aidan's house. When she'd finished her toast, Iris stood up. 'Gotta go,' she said.

'Me too,' said June. 'You seeing Neil tonight?'

'No, not tonight. He's away.'

'Oh, right. Well, I'll make a nice meal and we can watch *Orange is the New Black.*'

Iris would never have thought that her mother was the natural audience for a prison drama with lashings of lesbian sex, but she loved it and so did Iris.

On her way to Mansfield Cottage, she thought about Neil and how good June had been when Iris told her that they were sort of back on, in a way. She didn't crow or say, *I told you so.* She didn't ask, *What way?* She didn't say, *Shall I phone the wedding planner?* She had clearly decided to play it cool and unconcerned, and Iris was grateful for that. She was feeling seriously conflicted about Neil and dealt with this by not thinking about it too much, by working harder even than usual at R & T, and by taking life one day at a time.

Neil . . . They'd been meeting about twice a week, typically at the flat. He'd gone back to cooking tempting meals and they generally ended the evening upstairs and naked in his bed. Iris tried to make a point of going home at about midnight, but on a couple of occasions she'd stayed over. It was always a mistake. Neil annoyed her much more in the cold light of morning than at night after a couple of glasses of wine. Often, he struck her as plain bossy: giving advice when Iris hadn't asked for any and didn't need it. He criticized her involvement with some of the clients, which irritated her more than anything else. She was furious with him for what he'd been saying about Aidan and Vina last time she'd stayed the night. Their argument had started at breakfast.

'I don't see that what they do or don't do is any of your business,' Neil said, when Iris explained to him how pleased she was that they seemed to be getting together. 'I'd be very upset if I thought my estate agent took any interest in my personal life.'

'If you're dealing with someone on a regular basis, day in, day out, and talking about something that means as much to them as where they're going to live, then of course you take an interest. I do, anyway.'

'Well, I wouldn't,' Neil said.

'I love the way you always know so definitely that you're in the right about everything,' Iris said. 'What you'd do is right, and what anyone else might think just doesn't come into it, does it?'

Neil opened his mouth to reply, looking a little like an offended goldfish, but she spoke before he could get a single word out, 'I'd love to stay and fight, darling, but gotta go! Bye!' and sailed out of the flat before he could gather his thoughts.

Now she hadn't seen him for a few days and couldn't really say that she was missing him. She drove to Mansfield Cottage through the Hertfordshire countryside, which was pretty and green, and full of hawthorn in bloom. Iris hoped that Will and Josie would appreciate the beauty and contrast it with the crowded streets they were used to. When she got there, they hadn't arrived, and Aidan let her in. Iris hadn't seen him for a bit and he looked like a different man. Was this Vina's doing?

He wasn't wearing a tie: that was the first thing that struck her. His shirt (was it new?) was dark red. Since when had Aidan worn a dark red shirt? He was smiling, and seemed much less nervous than usual: positively chatty.

'House looks nice, Aidan,' Iris said, when the hellos and how-are-yous were over. He blushed. Why on earth? She was wondering why the state of his house would make him blush when he said, 'Yes, it does, doesn't it? Vin— Mrs Brownrigg came over and helped me to tidy it up for this viewing. We bought some flowers. They cheer the place up, don't they?'

'Right! They really do.'

The tulips standing on the hall table did more than that. They were pink and white, and their elegance seemed to spread around the house. Iris could see past Aidan into the sitting room, where there were more tulips, every cushion had been plumped and every book was in its place on the shelves. She smiled. 'I didn't realize you had vases,' she said.

'Nor did I. But we found some.' He blushed again, having worked out that *we* was a bit of a giveaway.

Iris was longing to ask for more details about Mrs Brown-rigg's visit but just then the bell rang and Aidan went to open the door.

What was it about kids? Why did they have to erupt through a door instead of walking in like normal people? Zak barrelled in and would have gone on a total rampage round the house if it hadn't been for his dad, who grabbed him by the sleeve and hung onto him as if he'd been a puppy. Leashes for small children: was that a commercial proposition? she wondered, before she remembered toddler reins. They certainly existed but Iris had never seen a pair in use. On the other hand, she hadn't been looking at kids wherever she went.

'Hold up, Zak,' Will said, then grinned at her and Aidan. 'Sorry about this, folks. We're used to it at home but it's a bit much in other people's houses.'

'That's fine,' said Aidan. 'Hello, Zak. Why don't you come with me? Miss Atkins will take your mum and dad round the house and I'll show you the garden, okay?'

Josie's eyes opened wide. 'Really? Don't you mind? That's terribly kind of you.'

'Not at all,' said Aidan. 'Come with me, Zak.' He held out his hand and Zak went to him happily. They disappeared in the direction of the back door and Iris heaved a big sigh of relief. It would be so much easier now, showing the property to Will and Josie.

Some estate agents never leave their clients' side during a viewing. They keep up a steady stream of chat, pointing out the blindingly obvious. That wasn't the way Iris did it. Her method was to take the clients on a quick tour of the place, then make herself scarce while they got on with looking at the house by themselves. While they were upstairs, she made a point of being downstairs and vice versa. In Josie's case, Iris had known what she thought the moment Josie stepped into the hall. She'd almost caught her breath. It was obvious to Iris that she was imagining herself in the house. She knew how she would *be* there. Josie hadn't even looked at any of the rooms but Iris knew she was in love. The look on people's faces when this happened was unmistakable. Will hadn't been bowled over: he just peered about, looking over Iris's shoulder to see what he could of the sitting room, and glancing upstairs to assess what was up there.

They were on their own now. Iris could hear the murmur of

153

their voices and could probably have scripted their conversation. She was saying, 'Oh, Will, it's perfect. I love it,' and he was holding back. What fault was he finding? The house seemed so ideal that Iris couldn't think of a single thing, except the distance from central London. That was probably his beef, though she had no idea why it should be. Josie had mentioned in their last phone call that he'd lost his job and it was clear from what she said that this wasn't the disaster it could have been. He was his own boss now, she'd added, and mentioned the possibility of his setting up his own business.

Iris sighed and looked out of the window. Zak and Aidan were playing an elaborate game, which might have been a version of Hide and Seek. Aidan was standing in the middle of the grass with his hands over his eyes, and Zak was peeping out from behind an enormous camellia. She sat down at the kitchen table and took out her phone to check for any messages.

There was a text from Neil: *Don't be late tonight. Cooking something really special . . . xxx*

Blast him. Iris didn't need so much special stuff cooked for her. He was assuming she'd eat with him. He took it for granted that she wouldn't have another date, and he was right. She texted him back: *Okay, ta! x* and took some pleasure in responding to his three kisses with only one of her own. In Iris's opinion, that summed up the proportions of the investment in their relationship. She'd just pressed send when the phone rang. *Unknown caller.* Most likely a bank. She answered anyway because she was killing time till Josie and Will came downstairs.

'Iris Atkins here,' she said.

'Oh, hi. It's Patrick.'

Patrick? Who was Patrick? Iris was just about to ask him for his surname when he kindly provided it.

'Taylor. Patrick Taylor. I'm looking for nice walls, remember?'

'Oh, of course! I thought you were in the USA so I wasn't pre-pared for a call. Sorry. Of course I know who you are.'

'Great. That's good. I'm sorry to ring you on your mobile, but you gave me the number.'

'That's fine. What can I do for you? Apart from the wall thing, of course.'

'I was wondering if I could come and see you to discuss house stuff . . . Is that possible?'

'Well, I'm out of the office now but I should be back about three o'clock or so.'

'Could you possibly manage later? Say five?'

'Okay. See you then. Looking forward to it.'

'Yes, me too.'

Iris put her phone back in her bag. That wasn't too clever of me, she thought. She should have put him off till tomorrow, but she hadn't. Why not? *Because*, said a voice in her head, *you're quite keen to see him again and check that he really is as good-looking as you remember.* This inner voice had other interesting things to say, like: *Because you want to be able to text Neil and tell him you'll be late. Because you will be late and part of you is quite pleased to be acting in an unpredictable way that will slightly put him out. Admit it.*

Iris did admit it. She texted Neil: *Can you delay meal? Will be late after all. Say 6.30? Soz. x*

The answer came back instantly: *Guess I'll have to.* He accom-panied this message with an emoticon showing a very sad face. Iris knew that he was waiting for an additional message, along the lines of *How wonderful you are*, but she wasn't going to give him the satisfaction. Iris didn't care what he was expecting. She had stuff to do. Josie and Will were coming downstairs, ready to go out and look at the garden.

Will seemed happier in the garden than he had in the house. He spent ages in what Iris thought of as the shed, which was much bigger than any shed she'd ever seen. It was called an out-building in the details.

Zak left Aidan when his parents appeared. 'Dad! Dad! Come and see, Mum, there's a tree with apples on it. Little apples are growing. Aidan showed me.'

'Mr Church, Zak,' said Josie, smiling.

'No, Aidan, really,' said Aidan. 'If a child calls me Mr Church, I feel as if I'm still a teacher.'

The Forsters went off to explore the delights of the garden.

'It's looking lovely,' Iris said to Aidan.

'Summer's on the way, isn't it?' said Aidan. 'I love this time of year.'

'I think they're keen, you know,' she whispered. 'She is, for sure. It's a matter of whether she can persuade her husband. I'm hoping the pressure of Josie and Zak combined will swing it. I really think this house is just what they need.'

Aidan was smiling. 'Do you know what I need, too?'

'I'm really sorry I haven't found you somewhere yet, but don't give up. I'm sure the right place for you is there somewhere and we *will* find it.'

'The right place was a bit pricey – the Forsters' flat. I loved that. Wish I could have made an offer.'

'I know. I'm sorry. And now this Russian chap has come along. Never mind. If there's one thing I know it's this. There's always another property. Often the second place is even nicer than the one you lost. I've seen it happen so often.'

'You're very kind, Iris,' he said. 'I'm sure you're right. Some-thing will come up. And I'd be in a better position, wouldn't I, if my house was already sold?'

'Yes, I think you would,' she answered. She didn't add, *But how will I ever find you somewhere half as desirable as the Forsters' flat?*

Patrick Taylor and Iris were still chatting when Bruce came over to her desk.

'Don't want to interrupt. No, don't want to interrupt, but got to rush off, I'm afraid. And I need to lock up, so sorry!'

'I'm the one who's sorry,' said Patrick, standing up. 'I've taken up far too much of Miss Atkins's time. I'll go.'

Iris stood up too, gathered up her handbag, and stuffed her phone into it as quickly as she could. Patrick was through the door. She muttered apologies to Bruce. 'Sorry, Bruce. Didn't notice the time.'

'No problem, Iris. He looks a good prospect. Night-night.'

Iris fled. Patrick was on the pavement outside, looking sheepish, or as sheepish as a dark, rather wolfish bloke can ever be.

'Hope I haven't got you into trouble, Iris.' They were Iris and Patrick now. They'd chatted for about forty-five minutes. The first twenty had been taken up with looking through house details but then they'd moved on to New York, his children, Iris's family, his paintings, walls and other things. Iris liked talking to him and she hadn't lied when she'd told Bruce she hadn't noticed the time.

'That's fine,' she said. 'I'm not in a hurry.' *You're such a liar, Iris!*

'No one cooking for you at home?'

How did he know that? 'Did I say someone was?'

He smiled. 'You didn't, but I'm assuming there's a boyfriend or similar . . .'

'*Similar* describes it better,' Iris said. 'He's not my boyfriend, not really.' *So what was all the sex about? And the holiday you're*

157

about to go on? 'And, yes, he is cooking but I did warn him I'd be late.'

'Okay! I'll be in touch. Nice chatting!' He loped off down the road towards a low black car parked across the road.

Damn, damn, damn. Could she have handled that any worse? Iris was sure he'd been angling to invite her to eat with him or at least have a drink, and she'd messed up the chance. She felt bad about that. Why, though? What was Patrick Taylor to her? Another person who was looking for a house, that was all. It didn't matter. Not a bit. Not really.

What did matter was Neil's foul temper when she rolled up at his flat more than an hour late. The silence from her phone was ominous. Iris would have much preferred an angry text. No text meant he was sulking. Her heart was sinking as she went to find her car.

JOSIE

'Can we live there?' Zak was in the back seat and, for once, not attached to Will's old iPhone, playing electronic *Peppa Pig* games. 'I want to live there. I like it. Can we live there?'

Will and Josie spoke at the same time.

Will said, 'No, we can't.'

Josie said, 'We'll have to see.' Then Josie said, 'Play with your *Peppa Pig* game now, darling. Daddy and I have to talk.'

Zak turned to the phone and Josie looked sideways at Will. Was it sensible to argue with him while he was driving? Probably not, but she couldn't help it. She had fallen in love with that house and she had to talk about it or she'd go mad. As soon as she'd stepped into Mansfield Cottage, she'd known it was home. She could see, in her mind's eye, the Christmas tree in the big hall, lit up, shining. She could envisage her furniture in every room. There was work that needed to be done but they could do it. Will didn't have a job, after all, and he was handy with a paintbrush and good at things like plastering and hanging wallpaper. The thought flashed through her mind, *He could start a decorating firm.* She filed it away for later, but she could already see him with a small business that took charge of everything and offered the personal touch: painting, decorating and interior design. What was the point of her training if it was not for that kind of thing exactly? She smiled at how

ADÈLE GERAS

speedily she had imagined their whole future. Daydreams moved very fast.

All that was for later. Now Josie had only one aim: to get Will to see that the advantages of that house massively outweighed the disadvantages. What were the disadvantages? The location. Would Will agree to live in what was as good as the country? Out of central London? Would he see how much better it would be for Zak?

'Go on,' said Will. 'You're dying to talk about it, aren't you?'

'Am I?'

'You know you are. I can see speech bubbles hanging over your head. Say it.'

'Okay. I love that house. I want to make an offer. I want to do it now, this minute.'

'Hang on a mo,' said Will. 'You haven't asked me what I think of it. And I think it would be madness. Just madness. How can we live there, miles from anywhere?'

'It's not miles from anywhere. It's very near Potters Bar.'

Will laughed. 'Potters Bar! You *cannot* be serious. I can hardly say the words without creasing up. Potters Bar!'

'It isn't *in* Potters Bar! It's near, that's all.'

'We don't know anything about schools,' said Will. 'I don't want Zak to go to crap ones, just to fulfil your dreams of living in the sort-of country.'

'They're not crap schools. They're rather good, as a matter of fact.'

Will turned to look at his wife, who said, 'Keep your eyes on the road, please.'

'Stop being a backseat driver. That's all I need right now. How do you know about the schools?'

'I've looked them up, that's how.'

'Might have guessed. When did you do that?'

Josie said, 'When I saw a picture of Mansfield Cottage and felt it was promising. That's when.'

Will nodded. 'Typical.'

'What don't you like about it? Tell me. Apart from its location, that is. You've made your feelings about that perfectly clear.'

'It's big,' said Will.

'And your point is? I thought we wanted big.'

'*You* want big. I just see miles of garden and trees and an outhouse. It's like a kind of estate. Do we want that? The upkeep?'

'Yes!' Josie tried to keep her voice even. How could he not see it? 'We do. We're going to have another baby. Maybe two. We're going to have a dog. Maybe two.'

'Blimey, Josie, you've got it all worked out! What if I don't want another child or maybe two? Or even one dog?'

'How can you say that? You *can't!* We agreed we'd have a dog when we moved. Zak wants a dog.'

That remark penetrated Zak's *Peppa Pig*-induced trance. 'I want a dog. Can I have a dog? I want one. You said I could have a dog. Didn't you? Didn't you, Mummy?'

'Yes, Zak. I did. You will. You'll get a dog.'

Josie waited till her son was playing on the phone again, then turned back to Will. 'We can talk about this more at home but, honestly, Will, it's as though we hadn't discussed it before. You *know* we have. You can't start saying you don't want another child. That's unfair.'

'Okay, okay, keep your hair on. I *do* want another baby but the rest – Potters Bar, miles of garden, dogs – have I said I wanted that? What about my work? I'm not going to be able to swan around on severance pay for ever, am I?'

'You said you wanted to start your own business.'

'In Potters Bar? You're joking, surely.'

Josie said, 'No, I'm not. I don't see why you have to be in London. Why can't your business be out of London? What's actually *wrong* with Potters Bar?'

'Okay, okay, I give up. Potters Bar is business heaven. I don't suppose for a moment you've given any thought to what this business might be that I'd be starting?'

'I've got a few ideas. I also know what I'd like to do, but I'm not telling you one single thing till you agree on principle that this house is too good to miss. I want to phone Iris. I want to phone her right this minute. Now.'

'You're mad, you know. Quite demented. The house has been on the market for four months or more, and no one's offered for it. Why d'you think that is?'

Sometimes Josie thought that in spite of his erstwhile high-powered job with J & S, in spite of his qualifications, in spite of his native good sense, her husband was just plain thick. She tried to keep any impatience or scorn out of her voice when she answered. 'It's probably because Mansfield Cottage is on the market for almost three million pounds. Not everyone is in a position to offer for it. And, thanks to the oligarch, we are. We can offer for it and move in tomorrow. Well, the next day. But we can go for it, Will, don't you see? And I don't want to run the risk of someone else being in the same position as us and beating us to it. I couldn't bear that. I want to live there.' She gestured with her head towards the back seat. 'He wants to as well. I can't believe you didn't like the house. Go on, tell me. Did you actually not like Mansfield Cottage?'

For a few minutes Will didn't answer. Josie thought perhaps she ought to say something but stopped herself. He was frowning slightly: a sure sign of deep thinking. After a bit, he spoke:

'Okay. Okay, I admit it. It's a beautiful place. I can see stuff I'd like to do with it. Decorating, I mean. Refurbing. That sort of thing.'

'If you weren't driving I'd kiss you. Right now. I could kiss you to bits. Oh, Will, I'm so happy you agree. Can I ring Iris? Can I ring her right now?'

'Go on, then. Make the offer.'

Josie had her phone out and was trembling so much that she could scarcely dial the number.

'Iris? Hi, it's Josie . . . Yes . . . Yes, fabulous. We love it. We all love it. I want to make an offer. Can I do it over the phone? . . . Yes, right now. Offer Mr Church the asking price. I don't want to take the slightest risk of losing Mansfield Cottage.'

As soon as she put her phone away, Josie noticed that Will was frowning again. 'What's the matter?' she asked.

'I hope we've done the right thing, Josie, that's all. I'm not a hundred per cent convinced it's right for us. Making an offer doesn't commit us completely, don't forget . . . We might find somewhere more suitable. Like, in London?'

Josie let out a moan. 'Don't do that, Will. Don't go back now on what we decided.'

'What *you* decided. I'm still undecided. That's my whole point.'

'I'll talk to you about it later on. When you've had something to eat. I can see you're getting tetchy.'

'Anyone who disagrees with you is labelled tetchy. I see!'

Will was smiling, but Josie felt weary. Was she really going to have to talk him into it all over again? She intended to do it if she had to. There must be a way of making Will as enthusiastic as she was. In any case, Iris was going to make the offer. That was what counted.

Summer

VINA

'Even if I had a fiver for every time I've said it,' Aidan was stirring his coffee and not looking at her, 'I'd be a pauper.'

Vina smiled at him, but he wasn't meeting her eye. 'Me too,' she said. 'Maybe it's generational. Maybe it isn't the kind of thing we said. We assumed it, took it for granted, perhaps. In my case, I had years and years of not saying it because I'd have been lying if I had. I stopped loving Geoff donkey's years ago. Anyway, he'd have thought there was something sissy about saying it.'

Aidan nodded. 'Not sissy exactly but, I don't know, somehow not British. Flowery. Foreign. I always loved Grace but I said the words more often towards the end of her life. I wanted her to know . . .'

Vina leaned across the table and squeezed Aidan's hand. 'Of course you did. And she knew, I'm sure, that you loved her all the time.'

'I think she did. I hope so.' He met her gaze for the first time since they'd started the conversation. A silence fell between them. This happened so seldom that Vina said, 'Are you okay?'

'I'm fine, Vina. Really I am. I just . . . Sometimes I'm taken aback by everything that's happened. I look at you and can't believe . . . Well. I don't know how to say it, but I'm feeling so many new things. Saying things I've not said before to anyone.

Talking more than I've ever talked in my life. I'm meant to have a reputation as someone quiet and quite shy. You're what's changed me, Vina.'

'You've changed me, too. Though no one ever called me shy and quiet.'

'Quite the reverse. Rowdy, I'd say.'

They burst out laughing, both remembering the same thing: Vina's lack of inhibition in bed.

She blushed. 'I'm sorry,' she said, under her breath.

'I love it. It makes me . . . Well, I love it. I love you. There. I've said it again. Three times in one morning. A record.'

'I love you, too. I don't care how many times you say it. Or where.'

They were in the National Gallery cafe. They'd gone to see Monet's painting of the lily pond. Vina realized that Aidan was not used to galleries. They'd walked through each new room slowly, and he'd peered up at certain paintings, the ones that attracted him, reading every single word of the information on the wall.

'I go to museums a lot,' he'd explained to Vina, 'and I love paintings, but I'm not used to examining them so closely. I think I don't know enough about them.'

'I go to a lot of art galleries,' Vina said. 'But you don't have to come with me, if you find it boring.'

'I'll come. I never find being with you boring.' They were in front of the Monet now. He turned to her. People were milling around them. Tourists, children . . . There was a school party of about fifteen kids sprawling on the parquet floor in front of the painting, making their own versions of the water lilies, coloured crayons lying around them. Aidan had taken no notice. He had gone on talking calmly, quietly, so that the words were only for her. 'I love being with you. I've started to wish away the time when I'm not with you. That's because I love you.' He closed his eyes. 'I love you, Vina.'

Vina took his hand. 'And I love you. I've been wanting to say that for weeks. To tell you. Since the first time . . .'

'Saying the words makes it different, doesn't it? I feel it does.'

'I think it does, too,' Vina said, and they'd gone back to looking at the painting. Changed the subject. Discussed Monet, his technique, Giverny, where he had made the Japanese garden precisely so that he could paint the water, the light and the lilies.

'Is this the inspiration for your pond?' Aidan asked.

'It is, in a way. I used to come here a lot and stand in front of it. I've . . .'

'What?'

'Never mind,' Vina said. 'I'll tell you later when we're having coffee. We *are* having coffee, aren't we?'

Now they were at the table, discussing their changed status. Saying the words, in Vina's mind, bound her and Aidan together somehow. Which was rubbish, when you came to think of it. People said the words every day without properly meaning them. *I love you* had never stopped anyone walking off into the sunset without a second thought. Nevertheless, she definitely felt they were a couple, linked in a subtly different way, now that they'd articulated their feelings.

'What did you start to say when we were looking at the Monet? You said you'd tell me over coffee.'

'I thought you might have forgotten.'

'You don't have to tell me if you don't want to.'

'No, it's not that. I don't mind telling you. It's about my holiday. I'm booked to go to Paris. From the fifteenth to the twentieth. When you said you loved me, well, I just thought you might like to come with me . . .'

'To Paris? You'd like me to come with you to Paris?'

'Yes, I really would. If you're free. I hadn't mentioned it because I was considering cancelling.'

'Why on earth?'

'I wanted to stay with you, see *you*, more than I wanted to go on holiday. But asking you to come with me hadn't occurred to me. Now that you've said . . . we've said . . . Well, if you'd like to come, if you *could* come, we'd have a wonderful time.'

'Gosh!' Aidan looked so shocked that Vina wondered whether she'd made a dreadful mistake. Maybe it *was* too soon in their relationship. Maybe he'd run a mile. Maybe—

'I'd love that,' he said, interrupting her thoughts. 'No one has ever asked me to go on holiday with them. I haven't been to Paris since I took my class from college on a trip to the war graves in Normandy twenty years ago or so. I'd like that more than anything I can think of. Thank you.'

Vina could feel the happiness in her body, a physical thing, like pins and needles. It was like bubbles rising through her blood, making her want to sing and shout. She restrained herself. What would these tourists think if she burst into song? She took Aidan's hands in hers and squeezed them. 'It'll be marvellous. I'll make all the arrangements. I've booked a nice hotel but they'll change my room to a double, I'm sure. And I'll go on the Eurostar website when I get home. Oh, Aidan, I can't tell you . . .'

'I know. Me too.' He took a last sip of his coffee. 'I think we should go back to your house, don't you? There's planning to do, isn't there? Lots to do . . .'

Her mind raced to a vision of how it would be when they

arrived. Everything was still new. The house was empty. On past form the door would hardly have closed behind them before they began to kiss. On a couple of occasions, they'd never even made it upstairs to the bedroom. Vina blushed. 'Yes,' she said. 'Let's go to mine.'

Aidan went back to his house after supper. He was working hard on his book, though he never referred to it as that. He called it *my research*. In the last few weeks, Vina had noticed a strange thing happening, something she hadn't expected. She'd begun to miss him when he wasn't with her. She'd begun to want him near her all the time. At first, she'd relished the hours alone after one of their meetings. She had leisure, as the knitted fabric gathered on her needles, to go over what they'd done, what he'd said to her, what she'd said to him. She'd sifted every remark for meaning, and tested each word for its level of affection. She ought to have had even more satisfaction today. He'd told her he loved her. He'd said it not in the fever of love-making but in a crowded art gallery. The knowledge drifted around her, like a cloud of happiness. It moved away from time to time, as she focused on other things for a bit, but then the joy returned to settle on her like a blessing. *He loves me.*

For a while in the late afternoon, she continued to be buoyed up by her new status. *I am loved*, she told herself. But soon that thought was followed by another: *I wish he was here now. I wish he could be here always.* Which brought her up short. When she was married, while she was living with Geoff, she had longed very often to be single. When he'd left her, after the initial misery of being rejected, thrown away, she'd enjoyed being on her own and being completely selfish. There was even, she discovered, something to be said for having an entire bed to yourself. Her bedroom and her life were set up for independence and she enjoyed her solitude. She had sworn that she would never live with a man ever again. *Even if I fall in love*, she'd said to herself during the days when this was a remote, far-fetched possibility, *I will not live with a man ever again*. What had changed? Why did she want to see Aidan sitting on the other chair, across from hers, in the sitting room? Why did she want to cook lovely meals for him? Why did she assume he'd be much better off if she could care for him, look after him?

The main reason she could envisage a life with Aidan, she realized, was that he was unencumbered by children, parents, siblings and, as far as she could see, close friends. He was on his own. Vina's heart ached to think of how alone he was in the world. Who had he talked to before he'd met her? On the other hand, anyone who shared Vina's life would have to factor in Libby, with her moods, and Rob, with the distance he'd managed to put between them. He lived quite close in terms of miles, but hardly ever got in touch, and it was up to his mother to do the emailing and arrange any meetings. Over the last few years, this had been Christmas and maybe a couple of times during the year. Her son and his wife were busy-busy-busy. And they liked travelling, too, during the holidays. Vina avoided examining the truth, to spare herself pain, but she found that her lack of contact with her children hardly worried her at all. I must be an unnatural mother, she told herself, then wondered whether other mothers felt the same and never admitted it.

Staring out of the kitchen window at her garden, in the golden light of early evening, she began to talk herself into a more reasonable frame of mind. Would I live with him if I got the chance? And how would it work? She'd seen the sort of house Aidan was looking for. He'd shown her the details of a couple Iris had taken him to and he was quite keen on, and she knew that, whatever happened, she didn't want to live any-where that looked like that: a new-build surrounded by other new-builds, something easy for a man to maintain. Something soulless, in her opinion. She sighed. However much she loved Aidan, Vina saw no need to sacrifice herself to the extent of liv-ing in a house that made her feel like screaming. There was nothing wrong with wanting to live on her own . . . except that she wanted to be with Aidan every day and every night. Per-haps she ought to take her own house off the market and suggest to Aidan that he moved in with her, but she knew she wouldn't, couldn't, do that. This house was tainted with her history: she wanted to close the door on it and live somewhere completely different.

Before she met Aidan, the need to do that had been over-whelming but now Vina felt less desperate. An early possibility of a buyer had fallen through and she'd had a job persuading Iris she wasn't all that disappointed. Now she sized up every couple who looked round her house with interest but also with a feeling of *I don't care if you don't like this house. I'll live in it till I can find somewhere special.*

So far, the houses she'd looked at were okay but there hadn't been a single one in which she'd felt at home. Also, there hadn't been a single one that would suit her and Aidan as a couple. Grow up, Vina, she told herself. You're not a couple in that sense. Just be grateful that he loves you and would happily come and see you wherever you end up. She picked up her knit-ting bag from where it was hanging on the back of a chair and left the kitchen, wondering why, when it ought to be comfort-ing, that thought depressed her so much.

From: bruce60@R&T. com
To: client mailing list; staff mailing list
Subject: Bruce's Barnet Bulletin, number 403

Hello everyone,

Now that the summer is with us, I hope you're all raring to go, keen on getting the news of our latest and best properties. Our list has grown a lot in the last few weeks and, whatever you're looking for, R & T has something for you.

Follow the links to NEW PROPERTIES and you'll see the full range, but here are a couple of highlights:

24, Selwyn Crescent, Barnet

A beautifully maintained two-bedroom terrace in a quiet street. One large reception, good-sized kitchen and two double bedrooms. Small but neat garden. On road parking. Perfect starter home.

The Limes, Broadway Close, Hadley Wood

A superior 1930s four-bedroom house set in a most desirable area. A large garden (100 ft) and conservatory enhance a property with enormous promise, in need of some updating.

Enjoy the sun and don't forget the sunscreen,
Bruce

IRIS

Iris deleted Bruce's Bulletin, without reading the rest of it, not even the bits that listed the latest sales. She'd made four in the last few weeks and that wasn't bad but, still, the people she most cared about hadn't found anything that Iris would have been happy to see them moving into. True, Josie and Will had offered for Mansfield Cottage and the oligarch meant that that sale ought to go through with no trouble, but Aidan was a problem. Until he found something, the Forsters were stuck.

He'd changed lately. Iris knew that he and Vina were seeing one another from time to time. They'd just been to the National Gallery, he'd told her, during their last conversation. Iris was really pleased with the idea of them getting together, and though she wasn't sure how far the relationship had gone, it was obvious that he had moved on from the man he had been when she'd first met him. His clothes were different: after the burgundy shirt, Iris had noticed others in teal and French navy linen. True, it was summer and Iris had met him when the weather was cold, so it was possible she was seeing his late wife Grace's choice of seasonal shirts, but somehow she didn't think so. She was pretty sure Vina had taken him shopping. His jackets and trousers had improved, too.

But the problem of houses persisted. He wasn't bothered. Iris could tell that his mind wasn't really on the subject. She had even asked him about it when they were going round another boring little box last week.

'You don't really care where you live, do you?' Iris said, when he dared to mention that he quite liked the house. 'It would never do for you,' she told him.

'Why ever not?' he said.

'Because . . . it's too . . . ordinary.'

'Well, I don't mind that so much. I'll have lots of neighbours.'

Too many, she thought, and too near to you. All she said was 'I don't see you here, that's all. I think you could do better.'

'I'm not sure I can, you know,' he said.

'I'm not giving up yet,' Iris said, trying to sound upbeat. 'And the Forsters have made you such a good offer that you can afford to spread your net wider. What about a flat on the river? Weren't we going to try for something like that too?'

'That was just a dream. I'd never have been able to afford their place.'

Iris kept quiet after that, but she couldn't shake the vision she'd had of him looking out at St Paul's, and going up to that lovely little bedroom (which she imagined he would probably turn into a study) to do his writing. She wished she could ask him about Vina, whose house still hadn't sold. That was another thing that bothered Iris. She continued to take people to see it but no one had made an offer. There had been interest from buy-to-let people but Iris had managed to divert them to other properties. She was pretty sure Vina wouldn't want her house to end up as a series of expensive boxes. Vina hadn't found anywhere that suited her either, but she was the opposite of Aidan. Nothing she'd seen was as nice as her own home, and although she claimed she was keen to leave it because of the memories it held of her awful ex-husband, she'd grown to like it a lot more after she'd discovered what she might have to move into instead. Iris sighed. Some chains went well, others badly. On this one, Vina and Aidan were holding her up. What if they really were an item? Could they buy a house together?

The idea was so startling that Iris must have made some sound.

'What's the matter?' said Holly. 'Why're you squawking?'

'I didn't squawk. I do not squawk.'

'You did,' Dominic pitched in. He started making chicken noises and Iris threw a balled-up page of advertising bumph at him. It missed.

'Shut up. I'm thinking,' she said. And she was. She had to talk to them, or to Vina at least, to find out if that was even a possibility. She didn't want to put her foot in it. Maybe they really were just good chums, but imagine if they wanted to live together. She could show them quite different properties: bigger ones, more expensive ones. There was no reason why they should stay in the Barnet area. Iris could look at all kinds of stuff.

She went to her email to write to Vina and found a message from Patrick Taylor:

If you're not doing anything this evening, do come along to the private view of my exhibition at the Contersby Gallery. I'd love to see you there if you can make it. I realize it's ridiculously short notice and that's my fault. I meant to give your email address to the gallery ages ago and didn't. So very sorry. If you can't come tonight, then the exhibition runs for three weeks. And do please bring someone along if you'd like to. The Gallery will provide canapés, which is art-gallery-speak for crisps and peanuts most probably. Wine too. Patrick x

Iris hesitated for a second and a half before typing, *Would love to come. Thanks very much. Iris*

After she'd sent the message, she began to wonder why she was so keen. She decided it was because she was nosy and wanted to see what they were like, the paintings that needed the right kind of wall. She already knew quite a lot about him. Patrick had told her a little about his life and she'd Googled him after their last conversation. He was divorced from an American woman called Myra Heidsink. They'd been married for twenty years and had two children, Paul, twenty, and Melodie, nineteen. Iris did some sums and could see that he'd married when he was very young, and the rate at which the kids had appeared meant that in the beginning, certainly, there had been no shortage of affection between Patrick and Myra.

He'd told her that the divorce had been 'a bit fraught', which was probably Englishman-speak for 'totally nightmarish'. The kids were both at college in the UK, and his mother wasn't getting any younger. Those seemed to be the reasons why Patrick was keen to move from New York and find new walls to hang his paintings on.

I also want to look at his friends, Iris thought. *And you want to get a look at his girlfriend*, said a voice in her head that she preferred to ignore. She was perfectly sure he had a girlfriend. That kiss at the end of his email meant nothing. Well, she had Neil, thank God, so she wouldn't have to turn up looking like someone who might be desperate. She picked up the phone to talk to Neil. This was too important for an email.

The Contersby Gallery was packed. Iris looked through the window and could scarcely make out what was on the walls for the press of bodies. She couldn't see Patrick anywhere. Neil, as Iris had known he would be, was excited at the prospect of diving into that scrum. He was good at parties and she was rotten at them. She hated not being able to hear herself think, and as soon as she saw what the other women were wearing, she began to regret what she had on. Her dress was dark green and would have looked okay at a racecourse, she thought, but on a dull June evening in London, it looked . . . wrong. Sleeveless, floaty, and probably the wrong length. Through the window, she could see that black was the order of the day and those women daring enough not to wear the uniform were somehow startling. She saw earrings made from what looked like knotted string, dipped in bronze. Very dark red lipstick on almost every woman's mouth. Lots of gold jewellery. Shimmery scarves wrapped around heads, turban-style. The men were in jeans and sandals, silk and linen shirts – Neil would blend right in.

'What are we waiting for?' he asked. 'Let's go.'

Iris had been looking at Patrick's paintings carefully for about half an hour, going around the gallery from one to another, taking them in. She had a wine glass in her hand and every so often a fiendishly skinny and youthful person passed near enough for her to grab a prawn in filo pastry or a doll-sized smoked-salmon sandwich and pop it into her mouth. Patrick had made contact of a sort. He'd waved at her from across the room, and Iris had smiled and waved back. He was with a dark young woman, who looked both fierce and beautiful: a female Patrick equivalent. Well, Iris told herself, what did you expect? And why does it even matter? Get a grip. He's your client, not your boyfriend.

Neil, with whom she still refused to live, was having a whale of a time. He was deep in conversation with a blonde woman. At first Iris could see only her back, but when she turned, it became clear that she was old enough to be Neil's mother. Perhaps she was rich. It would be just like Neil to do some serious networking at an occasion like this.

'What do you think?' said someone next to Iris. This woman was elderly, grey-haired and dressed in an understated outfit of black trousers and a grey silk shirt. She was leaning on a rather beautiful stick, with a carved ivory handle, and had spectacles on a gold chain round her neck. She put them on to examine the nearest painting.

'I love it,' Iris said. And as the words left her mouth, it occurred to her that she really did, though she wouldn't have been able to say why. They were all abstracts, like this one, and she didn't usually like abstract paintings. They were large, and she'd thought she preferred small pictures. In the end she said, 'I like the colours.'

'Magnificent, I agree,' said the woman. 'Influence of Rothko and Diebenkorn.' She walked away slowly and Iris stood in front of a huge picture that seemed to be made up of smudgy bands of colour: pinks and yellows and blues that looked like no other pinks, yellows and blues that Iris had ever seen. She had heard of Rothko but not the other chap and decided to Google him later. Or she could ask Neil, who knew more about art than she did. Most people knew more about art than Iris did, but Patrick was right. He *did* need a special wall to hang things like this on. A normal three-bedroom semi wouldn't do.

'Hello,' said someone. Iris turned and there he was, Patrick, without the dark woman he'd been with earlier. 'What do you think? No, don't answer. I shouldn't ask that – very bad form. You can't possibly do anything but lie if you hate them, can you?'

'I don't hate them,' Iris said. 'See that woman over there? She was here a moment ago and I told her I loved them. So there.'

He smiled. 'That's good. That's my mum.'

'Oh, I wish she'd said. How glamorous she is. Mind you, my mum looks pretty good too.'

'It's a baby-boomer thing. People who were young in the sixties don't really do old and frumpy, do they? But I'm glad you like the pictures.'

'I see your problem about walls, too. I know much better what you need now that I've seen these paintings. I'll send you some more details soon.'

'Look forward to that,' he said, and as he did, he reached out and touched her arm briefly, above the elbow. Then someone came along and took him away and that was that. A canapé-carrier appeared just then and Iris picked up a sushi-type thing and ate it so quickly that she had time to grab another before the tray moved away. Patrick had gone and Iris saw him only once more before they left, a bit later. He was with the dark woman again. No skin off your nose, Iris told herself, but she couldn't help feeling a bit . . . What? She didn't really know. Dissatisfied. Disgruntled. She went to find Neil to see if she could persuade him to leave.

When they reached June's house and Iris opened the car door, Neil said, 'I can't imagine you actually like living like this, Iris. Isn't it a bit sad to be with your mother at your age?'

'Wow! You certainly know how to make a person feel better, don't you? You've always got just the right words to put the finishing touches to what was a really nice evening up to now. Good night, Neil. Not bothering to answer, please note!' She kept the smile glued to her face and waved a jolly hand as she opened the front door. She had no intention of letting Neil see that he'd got to her. Because, of course, he was right and Iris was beginning to feel it more and more. To be living with your mother, she thought, when you were in your thirties (hello, dear Biological Clock!) was somewhat of a failure.

The whole situation was made worse because in her job she had to find precisely the right house for other people. Marilynne called it 'a bit of an irony'. Blast her. But why, Iris thought, can't I find a place for myself? As she undressed and got ready for bed, she went over the reasons. First, the kind of home she'd be happy in, she couldn't afford. Second, even though she saw hundreds of properties, nowhere, at the moment, was calling to her, demanding that she live in it. From the houses currently on R & T's books, the only one Iris really liked was Vina's, which was miles too big for a single person. So why not a pretty one-bedroom flat? That brought her to her third reason: Iris didn't like flats. She might have made an exception for Josie's, but that was out of the question. Also, in spite of what she'd said to Neil, she hadn't quite given up on finding Mr Right. Part of her wanted a family home, even though she didn't want a family. What's the matter with me?

She sighed and went to the kitchen, to make herself a cup of tea. After she'd drunk it, she went upstairs, suddenly tired.

As she lay on the bed, she couldn't stop thinking about Patrick's paintings. Walls that might suit them. Walls where they'd look good. She was just drifting off into a dozing state when she woke up again. Some inkling of where they would look wonderful had drifted into her head, then drifted out again. Where was that wall? She'd seen it in her half-dream and now it was gone. But Iris was sure it was a real wall she'd seen in a house she'd been round – but which house? *It'll come back to you if you forget about it*, she told herself. She wasn't sure whether it would, but she could hope and, meanwhile, there were other houses she and Patrick could look at.

JOSIE

'I thought,' said Josie, looking up from her desk, 'that you were getting to be as keen as I am. Clearly you're not. Am I going to have to have that fight all over again?'

Will had stretched out on the sofa with the newspaper unfolded over his chest. Josie had assumed he was reading, now that Zak was finally asleep. He hadn't said a word for ages. He'd probably been snoozing. Then he'd sat up suddenly and said, 'About Mansfield Cottage. Should we think again, d'you reckon?'

Josie sighed. Since they'd made their offer, she had been talking and talking, trying to reassure Will that, really, it was their dream house, that they would be fine and, most important of all, that he would find work. Talking and talking was one way of describing it. Actually, they'd had a couple of real arguments. She'd been near to tears more than once as Will appeared to be digging his heels in. Too far to travel from Mansfield Cottage to London. What would he do when he got another job? It was time to start looking for one. Hanging around the flat, occasionally going out with Zak and fixing every tiny thing that needed attention wasn't going to cut it for ever. But the last time they'd spoken, Josie had thought she'd nailed it.

'We agreed ages ago, I thought, that you could start your own business,' she said, 'if no one will employ you!'

'Doing what?' he'd replied.

'I've had a couple of ideas but I'm sure something will turn up.'

'That's mad,' Will answered crossly. 'What if nothing does? You have to agree that's a much more likely scenario.'

Since then they'd batted about lots of crazy ideas and a few sensible ones, like her original idea of a decorating firm. At least, they were sensible in Josie's opinion.

'You're good at so many things, Will,' she said. 'Just think of what you'd like to do.'

He'd shut up after that and, to be fair to him, he had started to think about what a business plan might look like, if he could only decide what the business might be. Now he was bringing the whole thing up again.

'It is ridiculously situated, don't you think?' he said.

'There's nothing so special about living in London,' Josie said patiently. How often could she repeat herself? How long would Will keep banging on? 'I can think of lots of advantages to living in a place where you look out of the window and see green stuff all around. Also, as I've told you already, the nearest school looks brilliant. The move'll be good for Zak. We promised him a dog, remember? You promised, too. He's going to have to wait ages as it is. Mr Church doesn't seem in too much of a hurry to move, does he? It took me hours to explain to Zak about house chains. He's got it now. He knows it might be weeks and weeks before we move in.'

'It's a hell of a commute if I get a job in London.' Will had stood up and gone to the kitchen. He filled the kettle and waited for it to boil. 'Want a coffee?'

'Yes, please. I don't think you *should* get a job in London. It'd be the same kind of job that you hated at J & S. Like I said, start your own business.'

'What are you doing over there anyway?' he said, turning the conversation away from himself. Josie recognized the tactic. Will got bored with arguments long before she did. Still, he did absorb things in his own way, and Josie was sure that if only they could move into Mansfield Cottage, he'd be as happy living there as she would.

They'd been back twice, to look at the house more carefully, and Josie had loved it even more than she had the first time they'd seen it. Zak loved it too. He'd spent most of the time in the garden by himself, just mooching about, which had allowed Mr Church to chat a bit to her and Will. Josie liked him and was pleased that he and his late wife had lived there for ages and been happy. She didn't believe in *feng shui*, but as she'd walked around the house and stood at every window examining the view, she could feel Mansfield Cottage settle itself round her, as if it was welcoming her, embracing her. She didn't mention that to Will because he would have thought she was bonkers, but Josie knew it was her home and the idea that she might not live here filled her with dread.

Now she answered Will, with an edited version of the truth: 'Oh, I'm just looking at stuff online.'

She turned off the computer and went to sit on the sofa next to Will, who turned on the news and put an arm affectionately around her shoulders. 'Okay! I'll back off. I expect I'll find something.'

'We've got time,' Josie said. 'You don't have to decide right now. I'm sure – surer than I am of anything else – that this is the right house for us. I'm positive.'

'Fine,' Will said, and turned his attention to the horrors unfolding on the screen.

Josie was still thinking of the dog breeders' websites she'd been looking at. It had started as a game with Zak. He'd been expecting a dog almost at once. After Josie had explained to him how the house-moving thing worked, she'd promised him they could have lots of fun looking on the computer at every sort of dog. It would, she said, help them to choose what kind they wanted. They'd spent hours looking and had drawn up a short list. Then, earlier this evening, Josie had had a brilliant idea. Zak's birthday was at the end of September and she'd thought of one present she could make herself and that she knew he'd like.

'Can I show you something?' she asked Will. The news had moved on and the lesser items were as boring as news was capable of being.

'Sure,' Will said.

Josie jumped up and went back to the desk. She picked up a piece of paper from beside the computer and brought it over to show Will. 'What does this look like?' she asked.

He took the paper and stared at it. 'It's fantastic. Who did it? It's brilliant.'

'I did.'

'Really? That's amazing. It's – it's ace. Is it for Zak?'

Josie looked down at the sketch she'd made of a Welsh terrier she'd seen on the internet. She'd been pleased with the likeness, and thought the dog looked as if he was going to bound out of the paper. She hadn't taken very long to do it, but as she'd worked, she'd known that Zak would love it. The next best thing to a dog was a portrait of a dog.

'I'm going to do a few of them, different dogs, frame them properly, and they can be part of Zak's birthday present.'

'That's really cool. He'll love it! Anyone would. Any dog lover. I had no idea you could draw like that.'

'I haven't done any drawing for years. I used to be good.'

'Well, you still are. You really are.'

Josie went to put away the sketch in a file. 'Don't mention it to Zak. It's a surprise.'

From: bruce60@R&T. com
To: client mailing list; staff mailing list
Subject: Bruce's Barnet Bulletin, number 404

Hello everyone,

Things have been a little quieter than we're used to here, but hey! That means things can only get better, right? We have recently acquired several most interesting properties, including three flats in a new development, which looks really beautiful and which, many of you will know, has just put its first homes on the market. Word travels fast around here!

There are three different price ranges in this development, including some suitable for first-time buyers. Most flats are between £345K and £645K and the location is a prime one as well.

To see details of these and other wonderful homes, please visit our website: www.R&T.com or call into any of our offices. We go the extra mile to find you the house of your dreams.

Bye bye,
Bruce

AIDAN

It hadn't been nearly as bad as he'd feared. They'd almost finished eating, so it wouldn't be long before Rob and Janice said their farewells and he and Vina were left alone. Then he could relax.

When she'd mentioned that she wanted her son and daughter-in-law to meet him, Aidan had said something along the lines of 'Yes, of course,' but he'd reckoned without Vina's organizational ability. Now here he was, only days later, sitting outside her kitchen again for Sunday lunch in the shade of a large umbrella, enjoying salads and quiches, coffee and walnut cake, and cold white wine. Rob and Janice were on elderflower cordial, even though only one of them was driving home. Aidan looked at Vina's son, who was blond and good-looking, if a bit on the beefy side. Janice was skinny and dark, with long hair that hung down over her tanned shoulders. She reminded him of a reasonably attractive rodent.

Before they'd arrived, he'd said to Vina, 'I'm nervous. I haven't felt this nervous since I had to meet Grace's parents who turned out to be daunting and Scottish and very formal. '

'Rob and Janice are nothing to be afraid of, honestly. I want them to meet you because you're important to me.'

'What if they don't like me? What if they disapprove?'

'It won't make any difference to how I feel, I promise you,

but why on earth would they disapprove? It's none of their business.'

'They might think I'm some kind of fortune hunter.'

Vina laughed. 'How mad! They could equally say I'm a gold-digger.'

He'd relaxed a bit after that, and in truth the meal had gone better than he'd expected. Rob turned out to be, if not fascinating, at least not boring. He seemed intelligent, too, and asked some quite perceptive questions about Aidan's research. He didn't look as though he disapproved of his mother's new lover.

Every time that word came into Aidan's mind, he felt an unfamiliar thrill. The image he had of himself, his idea of who he was, encompassed a number of things he gave a name to: husband, then widower. Teacher, then ex-teacher. On good days, historian or writer. Son, once upon a time, though not for years and years. He'd never been a brother and therefore not an uncle. Worst of all, he'd never been a father. He had been, and still was, a friend. In his teens, he'd even been a boyfriend a couple of times but he'd never, ever thought of himself as a lover. Now he was. His life had changed beyond recognition in a dizzyingly short time. The way he dressed had changed, because Vina had taken him shopping, so now he even looked different. The shopping . . . He'd dreaded it but it had turned out to be fun. Who knew there were so many choices? He now rather regretted letting Grace buy most of his clothes for decades. He'd missed out on the fun of choosing his own shirts and socks for far too many years.

'In a fortnight,' Vina was saying, when he tuned in again to the conversation round the table. 'We're going for four nights. Our hotel looks gorgeous. We're pushing the boat out a bit. '

'Not too far, I hope,' said Rob.

'It's none of our business, Rob,' said Janice, pursing her lips and looking more than ever like a pretty mouse. 'Vina can spend her money as she wishes.'

'Sorry, Mum,' said Rob. 'Don't want you falling on hard times, that's all.'

Vina smiled and ignored him. 'We're going to Giverny. To see Monet's garden.'

'That sounds nice,' said Janice. 'Hope it's not too hot for you.'

'I've got a sunhat,' said Vina. 'I'll be fine.' She then told the passport story: how Aidan had discovered his passport was out of date and how they'd had to scramble to get him a new one in time for their departure.

He and Grace hadn't been abroad for years and his passport had sat in a rarely visited section of the filing cabinet. He hadn't given it a thought till Vina had asked him about it. His old passport photo was ridiculously out of date. Vina had exclaimed about how handsome he'd been and he'd pretended to be offended. They'd examined the new passport in bed, a few nights ago, and he'd said, 'I look like an old man.'

Vina had answered, 'You don't feel like an old man.'

That conversation had ended in a most satisfying demonstration that she was right. He smiled, remembering it, but the others were busy talking about the euro, how good the exchange rate was, and didn't notice.

By the time Janice said, 'We really ought to be getting home, Rob. Early start tomorrow,' Aidan was prepared to admit that the lunch had gone well.

As Rob's car disappeared down the road, Vina let out a sigh, 'Thank Heaven that's over,' and sank into a chair. 'I need another cup of tea.'

'I thought it went very well. I liked them,' said Aidan.

'Well, that's a relief to me, I must say. I thought you might hate Rob. He can be so pompous, you know.'

'No, I thought he was . . . well, rather nice, actually.'

'He *is* nice, really. Not everyone can see it straight away, though. I do love you! But I'm relieved he liked you. That was really what I meant.'

'You said it didn't matter when I told you I was nervous of what he might think.'

'Well, it doesn't. Of course it doesn't, but I can't pretend that life isn't much easier if one's children do get on with one's lover.'

He leaned over her chair and kissed her. 'You've said it. I've never heard you say it. I think of myself as that sometimes, *your lover*, and it gives me a real thrill when I do, but it's even better when you say it. Is that how you think of me? Your lover?'

'Yes,' said Vina. 'You are. You're my lover. And you've been drinking and so have I, so neither of us can drive you home. You'll have to stay. Sorry.'

'No need to apologize . . .'

Aidan wondered why he'd never kept a diary. He wished now that he had a record of his life but it was too late, and he regretted those days and nights that had moved away into the past, leaving no trace. How accurate were his memories? How partial?

Vina was still asleep. He always woke up before her, and relished the time that was his own, in which he could go back over what had happened. How many nights, for instance, since he and Vina had first got together, had he spent in this house? He tried to add them up. Maybe eight or nine. He loved sleeping with her through the night and waking up in the morning in her bed and, if he was honest with himself, he would have been glad to live with her. All the time. For ever. They'd never discussed it. Each day unfolded with neither of them making an effort to push it in one direction or another.

Another thing they'd never talked about was money, and it was only Vina's mention of Rob taking him for a fortune hunter that had brought the subject into his mind. He'd never been remotely interested in financial matters, which he supposed was a luxury only available to those who had enough. He'd never thought to ask how much Vina had, or from what source. He wouldn't have dreamed of it. It wasn't his business. He knew about the Knitting Account, because she'd mentioned it, in relation to her work, and she'd also told him that her ex-husband no longer paid her anything. She would profit from the sale of the house if she moved somewhere smaller, which was what she intended, but he was truly not interested in her financial situation. The hotel they were going to was quite expensive, but for his part, he felt no guilt. He'd not been on holiday, not even to a B & B in Cornwall or Scotland, since Grace had become ill. He could afford it, so why on earth not? As Vina said, 'It's only the very young who revel in discomfort. The hotel's the most important part of the holiday for me. I warn you, I like spending my afternoons lying down, resting.'

'Don't know about resting,' he'd answered, 'but lying down in luxury sounds good to me.'

VINA

'So tell me. I want to hear everything. It's my only pleasure, other people's news. And you said you had news. Is it him? Your new squeeze?'

'For a woman of your advanced years, George, you're very modern. I hate *squeeze*. It makes Aidan sound like a soft toy.'

'What do *you* call him?' George had moved from a swift discussion of the month's knitwear to the more serious stuff: Vina's love life. 'I notice your work isn't suffering. Does that mean he's undemanding? Tell me about him.'

'I've got photos. Then you'll know at least what he looks like.'

She took her phone out of her handbag and stroked it into life. 'There you go. Swipe to the right.'

George looked and handed the phone back. 'Very nice too, if a little bony. I prefer cuddly men. Do you love him?'

Vina took her time answering, sipping the lapsang souchong in her cup. 'Yes,' she said at last. 'I do. Isn't it odd?'

'Not at all. Lucky, I'd call it. Some people, you know, go through their whole life without ever experiencing it.'

'Really? I feel sorry for them, then. But that can't be true. Everyone loves *someone* in their life, don't they? Children, parents, grandparents, siblings and so on.'

'I'm not talking about that. I'm talking about . . . well, love for a man. Or a woman, if that's your thing. Sexual love, I guess

I'd call it. Others might call it romantic, but romance is usually based on sex, don't you think?'

'I suppose so,' said Vina. She was not used to talking like this. George was the only one of her friends who would ask her about Aidan in this vein. The others were interested in the details but would never have dared to ask about them. They dropped hints, they invited confidences, but they wouldn't have pushed their questions too far. And they knew very well that Vina wouldn't spill any lurid beans whatsoever. George, on the other hand, was clearly about to embark on an interrogation that Vina would have to avoid. She spoke first, to deflect George before she'd worked up enough steam to ask for any more information of a kind Vina wouldn't have been comfortable giving.

'We're going to Paris next week. Four nights in a really nice hotel. And I've booked us a trip to Giverny.'

'It's heaven, pure bliss! I love Monet. Love the house – that yellow dining room. Divine. You'll adore it. But there are crowds, be warned. They don't spoil it – well, nothing would – but you sort of imagine it empty, don't you, when you book your tickets? And it isn't. So be prepared.'

'We won't mind.'

'Nor should you. That's the best way to go to Paris, I reckon, when you're so wrapped up in one another that you might just as well be in Luton.'

Vina laughed. 'I won't be taking any knitting.'

George leaned forward and poured herself another cup of tea. 'There's something I meant to run past you, Vina,' she said.

The way she was looking at her, the way she'd gathered herself into a more upright position on her chair, the way she made much of arranging the scarves that hung around her neck into a neater configuration alerted Vina: George was about to speak seriously. She did this so seldom that she sat up straight and put her cup down on the saucer.

'No easy way of saying this, darling, but I'm retiring. At the end of the year. There, I've dreaded saying it and now I have and I feel better. Even if you don't.'

Vina was trying to absorb the shock she was feeling. Before she'd assembled the questions she wanted to ask, George said, 'It means no more knitting work from me, I'm afraid.'

'Oh,' said Vina. 'I'm being fired. Am I?'

'Oh, no, love. No, not at all. It's just the work will stop. I am never, never going to fire you.'

'But why, George? The latest designs are some of the best ever. You're so . . . you have so much to . . .' Words failed Vina and she bit her lip to stop her eyes filling with tears.

'I'm a bit of a fraud, darling. I look energetic. I sound energetic, when you or any of my knitters come round, because I feel I have to be. But on my own I'm a wreck. I just sit around here in a chair watching telly. Every single design is a struggle. I'm over eighty. Did you know that?'

'I never think about it, but, yes, I suppose you do deserve to retire if you want to. I don't know what I'll do without you, though.'

'You'll still come round and see me, won't you? Even if you're not carrying knitwear?'

'Of course I will. Of course.'

'And there's still five or so months' work, isn't there?'

Vina nodded. She'd wait till she got home to think about what this would mean to her. How would she manage without the work, not so much for the money but for the pleasure it gave her? What would she knit now? Who for? A secret jumper for Aidan for Christmas was already hidden at the bottom of her wardrobe. She'd started it early because she could only work on it when she was alone in the house.

'There's one other thing, Vina,' George said. 'You don't have to say a word now, but I do want you to think about it.'

'You're sounding mysterious.'

'Not at all. It did occur to me that maybe there *is* a way to go on. To continue as we've been going on for years. People seem to like the woollies, don't they?'

'Because they're beautiful. That's why.'

'Well, I think you ought to carry on the business. I've thought so for a long time.'

'Me? Carry on . . . I'm not sure what you mean, George. How can I do that? You're the business.'

'I have been, so far, but there's no reason why you can't do what I do. Organize the knitters. Liaise with the shops who take my things. Pay everyone out of what you take. It's not hard, darling. Honestly. I could show you the ropes in a day. Less than a day. What I've thought is, you could become a partner instead of simply being on the payroll. Then, of course, I'd be here to advise you and so on, but you'd be doing the heavy lifting. You'd very soon learn how it works.'

Vina was silent, trying to process what George was saying. In the end she said, 'I suppose I could do the financial stuff and deal with the people, especially if you were here to help, but the main thing you do, the designing, how can I possibly do that? Georgiana jumpers are world-famous. That's the point of them. That's why we do it.'

'Have you ever tried? To design something?'

'Not since I improvised stuff for Libby when she was a little girl. The odd cushion and scarf, too . . . you know. I couldn't possibly do what you do.'

'You won't have to. You'll do something else . . . *your* thing. Your designs. Just think about it. That's all I'm asking. Think about your own patterns, your own combinations of colours and textures . . . and, *voilà*, you have a unique creation.'

'Wow! . . . Okay. I'll think. But it's mad, really. I don't think I could ever do what you do.'

'At the risk of sounding like a head teacher, you never know what you can do till you try. That's true. I've proved it myself. Now, you don't have to go yet, do you? Have another cup of tea. I want to get back to your man. Your Aidan. Does he love you? I never asked you that.'

'He does. He says he does.'

'They all say they do. Can you feel it, in your bones?'

'Yes,' said Vina. 'Yes, I think I can.'

There was so much to think about on the drive home that Vina decided to leave all of it till she got home and concentrate on driving. If she got too absorbed in working out what she had to work out, it was perfectly possible that she'd do something stupid and crash the car. By the time she opened her front door, she was exhausted by the effort of keeping her mind empty.

She took off her cardigan, threw it over the newel post, went into the kitchen and made herself a cup of tea, which she took into the sitting room. She felt nervous, uneasy. Not only because of George's suggestion but also because of what she, Vina, had said. Before she had spoken the words aloud to George – *He loves me, I love him* – what she and Aidan felt about one another had been private between the two of them, part of what sometimes seemed like a dream she'd been inhabiting. Inviting Rob and Janice to Sunday lunch had made it public. Vina was aware that she needed to Skype Libby and bring her up to date. She dreaded it and kept putting it off, hoping that perhaps Rob would have discussed Aidan with his sister, but he might very well not have done and she decided to do it today. Telling George, saying the word *love*, had taken it outside the family.

Vina knew, as certainly as she knew anything, that she loved Aidan. I wouldn't have said it in the first place, she thought, if I hadn't meant it. But was it all too quick? Had she spoken out of a mixture of lust and relief at finding, late in life, a person she could talk to as she'd never talked to anyone before? She'd told Aidan things she'd not articulated even to herself about her children, about Geoff, about her life before the divorce. She'd confessed to him things she hadn't confessed to anyone else, going back to her own childhood. And, which was almost as important, he had listened to her. When Vina noticed this, she'd realized it was a first. No one, not her parents, not her children and certainly not Geoff, had ever *truly* listened to her before, given proper weight to her words and responded to them.

Then there had been the words he'd spoken to her. They were important. On one of their very first walks, back in May in Kew Gardens, they'd sat outside the Palm House on a bench and he'd told her about Grace. They hadn't known one another well then, not at all. They hadn't even kissed properly, though she'd started to think about it and was willing to bet Aidan had too. But he'd said, 'I was married before, Vina, and I can't erase that experience. I don't want to. I'm going to tell you about Grace and me.' He'd turned to her and smiled. 'It may take some time. There's a lot to say.'

'Tell me,' she'd said.

He told her about meeting Grace, falling in love with her, living with her happily for many years and, at the end of her life, caring for her when she was suffering. Looking after her, in agony at his powerlessness to stop her pain, to make the cancer go away, to get her back to what she used to be.

Then he told her about Grace's death and the aftermath: the paralysis, the bewilderment, the grieving and also the guilt he'd felt at his relief that her suffering was over. He described the hours and hours of treatment in hospital. He spoke of the kindness and care of the doctors and nurses. He told her everything it was possible to tell. Also he told her the most important thing: 'I will never forget her. Our life together will be part of me for ever. I will keep on visiting her grave.'

Vina had nodded, unable to find the right words to say. He turned to face her directly, and added, 'None of which affects my feelings for you.'

At that point in their relationship, Vina wasn't sure what his feelings were, or her own, but she was pleased to know that he had *feelings* of any kind.

In the last few weeks, they'd spoken more freely, and since that morning in the Tate when he'd said he loved her, Vina hadn't had the slightest doubt that he'd meant it. He'd told her, a few days ago, that even though he didn't believe in an afterlife of any kind, if there *was* one, Grace would be glad to see him so happy. 'She worried about me. About how I would cope when she was gone. She was in charge of everything. She expected me not to be able to manage.'

Vina had never been jealous of Grace. That part of Aidan's life was over and this one was just beginning. He wanted to be with her. He was far too much of a gentleman to discuss his sex life with Grace, and what that had been like, but she suspected that making love to her, Vina, had been a bit of a revelation and she couldn't help feeling proud of that. Being good at sex wasn't something you could boast about in public, but it was a gift, like being good at dancing, and Vina was glad she had it. Looking back at her time with Geoff, she reckoned that must have been part of why he'd stayed with her for so long, through so many affairs. That and the good cooking, which was another of her talents.

She got up, went upstairs to the Knitting Room and opened her computer. What she really wanted to do was think about George's suggestion, which had been sitting in her mind, like a secret bar of chocolate at the back of a drawer, but in order to take it out and enjoy it, she had to get over the difficult thing first. She had to Skype Libby and talk to her.

Vina hated Skype. She used it as little as possible. Everyone looked half dead on the screen and it was hard to talk naturally. Or maybe she didn't do it often enough to get used to it. Rob and Libby were the only people she ever Skyped. As she went through the routine, she wondered, for the millionth time, why they never rang her, but again, for the millionth time, she pushed aside the thought and got on with finding a nice smile and a happy expression.

'Hi, Mum,' said Libby.

'Hello, darling. You look nice. Is that a new necklace?'

'Yes,' said Libby. 'I've started a line using amber. Expensive, but I like it.'

'Me too. Well done, love. It's gorgeous. Are you still thinking about updating your website?'

Libby made a face. 'Stop nagging, Mum. I'll get to it. I've got other things to think about at the moment.'

'Anything exciting?' (A boyfriend, a journey, a pregnancy, even?)

'Not really. A craft fair in St Ives next weekend. I'm working flat out for that.'

'Sounds super.' Vina took a deep breath. 'I've got news.'

'Really?'

'Yes.' Why did Libby sound surprised? Because, according to her, Vina was an elderly woman to whom nothing of any interest ever happened.

'I'm going on holiday soon,' she said 'and I've invited Aidan to come with me.'

'I know. Rob said. He Skyped me the other day and told me he and Janice had been to lunch and met him.'

The words came out before Vina could stop herself: 'Why didn't you Skype me and say? What did Rob say about Aidan? Did he like him?'

'Ask Rob. He said he was nice, actually.'

'Well, I'm pleased about that,' said Vina. 'I wish both of you were more forthcoming.'

'It's none of our business, really. I'm glad you're happy, Mum, and I hope you have a nice holiday with him.'

'I'd like you to meet him. You ran away, remember?'

'I was embarrassed. It's not every day you find out your mum's been screwing someone she's only just met.'

Vina let that pass because she couldn't think of a suitably scathing reply. She changed the subject. Libby clearly wasn't too bothered and that suited her. 'A couple of people have looked at my house, but I haven't had an offer yet. Iris says I shouldn't worry and someone will come along, but I must admit it's frustrating. Still, as I haven't found anywhere I really like, I'm not that worried.'

'Good,' said Libby. 'I can't think why you're selling, as I told you.'

'And, if I remember, I explained exactly why. Never mind, don't let's argue about that. Are you going on holiday?'

'No, Mum. I live in Cornwall. I feel as if I'm in a holiday place already. And I can't really afford to go away. '

That was as near as Libby would get to a joke so Vina laughed. 'Yes, you're right. It must be lovely at the moment.' As soon as she'd said it, she wondered if Libby had been asking for money in a veiled way. Vina decided that she'd be much more likely to ask directly so she didn't say anything. The conversation went on for few more minutes but the main information had been conveyed and Vina felt as if a burden had been lifted. 'Must go, darling,' she said. 'I've got a huge amount of work to do.'

Libby looked sceptical but Vina only smiled.

'Bye, Mum,' said Libby.

'Bye, darling. Speak soon.'

'Okay,' Libby said, and her face was gone.

Vina closed her laptop and picked up the piece of knitting she'd been working on. It was a simple pattern: one that allowed her mind to wander as she worked and her thoughts turned to her house. She had been warned about buyers who were interested in getting hold of properties to chop them up into tiny apartments that they could let at exorbitant rents. She'd mentioned this to Iris, and was glad to hear that Iris shared her opinion of that practice.

'Don't tell Bruce,' she'd said, the last time someone came round to look at the house. 'He reckons that a sale is a sale is a sale, but I have a good nose for who's really in love with a house and who wants to wreck it. I'd give you the heads-up if I saw a buy-to-let landlord coming after it. It can be okay in some cases when you're rescuing a place, but this house is special. It has to stay as it is.'

My problem, thought Vina, is that my mind is on other stuff. Loving someone takes up a lot of headspace, which is fine when you're young but not so much now. She sighed. Apart from house worries (selling hers, finding another that was fit to move into), there was the matter of George's offer. Could Vina do what her boss had suggested? She had to be efficient about it. Discuss it with the other knitters to make sure they were okay with her becoming the person who allocated their tasks. Would any of them be jealous? Vina didn't think so. Most of them were much older than she was . . . They would be glad not to have their income suddenly stopping, the most important aspect of the change to them. She smiled. I was talking to Libby about a website when I'm the one who needs one. George clearly hadn't wanted one, but if Vina had anything to do with it, there would be one that sold Georgiana knitwear, as well as other lovely things.

Vina was surprised to find that, once she started thinking about her future, all kinds of ideas began to creep into her head and flower there: ideas that might make what George used to do more modern, more profitable, more enjoyable for her. Once I get back from our holiday, she thought, I'll concentrate on all that.

Aidan. What will he think of my ideas? Will he approve? Why shouldn't he? Was it even his business? Vina was pretty sure he'd be fine with it and, like her, would consider that knitting and Vina's work had nothing to do with him. I'll deal with everything properly, she said to herself, as soon as we get back from Paris.

IRIS

Eating out with another couple made a nice change. When Neil suggested that they meet up with Dave, the chap who owned the lovely hotels and who'd said she and Neil could spend a weekend at one for free, and his wife, Fleur, for a meal at the Lebanese restaurant on Sunday night, Iris was happy to fall in with the plan. She liked Neil much better when he was diluted by other people. That was enough to confirm to her, as if she needed confirmation, that she really didn't want to spend the rest of her life with him. She was interested in meeting Dave, about whom she'd heard so much. He and Fleur had no children, which meant that there was a good chance of a pleasantly unrushed evening.

A big plate of hummus, olives, pickles, small falafels and cut-up pitta bread was set before them, and the talk moved to houses, the buying and selling of them, how the market was, how young people couldn't afford a house in London. Iris told them how things were at R & T (busy, selling houses, flats and bedsits all over the place but, yes, very pricey these days and hard for any first-time buyer). She didn't mention anyone by name but boasted a bit about the riverside flat under offer to an oligarch from Russia.

That led to a long conversation that took up most of the main course about oligarchs, Arab potentates of one kind and another, Qataris, the World Cup, the madness of FIFA . . . Iris said very little and just ate. She and Fleur were sitting opposite one another and Fleur was beside Neil. It was clear to Iris that she fancied him. Well, she thought, so do I, and so do lots of other women, so no surprises there.

With the pudding, the talk turned to holidays and, in particular, the wonderful hotel where, thanks to Dave, Iris and Neil were going to be staying. Neil and Dave then took over the conversation, going on and on about all the details that made the place so outstanding.

'That sounds fabulous. Doesn't it sound fabulous, Dave?' Fleur turned to Iris. 'He hardly ever mentions his own work. These hotels . . . I had no idea they were so fabulous. Maybe we could go there sometime.' Her eyes had lit up like headlights.

'Don't see why not,' said Dave. He grinned.

'Can we go when they go?' Fleur looked anxiously and flirtatiously at her husband, and Iris wondered how she managed that combination of expressions. 'It would be so fun to be there together, don't you think?' She beamed round the table, expecting everyone, clearly, to fall in with her idea of a perfect holiday.

Iris took a sip of wine. She wasn't at all sure that the addition of Dave and Fleur to the idyllic couple of days she'd been envisaging was altogether a good thing, but it was Dave's hotel, after all, so there was probably little she could do about it. She grinned at Fleur and said, 'Yes, huge fun!' as sincerely as she could.

At the end of the evening, as she stood up to leave, Fleur said roguishly, 'See you very soon,' then kissed Neil goodbye, first on one cheek, then the other. Dave kissed Iris in a similar fashion, and at last they were in the car driving home.

'That's a bit of a turn-up for the books,' Iris said. 'Who knew we'd be off on holiday with your boss? The hotel's owner, no less. We'll definitely get good service, won't we?'

Neil glanced at her. 'You're okay with it, aren't you?'

'Fine,' Iris said. 'It'll be fun, I think.'

Maybe it really would be. Iris was well on the way to persuading herself.

Because she overslept a bit on Monday, Iris didn't have time to look at her emails before she went to work. She raced into R & T and muttered, 'Sorry, Bruce, sorry, everyone,' as she sat down next to Holly for the usual Monday morning meeting. Bruce liked to call it a conference but, really, it was just the four of them sitting round Bruce's desk, talking through the week's work.

'Hello, Iris,' said Bruce. He was looking unusually sombre.

Surely he wasn't put out that Iris was ten minutes late. That wouldn't have been in character. 'I overslept, folks. Apologies. What's up?'

'You haven't read my email, then?'

'No, soz. I thought it best to get here quickly. I haven't even had a coffee.'

'Then you haven't seen the news?'

'What news?'

In the split second before Bruce told her, Iris raced through what news could have wiped her boss's permasmile from his pink features.

'Mr Raskoff has withdrawn the offer on Riverside Court.'

'What?'

'He's pulled out. He's investing in a Mayfair property instead.'

Iris couldn't speak. The air around her turned darker as she saw, in a dizzying slide, all the consequences of this news. The Forsters would have to withdraw the offer on Mansfield Cottage. Josie would be devastated – she loved it so much and would have been so happy to move in there. It would have fitted the family perfectly. Aidan would be sad because he had begun to see a kind of light at the end of the tunnel. Several properties had just appeared that looked quite promising. She sighed.

'I've got to ring Mrs Forster. Right now. And I think I might try to visit Mr Church. They have to be told at once.' Iris smiled at Bruce. 'Keep your chin up. It's such a fabulous property that it'll go very quickly. He's not the only oligarch on the block.'

Did she believe that? Iris wasn't sure, but she was quite sure of the desirability of the property and that it would go. She knew it would, but she had to persuade Josie. She punched in her number. Josie was out and Iris left a message: 'Josie, please ring me. I need to talk to you. Bye.'

Aidan was next. Iris was beginning to have an idea, but whether it was viable or not, she didn't really know. Still, whatever the case, she had to talk to him, but wanted to do that face to face. He wasn't answering his phone either. What was the matter with everyone? Iris left him a message too, and sat down to do boring admin, which she hoped would take her mind off the storm of disappointment that was going to break over her head very soon.

JOSIE

'What are we going to do?' said Josie. 'How are we going to explain to Zak that there's going to be no dog, that we're not going to move to Mansfield Cottage, that we've got to stay here after all and not have a garden? Oh, I can't bear it!'

Ever since Iris had rung, she'd been finding it hard not to cry. Now that Zak was in bed, and Will and she were well into a bottle of wine, the tears came to her eyes and some of them spilled onto her cheeks.

'Sorry, sorry,' she said, sniffing. 'I'm not going to cry. It's mad, I know it's mad, but I'm so sad. I loved that house so much.'

'We haven't withdrawn our offer, have we?' said Will.

'I know, I know,' said Josie. 'But it's not fair on Mr Church, is it, to let him think he's still got a buyer when he hasn't? We can't afford Mansfield Cottage unless and until we sell our flat.'

'And we will, darling. You know we will. It's such a fabulous flat. Who can resist it? London is packed with oligarchs and other rich people. You know we'll sell it.'

'Yes, but when? If we withdraw our offer, Mr Church's house will be sold to someone else.'

'Did Iris not say she'd ask him to hold off for a while? See if anyone came up to buy the flat?'

'She did, but she also said that Mr Church had maybe found a nice place to live and wanted to move out.'

'I feel bad, because if I'd stayed in my job, we could have got a bridging loan maybe . . .'

'That's mad. If you still worked in the City, we wouldn't be looking to buy a house near Potters Bar, would we?'

'Okay, maybe not. But what you don't need is Zak being miserable. I reckon you ought to stall with him. Explain that we have to wait for Mr Church to buy his new house. Don't say anything about this flat at all. He'll never know.'

Now Josie burst into tears. 'He will! He will know! You're not thinking this through. People are going to be coming here to look at the place. We're going to have to start looking at other properties . . . Of course he'll realize what's happening.'

Will looked glumly into his empty wine glass. 'All right, we'll tell him. Somehow or other. He'll be okay. We'll tell him we're going to get somewhere even nicer than Mansfield Cottage.'

'There isn't anywhere nicer,' Josie said.

'Now you're the one who's being stupid. Of course there is. There's always somewhere nicer. Didn't Iris say that?'

'She did, but she's wrong. For us, there isn't. Mansfield Cottage was ideal. See? I'm already talking about it in the past tense. Oh, Will, I'm so upset about this.'

'I know you are. I am too. But we'll be okay. We will.'

Josie sniffed and sat up straighter. 'I guess. I have to stop crying. That's not doing anyone any good.'

Summer Holidays

AIDAN

'I take off my hat,' said Aidan, 'to old Monet. He sounds a good chap. I think shouldering the burden of someone else's children is a noble thing to do and I'm pretty sure I'd have run a mile if I'd been him.'

'He was a good cook, too,' said Vina. 'He wrote a recipe book. What about this dining room? Yellow . . . Not sure I'd like to eat in here every night but it's a wonderful room, isn't it? This and the blue kitchen.'

'I like the view from the bedroom. And the studio.'

'And the garden. That's the best thing. I'll never forget it.'

They were walking round Monet's house in Giverny. Vina had been her usual efficient self and had booked a small minibus to take them to the house and back to their hotel. Two American couples (unusually taciturn for Americans, and one couple disturbingly resembled the farmer holding a pitchfork and his wife in the painting called *American Gothic*, by Grant Wood) travelled with them. Their driver let them out in a car park that was packed solid with buses. 'I didn't imagine anyone else being here, when I thought of us walking round Giverny,' Vina had said. 'George did warn me it would be crowded, though.'

'There are always people,' Aidan had answered. 'I don't mind that a bit.'

The crowds were no problem in the garden, which, even to

Aidan's untrained eye, was extraordinary. He couldn't put into words the effect on him of so many flowers, so much growth, so abundant a gathering of colours, fragrances and foliage, and especially the sunshine beating down on the whole thing from an unrealistically blue sky. He felt drunk: slightly dizzy, silly and lightheaded.

In the house, things were both better and worse. The people got in the way more but there was so much to look at, and so strong a sense of the family who had lived there, especially the man who'd put the whole thing together. The Japanese prints were beautiful, but Monet had also clearly been capable of loving something that bordered on kitsch.

'Look at this!' he said to Vina. They stared at a figurine of a pale grey cat, curled up on a cushion, almost sinking into it. She was asleep and had a pink ribbon round her neck.

'Lovely. The right side of kitsch, I think, though I couldn't say why,' said Vina.

On the way back, on the tour bus, with the still-silent Americans, they said very little and Aidan fell asleep for a few minutes.

'More than a few minutes,' Vina told him, when they were back in their hotel room. 'About twenty.'

'I'm sorry,' he said.

'Don't be,' said Vina. 'I was fine. I was thinking about houses . . . yours, mine and how long it's all taking.'

'I feel very sorry for the Forsters,' he said. 'They really wanted Mansfield Cottage.'

'I know,' Vina said.

'She came to see me, you know. Iris. I thought that was very kind of her. I asked her why she hadn't just rung me and she said she wanted to cheer me up. Make me realize that someone else would be along soon . . . She also hinted that the Forsters' flat was sure to go soon, and though she didn't actually say so, I think she was telling me to hang on a bit and wait to see whether they wouldn't be able to buy Mansfield Cottage after all.'

'You aren't in a hurry, are you?' Vina asked.

'No, not really. And I liked the Forsters' little boy. He's called Zak. I'd like to think of him running around the garden with his dog. He was perfectly sure that a dog would be part of the picture. There've been a couple of other near-offers but I wasn't too bothered when they fell through. And now I've seen a couple of things that might be okay. Maybe you can come and give your opinion. I don't think Iris likes either of them, to be frank. She says that, apart from anything else, they're a bit small, but the whole point of selling Mansfield Cottage is that I'm rattling around in it.'

'It's not up to her, though, is it? Not in the end.'

'No, but still. Besides, I'd like you to be happy with it. That's important. Actually, she asked me about us. I thought that was a bit . . . well, not exactly strange but you don't expect your estate agent to take an interest in your love life, do you?'

'Iris is not your usual estate agent. She has imagination. And I think she's a bit romantic, too. She likes the idea of people getting together. She looked so pleased when I told her you were coming to Paris with me.'

'I didn't mind her asking at all,' Aidan said. 'I could feel that she approved.'

Aidan watched Vina as she turned back to examine her image in the dressing-table mirror, getting ready to go out for dinner. Their room looked out onto a courtyard and the windows opened to a view of a wall covered with ivy, a high-rise habitat for a huge population of French sparrows. Their song was loud enough to wake him in the morning, but they were quiet now.

*

Aidan had got into the habit, even after two days, of lying in bed for a while as Vina slept, trying to read, but unable to stop thinking, *I'm here. I'm in Paris with Vina. I'm lying in a French hotel with the woman I love. I'm happy.*

'Hello,' she said, turning to face him. 'Have you been awake long?'

'Not really,' Aidan answered. 'I've been thinking.'

'What about?'

'Stuff. I like being here with you.'

'Me too!' She turned over to lie on her back and said, 'I'm thinking about croissants, though. And I've got something to run past you at breakfast. It's been on my mind.'

Aidan could feel his heart moving into a strange rhythm in his chest. Was this it? Surely she couldn't be going to drop him. Had he not been what she expected on this trip? All kinds of clichés went through his head. *Holidays bring out the worst in you. You really get to know a person properly if you go on holiday with them. Living cheek by jowl exposes the cracks in any relationship.*

He said, trying for a light tone, 'Nothing bad, I hope?'

Vina was standing up by now and she gazed at him from her side of the bed. 'Oh, God, Aidan, you look so worried! Nothing to worry about, honestly. A business thing, that's all. Relax.' She went into the bathroom, closed the door, and Aidan's breathing returned to normal.

The second croissant of the day was almost finished. Three would be greedy and one was not enough. Aidan had decided that two was just right. He took the last bite and said, 'I think it's a brilliant idea. You'll enjoy doing it and you'll be very good at it. You're a wonderful organizer, and something else as well.'

'What's that?' Vina had hardly touched her second croissant, but she'd been the one doing the talking. She'd explained George's plan for her to become a partner in the knitting business in great detail. 'I'm so relieved that you don't think I'm mad to be doing it.'

'Far from it,' Aidan said. 'I think you ought to expand it somehow. Online is the way to approach it. You might have to do a course or something to learn how to set up a good website, but that shouldn't be a problem. You could take on more knitters and set up a kind of internet shop of sorts. If you bypass Harrods, you'll get more money. You pay your knitters and so on but you'd have all the profit instead of just some of it.'

'Yes, I've thought of the internet shop idea. But it's having the jumpers in Harrods and Harvey Nicks and Selfridges that tells people they're buying something special. I'm also not sure whether it will be the same when customers realize that Georgiana knitwear is not being designed by George herself.'

'I don't know much about it,' said Aidan, 'but maybe you could have an arrangement with just one shop and no one else. You could make a limited number for that shop exclusively, then use the website for perhaps a different kind of item. Something that doesn't take as long to make.'

Vina smiled. 'Accessories – shawls, mittens, cushions on the website, jumpers and cardigans in the shop. You are clever, Aidan. Thank you for that. Perhaps I'll talk to Liberty. George never managed to get a foothold there. I wonder if I can. I can try, right?'

'Of course,' said Aidan. Vina picked up her croissant and finished it quickly. She poured another cup of coffee from the silver pot, and Aidan felt he could sit in the shade of the sunny courtyard and watch the sparrows eating small, buttery crumbs till the cows came home.

IRIS

'I'm so proud of Dave! Isn't it this an amazing place?' Fleur was smiling at Neil and the four of them raised their glasses and toasted him for being, indeed, very brilliant. Top of the class for Creating Nice Hotels, definitely.

The Unicorn near Dawlish was perfect. Holly, Iris thought, would have called it *heaven on a stick*. It had wooded slopes behind it, and the sea was only a little way down the road. The building was old without being dilapidated and it had been imaginatively converted into a state-of-the-art place: very minimal as far as décor was concerned but full of ancient, unexpected corridors and little flights of stairs that led magically to other rooms. There was a spa in the basement, and as soon as Iris saw it, she resolved to spend most of her time there. Wooded slopes and seasides were fine in their way, but there was nothing to beat a comfy lounger, a fluffy bathrobe and a good novel beside a pool with sauna, jacuzzi and all mod cons thrown in.

They were eating in the Unicorn's restaurant, which was just as good as the rest of the hotel.

'We can explore the area tomorrow,' said Dave. Neil and Fleur nodded enthusiastically, and Iris thought longingly of her lounger. She intended to take up residence in the basement quite soon and said, 'You can go by yourselves tomorrow. I might be sick of the spa by Sunday, but tomorrow is my day for lounging by the pool.'

She had to put up with a bit of grief for that, but nothing the others could say would persuade her. As they drank their coffee, Neil said, 'I'm off for a swim before bed, I think.'

Fleur and Dave made going-to-bed noises, and Iris said, 'I'll be okay in the room, don't worry. I've got some emails to write and I'm quite happy watching telly, too.'

When Neil eventually appeared in their room, Iris realized he'd been swimming for more than an hour. 'I'm knackered,' he said, wandering into the shower. 'Totally knackered.'

'Didn't you shower down there?' she asked.

'Naah. Like my own shower. What have you been doing?' The noise of the water almost drowned his voice but Iris heard him.

'Nothing much. TV's rubbish, but I did my emails. Let's go to bed, okay?'

Neil put on his pyjamas. Iris was quite surprised he'd brought them. She'd packed a nightie but that was mainly in case there was an unexpected fire drill and it was still in the suitcase. She was naked under the robe provided by the hotel, which was deliciously soft and the kind of white you never achieved after something had been washed even once. They got into bed and Neil said, 'I'm absolutely bushed, my love. Are you okay with that?'

'Oh, right,' Iris said. What else could she say? *No, I'm gagging for it, and will be slightly disappointed if you don't shag me for the next half-hour or so.* That was more or less how she was feeling.

Neil fell asleep at once. And as Iris lay awake, she began to go off the idea of some slap and tickle. She was quite tired, too, but wound up from having read work emails before getting into bed. The one that interested her most was from Patrick. He wanted her to help him look at a property in the East End, which another estate agent (How dare he have another estate agent?) had mentioned to him. If Iris agreed to this, he said in the email, could she perhaps not mention that she was an estate agent too? Would she be willing to do that? He really would value her opinion. Iris didn't see any reason not to agree. I could go in a private capacity, she told herself, and not in my professional role. She was quite excited at the idea and had written saying, yes, she'd love to and could they set up a date for next week? The answer came back at once. They would be meeting this time next week, on Friday. Iris was looking forward to it, which made her feel quite forgiving of poor, knackered Neil with his midnight swimming. Mad, she said to herself. That's what he is. Quite, quite barmy.

'I don't know where you got to last night,' said Dave to Fleur at breakfast. They hadn't arranged a time to meet but somehow had found themselves all sitting down together at about half past eight. Dave turned to Iris and Neil as he buttered a piece of toast. 'I fell asleep as soon as I got upstairs, but God knows what time Fleur came in. Can you believe it? She'd gone for a walk.'

'Nothing wrong with that,' said Fleur, calmly pouring milk into her coffee. Dave made up in toast-eating for Fleur's deficiencies in that department. Iris felt a bit ashamed of her full English, but not ashamed enough to do without it. Fleur went on, 'It was a beautiful night and I only explored the grounds. The garden was sensational, even in the dark. There's a gazebo.'

'Moon was pretty well full,' said Neil. 'I noticed that.'

'It was heavenly,' said Fleur, smiling at Neil. Was Iris imagining a special sheen to the smile? A glow and radiance that hadn't been there when she smiled at her husband?

The conversation moved on. The other three made plans and Iris went back to thinking about her lounger and her book.

JOSIE

How on earth, Josie thought, could this holiday be any worse? They'd made the effort, for Zak's sake, to book three days by the sea in Brighton, and what was the first thing that happened? He got earache. Fortunately, the hotel had a resident doctor. Zak was now on antibiotics and not in pain, which was obviously better, but he was peevish, hard to entertain, and watching children's telly programmes was beginning to pall for all three of them. The beach was out of the question today: rain was coming down outside as if it intended to go on for hours.

'It's Sunday. What about going to your mum and dad's?' asked Will. 'Didn't you tell me Stuart and co are going there today? We'd get a decent lunch. Zak could play with Bobby and see the twins. You could fill your mum in with all the news.'

Josie sighed. 'Can I bear it? All the interrogation? The coming up short on everything? The comparisons with Matty and Stuart's kids, Zak being spoiled rotten . . .'

'Coward!' Will laughed. 'Zak will love it. And the twins are only eight months old. No comparison.'

'But there's two of them, so twice as good. And what about my beloved brother? Stuart's got a job and you haven't. Are you up for all that talk?'

'I can take it. I'm not losing my hair for one thing. That gives me confidence. We *would* get a good meal and we wouldn't have to think about them again till Christmas time. Come on, it's surely better than sitting in a hotel room in Brighton on a rainy day.'

'Okay. I give up. Let me find some clothes that don't make Matty raise those very plucked eyebrows of hers. Come on, Zak, let's get ready. We're going on a ride to Granny's. We can play with Bobby.'

That did it. Zak leaped into action and before long they were in the car, driving through the lanes of Sussex towards Josie's childhood home.

'You ought to be more attached to Rock Cottage than you are, you know,' said Will. 'It's a fab place. And wonderful for children. If you played your cards right, we could probably leave Zak there for weekends in a year or two. Or we could go and stay when they're away.'

'They're never away. And I can't bear the thought of Mum and Dad getting hold of Zak. She's a control freak and wouldn't give him a moment's peace. I was only too happy to get out of there, as you know. By the time I was doing my A levels, I was standing at the gate with my eyes on the horizon, itching to leave. My mother never stops. You're never clear of her. She interferes.'

'All mothers interfere,' said Will, calmly. 'It's in the job description.'

'Yours doesn't,' said Josie.

'Bit hard to do from Australia. She's the other kind of mother. Uninterested in her children. I reckon that's much worse.'

'No, it isn't. I'd love not to hear from mine.'

'Well, plaster on your best smile, darling, because we're here. And we're going to enjoy the day if it kills us.'

*

Josie was very glad she'd brought her sketchbook with her. Lunch had been okayish. Gauntlets she'd had to run were:

(a) What were they going to do now that the oligarch had fallen through? Answer: wait.

(b) What did Will intend to do with the rest of his life, now that he had so recklessly (they said bravely, but meant recklessly) given up his job? Answer: get another one.

(c) Was Josie going to have any more children? Two being so much better than one – this from the parents of twins. Answer: none of your business.

(d) Had they found anywhere to live? Answer: still looking. Josie had no desire to go into the whole Mansfield Cottage situation.

(e) Were they thinking of getting a dog? Zak obviously loved Bobby, who was such a good dog and so wonderful about the twins. Because dogs did get jealous, did you know? Just like people. Answer: yes, eventually.

Josie looked round the table at her family and wished she could do a drawing of them all. Phyllis, her mother, was still handsome at sixty-two: very much the tennis-club type. She was wearing tailored grey trousers, a pink blouse, which had come, Josie was sure, from the Gray & Osbourn catalogue, and the two strands of pearls around her neck had been practically stapled there for decades.

Her father, Mike, was a small man resembling a nut: brown from a lot of walking and completely bald. He was not a problem in the way Phyllis was and never interfered in anything. He had his interests and for the most part just joined in by opening bottles and passing vegetables. He read volumes and volumes of military and naval history, each one fatter than the last. His saving grace was his devotion to Zak, and before lunch the two of them had had a good time looking at family medals from two wars. Mike explained what they were and Zak arranged them in different configurations and both were happy with that.

Matty used to be a model, and how Josie's very normal and pleasant-looking but not in the least glamorous brother had persuaded her to marry him was one of life's mysteries. She was tall, thin, and her skin looked permanently airbrushed. Josie would have liked to find fault with her looks and her taste but couldn't.

After lunch, the twins went upstairs for their nap, the men, including Zak, went out for a walk and Josie, Matty and Phyllis were left to spend the afternoon on the squashy-cushioned furniture that looked like something from the back of the *Radio Times* but was actually very comfortable. Bobby, a Cavalier King Charles Spaniel of uncertain temperament but great beauty, was taking a nap too, on the hearthrug. Josie took out her sketchbook and began to draw as they talked. The chat ranged from boring (the twins' schedule), to more boring (Stuart's latest promotion – he was a chartered accountant), to mind-numbing (the politics of the tennis club and who would do well in the club's *mini Wimbers* tournament. Phyllis didn't rate her own chances of getting past the quarter-finals). Josie didn't mind. It was quite soothing, this stream of nothing very much, and Bobby's likeness grew as she listened. She had fallen into a kind of a trance when Matty spoke to her directly, almost waking her up.

'Sorry, Matty, what did you say?' she asked, trying to remember what they'd been talking about when she'd zoned out.

'I said, that's amazing. Quite amazing . . . Were you always this talented? It's exactly like him. Look, Phyllis. Isn't it just like Bobby?' She held out her hand for the sketchbook and Josie reluctantly handed it over.

Phyllis didn't say anything for a bit. Then she looked up and smiled at Josie. 'I can't believe it. When did this happen? Were you always this good at drawing? How come I didn't know?'

'I've always been good at drawing,' she said, smiling to soften her words. 'You've just never noticed.' She added to herself: *Too busy encouraging Stuart. You didn't know because you didn't want to know.* 'I've got good because Zak likes dogs and we spend a lot of time looking at them.'

'May I keep it?'

Later, when she recounted this conversation to Will, she couldn't quite explain what came out of her mouth next. Immediately, without a second to consider the implications of what she was saying, she replied, 'Well, it's for sale, actually. You can buy it, if you like.'

Even more surprising than her cheek in asking her own mother for money for what was, if you looked at it like that, a mere doodle done in a moment of idleness, was Phyllis's reaction. She got up from the sofa, went to find her handbag, then took out her chequebook and a pen.

'Done. How much?' she said.

At which point, Josie felt bad and backtracked like mad. 'Oh, I'm sorry, Mum. Of course you must have it. I want you to have it. I can't possibly take money for it. Of course not.'

'Well, that's very kind indeed of you, darling. I'll frame it and treasure it.' She came to sit down again. 'However,' she went on, 'I think this would be a real money-spinner.'

'What would?' Josie asked.

'Well, when my friends see this, they'll all want a portrait made of their pets. You could certainly charge *them*. Do you do cats as well?'

Josie laughed. 'Do you honestly think people would be willing to pay? And, if so, how much?'

Matty said, 'I'd say a hundred pounds for a sketch and two hundred for a coloured portrait.'

'Blimey,' said Josie. 'Really? That much?'

'It's not a lot,' said Matty. 'You could probably ask much more. Go online and see what other people are charging.'

'Other people may be more, well, more qualified than I am,' said Josie. 'They may be artists.'

'You're an artist. And I bet they're not as good as you are,' Matty said. 'Bobby looks just . . . well . . . exactly like himself but better. I think this'll be a gold mine. An absolute gold mine.'

'Well, I'll look into it,' said Josie, feeling suddenly much friendlier towards her mother and her sister-in-law. A gold mine! What if they were right?

IRIS

Where the hell was Neil? Iris had been asleep and woken up, and he still wasn't in the room. Okay, she'd hadn't gone to bed that late, worn out by very energetic lounging and eating and a bit of walking around the garden before dinner but still. Where was he? His swimming trunks were hanging in the en-suite so he wasn't in the pool. Could the others still be in the cocktail lounge? She'd left them there at about eleven but it was now twelve thirty.

If there was one thing Iris hated it was waking up about an hour after she'd fallen sleep. It meant she would find it very hard to drop off again. Damn Neil and his ridiculous habits. One thing was clear: he was not in any rush to get into bed at the same time as Iris. She wondered what that said about their relationship. It was obvious to her that Neil wasn't desperate for sex (which was fair enough, she supposed, as he got it rather often. Could Iris still say she was living at home? She thought she could, just about) but also he obviously didn't much fancy the other things that were often fun, like gossiping about Dave and Fleur and dissecting every aspect of their characters. It crossed Iris's mind that if Marilynne, Anne or Penny were there, the conversations would have been much more interesting.

She got out of bed and went to the window. Their bedroom

looked out onto the garden. Iris could see a stretch of dark lawn. There were flowerbeds at either side, and some trees, with benches around them, dotted about. During the day, they'd all sat under an apple tree, sipped cocktails and told one another how blissful it all was. Which it was. Fleur had been wearing a rather skimpy top and a skirt Iris thought was too short, but her brown legs were, she acknowledged (and, God, how she hated the phrase!) *beach ready*. They also went on for far too long. Earlier that afternoon, Iris had noticed that Neil could hardly take his eyes off Fleur, who had a habit of licking her lips every time she took a sip of her drink. This had annoyed Iris so much that she came close to knocking the glass out of Fleur's hand.

Iris looked over at the gazebo, and as she stared into the darkness, she saw someone coming out of it. Two people. At first, she couldn't see them clearly. Later, she would ask herself, What would have happened if I hadn't been nosy? If I hadn't decided to wait at the window till they came close enough for me to make out who they were? But Iris did wait and she saw everything. It was Fleur and Neil. Could she have known it was, before she saw them properly? Was that why she'd waited? Iris had no idea, but there they were, right under her nose, and she was mesmerized. God, she thought, what a bastard. What a scuzzbucket. How could I ever, *ever* think of going anywhere near such a dickhead? I didn't even love him, for God's sake. I'm useless. A girl of eighteen would have known it was mad to go back to him. I knew what he was like, and I've wasted months – *months* – when I could have been free of all this hassle and grief. What made me do it? I *knew* it was a mistake – and worse than a mistake: just chucking away my days and nights. What on earth am I going to say to him? To her?

Iris took a deep breath. She knew she didn't want to talk to Fleur ever again or even look at her from a distance. All these thoughts took no more than a second or two to fly through her mind. She was still staring at the two of them making their way to the front door. Neil had his arm around Fleur and they looked so easy with one another that it occurred to Iris that the affair might have been going on for months. He could have been juggling the two of them for ages. Iris felt sick. There was a bay tree in a pot on either side of the door, and when they got there, Neil pulled Fleur into the shadow of one of them and kissed her. It was revolting. One of his hands was down the front of her low-necked T-shirt and the other was doing stuff under her skirt that Iris didn't want to see or think about. Fleur had her arms around Neil's neck and her mouth was glued to his. Revolting, revolting. She left the window and sat on the bed. Neil must have been with Fleur the previous night, she reckoned, when he'd said he'd been swimming. Images of Fleur's silky brown body flat on a lounger with those long legs spread and Neil pumping away on top of her came into Iris's head and she almost threw up.

As she sat there she took a few deep breaths and made up her mind what she was going to do. She would pack and leave. Right now. As soon as she'd told Neil where he got off. He could cobble together a cover story to tell Fleur and Dave, and Iris didn't care what he said. The whole thing was his problem and Iris intended to leave him to deal with it.

When he came into the bedroom, she was already dressed and in her jacket. Her bag was packed and at her feet.

'Hello!' Neil said. Full marks for nonchalance, Iris thought. 'What are you doing dressed up and packed? It's the middle of the night.' A frown came over his face then. 'It isn't an emergency, is it? Has something happened to June?'

'June's fine, but I'm off.'

'Now? It's the middle of the night, for God's sake. What's the matter with you?'

'I admire your ability to keep a straight face, Neil, I really do. Go to the top of the good acting class. I saw you.'

'Saw me?' He was playing for time, Iris could tell. He knew exactly what she meant and was working out his strategy. Fuck him.

'Yup! You and Fleur. So I'm off. That's it. Goodbye.'

Iris moved to the door, to give force to her words and he started babbling: 'No, no, Iris, honestly, it was nothing, please, it didn't mean anything. It's you I love . . . Fleur, that's just a, well, a holiday romance if you like. Nothing more.'

'I don't care. I'm out of here. I don't want to see you again. Ever. Please send any stuff of mine that's in your flat to June's. Ta.'

'But, hang on, can't you wait till tomorrow night? What will I tell them both?'

'I'll leave you to work that out. You have the rest of the night to do it. Oh, and I'm taking my car. You can go back with Dave and Fleur. That'll be fun.'

'Please, oh, please, Iris, I don't want to do that.'

Iris was glad she'd insisted on driving down in her car. 'Soz. I no longer care what you want and don't want.'

'But . . .' He was almost speechless.

'Out of the way, please, Neil. I want to leave.'

'But you can't drive all the way to London in the middle of the night!'

'I can and I will. It's no business of yours what I do any more. Sleep well.'

She managed a fairly dignified exit, wheeling her suitcase

behind her. She went down in the lift and walked straight out of the front door. The young man at Reception didn't even glance in her direction. She took a swipe at one of the bay trees, feeling like an escaping prisoner. As she started the car, Iris looked at her watch. Start to finish, from when she'd seen Fleur and Neil together to this moment, only twenty-five minutes had passed.

As she drove, Iris felt buoyed up with thoughts of what Neil might say to his fancy friends. She imagined the conversation at breakfast. *Iris had to go home. Her mother was ill. Her boss called her back for a very important client.* Yadda-yadda. She quite enjoyed inventing the scenarios. As the road disappeared under her wheels, she wondered how long the *flirtation* or *romance* had been going on. She didn't care and wasn't sure she wanted to know. What if, she asked herself, he'd been shagging Fleur for months? That made it worse. That meant he'd been deceiving her for ages instead of just the last couple of nights. She made up her mind to find out, somehow, even though it really didn't make much difference. I haven't loved him for a long time, she thought. Bastard.

VINA

There was a lot to be said for long train journeys if you were someone who enjoyed knitting. Aidan didn't think so, but Vina had held her ground.

'Why not go by plane and get there more quickly? And come back more quickly?'

'I like trains,' Vina had answered, quite honestly. 'Look at the fun we had on Eurostar.'

'That was different. That was . . . Well, normal trains aren't like Eurostar, are they?'

'No, that's true but I'm going first class.'

'Really?'

'Yes. I booked long in advance and got a good deal. Well worth it.'

Aidan was going to do some research in Nottingham, looking at archives and staying one night with his friend Edward, who lived nearby. He'd arranged the visit when he realized he would be alone over the weekend.

'I'll miss you,' he had said, when they parted. 'Why can't the workshop be in London?'

'Because the designer lives in Edinburgh. That's why. And you won't miss me. You'll have a smashing time with Edward.'

'I *will* be fine,' Aidan had agreed. 'Nevertheless I'll miss you.'

'Well, of course. I'll miss you too,' she said, but now Vina came to the conclusion that she wasn't really *missing* Aidan. Of course she wondered how he was, and intended to phone him every evening – all two evenings – that she was away but it would do them good to be apart for once. She loved him, she was sure of that, and she enjoyed being in love – she and Aidan had good times together – but what she *didn't* want was an infantilized creature for whom she was responsible. Never again. She'd done that with Geoff, who was as dependent on her as he was unfaithful to her. Any man she was involved with had to be his own person, who didn't rely on her physical presence for his happiness.

And we'll always have Paris . . . Humphrey Bogart's words from *Casablanca* came to her and made her smile. But she knew that as long as she lived she would treasure the memory of those days. They had both, somehow, gone back to the kind of unworried state that the young generally inhabit. They'd forgotten about houses, children, work, everything relating to their lives in England, and just gone from place to place looking at everything with eyes ready to be pleased. She remembered the long, long nights, full of talk and lovemaking, more talk, closeness and warmth. The hotel, with the sound of birdsong loud in the early morning. How intensely green the Jardin du Luxembourg was, and the way chairs were scattered about its paths inviting you to sit down, whenever you felt like it. She thought of the food – far too much of it – and how they'd lounged about on the pavement with a coffee, watching the people going by.

Giverny had been a revelation and, like much else they'd seen, an inspiration. She hadn't mentioned it to anyone, not Aidan, not George, but the morning after they'd arrived home, Vina had gone to the Knitting Room and worked out designs for three garments and five cushions, inspired by what was filling her head. No one would realize, she thought, but she would know that these colours, these shapes, this style, came directly from what she had seen. There was a series of patterns based on the *Lady with the Unicorn* tapestries in the Musée de Cluny. Those, she'd decided, would be the works of art she would choose to take to a desert island. Another set of ideas was inspired by Monet's house: the yellow room, the blue room, the flowers, the lilies. Her head was filled with images, but every time she sat down with a piece of graph paper to convey what she was seeing in her head on paper in a way that could reasonably be knitted into something wonderful, she felt inadequate.

She had done something about this inadequacy at once. She'd Googled *knitwear design workshops* and come across the one she was on her way to, which was taking place in what looked like an airy room in Edinburgh. She had booked the course, the hotel and the train within minutes, and now here she was. Her phone buzzed. A text from Aidan. *On my way. See you Monday. Love xx A*

She texted back: *Drive carefully. Love xxx V*

In fact, she was rather dreading next week. She'd promised to view a place with Iris on Tuesday and then they planned to pick up Aidan because he wanted her to see the latest place he was interested in – the one Iris thought was too small. She was apprehensive about showing enough enthusiasm. They had such different taste when it came to houses. Aidan didn't seem to care as much as she did about his surroundings, even though he'd shown himself to be very observant and informed while they were in Paris. He certainly knew a great deal of history, which was something Vina had mostly missed out on. She'd learned a lot from being with him.

Houses . . . When she was at home, and because her life had suddenly become interesting and full of new sensations, selling her house and finding another had become less important. Days and days went by with no one viewing. In the normal course of events, Vina would have worried about it but she had so much else to think about that it had taken a back seat. She still interrogated herself about what she wanted, and wondered sometimes why she was so hard to please.

'Maybe,' Aidan had said, one day, when they were in the Jardin du Luxembourg, walking along the paths, eating ice cream, 'you don't want to move at all and you ought to stay where you are.'

'You too, eh? That's what my children say and even some of the people who come round. *Such a beautiful house. Can't think why you're leaving.*'

'It *is* a beautiful house,' said Aidan, 'but I understand why you want to move. It's the same with me. The house – both houses, really – represent a different life. A life that has nothing to do with the present. That's it, isn't it? I want to leave the past behind. Plus the house is too big for me to manage. I seem to live in three rooms.'

'I know. But you're able to like what you're shown much better than I do. Iris despairs of me. I pick holes in every single property. I can't decide what's important. Sometimes I want a garden. But do I? Really? I'd be quite happy with a few pots on a sunny balcony, or something like that, especially if I'm going to be a knitwear tycoon. I won't have time to garden. You can't believe how much time I used to spend there while I was married to Geoff. It was the only place where I knew he'd never follow me.'

Aidan had laughed and said, 'Tycoon, eh?' but Vina had

begun to think of the financial side of the knitwear business. Once I get back, she decided, I'll get in touch with George and ask her to go over the figures with me.

Now she was on her way to learn. Once she knew how to set about designing and writing patterns, she would try again to transfer the pictures she had in her head to paper. Vina smiled. Already houses were slipping out of her mind. I've got room in my head for Aidan and one other thing, and for the moment, that's this workshop.

IRIS

Iris arrived at her mother's house at half past four in the morning. She tried hard to let herself in silently but it didn't work. She had only just gone into the kitchen when June appeared in the doorway. Most elderly women, Iris reflected, hearing someone padding about downstairs, would have either locked themselves in their room and phoned the police, or come down the stairs carrying an improvised weapon. June was clearly braver than most.

'Make me a cup, too,' was all she said, as she sat down at the kitchen table. 'And there's a bit of that fruit cake left. I could eat a slice and you could probably do with one. When did you last eat?'

'Hello, Ma,' Iris said. 'I thought I was being totally silent.'

'I was awake anyway. I'd just gone to the loo and heard your car. Did something happen?'

'You could say. Neil's been shagging Fleur.'

'Do I know her?'

'She's the wife of the chap who invited us to the hotel in the first place. Pretty, in an obvious way.'

June looked shocked and Iris felt some satisfaction at having been able to surprise her. Normally nothing fazed her. 'Bloody hell,' she said. 'That's a bit much.'

'Yes, it is,' Iris said, putting tea and cake in front of her mother and sitting down to pick at hers. 'Still, it's lucky I wasn't in love with him, right?'

'Mmm,' said June. Her mouth was too full for her to say anything sensible. When she gathered her thoughts, she said, 'Oh, well. Never mind. Win some, lose some, right? You're clearly not heartbroken so I won't bother sympathizing. You can't trust them, that's the bottom line. Though I have to say I'm very disappointed in Neil.'

'If by *them* you mean men, that's not true. Women are just as bad. Fleur's just as much to blame. Maybe more so. I rest my case. And I told you about Neil. I can't think why you were so attached to him.'

'Well, I liked him. I thought he was . . . well, very fond of you. I had hopes of everything coming right in the end. Mad, I suppose, but still . . .'

Iris laughed. 'What Marilynne would call a bit of an irony – me cheering you up for the loss of a useless git.'

June stood up. 'Never mind, eh? We'll recover, I'm sure. I'd go to bed if I were you. Send Brucie Bonus an email saying you'll be in on Tuesday. Or in the afternoon tomorrow, anyway. You need to sleep.'

Quite suddenly, weariness overcame Iris. She was just about to tell her mother that, no, she wanted to be woken at eight – only three hours away – when she realized that Mother probably did know best. 'Okay,' she said. 'I'll be no good to anyone if I don't get a few hours' sleep. I'll send Bruce an email and leave all my devices down here. I'm going to be unconnected till lunchtime.'

'You'll live,' said June. Iris, for her part, and considering how she felt, wasn't so sure but was too tired to argue. She took out her phone to email the office.

Once she was in bed, Iris felt more wide awake than she had been for the last two hours. She lay there, thinking, trying to make up her mind about certain things. First off, she did not love Neil. Did she? Was she kidding herself? She didn't think so. No, she decided, she really wasn't. So why on earth was she so upset? She came to the conclusion that it was the lies she hated. The lies and the greed. Iris could see the wheels whirring in what Neil liked to call his brain: *Why not shag two of them, even if the first doesn't really love you and isn't going to commit, and the second is married?* I was a bloody fool to go back to him, Iris told herself. He could have said something along the lines of *Let's both of us be free to continue seeing other people* but he hadn't. He'd made Iris think she was the only one, which was much harder to take. Maybe, she thought, I ought to get my phone from downstairs. She could imagine the texts piling up in it. But, no, that was for tomorrow. Iris turned over and buried her head in the pillow. She didn't cry. Iris hadn't cried a single tear over Neil and she was quite proud of that.

*

From: bruce60@R&T. com
To: client mailinglist; staff mailing list
Subject: Bruce's Barnet Bulletin, number 405

Hello campers – and villa-ers and hotel-ers and all other kinds of holidaymakers I haven't thought of.

I know that the last thing anyone feels like doing when the weather's fine and sunny (and haven't we been lucky this year? You should see my tan and that's just the back garden!) is go and view properties. But to tempt you away from the Pimm's and out from under the sun umbrella, here are some new houses that have just come on the market. Though I say it myself, they're real beauties. But I would say that, wouldn't I? Pick up the phone, arrange a viewing and see for yourselves.

The Larches, Meadow Way, Friern Barnet
Meadow Way is a new development of state-of-the-art houses, built to the highest specifications and imaginatively provided with communal and private gardens. Within easy reach of all transport systems, and near several good schools, these homes need to be seen to be believed. They are very competitively priced in the area of £500,000 and are deserving of your attention.

Flat 2, The Towers, Rathbone Road, Finsbury Park
A small but perfectly formed flat, which would suit a single person who wants somewhere convenient and modern without being soulless. This flat meets those specifications. One large reception room, one bedroom, modern kitchen and bathroom, and reasonably priced in the region of £400,000. Well worth your while!

AIDAN

This, Aidan thought, was definitely an adventure. He was doing something he'd never done before. He was on the road again, on a route that used to be familiar but which he hadn't gone near for almost four years. This was the way to Cornwall, and although he missed Vina, there was something about being on your own in a car on the motorway. He'd not driven very much, except locally, in the last few years and the sensation of speed and freedom was something that belonged to a life before Grace became ill. In those days, the two of them used to drive everywhere . . .

No one knew where he was. He'd lied to Vina. Putting it like that made him feel guilty and uneasy, but he comforted himself with the thought that he would be telling Vina the whole truth as soon as he returned to London. When he'd learned that he would be alone for the weekend, he'd begun to plan a visit to Libby in Cornwall. His idea was: go down there, introduce himself properly, take her out for a meal, talk to her about himself and Vina, then arrive back in London able to tell Libby's mother that he and her daughter were the best of friends.

Libby lived near St Ives. He had found her email address because it was on her rather old-fashioned website, and there was a mobile number too. Aidan intended to text her from a service station on the way down to the south-west and say he was in the area by chance. From then on, he had no idea what would happen, but he was ready to deal with whatever came up. Now he was making a journey that he and Grace had often taken and the road, even before he'd reached St Ives, stirred up memories of their trips.

Grace had loved Cornwall. They'd spent many holidays there, walking on the cliffs and over the countryside, and Aidan couldn't help comparing the modest bed-and-breakfasts they'd always stayed in with the hotel in Paris he'd just left. That's an unfair comparison, he told himself. We were young. We weren't well off. I wouldn't have missed our holidays for the world, but Paris . . .

He'd still not got over those four days, which seemed to him, looking back, a little removed from real life. At times, while they were there, Aidan had felt as if he was in a film. Every street corner was beautiful in Paris, and he'd felt constantly as though he was outside his own life, his comfort zone. He was always happy to be back in his own space, always happy to see his books and reacquaint himself with his papers and familiar things from long ago, but occasionally, since coming back, he'd stop in the middle of a room and remember something: Vina in a red scarf, walking by the Seine with Notre Dame behind her – why had he not taken a photograph of her? The two of them in a cafe, sharing a brandy before bed. That kind of thing . . .

Grace . . . Part of him could imagine her sitting in the passenger seat. In those days, he'd had no sat-nav but Grace had become a good map-reader. Those happy memories were overlaid, though, with worse ones. Times when he'd taken her in this very car to her appointments at the hospital. Times when he'd brought her back after chemo. Times when she'd had to lie on the back seat, unable to sit up without pain . . . No, he told himself. Don't think about that. This is something else. This is an adventure.

Iris was the one who'd put the idea into his head. Not the idea of going to Cornwall, or not exactly, but she'd articulated what he hadn't dared even to think, but which had become true when she'd said it. He would have to tell Vina, of course he would, but how and when he hadn't yet decided.

Just before they'd left for Paris, Iris had come to see him to find out how he felt about the Forsters having to pull out of the sale. He'd given her a cup of tea. 'And I've got some cake today,' he'd added. 'You're in luck.'

'I'd love a bit, thanks. Have you taken up baking?' Iris sat down at the kitchen table and Aidan had admired her ability to be at home in any setting. Whenever he'd had anything to do with Iris, she'd looked comfortable and at ease.

'Oh, no,' he'd answered, and found himself blushing. 'A friend made it.'

'Well,' said Iris, taking a bite, 'it's wonderful.' She took another slice. 'Is the friend Mrs Brownrigg by any chance?' She'd rattled on, giving him time to prepare an answer. 'Forgive me, I shouldn't really ask but I have sort of noticed . . . and Mrs Brownrigg herself said . . .'

'Yes, it's Vina's cake,' Aidan said, and Iris went on eating it.

When she'd finished, she said, 'Please forgive me for asking this, but are you two . . . I mean, is it? I mean . . . oh, God, I don't know how to put this! It is *soooo* none of my business!'

'I don't mind. I'm not ashamed of my feelings. I'm very much in love and that's the truth.'

Now Aidan smiled at a passing truck, remembering how happy Iris had looked when he'd said that. What was it about love that made people so delighted to encounter it? After all, it often brought pain and heartbreak. Why was everyone so bloody chuffed when they learned you'd fallen for someone? She'd said at once, 'I'm *really* thrilled for you, Mr Church.'

'Aidan,' said Aidan. 'You find it hard to say because I'm old and remind you of your dad, probably, or a teacher or something but, really, I've just confessed something deeply personal, so I think we can lose the Mr Church. Okay?'

'Yes, I'm so sorry . . . but it's marvellous news. I don't think you're good at being on your own, are you? Most men are rubbish at it. Especially if they've been happily married before. Are you thinking of asking her to marry you?'

That question knocked Aidan sideways. 'Well,' he said, taking another bite of cake, slightly disconcerted at having to admit to himself something that had been buried so deeply at the back of his mind that he hadn't really acknowledged it. 'It had crossed my mind . . . I would be . . . I mean, I had thought of it but not in any practical way. And I haven't mentioned it to Vina . . .'

'I won't say anything, I promise you. But as for practicalities, if you were married, you'd only need one house to live in. I'm sorry to think of it from an estate agent's point of view . . .' She put her hand over her mouth and gasped. 'But would it be possible to rethink the Forsters' flat? If there were two of you, perhaps together there wouldn't be any need for a mortgage?'

'The flat? Really?' Aidan blinked. 'Oh, I don't know about that . . . It's still . . . Well, of course I don't know what Vina's position is.'

'But she should see it, don't you think? Can we show it to her somehow? I'd so love to know what she thinks of it.'

'But . . . Well, I'll get back to you, Iris. I have to think about this more carefully. I have to think what I want to do about everything. I'll consider it carefully, though.'

'I'm sure you will,' Iris said.

It was partly because of that conversation that he was on his way to talk to Vina's daughter. He still hadn't raised the possibility of them living together with Vina, and he didn't know how, where or when he'd do it, but as soon as Iris had put the thought into his head, he realized that that was exactly what he wanted. Okay, maybe not marriage, but he wanted, more than he'd wanted anything else ever, to live with Vina. And, moreover, he saw Riverside Court, to which his thoughts kept returning, as being exactly what Iris had said it was: quite possible if the two of them bought it together.

Why had he said nothing about their living together while they were in Paris? He searched about for excuses and none of them was any good. Partly it was because he'd wanted nothing to spoil the time. He was frightened of raising subjects on which the two of them might disagree. Or maybe it was because he knew how much Vina enjoyed living without a husband. She'd told him often enough how much she valued her own space. She might be horrified at the very idea of living with him. But, whatever happened, he wanted to meet Libby. Vina wouldn't base any decisions she made on what her daughter thought, but for his part, he had no desire to antagonize anyone and he felt, perhaps irrationally, that if he managed to hit it off with Libby, it would go some way to persuading Vina to live with him. It was silly, perhaps, but he wanted to know that the family was on his side and didn't regard him as some kind of fortune hunter.

He and Vina had never discussed money. He had more than he'd thought he had, and she clearly wasn't poor. Geoff, he knew, had given her the house and a settlement of some kind when they divorced. He'd wanted out, quickly, and was in a position to pay for it. Aidan smiled to think how happy so many people would be if he and Vina acquired the Forsters' flat. Will and Josie and Zak especially, of course, but him, too, and, hopefully, Vina. I have to get her there, he thought. She needs to see it.

He stopped for lunch in a service station. As soon as he sat down, he texted Vina: *At Edward's soon. See you Monday. Love xx A*

A lie. He felt bad all over again but had to smile at how immediately the answer came back: *Enjoy yourselves. Love xxx V*

She would be sitting on the train, knitting. He looked down at his phone, the magic machine that meant you were never out of touch. He resisted the temptation to send her yet another message. Instead he texted her daughter.

Libby was a pretty young woman, Aidan thought, though he struggled to see anything of her mother in her. She was not much of a smiler and her expression was one of deep suspicion, which was, Aidan thought, only to be expected in the circumstances.

After a series of rather stiff messages between them (in which he'd told her he was passing through on his way to somewhere else to see an old friend, one lie leading to another), they'd arranged to meet at an Italian restaurant called Venezia, which suited Aidan because it was near the B & B he'd chosen as soon as he knew Libby was free to talk to him. It wasn't as though there was much choice but the Belmont was okay. Clean at least, and near the centre of town. Certainly good enough for one night.

He stood up as she approached and shook her hand.

'Lovely to meet you, Libby. Thanks so much for agreeing to have dinner with me.'

She sat down. 'It was very kind of you to invite me.' She looked at Aidan and added, 'A bit of a surprise, though.'

Aidan murmured something, then the waiter appeared, with huge flapping menus in his hand. Aidan said, 'Shall we choose our food?'

'Okay,' said Libby. She bent her gaze to the menu, and when the waiter came for their order, chose tomato and mozzarella salad and a mushroom pizza to follow.

'I'll have the same,' Aidan said, 'and a bottle of sparkling water. Or still, if you prefer that, Libby? Or maybe you'd like some wine?'

'No, ta. I'm driving. Fizzy water is fine.'

The waiter scooped up the menus and vanished.

Aidan smiled, mainly to see if Libby would smile back at him and, after a moment's hesitation, she did. The smile transformed her face from pretty but ordinary to almost beautiful.

'I ought to explain a little. I have to tell you this, before anything else. Your mother doesn't know I'm here.'

'What? She doesn't know? Where does she think you are? What did you tell her?'

'A lie, I'm afraid. She thinks I'm with my friend Edward in Nottingham.'

'Where's she?'

'On her way to Edinburgh. For a knitting design workshop. She'll be there by now, I expect.'

Libby took a sip of her drink. 'I don't fancy your chances when you do tell her. She's going to go ballistic, you do realize?'

'Why, when I tell her I only wanted to meet you properly?'

246

Libby shook her head. 'You deceived her. You lied to her. Mum doesn't take kindly to being lied to.'

Aidan was silent. Suddenly he saw it. Why had it not occurred to him before? Vina would put him on the same level as Geoff, as anyone else who'd ever deserted her. Surely if the motive were better, the crime wasn't as bad. Surely he could convince her that the deception was only done out of love for her. What if she was really, really angry? He cringed to think of the harsh words she might speak to him. What would he say?

'Well,' he said to Libby, after a long pause, 'I'll confess all. As soon as I can. I'll throw myself upon her mercy.'

'Good luck with that,' she answered. 'But why on earth *didn't* you tell her? Would she have minded? Don't see why she would have done.'

'Okay, I see what you're saying. It was . . . it was wrong of me. I'll phone her as soon as I can and tell her about our meeting.'

'But why on earth did you come all this way just to see me? We'd have met eventually.'

'I'm in love with your mother,' he said

He wasn't expecting the reaction. Libby burst out laughing.

'What's funny about that?' he said.

'Nothing, nothing. Not really. But have you come to see me and taken me out to dinner just to tell me that?'

'Put in those terms, it seems ridiculous, I agree, but I wanted you to know how serious I am. I did *not* want you to think that I was (a) after your mother's money or (b) a mere passing fling of some kind. I love her. She says she loves me. And, what's more, I want to spend the rest of my life with her.'

'Marry her? You want to marry her?'

That caught Aidan so much by surprise that it took him a couple of seconds to get his thoughts back in some kind of order.

Marriage? Did he mean that? Was that what he wanted? Two things came into his head at the same time. Yes, that was precisely what he wanted. He hadn't thought so when Iris had asked him the same question but now he knew it was. Why had he never before articulated a desire to be married, even to himself? Because I was scared. Because I thought Vina wouldn't want to get married again – *once bitten twice shy*. He said, looking Libby straight in the eyes, 'Yes, now that you mention it. I'd love that. I don't know what Vina would think of such a suggestion. Please don't tell her we've had this conversation, Libby. You won't, will you? I intend to ask her to live with me. That's a first step, right?'

'Shan't say a word.' Libby smiled. 'Don't worry.'

The first course came, and they paused while the waiter set the plates on the table. 'I suppose it was a bit of a shock seeing me back in London,' Aidan said, when the man had gone. 'With no warning or anything.'

'It was. I couldn't believe it. I was . . . Well, Mum is normally so . . .'

'What? What do you think your mother is? I'd be very interested to know, if you don't mind telling me.'

'I don't mean to be horrible about her. I do love her really, but I hated the way she was when I was a girl. She was . . .' Libby ate a mouthful of salad '. . . spineless. I couldn't forgive her for not standing up to my father. He was bossy and bullying, and she just disappeared into the garden and worked on her bloody pond, instead of telling him to fuck off. Sorry, sorry, didn't mean to swear but it still makes me angry. I felt like shaking her so often. Does she talk about me? Our relationship?'

'No, of course not. She has only good things to say about you, but she did say you were a bit of a daddy's girl when you were small.'

Libby blushed. 'I was, I guess. If you side with the strong person in the marriage, you get your way far more often. I'm a bit sorry I did now, but I find it hard to apologize.'

'I'm sure she isn't expecting you to do that,' Aidan said. 'I think she'd like to see more of you, that's all. Perhaps feel you take her into your confidence more. I'm saying this for myself, you understand. Vina hasn't mentioned anything like it.'

'I'm not very good at telling Mum stuff. There always seems to be some kind of blockage in the conversation. I don't know why, really. I suppose it's the habit of a lifetime. So I avoid it. She'd want to know about my love life and stuff.'

'I'm sure she would, but I don't see anything wrong with that. She'd want to meet anyone you're keen on, I'm sure.'

'There's no one at the moment. I'm not good at men. I fall for the wrong sort of person.'

'What sort is that?'

'Someone stronger than I am who gets shirty when I want my own way. It's pathetic. I keep getting involved with men who are younger versions of my father. Flashy, attractive, but not kind. I'm a walking psychological cliché.'

'Kindness is an underrated virtue. I think it's the most important thing in a relationship. Sorry, I'm sounding like a marriage guidance counsellor. But don't worry. You're very young. The right person will come along. Now, I'm the clichéd one . . .'

Libby looked at him. 'Are you like this with your own children?'

'I haven't got any,' said Aidan. 'That's always been a matter of regret to me.'

'God, I'm sorry.'

'No need to be. I'm surprised your mother hasn't told you.'

'She would have done, I'm sure,' Libby said, 'but I've never really . . . Well, I've never asked her stuff like that.'

The time had come, Aidan felt, to change the subject. The main course arrived and the talk became more general: Cornwall, the sea, and the benefits of not living in London. Then Aidan asked, 'Would you like a pudding?'

'Yes, please. I love tiramisu. And it's the best in this place.'

After the meal, they walked together to where Libby's car was parked.

'Are you going on to Devon did you say tomorrow?' she said.

'That was a lie too,' Aidan replied. 'I only came to see you.'

'Have you got time to visit the cottage in the morning? I'd like you to see the stuff I'm doing now – I make jewellery. Maybe you're not interested in that, though. Not many men are.'

'I'd love to. I'd be most interested. Thank you. What time?'

'About ten or so. And thanks so much for dinner. I'll text you my address and a link to a map.' Libby hesitated, then smiled. 'I'm really pleased to have met you. It would be good if you and Mum do end up living together. If she ever forgives you for this trip, that is.' She walked towards her car.

Once she'd gone, Aidan felt like someone who'd been standing outside the head's office for a long time and was now having to go in and face his punishment. It was time to phone Vina. He walked towards the Belmont, filled with dread.

IRIS

After the split, the post-mortems. When Iris left her bedroom at lunchtime and turned on her phone, it took about three minutes for all the texts to appear. There they were, pinging into her inbox, mostly from Neil. She read every one, even though she could have predicted what they would say. They were all a version of *We must talk*. Or *Let me explain*. She deleted them, deciding Neil could wait a bit for an answer.

Another ping. Iris nearly deleted the message before she read it, but it wasn't from Neil and it wasn't from any of her friends. It wasn't from anyone at work. The message was from Patrick. *Can you phone? Need to chat asap. Ta! Patrick*

That was intriguing. Why did he need to chat ASAP? Iris rang him straight back.

'God, that was quick! Thank you!' he said.

'Had the phone in my hand when your message came. It sounded urgent.'

He laughed, and Iris could almost see him doing it. He had a nice laugh. *Don't be silly, Iris. This is the rebound. You've cut loose from Neil, inadequate as he was, and, like a newly hatched duckling or something, you're fixating on someone else – anyone else. Don't forget his beautiful girlfriend, not to mention his student children, his mother.*

'Not really urgent, but I could use your help, if you're free.'

Iris thought of Bruce. She thought of R & T, Holly and

ADÈLE GERAS

Dominic, how much of her work they were picking up in her absence. 'Yes, I'm free,' she said. 'Happy to help.'

'That loft I mentioned, with the other estate agent, can you come round it with me now instead of on Friday? I'd really value your judgement. I'm conflicted. This one has too much walls, I think.'

'Too much walls, eh? That's a new one. But, yes, fine,' Iris said. 'Happy to do that. Give me the address.' She took it down. 'I'll see you in an hour or so.'

'Okay. I'm not in my car, but I'll get there before you going by Tube, I think.'

'Right. See you soon.'

Iris decided she would ring Bruce, apologize for her no-show at work and say she couldn't come in now as she was helping one of R & T's clients, which was not a lie. She would do that as soon as she'd showered, washed her hair and decided what she was going to wear. She couldn't deny it. She was feeling much better than she'd felt five minutes ago.

VINA

'Hello? Aidan? How lovely to hear from you. I was going to ring but I thought you and Edward would still be busy. Out to dinner or something.'

Vina settled down on the bed, ready for a long conversation. She was tired from the train journey and meeting her fellow workshop companions. The prospect of learning things about knitwear design that she'd never even considered before made her feel like a child about to start in a new class: a mixture of excitement and anxiety. And now here was her beloved Aidan, ringing her up for a chat. How lovely!

'I'm not with Edward,' he said.

'Why not?' There was a silence at the other end and she heard him sigh. 'Is anything wrong? Are you ill?' Her heart had started jumping about in her chest. Something like terror crept over her, making her feel cold.

'No, no, not at all. Nothing's wrong. Quite the opposite, in fact, but I wasn't with Edward because . . . Well, there's no way of saying this except saying it. I took Libby out to dinner in St Ives.'

Vina sat up. 'What? St Ives? How . . .' Aidan was not with Edward. He'd lied to her. *He'd lied to her.* How did this happen? Wasn't there total honesty between the two of them? She took a deep breath. 'You never said you were going to see Libby. Why did you? What possible business do you have with my daughter? And how *dare* you lie to me? You *deceived* me, Aidan. You lied to me. You didn't tell me you were going to see *my own daughter*. What if I hadn't wanted you to? Did you even think about that? I don't know what to say . . . I don't . . .' Suddenly the horror of what she'd just discovered came over her and she started to cry.

'Vina, Vina, listen. Please, please, don't cry. And listen. I want to explain.'

'I don't know,' her voice was thick with tears, 'how you could do that. How did you find her address? Why . . . Oh, I really, really thought there would be no lies between us. I'm sick to death of lies! Don't you understand that? Don't you see that this makes you like Geoff? Like bloody *Geoff*, Aidan. He lied to me the whole time and I hated it then and I can't bear it now . . . I don't know what to think. What to think of you.'

'Vina, honestly, please. I didn't mean to lie to you and I didn't mean to hurt you . . . really. I wanted everything to be perfect. I wanted to meet Libby so that I could tell her how much I loved you and that I wanted us to be together for ever. I didn't want her to disapprove, that's all.'

Vina listened to his voice wavering and trembling.

'Why on earth didn't you ask me? You could have asked me,' she said. 'You could simply have consulted me. I'd have given you her address, and then I wouldn't be feeling now as if you've been going behind my back and keeping stuff from me.'

'I'm *not* keeping it from you. I'm telling you. I always intended to tell you at once, as soon as I'd seen her. I wouldn't have kept it from you for long. I didn't hide my visit to deceive you . . . I wanted it . . . I wanted it to be a kind of surprise. I wanted to be able to say: *Guess what? Libby and I got on very well. We like one another*. That's what I wanted to say to you . . . I didn't mean to hurt or deceive you, my darling. You *must* believe that. Please say you believe that. And please, please, forgive me. I won't be able to sleep if you don't.'

Vina sniffed and blew her nose on a tissue from the box at the side of her bed. She sighed. 'I *loathe* this. D'you see? I hate the stuff that goes on around lies, as much as I hate the lies. You'll have to promise me *solemnly* to tell me the truth always. Do you promise? Can you do that?'

'What about presents? And surprises? That sort of thing? Can I hide things like that from you?'

'Oh, God, you're impossible. Pedantic, too. *Of course* I don't mean things like that. You know exactly what I mean. Making decisions without consulting me. About my own daughter, what's more.' As she spoke, Vina could feel her anger, which she'd managed to squash down for a few moments, rising up again. Libby. Her own daughter . . . How on earth could Aidan decide it was okay to go behind her back to meet Libby? She said, 'It never occurred to you to suggest we both go down to Cornwall? I could have introduced you . . . That would've been okay, wouldn't it?'

Silence. Then, 'Well, no, actually. It wouldn't have been the same. I wanted to meet Libby on my own. I wanted her to see me as me, and not as someone attached to you. I wanted her not to be under any obligation to be polite because you were there. It's much harder to disguise your feelings if you're across the table from someone. I wanted to know she liked me because she liked *me* and not to please you . . . Oh, God, Vina, I'm so sorry but there were good reasons, really. None of them has anything to do with wanting to pull wool over your eyes, honestly. And I won't do anything like this ever again, I promise you.'

'Okay,' Vina said. 'Okay, Aidan . . . So now you can tell me about your dinner with Libby. I *am* glad she likes you, you're right. Only, please, never lie to me again.'

'I won't. I never will. I promise. '

Vina settled back against the pillows and listened as Aidan told her about Libby and their dinner together.

JOSIE

The cafe in the park was full. Josie and Will had got to know it rather well because they often went there before or after looking at a house. Today, they'd seen a place that was just about possible, but which didn't fill either of them with joy. The park was often quite busy at weekends, especially during the school holidays, but today, because of the sunshine, whole families were there, complete with dads, even though it was a Wednesday. You didn't, Josie thought, see many fathers in the normal course of events, but it was August and the weather had tempted some brave ones to risk an hour or two overlooking events on the bouncy castle and having ice cream with their kids and their kids' mothers.

There was no question of occupying a table to yourself at the outdoor cafe. Josie, Will and Zak (who didn't take up a chair but spent his time rushing between one piece of equipment and another, then bouncing and bouncing on the castle) were sharing with a man of about fifty who had seemed at first to be on his own. Josie examined him with some suspicion to begin with but soon after he'd sat down at their table ('Hope you don't mind?' with a big smile to disarm them) a girl of about five came up to him, jumped onto his lap and he introduced her to Josie and Will, as though they were sitting together as friends.

'This is Milly, my first granddaughter. I say that because Milly's mum is expecting again. My name is John Holder.'

'Nice to meet you,' said Josie, and Milly hid her face in her grandfather's neck and said nothing. Just at that moment, Zak whizzed over from the castle, asking for a drink, and Josie got up to take him to the cafe. When they came back to the table, Zak imitated Milly and climbed onto Will's lap. Josie noticed that the men had got a good conversation going. It seemed to be about houses and builders.

'This is John, Josie. He runs a firm of builders and decorators. Totally fascinating.'

'Great,' said Josie. 'I'm surprised to see you here in the park. Aren't builders always in demand? And decorators.'

'Well, yes and no,' said John. 'And I'm not on holiday, just doing a few days' grandfather duty, which is my idea of a holiday. I'll be back there tomorrow. This is a treat for me.'

The chat went back and forth. Will was starting to tell John about his situation. Josie tuned out and turned her mind to the unsatisfactory state of their own house hunt. Three people had made ridiculous offers on the flat, which they'd turned down. Iris thought that was fine and told them there was no hurry, and until Josie found a place as perfect as Mansfield Cottage, she wasn't in a rush to leave. She woke up every day convinced that today Iris would phone or text and tell her that Mr Church had sold the place to someone else.

It wasn't as though they'd stopped looking for a replacement and, indeed, there had been a couple of other houses that were better than the one they'd seen today, houses she'd quite liked, but as long as Mansfield Cottage remained unsold, Josie still held out hope for that. Her daydreams were always about *those* rooms, *that* garden. She imagined her family there, in great detail, rather too often. Pathetic.

She surfaced to hear John complaining, basically, that you couldn't get the help.

'I don't have a problem with brickies or plasterers. Plenty of those about. I pay a decent wage and word gets round. I treat my people as well as I possibly can. But what I need is someone to take care of the business side of things. I've got an accountant, but I need someone to oversee future plans, arrange things, to be aware of what's going on at every site. A manager, I suppose you'd call it. He'd need to know a bit about the building trade, but that's easy enough to pick up. And I could do with getting my website to be a bit more than an online entry in the *Yellow Pages*.' He leaned forward, took a swig of his coffee and looked directly at Will. 'You've not got a job at the moment, have you?' he said.

'Well, no, I haven't. I hadn't thought of . . .'

'How about coming to work for me? You could try it for a couple of months and see how you liked it.'

Josie could see that Will was disconcerted. This wasn't how jobs happened: over a cup of coffee in the park. And who was John? He might be a criminal, for all Will knew, though he didn't look like one. He seemed like a nice person. He was certainly friendly and easy to talk to. Did that count for anything? Will would have expected interviews, panels, discussions, competition. And did he want to go back to work as a manager to a builder? Should she say something?

'Well,' Will began, 'managing a building business wasn't something I'd considered, really. But—'

'It's good work,' said John. 'Building something where nothing was before and making sure people's houses are as beautiful as they possibly can be. That's good work, surely. Interesting work. Plus, and I haven't said this before, it's very profitable. There's money in building.'

'Can I think about it, John?' said Will. 'Could I come and see you at work? It sounds . . . interesting but—'

'You don't know me from a bar of soap and for all you know I'm a criminal mastermind. Okay, no worries. Come and see me whenever you like. Here's my card.' He gave it to Will. 'But I have to be frank. I liked you at once and I'd be very glad to give you a chance to come in with me. And,' he turned to Josie, 'it was a pleasure to meet you and Zak. Goodbye.' He went off to separate his granddaughter from the crowd on the bouncy castle.

Josie noticed that Zak was very near Milly. Had they made friends? It would be hard to get this information from her son, she knew, but she'd have a good try.

'Phew,' said Will, when John had left the park. 'That's a bit of a turn-up for the books.'

'Might you be interested? I liked John.'

'Yes, I liked him too, but I'll have to do some research into his firm before I arrange to go and see him. I'm not sure an informal chat in the park on a sunny day with kids screaming around you is the perfect place to find a job. And what about me, from his point of view? How does he know I'll be any good at what he wants me to do? How does he know I'm not a liar? I could have been sacked from my last job for embezzlement.'

'Rubbish. You'd be in prison if you had been. He's just willing to take a bet on you. Whether you're willing to try a couple of months' working for him is another matter.'

'Like I said, I'm going to look him up.' Will pulled out his iPhone and began searching.

Josie took John's card from where Will had put it, next to his coffee cup, and examined it. 'Look,' she said. 'There's an address here just off the high street. Let's go and see it on our way home. Can we?'

'Okay,' said Will. 'Why not? He's right about his website. It could be a whole lot better. If I go and work for him, I could sort that out.'

'Right. So you're taking time to think about it.' Josie laughed. 'I was beginning to think I'd never have to work again, what with you becoming a famous dog portrait artist and all.'

'Don't be silly! I've made exactly two hundred pounds. That's not going to butter many parsnips.'

'You're just at the beginning of your brilliant career. I think for once your mother was inspired.'

'You're right. It *was* quite a good idea.'

Her mother had done exactly what she'd said she was going to do: she'd shown the portrait of Bobby to her friends in the tennis club. Two commissions had followed almost at once and Josie had charged a hundred pounds for each portrait, including the frame. Okay, that worked out at sixty pounds for the picture and forty that she'd had to spend on framing it properly but, still, it seemed like easy money. Both buyers had been so pleased that they'd passed the word on. Josie now had three new commissions, with three photographs (two dogs and a cat) to work on. Maybe Will was right and she would become the John Singer Sargent of the pet world. The thought made her laugh and Will said, 'What's so funny?'

'Nothing,' she answered. 'Let's get Zak off the bouncy castle and go and see John's premises.'

John's premises were a builder's yard. There was a small office, staffed by a pleasant-looking young woman who sat at a desk facing the street. There were pictures in the window of various properties they must have built and decorated.

'This must be,' said Josie, 'where you come to discuss what you want before John gets going on the actual building. Looks nice.'

They walked round to the yard, which was neat and tidy, with cement mixers and piles of bricks under tarpaulin and a long black shed.

'They'll be out on their sites,' said Will, 'so this doesn't tell us much. I wonder how many other people John has accosted in the park? Maybe he does it all the time.'

'You'll only know if you try. I reckon that if there's a way of getting out if you don't like it, copper-bottomed and legal and everything, you've got nothing to lose. That's if you want to be a builder. Do you?'

'I don't know. Think I might. I'll ask around when we get home. There's a chap at J & S who knows about such things. I'll talk to him about it. It might turn out to be just what I was looking for.'

On the drive home, it occurred to Josie that if Will had a job in this part of the world there was even more reason to buy a house there. Mansfield Cottage was only a couple of miles down the road. Once again, regret washed over her. Stop it, she told herself. Do what Iris always says: never stop hoping.

IRIS

Iris was enjoying herself. She didn't have anywhere else to be, and sitting around a gigantic box with Patrick was – well, she had to admit it was fun.

They'd met about twenty minutes before he came out with his apology. The loft he was about to be shown was in a battered converted warehouse in the East End. This particular part of London hadn't yet been gentrified in a way that Iris could immediately see, and the estate agent who met them on the pavement in front of the building didn't inspire much confidence. He was one of the too-much-hair-gel brigade, who make people think of estate agents with some suspicion: very young, and with a tie he must have thought made him look sophisticated but did the opposite. This person, whose name was Nigel, kept up a steady stream of chat as they went up in the rackety lift, and as there weren't any actual *rooms* to look at – the space was huge: one enormous square with windows on two sides and a bathroom stuck near one corner – he kept up the patter until interrupted by a phone call. 'Sorry, I've got to get this. The boss!' and went off into the bit of the space furthest away from them to take it. They could hear him clearly, even though he was making an effort to keep his voice down. The acoustics in the fancy loft made privacy impossible.

'What? The keys to twenty-seven Langford Close? No, I'm

sure not . . . I'm sure I didn't . . . Hang on a sec.' He stopped and patted his pockets with one hand while holding his phone in the other. He looked frantic, like someone swatting a wasp. 'No, sorry, you're right. I have them. I'll bring them back at once . . . What? . . . No, I'm fine. I'll be there in fifteen minutes . . . Okay . . . Okay.'

Nigel came up to Iris and Patrick and began to explain, looking as though he'd just committed a serious crime. 'I'm most awfully sorry. I'm not sure what to do but I have to go now. I need to return some keys I'm not meant to have to the office. They're from another house. Someone's waiting to view it. I'm afraid I'll have to cut this session short.'

'I'll bring back the keys to this place when we've finished,' Patrick said. 'You can leave us and take your keys back.'

'I can't do that. I'm sorry. I'm not allowed to. But if I go and drop the keys I can be back very soon. Twenty minutes. If you wouldn't mind waiting here? Half an hour tops.'

Patrick looked at Iris and she nodded, to indicate that she was quite happy to hang around a featureless loft. He hadn't suggested they leave with Nigel, which might mean he was keener on this place than she was, but she was fine with staying longer because Patrick was with her. He said to Nigel, 'Okay, but don't hang around,' which Iris thought was kind of him. They were sure to be finished in five minutes or so. Patrick had undertaken to kill time for twenty-five minutes so that Nigel wouldn't get into too much trouble. That struck Iris as kind. She liked him even better.

Once Nigel had left, muttering apologies all the way to the lift, Patrick said, 'Well, we'd better look around carefully now that we've got time to kill. You see what I mean about *too much walls* now, right? '

'I do.' Iris laughed. 'Nothing but walls, really. Apart from windows. They're pretty spectacular. And floors. Shame you can't hang pictures on floors.'

She went over to the window. 'You could make a fortune. Set yourself up as competition to the Shard and let people pay to look at London from here. It's an amazing view.'

'It is, but how much time can you spend looking out of the window? And call me old-fashioned, but I like a separate room in which to sleep. This place makes me feel agoraphobic.'

'I've got clients who love lofts like this: one room, basically, to do everything. Kitchen stuff over here, living room stuff over there, bedroom somewhere near the bathroom . . .'

'And my studio. I have to have space for my painting. If it's not shut off from all the other functions, it'll spread. I'll find brushes in my bed and splashes of paint on my sofa. Turpentine in my soup.'

'I take it you're saying you're not very tidy,' Iris said.

'I am, actually, but you'd have to be a bit OCD to keep track of your possessions when you have only one room. And even though it has lots of hanging space, seeing it like this has made me realize something. I want domesticated walls. I want walls in a house. I want my pictures to hang in other people's houses, not in a desert of wall. Most of what I'm doing now is much smaller than what you saw at the gallery.'

They went to look at the bathroom, even though Iris could now see he had no intention of buying the loft. They found a minuscule shower in a tiny room. It was very modern and sleek, with a small separate loo, but it was soulless and Iris said as much.

'True,' Patrick said. 'I never thought that soul was something I was looking for in a bathroom but you learn something new with every property you see.'

'That's what I think!' Iris said. 'I'm so glad you agree.'

They went back into the big space. The previous owners had kindly left a mattress in one corner, which gave the loft the air of a posh squat.

'Let's sit down,' Iris said. 'I don't fancy standing at the window for half an hour.'

Patrick sat down, leaned against the wall and made his apology: 'I'm truly sorry, Iris. I've landed you in this situation.' Iris promised him it was fine. Then she hesitated. Where would she sit? If she sat down opposite Patrick, there'd be nothing to lean against. She'd have to twist her legs into an elaborate pretzel shape to avoid showing her thighs. She wished she'd worn trousers, but it was too late for regrets. In the end she sat next to him, also with her back against the wall, a couple of feet further down the mattress. They probably looked like two characters from a BAFTA award-winning gritty TV drama, or some documentary about urban living.

'You couldn't consider living here with children either, could you?' Patrick remarked.

Iris was surprised. She'd been assuming that Patrick wouldn't want any more children, then remembered the beautiful girlfriend she'd seen at his exhibition. She might want children and he'd want what she wanted. Everyone but Iris seemed to take children for granted.

'No,' she said, 'you couldn't. But . . .' She'd been turning an idea over in her mind as they'd looked at the loft but now she was determined to try it on Patrick. 'Are you free for the rest of the afternoon? There might be somewhere that would be just right for you. What do you reckon? Are you willing to wait till he gets back, then come with me?'

'Sounds intriguing. Do you want to give me more details?'

'Let me ring someone up first. Okay?'

'Okay. There's nowhere you can do it privately, though. Another disadvantage. Everyone who lived here would have to invest in massive headphones. Oh, it's too horrible for words.'

'I don't mind. I'm not going to be saying anything private.'

Iris clicked on Vina's number and she picked up at once. 'Oh, hello,' Iris said. She batted about a few items of small-talk, then said, 'I've got a client here who may be interested in your house. Is it okay if I bring him round?' She explained about the time and not knowing when they'd get there, but a few minutes later it was arranged. Vina was going to be in all afternoon and didn't mind when they came to view the house. 'Thanks, Vina, see you later.' Iris ended the call.

'Sounds intriguing,' Patrick said.

'I'm not saying anything.' Iris did her best to look enigmatic. 'I'm not even telling you where it is. It'll be a mystery ride.'

'Lucky you brought your car,' he said.

Suddenly they seemed to have run out of things to say, so Iris started telling him how much she'd liked the exhibition, even though she'd already told him in an email.

'Actually, my paintings are a bit different these days. Tatty isn't sure about them, but I like them, I think. You'll have to tell me what you reckon.'

'Is Tatty your girlfriend? The one who was at the gallery wearing red, and looking gorgeous?'

Patrick laughed. 'She's my sister, Tatiana. And she has very strong opinions, most of which I don't pay any attention to, of course. I'm only telling you what she thinks because I'm living at home at the moment. That's why finding a house is so urgent. I do love my family but I need my own place. I'd like my kids to be able to visit me from time to time. Most of my stuff from New York is in storage.'

Why, Iris asked herself, do I feel as though the sun has suddenly come out, and as if a weight has fallen off my back? Could it be because Patrick is now girlfriendless? Hang on a mo. He's only said that *that* girl isn't his girlfriend, not that he doesn't have one. The sun went behind a cloud again. Perhaps he had a girlfriend in New York. Maybe she was planning to come over here to join him once he'd got a house. They still had, assuming the over-gelled Nigel was punctual, at least fifteen minutes alone together. Iris embarked, as tactfully as she could, on a more detailed interrogation.

'Do you miss New York?' she asked. She meant, *Do you miss anyone specific in New York?* 'I do, in a way. It's a thrilling city, but it's not home. Not really. It's too cold in winter and too hot in summer. The weather in this country is almost the best thing about it.'

He was starting to get too general. Iris steered him back. 'But what about friends? You must miss them a lot.'

'Email, Skype, it's easy these days to keep up,' he said. 'Lots of them come over here often, and I go over there.' He fell silent and Iris was still trying to think where the conversation might go next when he said, 'To tell you the truth, I was quite glad to get away from a toxic relationship. I fell in love with the wrong person too soon after my divorce and it took me ages to sort myself out and realize how awful we were together. Have you ever been in a toxic relationship?'

Iris was furious with Neil but toxic was not the right word to describe what they had had. 'No,' she said. 'I've also just come out of a relationship but it wasn't toxic. I just didn't love him. He was bossy and demanding.'

Patrick said nothing for a few moments. Then, tentatively: 'Iris? Can I say something?'

'Of course. Anything.'

'So . . . the thing is, I've liked you from the very first time I met you. I fancy you, too.'

They were still sitting with their backs against the wall, looking towards the door of the loft. But now Patrick moved to face Iris and took hold of her right hand. 'Iris?' he said. He didn't need to say more. She turned her body a little to the right and he came closer. 'Is it okay if I kiss you?' he asked.

Iris didn't answer. She just leaned forward a little and he was there, holding her, and they were kissing and Iris felt as though every bit of her had dived out of the picture window and was flying up into the blue sky.

A key turned in the lock. 'Hello, folks!' said the cheery Nigel, and Patrick sprang away from her. 'I'm back in less than half an hour. That's record time, I think.'

They got up from the mattress trying to look as though they hadn't been kissing but had just, somehow or other, been caught twined together. They managed to bring the viewing to a speedy end, and the three of them went down together in the lift.

On the pavement, Patrick thanked Nigel and said that he thought on balance the place was not for him. The poor man looked disappointed but he said goodbye quickly. Patrick and Iris were alone again.

'Mind you,' he added, as Nigel drove away into the traffic, 'I now have something of a sentimental attachment to this place.'

'Me, too!' Iris said, and they brought the pedestrian traffic on a busy London pavement to a standstill while he kissed her again.

Two people shouted, 'Get a room!' and he murmured into her hair, 'God, that sounds like a good idea.'

'Stop it,' Iris said, pulling away and starting to walk towards where she'd parked her car. 'I'm going to show you a house.'

The drive to Vina's was strange. Iris was processing what had just happened, and she thought Patrick was doing the same. She didn't say very much to begin with, just concentrated on manoeuvring her car through the horrendous traffic. Perhaps it was the room, that vast space, and the two of them almost sheltering there, marooned on the mattress in a sea of parquet flooring, that had made them lose it emotionally. She glanced at Patrick and saw that he was gazing at her.

'You look,' he said, 'as if you're having second thoughts. Are you? I hope not . . .'

Iris shook her head. 'No, of course not. Just trying to . . . well, work out what happened back there. Not that I regret it, not at all, but it was sudden. Out of the blue.'

'For you, maybe. I've been laying plans since February.'

'Really?' Iris wanted to say, *Why weren't you more up front about it then? Why did you wait? Why haven't you given me even so much as a hint in all these weeks?*

'Well, as soon as I met you, I knew I fancied you. And, okay, maybe *made plans* is a bit exaggerated, but you've been on my mind since that first horrible house. That's true. Also, you said you had a boyfriend. I wasn't about to wreck that relationship.'

'Okay,' Iris said. She could see it now. She ought never to have gone back to almost living with Neil. She had wasted a lot of time. 'I hope you don't think I'm on any kind of rebound. I should have ended it with Neil ages ago. I *did* stop living with him – actually, on the very first day I met you. I'm staying with my mum now but in the last couple of months I'd got kind of lazy and started going out for meals with him and . . . you know. Line of least resistance. But that's over now. He's been shagging someone else at the same time, apparently. I only found out very recently. It was a bit of a shock, but I got over it almost at once. I'm not on the rebound, honestly.'

And she wasn't. Iris was quite sure about that. Thinking back, remembering how pleased she always was to get messages from Patrick, how diligently she'd Googled him, how much she'd enjoyed seeing him at his exhibition, her disappointment when she saw the person she'd thought was his girlfriend, and especially her relief when she found out that that woman was his sister: all of it persuaded Iris that her feeling for Patrick was genuine. It was new; it was coloured by desire; it was something precious that Iris wanted to nurture and grow, and it was real. When she thought about him, she was happy.

Iris told him a bit about Vina, but didn't mention her romance with Aidan. She felt like more than an estate agent to both of them, but was still professional enough not to gossip about her client's private business.

'I don't know why I didn't think of it for you before. I guess I was focused on walls and imagined those walls as huge. But see what you think.'

'Will you come and have a meal with me when we've looked round? I don't want to say goodbye to you yet.'

'I'll do that, but then I have to go home quite early. I wasn't at work today and didn't sleep much last night. I need to regroup.' Iris wanted to say, *I need to take in what's just happened to me. I think I've fallen in love*, but she stopped herself in time.

'Okay,' Patrick said. 'No worries. I'm going to make another date with you, once we're sitting down with our phones. I feel like filling your entire diary, if I'm honest, but I'll restrain myself.'

'Good!' Iris smiled at him. 'Here we are.'

'Can I kiss you before we get out of the car?'

The kiss went on a bit longer than Iris thought it would. After about five minutes, they were walking down the front path to the house. Iris had almost got her heart under control by the time Vina answered the door.

Autumn

From: bruce60@R&T. com
To: client mailing list; staff mailing list
Subject: Bruce's Barnet Bulletin, number 406

Hello all,

Well, it's almost time to put the barbies away for another year. Back-to-school stuff appeared in every shop window a couple of weeks ago, and now that it's September and the little darlings are safely stowed away in the classroom, mums and dads have lots more time to go about the business of looking for the house of their dreams!

And, as it so happens, we have several very desirable properties to tell you about.

First up, a property on the fringes of fashionable Highgate. A three-bedroom Edwardian semi, in need of some refurbishment but rewarding for the family who would enjoy undertaking this project. In a highly sought-after catchment area for one of Highgate's most admired schools.

Second, a state-of-the-art flat with a wonderful view. Tufnell Park, one bedroom. The ideal starter property for a single person.

Looking forward to showing you these and the many other properties on our website.

Bruce

AIDAN

When the email came through from Michael Procter, Aidan wondered who he was. Then he remembered. A few weeks ago, after a meal with Edward on one of his friend's visits to London, Aidan had written to him on Edward's recommendation: 'I knew him at college and he's now something high up at Irving & Scott. Non-fiction editor. It's worth writing to him with a proposal. What's the worst thing he can say?'

'He can say no,' said Aidan, pouring himself another glass of wine. He'd been happy that night: about to go on holiday with Vina, quite pleased with a house that Iris had shown him the day before. 'I don't care,' he'd added. 'I'm okay whatever he says.'

'But he might say yes,' Edward had pointed out. 'And in that case you'll be more than okay.'

So Aidan had gone home, buoyed up and feeling generally optimistic. He'd sat down and written an email to Michael Procter, in which he'd introduced himself, said that he was a friend of Edward's, then given an account of the book he'd begun to write. He added, as an attachment, the first two chapters of what he was proposing. The words just flowed out of him: his guard was down. That must have been the wine. He hit send after reading what he'd written only once, which was most unusual for him, but Vina had changed him and made him feel, in every bit of his life, more relaxed and spontaneous.

He'd gone to bed and, on waking, he'd reread the email from the night before. He knew very little about publishing, but it seemed to him the kind of book that a great many people would enjoy reading.

Now it looked as though Michael Procter agreed with him.

Dear Mr Church,

Thank you for sending me the first two chapters of your proposed book, Names from the Great War *(the title needs some work, I think) and I'm sorry I've taken so long to get back to you.*

I like the sound of this very much and I have shown your material to my colleagues, who are similarly impressed. I wonder if you would be willing to come into the office to discuss it further? If you are, I'll email some dates.

Yours sincerely,
Michael Procter

Aidan read the email three times. He then went into the kitchen and made himself a coffee, which he began to drink without really tasting it. Then he read the email again, half expecting it to have disappeared during the time he'd been away from his laptop. It was still there. He picked up his phone and rang Vina.

'Hello, Aidan,' she said.

'Vina?'

'Yes, it's me. Is anything the matter?'

'No, not at all. Quite the contrary. Can I read you an email I've just had?'

'Well, yes, of course, but—'

'Listen.' Aidan read the whole email through.

When he'd finished there was silence at Vina's end, then a sort of shriek. 'Oh, my God, Aidan! Are Irving & Scott really going to publish your book?'

'Hold on, no. It's not a contract. It's just a meeting.'

'But he wouldn't ask to meet you if he wasn't keen, would he? That's brilliant, my darling. Just marvellous. We must celebrate.'

'I'm going to send him some dates right now.'

Aidan ended the call, amazed all over again at what had happened to him since the spring. Sometimes he didn't recognize himself. He looked down at his phone. Vina had made him upgrade to a modern device to which he had become ridiculously attached. His whole life, he sometimes thought, was enclosed in that dark, flat rectangle. His diary was also on the phone, so he consulted it for some dates and wrote to Michael Procter. To his amazement, an email came almost straight back. The man must have been crouched over his machine at the other end. He had picked the day after tomorrow and a restaurant in Covent Garden. Aidan emailed Vina to tell her and added: *Come and meet me afterwards and we'll do something nice. Have tea somewhere or something.*

They went to Fortnum & Mason for tea. The Ritz would have to wait, Vina said, for when his book was top of the bestseller list.

'It'll never be that, but still, I can't believe it,' Aidan said, for what must, he felt, have been the thousandth time. But it was true. Ever since the lunch with Michael Procter (who looked about twenty years old, though he was actually forty-two), he'd been having great trouble imagining that, about a year from now, he'd be able to walk into Waterstone's or Hatchards in Piccadilly and see his own book on the shelves. With his name on it. He said as much to Vina.

'I can imagine it very well. I think it's the most wonderful thing that could possibly have happened.'

'And your news is good too.' He didn't dare to add that things seemed to be going well all round for fear of jinxing everything.

'Yes,' said Vina. 'The chap who came round with Iris seemed keen. He hasn't made an offer yet, but he loved the house. He kept going round and patting the walls and grinning at Iris. She was blushing. I reckon they might be . . . Well, it's hard to tell but I think he's more than a client, or about to be more than a client. She seemed extra happy. Also, she wants to take me to see the Forsters' flat, even though it has no garden and is totally out of my price range. She's very insistent. I'm going tomorrow.'

'Can I come with the two of you when you go? I'd like another look at it myself.'

'Are you still considering it? I thought it was too expensive.'

'It is, but I'd like to see it again. The house Iris showed me last week was okay. Will you come and look at that with me?'

'Of course,' Vina said. 'I'd love to.'

Aidan took another dainty cake from the plate. 'Do you feel like going to see something? At the British Film Institute if there's something good on?'

'No, I don't think so. Home, that's where I want to go. Maybe a couple of episodes of *House of Cards*.'

'That's gone downhill since Claire dyed her hair black.'

'I know, but we can't give up now. Got to see it through to the end.'

'I don't actually understand why we have to, but if you still enjoy it, I'm happy to sit next to you.'

As they left Fortnum & Mason, and stepped out into a sunny

Piccadilly, Aidan stood still for a few seconds and thought, *This is happiness. I must remember it. I mustn't let it pass into the mud of other memories.*

'You okay?' Vina took his hand.

Aidan nodded and they walked towards the Tube together.

VINA

Vina stood on the balcony of the Forsters' flat and looked down at the river. Then she glanced to her right, towards London Bridge and the Shard, and to the left in the direction of the Houses of Parliament, which she couldn't see but which she knew were there, beyond the bend of the river. She took a deep breath. It's cruel, she thought, of Iris and also of Aidan to bring me here. They must have known I would fall in love with everything about it. Finding and choosing a house after seeing this was, she reflected, a bit like dangling an Armani jacket in front of someone, then saying: *No, you can't have it. You have to have something from M & S. This is just for you to look at and covet.* Actually, it was worse than that. Somehow, it was possible to find good, reasonably priced imitations even of Armani, but property couldn't be copied in the same way. Sad but true. Vina turned to walk into the living room again and there they were, sitting on beautiful sofas, discussing, in jokey tones, the possibility of an oligarch coming along soon.

'We should go, I think,' said Iris, standing up. 'I'm sure you're very busy.'

'Well,' said Josie, 'it's been so nice having you. I feel much happier now.'

As they said their goodbyes, with the little boy, Zak, clinging to Aidan's trouser leg, till he was detached by his father,

Vina wondered why Josie felt happier. What had Aidan said to her?

Iris offered them a lift back to Barnet but Aidan looked at Vina and said, 'Fancy walking along the South Bank?'

'Yes, let's do that,' she answered, and they waved as Iris went off to find her car.

Vina was silent as they began to walk.

'You okay?' Aidan asked, reaching for her hand.

'I'm a bit stunned, to tell you the truth. I never expected . . .'

'What? I did tell you what an amazing place it was, didn't I?'

'You did, but still. It's . . .'

'Not what you're looking for, right? You want a garden.'

Vina thought for a moment. 'You could have pots of lovely things growing on that balcony. Quite a few of them, actually. Also, didn't Iris say there was space for a roof garden? It needed to be made, she said but that sounds . . .'

'Sounds what?'

Vina turned to look at him. 'I was going to say *possible* but the whole place is actually impossible. Cloud Cuckoo Land impossible.'

'Well, I think it *may* be possible. Just.'

'No! It can't be. Have you let yourself get carried away with that advance? Ten thousand pounds isn't all that much, you know, and you don't get it all at once. You're letting your success go to your head, and you can't do that when it comes to moving house.'

Aidan stopped walking. 'Here's a bench, Vina. Can we sit down for a bit?'

She frowned. 'Are you feeling okay? What's the matter?'

'Nothing, only I want to talk to you and I can't really do it effectively if we're walking along. I'm not someone in *The West Wing*.'

Vina laughed. They sat down and looked together at the opposite bank, to where the dome of St Paul's rose above the office blocks.

'I love this view,' said Vina, when she saw that Aidan wasn't about to say anything.

'Me too.' He turned his whole body to face her. 'Vina, I've been thinking. I love you. I've wanted us to live together since – well, since ages ago. But now I realize that what I really want is to be married to you. There, I've said it. Then we could buy the flat together. What do you think? Will you marry me?'

It was like being hit by a truck, Vina thought, as the meaning of Aidan's words came to her. Like being taken and flung over that parapet and into the fast-flowing river. Like being shaken. Like being whirled up and up into the clouds till she could see the whole of the city spread out in front of her. And then dropped.

Aidan looked white and drawn. Vina noticed this while being totally caught up in her own feelings. I must love him, she thought, to notice such things. I *do* love him. So why was she feeling so . . . 'Aidan,' she began. 'I don't know. I feel . . .'

'What? What do you feel? Oh, Vina, darling, please say yes. I couldn't bear it if you said no. Why would you say no?'

'I'm not saying no. I just . . .'

'What? What just . . . I don't understand.'

Vina put her hands over her eyes, so that she didn't have to see Aidan's face. What she was going to say would be hard anyway and impossible if she had to look at him. How to explain to him what she was thinking without hurting him? But if what she thought was even the smallest bit true, then he needed to know how upset she was by his calculations.

'I think . . . I think we're fine as we are and I also think your suddenly wanting us to get married is for the wrong reasons. And I've told you, I hated being married to Geoff.'

As soon as the words were out of her mouth, she regretted them. Of course Aidan wasn't Geoff, and it was unfair to think of them as if they were anything like one another.

Before she could apologize, Aidan spoke. 'What on earth are you saying, Vina? I don't believe you can mean it.'

'It's the flat, isn't it? You want us to get married so that we can buy the flat together. That's it, isn't it?' As she spoke, Vina could feel rising within her . . . not anger exactly, but a wash of disappointment, like the brownish scummy waters of the river creeping over the sandbanks below them. 'I thought you were different. I thought you loved me for myself and now it seems you've had a − an ulterior motive. You've made me fall in love with you, and now you spring this on me and what am I supposed to think? Part of me wants to believe you but part of me, and it's part of me that I don't recognize, thinks, *He saw you coming. He had this planned from the beginning. He wants that flat and will stop at nothing to get it.* I don't know what I think or feel any longer.'

While she was speaking, Vina had been prepared for anything. She longed for Aidan to shout at her. She wanted him to deny it, deny every word of her horrible suspicions. She wouldn't have minded rage. She wanted confrontation. She was looking for a strong reaction of some kind. Instead, he had sat silently as she unburdened herself. His face was a mask, frozen in horror. He went red, then white, and his lips were pressed together as if to prevent the words he wanted to say from escaping. Then he rose from the bench and walked away without a word.

Vina watched him as he left, growing smaller and smaller as he strode rapidly towards Waterloo. *This isn't happening,* she thought. *He can't do this to me. I ought to run after him.* Why . . . why wasn't he staying to face her? To quarrel with her? Did that mean she'd been right? That she'd hit on the truth of his feelings for her? The thought was so awful that she felt it in her stomach and doubled up in pain.

'You okay, missus?' Vina looked up to find a young woman standing in front of her. About twenty, clearly worried.

'Fine, fine. I'm fine, really. It's nothing. I'm okay now, honestly.' She wanted her to go away, to leave, to let her think. She did go away in the end but only after insisting Vina had a sip of water from a thankfully previously unopened bottle of water.

Two o'clock in the morning, and Vina couldn't remember when she'd felt worse. Surely, she thought, all those bad times with Geoff had been worse. She tried to recall what she'd felt on the long journey home on the Tube and couldn't. She'd been like a zombie. Dead in the head. Frozen solid with misery. Once she'd got home, she'd tried to eat something and couldn't. Then she'd sat drinking cups of tea till it was time to go to bed, and all the while her thoughts were spinning out of control.

How had things come to this? What had just happened? Aidan wanted to marry her. When she tried to piece together their conversation, the only thing she could summon up was a feeling of terror, a dread of everything they'd found, everything they had, or which she'd thought they had, sliding down and down into some kind of hideous wateriness. The River Thames, which, before he'd proposed, had been so much a part of what she'd loved about the flat, had turned into a flood of muddy, polluted water.

Stop it. Think. Vina tried to pull herself together. She got into bed and at once began to go over the whole relationship. She tried to bring back, one by one, the things he'd said to her; she went through their time together, scene by scene, as if remembering a movie. Lying in this bed, she could so easily conjure up the lovemaking. The caresses. Only yesterday . . . Oh, God, she could still almost taste him and smell him. So why not? she asked herself. Why not marry him and have him here beside you for ever? Don't you want that?

She did. She knew she did, in spite of her brave talk about loving being on her own. That was quite true. She did enjoy living alone, but if you loved someone, you wanted them there, right next to you. For ever. So what's the matter with me? she wondered. Hasn't he asked me to do exactly that? He wants me to be with him for ever.

And yet, like a black stone in her heart, Vina couldn't stop herself thinking: *It might all be a lie. He could have deliberately started the whole relationship knowing he wanted that flat; knowing that sharing with someone else was his only chance. I happened to come along at the right time and he seized on me. He's what Geoff warned me about. A fortune hunter. Just because he seems to be unworldly and a little naive doesn't mean a thing. He's clever. Also, what do I really know about him? I've never met any of his friends. He has no family. He could be an axe-murderer for all I know.*

Oh, God, Vina said to herself. I'm delirious now. Where does it come from, this crap I'm thinking? Aidan's not devious. He's completely transparent. Still, the voice in her head wouldn't stop: *That's the point of devious people. They deceive you. They don't mean what they say. They can look completely innocent.*

There wasn't any hope of sleep now, so Vina got up and checked her emails. Nothing from Aidan. No text. No phone call. She went into the kitchen to make another cup of tea. More keenly than she'd ever wanted anything, she wanted to talk to Aidan. But it was down to him. He was the one who'd walked off without a single word. It isn't up to me, she told herself. He left me there. He didn't contradict me or say a word in his own defence. He just walked away. Well, fuck him. I'm not going to be the first one to get in touch again. It's for him to get in touch with me.

She sat down on the sofa in the kitchen, and before she'd even picked up her teacup, the tears came and she began to sob as she'd not done since childhood. *Text him*, said a voice in her head. *Be grown-up about it. You're too old for this.*

IRIS

'You're looking very pleased with yourself, my dear,' said Bruce. 'Sold any good houses lately?'

'As a matter of fact,' Iris said, 'I think I might have a buyer for Mrs Brownrigg's house.'

'Really? Well, I always did say you had the magic touch.'

He'd never said anything of the kind, but Iris smiled at him. 'It's early days but I'm living in hope. A first-time buyer, what's more.'

'Oligarch?' Bruce looked interested. He always perked up when someone with lots of money came along.

'An artist, actually. Patrick Taylor.'

'Don't they generally starve in garrets?'

'Not this one, for sure. He's been living in New York.'

'Aah, a Yank. That would explain the money.' Bruce's world was lacking in subtlety and nuance.

'British, actually. Just living in the States for the last few years. He's coming back now and wants to settle down.'

As Iris said the words, she had a mental image of them walking round Vina's house together. Vina herself had been looking really happy and gorgeous. She'd been wearing a necklace Iris would have loved to own: amber set in coils and complications of silver. She made a mental note to ask Vina where it had come from. Maybe Aidan had given it to her. Those two were in love,

Iris could see it in everything they did, and it was good news as far as she was concerned. Just before coming into work this afternoon, she had taken Aidan and Vina round to the Forsters' flat and she'd seen how much Vina had loved it. What if they bought it together? She hadn't said anything, but that was what she was hoping for. There were other people booked in to see it, but as it wasn't easy for most people to find the asking price, Iris was optimistic.

The other part of her plan concerned Josie. She was so desperate to buy Mansfield Cottage that she would probably consider lowering the asking price of the flat at least a little to get the move going. And if Iris knew anything about her, she'd bet on her being extra pleased to sell the flat to Aidan. It was a swap of the very best kind. Iris hadn't mentioned any of this to Bruce, but he was still pleased with her. Iris opened her laptop feeling happy with her morning's work and ready to do a lot more this afternoon, before going to meet Patrick for dinner.

She did try. She made a valiant attempt to concentrate on the details of some new houses that had just come onto the market, then type them up into a state where they'd look good on the website and on printed details. This was generally Holly's job, but she was on holiday and it fell to Iris to do what she always thought of as the more boring stuff. She fiddled around for a bit answering emails.

One was from Marilynne, suggesting a group meal next week to find out exactly what Iris's feelings were about Neil and the Devon Disaster. Iris had mentioned this briefly to her friends but they would want to pick over the details. The truth was that, since kissing Patrick, Iris had hardly given Neil a thought. How fickle and trivial you are, she told herself, then immediately thought, No, you're not trivial. You'd ditched Neil back in February and it was only circumstances that brought you together again. Drink and lust: that was what had done it. There was nothing about the relationship that Iris needed to mourn. She had examined her feelings minutely, scrutinizing every last one in great detail, and concluded that Neil was well and truly out of her system. That left plenty of room for thoughts of Patrick.

Falling in love, Iris decided, was a bit like getting a cold. You could feel the early symptoms long before you got the full-blown disease: a tickle in the throat, an almost-headache, prickly eyes. Love was like that. Her heart was speeding up every time she remembered Patrick's kisses. She saw his face in front of her eyes whenever she was not actively looking at something else. Also, Iris had spent hours on the internet, Googling every single thing she could find about him, and there were lots. She gazed at his paintings on her phone. And she remembered, on a kind of video loop in her head, a few minutes in Vina's garden.

Vina had shown them round the whole house and Iris could tell that Patrick was impressed. Then she'd said, 'But you must see the garden. Why don't you look around by yourselves?'

They'd gone out together. Iris hadn't been in Vina's garden since before the spring when nothing much had been flowering. Now it was full of roses, dahlias and many shrubs she couldn't identify.

'Vina could have told you all the names,' she said.

'I know a few,' said Patrick. 'Those are peonies. They're not in flower now, but I love them.'

Iris hadn't given peonies much thought before, but now that Patrick had drawn her attention to them, she tried to imagine how beautiful they would be when in flower and decided to adore them on the spot. They walked along the path to the pond.

'Like a small-scale Monet,' Patrick said. Iris looked puzzled. He then told her about Monet creating an amazing garden, complete with a lake and waterlilies, just so that he could paint it.

'If you bought this house, you could do that,' she said. Iris was joking but Patrick stood gazing at the pond and the lilies and saying nothing for ages. She began to wonder if she'd said something wrong.

Then he turned to her. 'Yes.' He was smiling. 'I might.' He looked back at the pond and again seemed to fall into a daze. He was silent for so long, staring down at the water, that Iris said, 'I think we should go back now. Vina will be wondering what's happened to us.'

'Not yet,' he said. He took her hand and Iris turned to him. 'Not yet.' Then he kissed her.

Iris had been kissed before, many times, but Patrick's kiss, there by Vina's pond, was the one she kept coming back to. Top kiss, she told herself, without a doubt. Every time she thought about it (and it hadn't left her head since it happened), a kind of ripple went through her whole body. If she wasn't doing anything else, like working or talking to Bruce or Dominic, or speaking on the phone, if she let herself, she could get quite carried away, and her insides felt as if they were in meltdown.

By the time they came back inside and began talking to Vina again, Iris had calmed down a little but she felt sure she must have been red in the face and looking flustered. Patrick left soon afterwards for a meeting with his art dealer, and promised Iris he'd get back to her. Vina must have thought it was about the house, and Iris hoped it was, of course, but she knew it was also a remark meant for her.

Since the viewing, Patrick had sent four texts and they had spoken on the phone twice. The last time was to arrange to meet. Patrick was going to pick her up in just over two hours and Iris knew she would have to try to work till then, but it was going to be hard. She tried to concentrate on 36 Abergavenny Terrace, which was a very desirable three-bedroom Edwardian with almost all the original features, but it was Patrick's features that kept floating into her mind as she was typing the details. Dark hair, falling onto his forehead, unexpectedly blue eyes, and that mouth. When Iris thought of his mouth she was right back by the pond and had to stop typing for a few minutes to take deep breaths. Pull yourself together, she told herself. You'll see him soon enough. Actually, *not* soon enough. Iris sighed. She wanted to be with him all the time. She recognized the symptoms. This was it. A full-blown attack of something that bore at least a passing resemblance to love.

'We know,' said Patrick, 'very little about one another,' He helped himself to some prosciutto. They were in an Italian restaurant in Hampstead, which was, he said, his local. It looked to Iris like a very expensive local, but she would have been happy eating anywhere with him. He was right, though, in a way.

'I know a lot about you,' Iris said. 'I Googled you. I've looked at your work. I've seen your sister.'

'I've seen your boyfriend.'

'My ex-boyfriend.' Iris twirled her spaghetti around her fork as elegantly as she could and ate a mouthful. 'He shagged the other woman when four of us were on holiday together. As I told you, I gave him the push in February. But he came smoothing back for a bit.'

'Were you serious? Living together?'

'For a while. But he wanted me to do stuff I didn't want to do, like marry him and have kids. I don't want kids. I really didn't want to marry him. So I moved back to live with my mother.'

'Snap. Me too.' He grinned. 'We're like a couple of teenagers. Nowhere to go where we can be on our own.'

Iris said nothing. Did he mean what she thought he meant? He had assumed (had he?) that they were about to spend the night together. On what was technically a first date, even though they'd met and talked a few times. They'd done more than talk. Iris would have gone back to his place if he'd had one. She ate a few mouthfuls without saying a word. Patrick was silent too. What was he thinking? Would he be assuming that the evening was maybe going to end when the meal did? Iris wanted their time together to go on till it turned into tomorrow morning. She had even prepared for it by putting a small bag with a change of clothes and her toothbrush into the boot of her car. She'd taken a long time this morning to decide to do this, and she chided herself over and over again: *If it does happen, if he asks you to stay over, you'll look calculating if you come prepared.* But if she didn't come prepared how could she go to work the next day? In the same clothes she was wearing today. In the end, she made up her mind to lie and say that she always had a bag ready in the boot, in case of emergencies. No one could prove that she didn't.

'I want this evening to go on,' Patrick said, and Iris looked at him in astonishment. Had he been reading her mind? 'After the pudding and coffee.' She didn't say a word, but nodded.

'The Broderick is near here,' he went on. 'It's a small hotel. Not the Ritz but nice. Should I ring them?'

Iris hesitated for about ten seconds. Then she said, 'Yes. Ring them.'

She went to the Ladies then, because she didn't want to hear him actually making the call. She hated being overheard when she was on the phone and she assumed Patrick would feel the same. When she came back to the table, he said, 'All done. Would you like a pudding?'

'No, just coffee, thanks.'

Iris's instinct was always to have a pudding but her appetite had entirely left her. The only thing she could see was the two of them walking into a hotel together. Going up to the room. Kissing. At this point, the screen in her head went . . . not exactly dark but somehow misted over. Iris couldn't imagine any further than the hotel-room door closing behind them.

Patrick was busy paying the bill, waiting for the receipt to come out of the card machine, when Iris's phone rang in her bag. She reached in, found it and looked to see who was trying to reach her, quite determined to turn it off at once. Penny. Why on earth would Penny be phoning her at ten o'clock at night? What couldn't wait till morning or, even better, be put into a text? She was on the point of switching off the phone and letting Penny leave a voicemail, when curiosity overcame her and she signalled to Patrick that she was going to take the call. He nodded and mouthed, 'No worries.' He even seemed to mean what he was saying. Iris could detect no sign of impatience of the kind she'd become used to while she was with Neil. Fleetingly, she wondered why she'd put up with it. Why she'd put up with plenty of things.

'Iris?' Penny sounded as if she'd been crying.

'What's up, Penny?' If you'd known someone since you were ten years old, you knew at once when things weren't okay. Iris waited to hear the story: in the background, she could hear a child crying. That must be Maria, Penny's little girl, who was about two. Could Penny *really* not get her to shut up when her mother was on the phone? Iris wasn't sure about when kids were able to take instructions, such as *Keep quiet for a moment, would you, please?* but Maria was clearly in some distress.

'It's Maria,' Penny said. 'I don't know what to do. She's ill. She's had this sort of thing once before – bronchiolitis it's called, and she has trouble breathing when she gets it, but last time it was during the day so I could take her to our GP. I've got to take her to A and E, Iris. They said I had to on the phone – I rang the helpline – but I can't drive! I've hurt my hand! Ian's away but I rang him before I rang the helpline even and he's coming as soon as he can. He's in Manchester and he's on his way home now, but he's not here yet – and my mum and dad are on holiday. God, I'm sorry, Iris, but I didn't know who else to phone.'

'Calm down, Penny. It's okay. Take a deep breath.' Iris had an idea that there were questions to ask that Penny needed to answer, but she couldn't think what they were. Patrick was peering at her and frowning from across the table. She couldn't work out what that meant. Was he pissed off? It must have been clear to him, even without knowing the details, that their night together in a hotel was growing less and less likely by the minute. But then he smiled at her and reached across the table to touch her hand, which was gripping the side of the table so hard that her knuckles showed white. She smiled at him, while speaking to Penny in the calmest voice she could muster. 'It's fine, Penny. I'm coming. Right now. I'm in Hampstead. I won't be long. Keep calm if you can. I'll be there soon. Bye.'

'Okay,' said Patrick, standing up. 'Some kind of emergency, I get that. Let's go.'

'You don't have to come. I'm so, so sorry. Really. I have to take

my friend to A and E, so I need the car. Are you okay to get a
cab? I haven't even got time to take you home. Her baby's ill
and she's panicking. I feel awful. I really, really wanted. . . Can
we do this again?'

'Ssh. I'm coming with you. You can give me details on the
way. And I'll ring the hotel, don't worry. I'd offer to drive but
I've been drinking.'

'It's okay. I'm fine. Really. But you've left your bag, look.'

'God, thanks, Iris. My whole life's in there.' He went back to
the table and picked up the battered leather bag he had hung
over the chair next to where he'd been sitting. As they left the
restaurant, he slung it over his shoulder and they almost ran to
where the car was parked.

All the way to Penny's house, Patrick kept up a stream of
quiet, comforting talk. He asked sensible questions, looked up
the nearest A and E on his phone and worked out the quickest
way to get there from Penny's house.

'She'll know how to get to the hospital,' Iris said. 'She must.'

'Well, that depends on how panicked she is. Sometimes normal stuff goes out of your head when you're really stressed. But
why has she phoned you? Where's her husband?'

Iris explained Penny's situation. 'And I didn't ask why she
couldn't take a cab. That would have seemed . . . I dunno.
Heartless.'

'She wants someone with her,' Patrick said. 'Someone to talk
to. I understand that perfectly. And before you suggest again
that I go home, I should make it clear that I'm staying. I don't
think you and Penny should do this on your own.'

'I can manage,' said Iris. 'Honestly. You don't even know
Penny! You don't have to do this, Patrick.'

'I feel I do. I don't want to leave you alone to cope, that's all. You don't mind, do you?'

'No, of course not. Thanks, Patrick. It's really nice of you. Did you ring the hotel?'

'Yup. It's fine, don't worry.' He paused and said in quite a different tone, 'Iris . . .'

At that moment, they reached Penny's house and the moment vanished. What had he been going to say? Iris wondered briefly, as they got out of the car in a rush, like cops on the telly, and ran up the short drive.

The door was open and Penny was waiting for them. One of her hands was bound up in an elastic bandage. Maria was in her arms, clinging to her, no longer crying but whimpering gently. 'Oh, Iris, I can't . . .'

'Don't speak, Penny. You ready to go?'

'Yes, I am. Thank you.'

Patrick stepped forward. 'I'm Patrick, by the way. I'm coming with you both. Is that a baby seat?'

'Oh, God – I forgot that. Yes – yes, it is. I took it out of Ian's car and hadn't put it into mine yet. And now . . .' She held up her injured wrist.

No one spoke while Patrick fixed the seat into Iris's car. As soon as they set off, Iris said, 'That was impressive. I didn't know you could do that sort of thing. And so fast.'

'I watched Prince William doing it on the telly and thought, That doesn't seem hard. Everyone was impressed with how he did it but, truthfully, it's a doddle. Things have improved a lot since my kids were small.'

'This is so kind of you both,' said Penny, sounding a bit more cheerful, now that they were on their way. 'And I'm sorry I've messed up your evening.'

'It's fine,' Iris said. 'No worries. We were just in a restaurant, that's all. And we'd finished our meal. Have you eaten?'

'I can't remember,' said Penny. 'I don't think so.'

'There's a bar of chocolate in my glove compartment,' Iris said. 'Patrick, can you find it?' To Penny she said, 'We don't want you falling over, Penny. For Maria's sake.'

Iris felt quite proud of sounding a bit like someone from *Holby City*. She concentrated on getting to the hospital as quickly as she could without breaking the law and put thoughts of herself, Patrick and the room at the Broderick Hotel firmly out of her mind. She glanced at his profile and was happy that he was with them. Maria had now stopped whimpering and Iris could feel a chilly dread creeping over her. Would she be okay? What if she wasn't? What if they were too late? While they were stopped at a red traffic light, she turned to look into the back of the car and saw Maria's little face peering out of the blanket she was wrapped in. Her cheeks were red but otherwise she was as pale as a china doll. Iris felt an unfamiliar clutching sensation in the region of her heart.

'Right,' said Patrick, as the car approached the comforting glare of the neon-lit A and E. 'I'll go in with Penny and Maria while you find a place to park. Come in and find us. Okay?'

'Yes,' said Iris. 'Yes.'

She watched him hold the big swing door open for Penny and Maria and found that her eyes were full of tears. Stop it, she told herself. Pull yourself together. It'll be fine. Patrick will be there. She turned towards the car park.

JOSIE

'Will, you're being ridiculous.' Josie was down at the kitchen end of the flat, making a birthday cake for Zak, who was going to be five the day after tomorrow. She'd made a chocolate cake, decorated to look like an owl, with white and dark chocolate buttons for eyes and feathers, and talons made from cut-out marzipan. She felt quite proud of it, although Paul Hollywood might have criticized the talons for lack of symmetry, and took a photo to put up on Twitter. Zak would love it. She'd been so absorbed in it that she hadn't listened properly to what Will was saying. Still, she knew it was ridiculous.

'I'm being sensible,' said Will. 'We've got four lots of viewers coming to see the flat in the next day or so. If one of them makes an offer, we should take it. That's all I'm saying. If no one else shows up, then of course Mr Church is in with a chance. There's always the possibility that he won't offer, isn't there? You can't be sure he will.'

Josie was still gazing at the owl. 'Come and have a look at this cake!' she said.

'You're trying to change the subject because you know I'm right.'

'No, I'm not,' Josie said.

Will stood up and came to admire the cake. 'That's great.

Zak'll be thrilled. Well done, you.' He began to nibble some celery from a bunch stuck in a glass on the work surface.

Josie glanced at him. 'You're restless. Something wrong?'

'No, not really. I suppose I'm a bit nervous. About tomorrow.'

'Honestly?' Josie was surprised. Will had arranged to meet John at the builder's yard and discuss the job. 'I didn't think you cared so much. Do you fancy it, really?'

'I do, actually. I'm quite surprised by how much . . . I looked up the firm and it seems okay. They're doing interesting stuff, affordable housing that doesn't look like a brutalist nightmare. But there's the small matter of Mansfield Cottage. What if someone else buys it?'

'Then,' said Josie sounding calmer than she felt, 'we'll find some other house near your work. A job you'll enjoy seems too good to miss. Anyway, see how you go. I have a good feeling after Mr Church and Mrs Brownrigg's visit. I'm sure, even though he hasn't said anything, that Mr Church would actually prefer to sell to us and not to someone else.'

'Just because he liked Zak.'

Josie smiled. 'I think he's an old romantic and the idea of Zak and a dog in his house appealed to him. I'm also pretty sure he'll do what he can to offer for this flat. Wouldn't it be great if we could just do a straight swap? Think how happy Iris would be!'

'I'm not in this to make Iris happy,' Will said, but he stopped chewing celery and went to sit at the table.

'I'll speak to her soon,' said Josie. 'Mr Church or Mrs Brownrigg might have been in touch with her to say what their intentions are. I know Iris would like that outcome.'

'Estate agents want to sell their properties. That's all.'

'Not Iris. She's different. She wants everyone to be happy. And she knows where people will be happiest. It's a gift.'

'I love you to bits, Josie,' said Will, grinning, 'but you don't half talk some rubbish sometimes.'

Josie said nothing. She was right, she knew it, and she wasn't going to waste any more breath convincing someone who clearly hadn't the least idea of how Iris operated. He didn't need to agree with her: he just needed to follow her lead, and at the moment that was exactly what he was doing. Still, Josie thought, I'll be a lot happier when I know what's going to happen about this flat. Was hoping that Mr Church would offer completely mad? Maybe, but she knew he would if he possibly could. Fingers crossed.

AIDAN

Later, Aidan was to acknowledge that it was rage. Never in the sixty-odd years of his existence had he felt anything remotely like it. What came over him as he walked away from Vina on the bench beside the river was so unfamiliar, so total in its effect, that it was all he could do to stand upright and walk in the direction of Waterloo. Even that was wrong. At the time, he couldn't have said where he was walking. He saw nothing. He didn't know where he was going. He simply walked because if he stopped, even for a minute to catch his breath, he felt he would dissolve and break out screaming in the throes of this hideous, hitherto unknown emotion.

He didn't notice where he was going but found himself, eventually, in Trafalgar Square. The autumn sun was warm. The square was full of tourists and performers of one kind and another. There was the National Gallery. Fleetingly, he wondered if he should go in, but galleries reminded him of Vina, and to think about her was like putting a hand on an open flame. That's what it feels like, he decided. I can't think about her. My mind just shies away from it. But I have to. What happened? How can I assemble all the bits of our conversation in such a way that they make sense?

All his life, he'd analysed facts. Data. He would do it again. Soon. But now the only thing he wanted to do was get home.

Hide. Never come out again. The thought of life without Vina . . . He set off towards Leicester Square Tube station. I won't think of that, he told himself. It won't happen. I have to do something. Now. I have to do something now.

Then he stopped, right in the middle of the pavement. I can't, he thought. She said she didn't want to marry me. That was what she said. *She didn't mean it,* a voice in his head told him. *She loves you. She's said so over and over.* Another voice, which Aidan regarded as the sensible, rational side of himself, answered: *How can she love me if she doesn't want to marry me? If she reacted in the way she did?*

Tears blurred his vision as he thought of what that meant. What she'd said. It was easily, *easily* the most hurtful thing anyone had ever said to him. She'd accused him of deviousness, deceit, of not really loving her. How could she do that? And if she could, how much did she really love him? Maybe she didn't. That was the worst, the very worst, thought of all. Perhaps the last few months were just . . . just what? A kind of game. A fling. A woman allowing herself a bit of fun and nothing more.

He didn't, he *couldn't,* believe it. Vina loved him. She couldn't, could she, *pretend* or cynically act those cries, that passion? Aidan realized that what he knew about women was precisely nothing beyond his limited experiences with his wife over many years. He had no knowledge of what women could or could not do. Vina had turned down his proposal. *Ergo,* she couldn't love him as he loved her. She did not believe he loved her. That, to Aidan, was unbearable.

The long journey home passed like a bad dream. The people in the carriage were ghosts to him: he hardly saw them. He checked his phone over and over again in case Vina had texted him but there was nothing. No signal underground, of course, but it took him some time to work that out. He looked at the photographs they'd taken in Paris and had to shut his phone down. Seeing how happy they'd been made him want to howl. Had she really been happy? How could you tell if another person was being honest? When he thought of what she might be thinking of him now, that he was a fortune hunter, and only after the flat, his insides gathered together in knots of agony. The pain he felt was physical. His stomach was churning. His face was burning with the effort of not crying. His hands were unsteady as he swiped his Freedom card. How he reached home he had no idea but at last he was there, in his study. Staring at the screen, thinking of what to say.

Because, of course, he would have to write to Vina. What words? How to convince her?

By the early hours of the morning, he had written about three thousand words and deleted them. Sleep was out of the question. When Grace was ill, he'd become used to losing sleep. There had been many white nights. And now here was another . . . a different kind of pain but, still, a night when no sleep would be possible. He had to go and see her. That was the conclusion he'd come to as the words spilled out of him. He stood up. He had to go now. This minute. What was the time? Three a.m. Vina would be asleep. He would have to wait till morning. *But I can't*, he thought. I'll go now. I'll wake her up. I'll have a shower and a cup of coffee, then go.

IRIS

Iris had never been in an A and E department before but she knew a little of how they worked from watching television. While Penny was giving details to a nurse behind the desk, she and Patrick sat on blue chairs and waited. The white electric light was horrible and every single person in the waiting room looked hideous: miserable and tired and as if they'd been there for hours. Iris was holding Maria, who seemed to be not quite asleep but drowsy. Her breathing was laboured and wheezy. She was still pale and felt very light in Iris's arms. Looking down at her, Iris thought, *A child. I'm holding a child for the very first time in my whole life.* She said to Patrick, 'I've never held a kid before, you know. Not once. Isn't that strange?'

'Are you okay with it?' he answered. 'D'you want me to take her? I'm used to it. Apart from my two, my older sister, not Tatty, has two children and my elder brother has three. They're all in Scotland.'

'Wow,' Iris said.

'I'm quite good at kids, actually. I like them.'

'I don't think I've ever really met any, not properly,' said Iris. 'This is my first close-up experience of one.'

She was spared giving him any further details of her feelings about children by Penny coming to take Maria into the cubicle where a doctor would be looking at her very soon

indeed. That was what the nurse said but *very soon indeed* turned
out to be three-quarters of an hour later.

'I'm sorry about the hotel,' said Iris. 'I was really looking forward to it.'

'I didn't cancel,' said Patrick. 'I thought I'd go there when
we've finished here.'

Later, Iris would wonder where she got the nerve from to say
what she said next. 'If you wanted to go now, I wouldn't mind.
Honestly. I'm not scared any longer. Not now we're in the hospital. I could . . . I could come along later.'

Patrick shook his head. 'I'm not leaving here till you do. It
may be some time till they fix Maria up. Also, if Penny's going
to be alone after they've been discharged, we'll need to take
her home and possibly stay with her till her husband gets back.'

'Okay,' Iris said. 'Though she did say he'd be here quite soon.
That's fine. I'm going to email Bruce – I'll do it now. I'm not
going in to work tomorrow.'

'Excellent. Then we'll have the whole day together . . . and
tomorrow night.' He put an arm around her and pulled her
close to him. Iris leaned her head against him and shut her eyes.
She felt completely safe. She smiled as he kissed the side of her
head and felt relieved that she'd put the case into the back of
her car. He added, 'I don't care how long we have to sit here. I'm
just happy you're going to come with me when we leave.'

'Mmm,' Iris said. 'Me too.' She was definitely falling asleep
now, her eyelids growing heavy . . . She shook herself awake.
'Sorry, sorry,' she said. 'I'm knackered, that's all. But I have to
stay awake . . .'

'I'll go and get us coffee from that machine.'

He sprang up and crossed the waiting room, and Iris watched
him feeding coins into slots and pressing buttons. He was

smiling as he came towards her. 'I always feel as if I've won some kind of battle when I get coffee, or something like it, from one of those monsters.'

Penny came out of the cubicle and walked towards them. She wasn't smiling exactly but Iris could tell she was feeling better. She sat down in the chair next to Iris and said, 'Oh, God, is that coffee? Can I share yours, Iris?'

'I'll go and get you one.' Patrick sprang up again. 'It's far too delicious to share!'

'He's joking,' said Iris, as Patrick went off once more to battle with the machine.

Penny nodded. 'Maria's going to be okay. She needed a bit of help for her breathing, but that's much easier now. They're keeping her here for a few hours, just to make sure, so I've got to wait but there's no need for you two to stay. Honestly. I'll be fine.'

'I'm staying as long as you do,' Iris said. 'Don't bother to argue.'

'I'm so grateful, Iris. This is so kind of you.'

'Nonsense! It's nothing. I'm glad you asked me and I'm glad I could help, Penny. Really.'

Penny hugged her, then stood up. 'I'm going in to sit with Maria.' She waved towards the cubicle. 'She's asleep, but I want to be right next to her. Okay?'

'Of course,' said Iris. 'You go. I'll bring your coffee.'

Penny went off and Patrick waved to Iris from his place in the coffee queue. When he returned, Iris took the cup from him and said, 'Penny's gone back to sit with Maria. I'll take it in to her.'

Maria looked very small indeed on the regulation hospital bed. Iris could see at once that her colour was better and that her breathing was easier.

'She's been on a nebulizer,' Penny whispered. 'Much happier now.'

'She's lovely,' Iris said, looking at Maria's small pink hand and feeling suddenly overwhelmed with relief that she was okay. That the golden hair, which was now snarled and sweaty, would soon be clean and in the bunches held with pretty bobbles that Penny always favoured. I'll buy her some new ones, Iris resolved. I'll get her the best and most sparkly hair bobbles in the whole world. She bent down and kissed Maria's forehead gently. 'I'll go and wait with Patrick now. You sit there and try to sleep a bit.'

Penny sat down in the armchair and said, 'Ian'll be here soon. He just texted me. An hour at most.'

'Okay. I'll wait till he's here and then we'll go.'

Penny had her eyes closed. 'He's lovely, your Patrick. I meant to say that before. Really lovely. Is he the one?'

'Honestly, Penny, what a thing to think about now. He is lovely, I agree, but how should I know if he's the one? We've only just met, really.'

'Didn't look like that to me,' said Penny, sleepily. 'I wouldn't let him get away, if I were you. He's kind.'

'Yes,' said Iris. She was going to elaborate, but Penny was asleep in her chair, the coffee untouched on the table next to her, so she went to sit next to Patrick. He, too, was asleep. He was leaning against the wall and seemed completely relaxed. His eyes were closed and his breathing was even. His shoulder bag was on his lap and his hands were crossed over it to keep it safe. Could you fall in love with a person because of their hands? They seemed beautiful to her, as did the folds of his sleeve, and the way he was sitting . . . Oh, God, she thought. I need to sleep. I'm probably hallucinating. Feeling things I wouldn't feel if I was more together. And Maria: what she'd felt looking at her was very peculiar indeed. Tenderness. Something like love.

AIDAN

Vina's bedroom, which faced the front of the house, was dark. She must still be asleep, Aidan thought, and wondered if he ought to wait till she woke up before knocking on her door. No, he thought. I can't bear to be here and not see her. I'm going to wake her up. He was on the point of getting out of the car and marching up the drive to press the bell and fill the house with the ringtone, which Vina hated, when his courage failed him. I'll text her, he thought. Maybe she's lying awake. If she is, she'll read it and answer. Or not. That possibility hadn't occurred to him, but if she was still angry, it was quite likely that she would ignore it. No, better to wake her up and risk her anger. Frighten her, quite possibly. It must be frightening, mustn't it, to be woken in the early hours by that horrible tune on her doorbell?

Aidan had his back to Vina's house as he locked his car. When he turned, he saw her in the doorway and stopped moving. What was she doing there? Where had she come from? The light was on in the hall behind her and her face was in shadow: just a pale blur with no features. For what seemed like a very long time, they stood there. Then Aidan started moving towards her, feeling Vina's eyes on him as he approached. 'I didn't mean to wake you,' he said.

'You didn't. I haven't been able to sleep.'

'Nor me.'

'Well,' said Vina, turning and going into the house, 'come in.'

'Vina?'

'Yes?

'I don't want to come in if . . .'

'If what?'

'You know . . . if you and I aren't . . .' The words he was look-ing for refused to be spoken. 'I can't say . . . I'm so very . . . I don't know how . . .' Then he did what he had never intended to do: he stopped talking altogether and the tears he'd been keeping back for hours poured from his eyes and he did nothing to stop them but stood there and fumbled for a handkerchief.

Vina ran to him and put her arms around his neck and brought his face close to hers. 'Oh, darling Aidan, don't. Don't cry. Please don't cry. I can't bear it. I didn't mean it. I was hor-rible. How could I have said those things to you? I'm sorry, so sorry . . . I know I was unfair to you, I know I was, but you – you walked away. Just walked away without a word. How could you *do* that? How could you leave me and not say a single thing? No, don't answer. Come and sit down. Come and have a cup of tea. Cake . . . I bet you haven't eaten, have you? Maybe not cake – maybe porridge or eggs . . .'

'Vina, I must speak. It's important. I need to tell you some things.'

'Yes. And I need to tell you some things as well. But let's at least go inside. Oh, Aidan, I can't tell you how happy I am to see you. I thought I'd lost you.'

'Never. You'll never lose me. I promise. Never.'

Vina clung to him as if she had no intention of letting go. *I mustn't forget this*, Aidan thought. *Mustn't forget how good it is to have a happiness restored that you thought you'd lost for ever.*

Aidan and Vina were having a meal that was breakfast in every particular except that they were eating it at four o'clock in the afternoon. They'd gone to bed at six in the morning. Falling asleep like that, Aidan reflected, was like being knocked on the head. He hadn't even registered the pillow, so sudden and overwhelming was the drop into blackness.

Waking up, he looked around for Vina but she wasn't there. He could smell bacon cooking, so he went downstairs to find her.

'Hello!' she said, turning round and smiling at him. 'I've made breakfast, and if we eat enough, it can be our supper too!'

'Lovely. Thank you,' Aidan said. He looked at Vina, who had already showered and dressed. Her hair was still damp, and over a black T-shirt she was wearing a rose pink cardigan he loved. He watched her putting stuff on the table and said nothing. Now that the worst was over, now that they were together again, his question still stood. He wanted to marry her. Was this the time to ask her again? And the flat, what about that? He opened his mouth to speak and shut it again but Vina was too quick for him: she'd seen his hesitation.

'Okay,' she said, sitting down behind the teapot and pouring them each a cup of lapsang souchong. 'We have to talk about the flat. We have to talk about us. We have to discuss the things we should have discussed long ago. The future. Our whole life together.'

'Yes,' Aidan said. 'I agree. I can't say I've had time to think because I haven't. I didn't think a single thing till I came here this morning, just that I wanted to see you. That was literally the only thought in my head. I've only just woken up, so I've not had time to—'

'I have,' Vina said. 'I want to apologize, first of all. It was a mean and horrible thing for me to say: that you only wanted to get to know me so that you could buy the flat. I know it was mad, and I've got no excuses. It was just *mad*, and I don't know what made me say it. I knew it was awful as the words were coming out of my mouth. I am so, so sorry, my darling. '

'No need to apologize. It was fear.' Aidan took a croissant from the basket in front of him. 'That's what made you say what you did. You are, quite understandably, wary of anyone wanting to marry you. But I don't want to marry you in that way, in the Geoff way, if you know what I mean. I don't want to control you. I want to help you. I want you to help me. I want us to be together so that we can be happy. That's it. And I thought of it long ago, too. If you don't believe me, you can ask your daughter. I mentioned it to Libby when I had dinner with her.'

'Are you serious? You mentioned it to Libby? Am I going to have to be angry with you all over again about that? It was bad enough that you went without telling me, but I got over it. And now you're telling me you discussed *marrying me* with her? And didn't tell me? And she didn't say a word? Bloody hell, can I trust anyone?'

'Please don't be angry, Vina. Not about that . . . please. I kept it quiet because I was scared you'd take fright if I mentioned marriage. As, indeed, you sort of have. I also told Libby I hadn't mentioned it to you yet.'

'What did she say?'

'She was fine about it. But that's not the point I'm making. I told her this at a time when the flat was out of the question. I'd put it entirely out of my mind and was quite keen on thirty-six

Harris Gardens, if you remember. I am only' – he put out his hand to take Vina's – 'trying to show you that I've been wanting to ask you to marry me for ages. It's been a dream of mine. Please say you'll think about it.'

Vina stood up and took their plates to the dishwasher. She turned round when she'd stacked them and said, 'Aidan, I do need to think. Do you mind? It's not that I don't love you but I want . . . a bit of breathing space. Time . . . Just a few days? Do you mind? Please say you don't.'

Aidan stared at her, feeling as if she'd dealt him a physical blow in the face. What was this? Hadn't they made up? They'd just spent hours asleep in one another's arms. They'd just had a comfortable, pleasant meal. He found he was blinking to keep the tears from returning, feeling like a man who'd been pulled out of the sea on to a rescuing boat only to find himself tossed back into black waves. He found it hard to speak, but eventually he said, 'I suppose so. I'm not sure why.'

'A marriage proposal is not what I was expecting. A couple of days, Aidan, that's all. Give me a couple of days.'

He nodded, struck dumb with misery. 'Okay. I'll go now.'

'Thanks. And, Aidan . . .'

'Yes?'

'No texts or emails either, right? I'll phone you in a couple of days.'

He didn't trust himself to speak. He kissed her goodbye formally, on the cheek, and left the house quickly. He then drove home on a kind of automatic pilot, which he was sure was probably unsafe, and went into Mansfield Cottage feeling like Adam being exiled from the Garden of Eden.

IRIS

As they walked into their room at the Broderick Hotel, Iris felt more nervous than she had for years. They'd arrived at half past five in the morning. Patrick signed the register at Reception and the night porter gave them a key without even glancing at them. He looked almost as tired as Iris felt. She was carrying her overnight bag. Patrick had smiled when she took it out of the boot and she'd immediately said, 'Lucky I always have a bag in my boot, isn't it?'

'It's good to be prepared. That's why I carry my life around in mine.' He patted the bag slung over his shoulder.

Now she put her little case down beside the enormous wardrobe and sat on the edge of the bed.

'Iris?' Patrick came to sit next to her. 'We're tired. We've had such a long night. Let's just go to sleep now, okay?'

'Okay,' Iris said. 'Only . . .'

'Only what?'

'I didn't pack a nightie.'

Patrick grinned. 'Nor me. Not a nightie but you know what I mean. Never mind. I have my toothbrush. D'you want to go first in the bathroom?'

Iris brushed her teeth and took off her makeup. The only thing she could think of was how much she wanted to get into that bed, which had felt so soft and inviting when she was sitting on it, get into it and shut her eyes. She could sleep in her camisole and pants. It would feel a bit revolting, but she could. That's mad, she told herself. You know what's going to happen. It's why you agreed to come here in the first place. What's the point of being mealy-mouthed about it? She took off her camisole, tights, bra and pants and stood there completely naked, feeling brave and reckless. She opened the door between the bathroom and the bedroom and saw that Patrick had stretched out fully dressed on the bed and fallen fast asleep. Okay, she thought. Okay. She tiptoed across the carpet and made sure that the curtains were properly drawn. She turned her phone to silent. Then she slid under the duvet on her side of the bed, and before she let the lovely waves of sleep close over her, she was aware of the solid mass that was Patrick's body, warm against her right arm. Patrick, she thought. He's there.

When had she ever slept like that? Iris felt herself swimming up and up through darkness, the shreds of a dream she couldn't remember, and opened her eyes. She knew where she was at once. She had time to register the efficiency of the hotel's blackout curtains and the fact that Patrick must have undressed and got into bed beside her during the night. She was lying on her back and he was beside her, turned away from her. She couldn't see him but the warmth coming from his body, so close to hers that they were almost touching, was both comforting and arousing. She put out a hand and, as gently as she could, she stroked his back, running her fingers over his skin. He didn't move.

'I've been awake for ages,' he said, and the unexpected sound of his voice made her catch her breath.

'You gave me a fright,' she said. 'You were lying so still.'

'Didn't want to wake you up.'

'I'm awake . . .'

Patrick turned over in bed and faced her. 'You look lovely,' he said, and began to stroke her upper arm.

'I feel grotty. I'm going to brush my teeth, okay?'

'Okay.'

This had never happened to her before. She brushed her teeth and thought about going to bed with someone, making love with them for the first time. It had always, before now, happened at night. Typically, you went on a date, you drank a bit, you rolled into the bedroom feeling tipsy and generally up for it, and you both set to with abandon. You didn't look at one another too closely . . . not till later. It was a mixture of excitement and passion, recklessness and thrill. Having a long sleep with someone and getting up in the morning and brushing your teeth and hair, then getting back into bed, knowing exactly *why* you were doing that and not getting dressed at once . . . It was like being married. It was sedate. It was . . . well, it was strange, and she didn't quite know why she felt so peculiar. She would, she decided, simply go and lie down in bed and see what happened.

'Hello,' Patrick said, as she opened the bathroom door. He didn't sound a bit nervous.

As soon as she was lying next to him, he turned her gently towards him, so that their faces were almost meeting, but not quite. Iris could feel his breath on her face.

'I love the taste of toothpaste,' he whispered, and then he kissed her, gently at first and then more deeply. His arm slipped round her waist and he drew her to him. Iris closed her eyes and felt herself being pulled in, closer and closer to a source of heat and then her legs and Patrick's legs were tangled up together and he was still kissing her and then he covered her body with his and whispered to her, all sorts of words and more words, and she was too far gone to understand them or know what he was whispering to her, but Iris gathered him into her body and wound her arms around his neck to hold him and they moved together till she was ready to cry out with the sweet anguish of it and then, at last, it was over and she cried out as she came, and somewhere, somewhere close to her, he was crying out too.

'Iris . . .' Patrick kissed her again. 'Lovely Iris.'

Iris said nothing. She'd never known the right words for afterwards. What could you say that wasn't inadequate? She was still trembling, still shaken, and couldn't bring her mouth into gear to speak.

'I'm starving,' said Patrick, sitting up in bed and reaching for the hotel phone. 'I'm going to order food, okay?'

'Yes,' Iris said. She realized as she spoke that she was hungry too. 'What time is it?'

'Six o'clock. Evening, I guess. What do you fancy eating?'

'Continental breakfast,' Iris said. 'Croissants and maybe a bit of fruit and lots of coffee. Possibly smoked salmon as it's actually almost suppertime . . .'

'Right!' Patrick rang Room Service, and ordered the food. 'And,' he said into the phone, 'please could you leave the trolley outside the door and just knock? . . . Thanks. We're not really awake yet.'

Iris marvelled at his lack of embarrassment and said so. He smiled. 'They don't mind. They know what goes on, don't worry. They've seen everything.'

'Still . . .' Iris blushed.

'I bet I know what you're thinking, that I've done this before. Well, you're wrong. It's a first for me, too. I just don't get embarrassed about much and certainly not about being naked in a hotel room at six o'clock in the evening.'

'I wasn't thinking that,' Iris said, but was conscious as she said it that she wasn't being entirely truthful. She sat up. 'I must turn on my phone, if you don't mind. I feel as if I've been on another planet since last night and I should catch up. Okay?'

'Fine,' Patrick said. 'I'll shower first.' He went off humming under his breath and closed the bathroom door behind him.

There was a knock at the door just as he emerged with a towel around his waist. 'Breakfast and/or supper,' Patrick said, and answered it.

'We've got this room for tonight, you know,' Patrick said. 'Let's have breakfast/supper and go back to bed. You don't have to be somewhere else, do you?'

'No,' Iris said. 'Nowhere else.' She didn't add, *And there's nowhere else I'd rather be*, but the thought was in her mind.

*

From: bruce60@R&T. com
To: client mailing list; staff mailing list
Subject: Bruce's Barnet Bulletin, number 407

Hello everyone,
Well, the pumpkins are being carved even as I write and the nights are drawing in. Almost Hallowe'en, and you all know what that means: a very short time indeed till Christmas.

Traditionally, it's not the best time of year for selling but we at the Barnet branch are over the moon with our latest sales! We have just recently had offers on some of the most desirable properties we've handled this year, but fret not! We have lots more where those came from. For example:

11, Wilbraham Terrace, London N5
A highly sought-after area, with good connections by both bus and Tube into the West End. This property is a Victorian terrace house, with two bedrooms and an extended basement kitchen. In need of a little TLC, it is still a bargain for any enterprising couple looking for a starter home.

The Poplars, Baron Road, off Dancer's Hill Road, Potters Bar
This house would suit a large family. Five bedrooms, large gardens, and three reception rooms. A new conservatory adds value. Viewing essential. This property has been maintained to a high standard and, although set in green fields, is very close to Potters Bar station, with fast direct access to King's Cross.

Happy Hallowe'en.
Bruce

VINA

Vina hadn't slept properly for three nights. Days were slightly better because she made herself busy: knitting was good when your mind was in turmoil, and it occurred to her to wonder whether she was such a fast knitter because, all during her marriage to Geoff, she'd spent hours frantically concentrating on the needles. All that practice had made her quicker than most of George's other knitters at finishing her garments. Aidan was on her mind constantly. She'd made him promise not to get in touch but now she was regretting it. She missed him. She knew, as surely as she knew anything, that he was missing her. Vina could picture him, sitting at his desk, working on his book because everything else he liked doing, such as walking, allowed his thoughts to wander and he'd think of her: of *them*.

Vina kept coming back to this: she could choose to be with Aidan or she could choose to be alone. They couldn't go back to being friends, going to movies, galleries and restaurants, not after what they'd said to one another. I love him, Vina said to herself. And he's wrecking my sleep.

This was the third morning she'd woken up too early. She stretched out in the wide bed and wondered if she wanted to be married. They didn't have to marry. They could quite easily continue along the lines of the last few months and no harm would be done. I would move, Vina told herself, and he would move into one of the little box houses he's been looking at, and we'd go on holiday together and an oligarch would buy the Forsters' flat. Aidan would settle for that, she knew. He'd settle for anything that meant they could be together.

She sat up in bed and turned the light on. The early mornings were getting darker and a longing to have him with her, to live with him, suddenly overwhelmed her. And, yes, she thought, I'm not going to lie to myself. The Forsters' flat *does* come into it and I can't pretend it doesn't. But why do I have to marry him? Why can't we live together? Reasons came to mind at once: Aidan wanted to be married. He'd liked being married before and wanted, like so many men on their own, to repeat the experience. And I hated being married, she told herself, but that in itself shouldn't mean I'm scared of something that would be quite different. Am I scared?

Vina got out of bed and put on her dressing-gown. I'm not scared. Also, from a financial point of view, everything would be so much easier. All the financial and legal stuff would be far simpler if we were married.

The sun was shining into the kitchen as she made a cup of coffee. She sat down at the table, looking at the pale green ceramic fruit bowl, and tried to imagine herself on that balcony over the river, looking at St Paul's on a fine summer day. They could fit a small table and two chairs out there. Oh, for Heaven's sake, she chided herself, *do it*. What's the matter with you? She was on the point of picking up her phone when it rang.

'Iris? Hello!'

'Hello, Vina. Are you sitting down?'

'Yes . . . yes, I am.' Vina could feel her heart beginning to beat a little faster.

'I've got an offer for your house from Patrick. Mr Taylor. The artist, remember?'

'Of course I remember. Really? Does he really want to make an offer? I thought he seemed keen but I've been wrong before . . .'

'He loves the house and is offering the full price.' Iris sounded triumphant.

'Oh, Iris, that's brilliant. I couldn't be more pleased. Thank you. *Of course I accept.* That's the best news ever. Thanks so much for telling me.'

'Vina? May I ask you something? What did you think of the Forsters' flat?'

'Is it still unsold?'

'Yes, but I'm holding off a couple of oligarchs. Not really, but as you can imagine there's a bit of interest.'

'I loved it. There's something I have to do now but I'll be back to you soon. Okay?'

'Fine,' said Iris. 'I'll be waiting for your call. Patrick will be so thrilled. Thank you.'

Vina noticed the *Patrick* and wondered whether she was right about him and Iris. Then she picked up the phone and texted Aidan. *Hello, Aidan. Can you meet me for coffee? I can be there in an hour. Prestwick's at 11.00?*

She thought for a moment, then added two kisses. Aidan noticed things like that, and she wanted to kiss him, so they were telling the truth. His answer came at once. *I'll be there. A xxx*

He was there when she arrived, and seeing him peering anxiously through the window, looking out for her, made her realize how much she loved him and why. He stood up as she approached the table and they hugged, clinging to one another till he whispered, 'The waitresses are a bit shocked, Vina. Let's sit down.'

The waitresses in Prestwick's were in fact taking no notice, or at least pretending to.

Aidan and Vina spoke in unison.

'Vina . . .'

'Aidan . . .'

'You first . . .' he said.

Vina was about to speak when the waitress approached, and they ordered two cappuccinos.

'Cake?' Aidan asked.

'No, thanks.' Vina couldn't imagine eating anything till she'd spoken. As soon as the waitress was out of the way, she said, 'Aidan, I'm so sorry. I am, really. I haven't been able to sleep since the last time I saw you. I had to think but it's been, oh, it's been awful. I hate being without you and I'd love to marry you.'

With the relief of saying those words, the happiness that filled her immediately they'd left her mouth, Vina felt as if she'd drunk a magic potion. Aidan stared at her, astonished, hardly able to believe what she'd just said. 'I am . . .' he began. 'I'm happy. You've made me really, really happy, Vina. I feel like shouting!'

'And I feel like a bit of cake.'

When the waitress brought their coffee, they ordered two slices of apple and cinnamon cake.

'I had a phone call from Iris before I came here,' Vina said. 'A chap called Patrick Taylor, an artist, has made an offer for my house and I've accepted. Do you think we can really afford the Forsters' flat, if we're married?'

'I'm pretty sure we can. We'll have to talk to our accountants but, yes, I think it's doable.'

And, Vina reflected, that meant the Forsters would be able to buy Aidan's house. Sometimes, she thought, things *do* work out as we want them to.

AIDAN

Aidan and Vina were in Mansfield Cottage doing what Vina called 'culling'. This involved going through all his possessions (and, surprisingly, a great many of Grace's too) and deciding what needed to be taken to charity shops, to the skip or recycled. Some things would be kept, of course, but the 'keeping' pile was satisfactorily small. Aidan wondered yet again at the way stuff accumulated. Grace had gathered a great many ornaments, for instance, that Aidan had not even been fully aware of. When Vina picked up a vase or a dish and asked him, 'What about this?' he found himself having to focus quite hard to take in what he was making a judgement about.

'I haven't been looking at things,' he said. 'This was all Grace's stuff. I like some of the pictures, but as far as crockery and cutlery and ornaments are concerned, I don't mind what you dispose of. Honestly.'

'Fine,' said Vina. 'But I still feel I have to ask you.'

She was sitting on the floor, handing Aidan the books she had managed to get him to part with. He was putting them into boxes, reflecting that they would be doing far more good in someone else's hands: someone who would actually read them. So many volumes had sat on the shelves unopened for many years.

'What about jewellery?' she asked. 'I'm sorry to have to ask you this, but did Grace have any?'

'I gave it all to her sister. Her daughter, Grace's niece, we thought might like it. I didn't . . . Well, I saw no reason to keep it. And there wasn't much. Grace wasn't a great jewellery wearer.'

Vina smiled. 'Not like me.'

'No.' Aidan leaned over the box they were packing, and managed to reach just far enough to give her a quick kiss on the nose. 'I know about you and jewels.'

'I can't help it. I love them. Speaking of which, have you given any thought to wedding rings? An engagement ring? I'd love an engagement ring. I never had one from Geoff and I can't think why. He's such a conventional chap but he fell down there. Could we choose a ring for me together? And our wedding rings?'

'I'm afraid that won't be possible,' Aidan said. 'I've already made plans. The rings are completely under control.'

'What?' Vina rocked back on her heels and laughed. 'Under control? What on earth d'you mean? You're not someone who has plans about rings.'

'Well, I have, so there you are. I'm happy to see I can still surprise you. The rings are a secret. Will you trust me?'

'I suppose I'll have to. You're a dark horse.'

'I am. I really am.'

'Then I'll stop nagging you. Let's change the subject. Are you okay to come to George's with me tomorrow? She's been begging me to bring you round since I first mentioned you.'

'I'm fine. I'm looking forward to it.'

They went on packing together without talking much. Aidan loved times like this, when he could go into his thoughts and be silent, knowing that Vina was next to him, happy to be near him just as he was happy to be near her.

The last couple of weeks had been full of comings and goings about the house move. It had been so long since he had moved house that he'd forgotten the hoops you had to jump through. First the financial stuff – that had been exhausting. They'd spent hours working out the money and it had become clear quite soon that it was going to be a tight squeeze, but they'd both agreed it would be worth it. They'd sorted the finances now, and the lawyers were doing what lawyers do, and very soon, there would be an exchange of contracts and Mansfield Cottage would turn into the Forsters' ideal home. It would no longer be his house and, however much he searched his heart, Aidan couldn't find a speck of regret or nostalgia when he thought of leaving it. He'd taken it for granted for years, and since Grace had died, he'd not felt particularly attached to it. Now he and Vina would be married and move into that flat. At times he couldn't believe that things had worked out so well. So symmetrically. The last time he'd spoken to Iris, he'd asked her about it.

'Does it often happen? A straight swap, I mean?'

'Not often,' she said, smiling at him. 'But I'm so pleased it's happened for you.'

'I think we have a lot to thank you for, don't we?'

'I suppose so,' Iris said. 'Look at it this way. Sometimes things come up and I just *know* that certain people belong in certain properties. It doesn't always go so smoothly, I can tell you. I sometimes fail and people make quite avoidable mistakes, in spite of what I've tried to tell them. But in this case, it's worked out beautifully and I'm so happy for you and Mrs Brownrigg.'

At that point, he'd told Iris about the wedding and she'd leaped out of her chair and hugged him. 'Oh, that's wonderful! I mean, I knew you'd be living together, of course, but this is extra wonderful. When are you getting married? That is really, really brilliant.'

'Please don't tell Vina I told you. I swore I wouldn't tell a soul. We're having a silent wedding. That's even quieter than quiet. No one is coming. Just us.'

'Shan't say a word,' Iris had promised. 'You can trust me.'

Vina interrupted his thoughts and he came back to the present. 'Have we done enough, d'you think? I'm tired. Let's go for a walk before it's dark.'

'Good idea,' said Aidan. 'I was getting a bit fed up with packing things into boxes.'

'I could tell. You were miles away. What were you thinking about? Your complicated plans for the rings?'

'I was thinking about how circular everything was: us going to the Forsters', them coming here and, from what you say, your house going to a chap who's keen on Iris.'

'More than keen.' Vina stood up. 'Besotted more like. And I reckon she's quite taken with him, too, so that's good.' She put out her hand to help him to his feet.

'Come on,' she said. 'Let's take advantage of the fields and things while we still can. We'll be taking walks by the river quite soon.'

Aidan had never met anyone quite like George before. Vina had told him a great deal about her: how she'd been a famous dress designer in the sixties, known for her extravagant colours and daring tailoring. He'd had no idea what *daring tailoring* meant and Vina had tried to enlighten him.

'Different ways of cutting jackets. Asymmetrical hems. Seaming on the outside. All sorts of things. Unexpected fabrics for things, like tweed ballgowns.'

'Really? Tweed ballgowns? I can't imagine that.'

'She did lots of stuff that people couldn't imagine at the

time. A real innovator. Then she turned to knitwear and became famous for putting colours together in unusual ways. She's great. You'll like her.'

Aidan decided he did like George. She looked a little strange, draped in scarves and with a few necklaces clanking around as well, but she was friendly and shrewd, and had put out a very delicious cake, which they ate with cups of strong Earl Grey tea. She was also far more frank than he had been expecting.

'Well, Vina, you didn't exaggerate. He's dishy,' George said, turning to Vina and winking. 'You're a very lucky woman.'

He hadn't heard anyone say *dishy* for decades. Aidan didn't know where to look or what to say. That didn't matter because George simply ploughed straight on: 'And you, of course, are a very lucky man. Vina is a jewel.'

Aidan nodded and ate his cake and half listened and half daydreamed as the women discussed the business side of the handover of the day-to-day running of the business from George to Vina. After much discussion and chat, which often veered away from the matter at hand to gossip and jokes, it was decided that the two women would initially enter into a partnership agreement, which meant that George could still be involved in an advisory capacity, and they could decide on a split of the profits. George would bow out in time, but while they were partners, each would still be responsible for her own accounting and tax.

Aidan stopped listening to the details as they were discussed. The flat was very warm and he could feel his eyes closing. I mustn't, he thought. It's only old men who fall asleep in armchairs. He sat up straighter and concentrated on looking at Vina, and smiled when he thought of how cunning and inspired he'd been in the matter of wedding and engagement rings.

JOSIE

'You must be completely fed up with us coming round for this and that,' said Josie to Aidan.

'Not at all. I'm always delighted to see you. But you'll forgive me if I go upstairs and do a bit of work while you're here? I'll come down when I've finished what I'm doing and play with Zak for a while.'

'You don't have to, really. He doesn't expect it. He's perfectly happy running round the garden. Will is in the shed, planning stuff. It's just, well, this is so much fun for him. And for us.' She smiled. 'Isn't it marvellous how things worked out with us doing a swap? I'm so grateful to Iris for arranging it.'

'Oh, so am I,' said Aidan. 'I'll see you later. Please help yourself to coffee or tea and so on.'

Once he'd left the room, Josie stood in the kitchen and closed her eyes. Everything was coming together in a way that was so neat and so well organized that she frequently found herself offering up fervent prayers to the gods who looked after house moves that nothing should go wrong at this stage. She couldn't bear that. Other things too: the way they'd met John in the park, Will's new job as his manager and general financial, online whizz-kid, the pet portraits, which were still keeping her busy . . . I'll have to get a proper website, she thought. Will can help me set it up. A sudden strong feeling of what their life would be like in Mansfield

Cottage came over her and she began to imagine the kitchen she was standing in stripped of Aidan's stuff and how it would look once some of their furniture had been moved in. The red sofa in the corner. The antique dresser over there . . .

It was time to go and check on Zak. She went out of the back door into the garden, where he was busy building a house for some snails he'd come across, using an assortment of flower pots arranged in a complicated pattern. She grinned. The whole point of snails was that they carried their houses on their backs but that didn't stop Zak from trying to get them to live cooperatively in what looked like a kind of snaily Shard.

Josie called, 'Hello, darling,' as she passed him. He glanced up at her briefly, waved and returned to his task. She went down the path to the shed, to find Will as absorbed as Zak had been. He was sitting on a bench looking at his iPad and Josie went to sit next to him.

'First things first,' he said. 'I've measured up. It ought to be very easy to get this wired and ready to go with heat and light and stuff. It'll make a fantastic office. John's coming over later to have a look.'

'Ace,' said Josie, as the phone in her jeans pocket began to ring. Her mother. Did she want to talk to her? Should she let the call go to voicemail? No, she decided. That would only put off the conversation till later.

'Hello, Mum.'

'Hello, darling. Is this a good time to talk?'

'Yes, it's fine. We're at the house.'

'How exciting! But I'm ringing about something specific, dear. D'you remember Florrie?'

'No, who is she?'

'You did a portrait of her only a couple of weeks ago. I'd have thought you'd remember, honestly. A black and white Collie cross. Lovely dog!'

It was coming back to Josie. 'I do remember. The photo had her on the bed with a Moomin toy, right?'

'Yes, but you left that out. I thought Marjorie would mind but she didn't at all.'

Why would she? Josie thought. Surely even dogs wouldn't like an image of themselves that included a much-chewed toy they'd had since they were a puppy. And her brief didn't extend to Moomin portraits.

'What about Florrie, then?' said Josie.

'She's pregnant!' Josie's mother sounded as though this were a personal triumph for her.

'Congratulations to her, but I still don't know why you're telling me.'

'Then you're being slow, if you don't mind my saying so. I'm ringing because there will be puppies very soon and Marjorie is already looking for good homes for them. I thought you were about to get a puppy for Zak.'

'Oh! Right! Well, that's very kind of you, Mum. That's a great idea.'

'You have to be careful with dogs. We know the parents of this litter so you'll have none of the worry about puppy farms and so on. Also, Marjorie will charge far less than another breeder, whom you don't know. She'll be so happy to find a kind owner who's known to her. She's very particular, you know, and she wouldn't let just any old person take one of Florrie's children.'

'Puppies.'

'Puppies, children, same thing, really.'

Josie raised her eyebrows, but she saw the point her mother was making.

'The puppies are due in a couple of weeks. Why don't you all come down when they've arrived, and see what Zak thinks?'

'Yes, I suppose so. Thanks very much. I've got to go now, Mum. I'll be in touch.'

'So will I,' came the reply. 'As soon as Florrie's given birth. I'll send you a photo of her now. Watch out for it coming through. Bye, darling!'

'Bye, Mum.'

Josie was about to tell Will what her mother had said when the photo came through as promised. She was looking at it when Zak came barrelling through the door, asking for a drink.

'Look, Zak,' Josie said. 'What d'you think of this dog? She belongs to a friend of Granny's. I did a picture of her, remember?'

Zak looked. 'Florrie,' he said. 'I like her. She's got a nice nose.'

'She has. What about getting a dog like Florrie?'

Zak's eyes widened. 'Really? When? Can we have a dog today?'

'No, not today and not just yet, because we're not moving in till December, but quite soon. How would you like that?'

Zak was still staring at the phone, at Florrie's intelligent face. 'I really, really like this dog,' he said solemnly. 'Can I have a drink now?'

'Okay, let's go back to the house,' Josie said, then to Will: 'You coming for a coffee?'

Will shut his laptop. 'Why not? Getting a bit nippy. And from what I've overheard, we seem to have a solution to the dog problem. Is that right?'

'Yup! I think we've found our puppy,' Josie said. 'Fingers crossed. Unless every one of Florrie's litter is hideous and Zak hates them all. He can take his pick.'

'He'll want to bring the entire litter back with him. You watch.'

'Well, he can't. He'll have to choose the one he likes best.'

IRIS

'He's gorgeous! And he was a hero, honestly,' said Penny. 'I wasn't in a fit state to notice much that night, but how he was with Maria was just – you'd think he'd known her all her life. Like a real friend. And gorgeous. I did say that, didn't I?'

'You did,' said Marilynne, and Anne nodded. 'Iris, you're blushing! We need an update.'

Iris smiled at her friends, sitting around the kitchen table in June's house. June had left for her shift at work, having given the girls, as she still called them, the same meal she'd provided many times while they were at school together: spag bol. Even Marilynne, whose diets passed in a kind of endless loop through her life (gluten free, sugar free, low fat, GI) without having much effect on her shape, had abandoned her fussiness for the evening, unable to resist the lure of this childhood favourite.

Iris had spent the last couple of weeks in a daze of happiness. What had happened, she wondered, to make everything come so right in so many directions? There was Patrick, most of all. She had to stop herself texting him every so often to ask: *Is it true? Is it happening?*

They'd met every day (for meals, for movies, for another night at the Broderick, which had become a sort of home from home), and Iris had even brought Patrick to meet June. He'd come to tea last Sunday, on his way to do some measuring up in the Brownrigg house, and Iris held her breath. She needn't have worried. Her mother liked him.

'He's nicer than Neil, isn't he?' Iris had asked her, when Patrick had gone. 'Admit it.'

'Well, I don't know him as well as I knew Neil,' said June, 'but he seems very nice, I must say.' She couldn't help adding, 'D'you ever hear from Neil?'

'He's been totally silent since that weekend, thank Heaven. He's got the sense to know there's nothing he could possibly say, right?'

'S'pose so,' said June. She'd poured herself another cup of tea and looked searchingly at Iris. 'Is Patrick going to be . . . well, is it serious?'

Iris hadn't known quite what to answer, so she said, 'I'm taking it one date at a time for the moment. It's all very . . . well, it's very new.'

Which was still true. Her friends, in their way, were asking the same thing: *Is it serious?*

She turned her attention back to Marilynne. 'An update. Well, I'm not sure how much I've already told you.'

'We want a blow-by-blow account. Have you . . . I mean, are you . . . ?'

Iris grinned. 'Okay. We've spent a few nights together. Is that what you want to know? I'm not about to go into any more detail than that.'

'We sort of knew that much,' said Anne. 'Penny told us you'd gone off together from the hospital.'

'But are you . . . is it serious?' Marilynne persisted.

'My mum asked the same thing.' Iris laughed. 'You are predictable! You want to know if he's the one, don't you?'

They all nodded emphatically.

'Well, you'll be the first to know when I know,' Iris told them. 'Now, can we change the subject, please?'

'Not quite yet,' said Penny. 'Have you met his family?'

Iris nodded. 'Some of them. Not his kids – they're both at college, but I'll be meeting them any day now. His parents live in Dulwich in a very nice house indeed. They're well off, no doubt about that. Cynthia, his mother, is one of those grey-hound women – you know, beige and grey cashmere and lots of gold and too thin. You see them in pictures at the back of *Harper's Bazaar* and *Tatler*. His dad is some kind of City person. Haven't met him yet. One sister, Tatty, is very beautiful and she works as a physiotherapist though she looks like a model. There's another sister and a brother but they all live in Scot-land so I haven't met them yet. But Tatty and his mother were very nice to me. '

'Didn't they make you feel as if you should be tugging your forelock? Or is it fetlock? I never know.' Anne giggled.

'Forelock, and no, not at all. They were great. Maybe they think I'm his best hope of getting a nice house of his own. And I think I have. I've found him a wonderful house.'

Iris smiled, glad that the talk had turned to property. She was much happier to discuss houses than she was to talk about her love life. 'I'm very proud indeed of bringing Patrick and that house together. Gorgeous garden, elegant sort of place with stained-glass windows, you know the kind of thing. Edwardian. Four bedrooms.'

'But he's a single man,' Anne said. 'Why does he need four bedrooms?'

'He doesn't, I guess, but he wants them. He likes walls.'

'Walls?' All three of Iris's friends looked bemused.

'To hang a lot of paintings on,' said Iris, and they nodded

wisely. She stood up. 'Anyone fancy a slice of lemon meringue pie?'

'This meal,' said Marilynne, 'is turning into a total nightmare. But yes, please. In for a penny, eh?'

Much later, Patrick Skyped her as she sat at the ridiculous dressing-table of her teenage years.

'You look drained and ghostly,' he said. 'Are you okay?'

'Full of flattering comments as ever, I see. I'm fine. It's Skype that's responsible. I hate it.'

'I love it. I can see you. I wish I could leap out at you through the screen.'

'Have you done everything at Vina's house that you wanted to do?'

He nodded. 'But I need your input. You're good at decorating-type stuff, aren't you? Furniture et cetera. My mother says I can have some things from her house but I have to fill all these rooms. Well, not fill them but you know what I mean.'

'I'll help you,' Iris said, and suddenly there was nothing she wanted to do more than make Patrick's house beautiful for him. For them both, perhaps, because it did seem as though she would be spending a great deal of time there too.

Once again, he read her mind. He did that often. 'It's got to be what you like because you're going to be here a lot too, right?'

She nodded. He prompted her. 'Say you'll be here a lot, Iris. Please say it.'

'I will. I'll be there a lot. You'll have trouble getting rid of me, I promise.'

'I won't ever want to get rid of you. Never.'

After they'd spoken for another quarter of an hour or so,

Patrick said, 'I'm off now. Night-night.' He blew a kiss in her direction, and it was all Iris could do to stop herself leaning forward and kissing the actual screen, which held Patrick's slightly distorted image.

'Night-night,' she said, blowing a kiss back. 'See you tomorrow.'

The screen went dark and the echo of Patrick's words was still with her. *I won't ever want to get rid of you, Iris. Never.*

Lying in her narrow bed, staring up at the ceiling, Iris went through all the other things she was happy about: Josie and Will getting Mansfield Cottage; Vina and Aidan getting the flat they loved, especially now that they were going to be married. That struck Iris as the best news of all.

What about you? a voice in her head asked. If Patrick were to propose to her, what would she say? *You're getting way ahead of yourself,* she answered. He's an artist, with a career and a new house. A wife doesn't necessarily come into his plans. Did being a wife come into *her* plans? Wasn't it enough that he wanted her to be with him? *I won't ever want to get rid of you, Iris. Never.*

That's what I feel, Iris wanted to tell him. *I don't want to be rid of you, either. I want to be with you. Always.* She turned over to bury her face in the pillow. To her that meant Patrick was what Penny and the others still persisted in calling *the one,* even though they were no longer seventeen. The idea that the two of them might not be together for ever made her feel desperate. Something might part them: a quarrel, some external thing (he might meet someone else on his travels) or, in her worst nightmare, something might happen to him that she had no control over (accidents, illnesses). Those thoughts tormented her. I give up, she told herself. I can't pretend any more. I love him. This must be what love is, what I'm feeling now.

Iris sat up in bed and turned on the light. *I love him so much. What will I do if he doesn't love me?* She found that her stomach was doing strange things and her heart was beating very fast.

She put on her dressing-gown and went downstairs for another slice of lemon meringue pie. That would help her get to sleep, if only her heart would stop leaping about in her chest.

VINA

'You're up early,' said Aidan, putting his head around the door of the Knitting Room.

Vina turned from her desk to smile at him. 'So are you. It's only seven o'clock. I woke up at five and couldn't sleep so I've come in here to work on some designs. It's relaxing, like filling in a crossword.'

'Why couldn't you sleep? Are you nervous?'

'No, not nervous. Excited. I'm really excited.'

'Me too. Hang on a mo. I'm going to get something.'

He disappeared in the direction of the bedroom and Vina turned back to her work. She was designing a cushion with a complicated Fair Isle pattern in shades of beige and grey and cream; filling in the colours on the graph had been keeping her mind off her first wedding, which she hadn't enjoyed in the slightest. It wasn't that she hadn't loved Geoff at the time, but she had hated the fuss. His mother was an obsessive person who'd taken the Big Wedding bit between her teeth and over-ridden all Vina's wishes, so that her bridesmaids (*You can't have a wedding without bridesmaids*) were togged out in a hideous shade between fuchsia and purple and had had to carry bouquets of yellow flowers. Vina shuddered.

Today would be nothing like that. Aidan had booked the time at the register office. They would be married, then have a pleasant lunch somewhere. She'd already decided what to wear: a plain, elegant dress in the shade of blue she particularly liked – French navy. She would put her dark red cashmere jacket in the car in case it turned cold.

'I'm back,' said Aidan. He was carrying two small boxes. He sat down in the armchair near her desk and put the boxes next to her computer. 'I've been worrying about how and when to give you . . . Well. It seemed to me that there ought to be a significant place and time for this but I haven't managed to find it. So I think I'll just give you my wedding present right now. Okay?'

Vina touched the boxes. They were very pretty: dull gold and tied with black satin ribbon. 'I've got you a wedding present, too, but I can't give it to you yet for reasons I can't go into.'

'You didn't have to, Vina. Really.'

'I wanted to.'

'Please will you open the boxes?'

'Why are you so impatient? I like thinking about what might be inside.'

'This present has been burning a hole in my pocket, as they say, for a good few days. I've been longing to give it to you. Open the little box first.'

Vina untied the black ribbon and opened the box. A plain white gold ring set with a large, perfectly round moonstone lay on a bed of black velvet, and as she looked at it, Vina's eyes filled with tears. She opened her mouth to speak and couldn't. After staring at the ring for a few seconds, she managed an 'Oh', which was more like a sigh than a word.

'It's an engagement ring, my darling. From me to you. D'you like it? Say you do . . . Say I haven't made a terrible mistake.'

Vina stood up and went to hug him. 'Oh, my love, it's *so*

339

beautiful. The utterly perfect ring. How did you – where did you get it? Why didn't you say? I can't believe it.'

'Let me put it on your finger, Vina. Give me your hand.'

She put out her left hand and Aidan slipped the ring on. It fitted perfectly. 'How did you know the size?' she said.

'I asked Libby.'

'Libby? When?'

'Come down for a bit of breakfast and I'll tell you the whole story.'

'Hang on a sec. Is this . . . did Libby design this ring?'

Aidan beamed. 'I commissioned it from her. Ages ago. And now you must open the other box.'

'You commissioned jewellery from my daughter without telling me?'

'I couldn't, could I? It was a surprise.'

Vina laughed. 'So what's in this box, then? I assume it's also Libby.'

'You should be able to guess.'

'I'm guessing wedding rings. Am I right?'

Aidan nodded. 'Have a look,' he said.

The wedding rings were also white gold and each of them had two delicate raised lines of thin, pale gold going round the circumference, like tiny waves. 'These are,' Vina said, 'simply beautiful. Beautiful. I hate to think how much you must have paid Libby.'

'I'm starving. Come down and have some breakfast.'

'I spoke to her on the phone a few weeks ago,' Aidan explained. 'I told her exactly what I wanted. She was very amused by the whole thing. She knew your size and told me how to get mine, so I went into a jeweller's and did it. Also while I was there, I looked around to make sure I wasn't making a mistake, but I wasn't. Nothing I saw was nearly as nice as these are.'

'*Nice* isn't quite how I'd have described them. They're . . . Well, I'm speechless. Not just because I love the fact that you did that, that you asked Libby, which makes me so happy, but that she didn't let you down. That she really *is* as good as I've been telling her she is for the last few years. She lacks confidence, you know, but these . . . I bet she's thrilled with them too, you know.'

'Well, when I Skyped her the day I got them in the post, she did seem pleased. She also said a nice thing. I must tell you. It was along the lines of things always coming out better when they were made with love.'

'Really? Libby said that? That's wonderful. I'll ring her as soon as we're married and thank her. And I don't know how I can possibly thank you.'

'No need. None at all.' He stood up from the table. 'I'm going to shower and dress and then we ought to get going.'

People, Vina reflected, as she loaded the dishwasher, are very odd. Who would have thought Libby could make such things? They were so different from her usual designs. How much must they have cost Aidan? Libby would have been delighted with the money and Vina was pleased to have still more evidence of his great kindness. She opened her phone and took a photo of her left hand, then sent it to Libby with a message: *This is the most beautiful ring in the whole world and I love it and you. Thank you so much, darling. Mum*

She left the kitchen and went upstairs to dress, wondering whether she had a necklace to match the magnificence of her beautiful moonstone. Before she'd reached the bedroom the phone in her dressing-gown pocket pinged and she stopped on

341

the landing to read Libby's reply. *Love you too. Have a happy wedding day. Love to Aidan. L x*

They took a taxi to the register office and were waiting for their turn to go in, sitting on hard chairs in a pleasant sort of corridor. Vina whispered to Aidan, 'It's like waiting to go and see the head, isn't it?'

'Or the doctor,' Aidan whispered back. Their witnesses, a very respectable-looking pair of middle-aged ladies, were sitting alongside them. Aidan had been uncertain that they'd find anyone suitable. He'd worried in the car. 'I don't want just any old bod,' he'd said.

'Then we should have asked someone we knew.'

'But you wanted a silent wedding, as you call it.'

'Too late now,' Vina had replied cheerfully. 'We'll find someone lovely, don't worry.'

'I *am* worried. A bit, anyway.'

'I'll fix it. Leave it to me.'

And she felt very satisfied with Sylvia and Dulcie, who had 'just come out for a little walk'. They lived in flats nearby, and were only too happy to witness a marriage between two people they'd never met before and would never see again. Aidan had shaken their hands, and Vina had noticed how they fluttered and simpered around him. She was getting used to the effect he had on women of a certain age and felt ridiculously happy at the idea that he was marrying her.

At last, the doors opened and a jolly gang of young people and their older relations, about twenty of them, came out. The bride, Vina noticed, was wearing a dress that wouldn't have been out of place in Westminster Abbey, and all the women guests were in fascinators and teetering on very high heels.

The room they were called into had been designed for weddings. There were jardinières overflowing with flowers in every corner and the registrar was dressed in a pale grey suit. She was a pleasant woman of about fifty, with a helmet of Margaret Thatcher-ish hair. Vina scarcely heard the words. She was conscious of Aidan trembling beside her. She fixed her gaze on the wall behind the registrar's head and said the words. Then the time came for the ring to be put on and there was her hand, held in Aidan's, and the wedding ring slid over her knuckle to take its place above the moonstone. Then she put Aidan's ring on his finger and it looked strange there. He'd never worn a ring before, he'd told her, but wanted to now. Vina felt more touched by this than she could easily explain.

After they emerged into the early November sunshine, Sylvia said, 'Thank you so much for asking us to be witnesses. It's made our day. Wait till we tell them at the bridge club!'

'We must thank *you*,' Aidan said. 'We couldn't have got married without you.'

Everyone laughed at this kind but obviously silly remark, and Dulcie said, 'Now, we have to have some photos, don't we? Shall I take a picture of you both?'

There was no way of refusing, so Aidan put his arm gallantly round Vina's waist and she leaned into him. Dulcie made them stand there while she took about a dozen shots. 'Because you never know which one is going to be good, do you? Could you face one another, d'you think?'

Dulcie obviously fancied herself another David Bailey, but Vina turned and looked at Aidan and he at her, and that turned out to be the shot that encapsulated the day for her: Aidan more than ever like an old-fashioned movie star and she gazing up at him, looking not bad herself, with the rings visible in the foreground.

'Thank you,' she said to Dulcie. 'I'm glad you suggested it.'

The two witnesses trotted off down the road, and Vina said, 'I've never wanted lunch more in my life. But, first, I'm going to send Libby and Rob this photo.'

Over lunch, they discussed the matter of what Vina would call herself now that she was married.

'Why haven't I even thought about it before?' she said, running her spoon round a small glass bowl that had contained tiramisu. 'Not Brownrigg. I've always regretted that name and I'll be glad to shed it. My maiden name isn't much better. Hopson. Not even Hobson. D'you mind if I become Mrs Church?'

'I'd be honoured. But isn't it deadly boring? I've never been that keen on it.'

'Not boring at all. Aidan Church is most distinguished and just the name for a book cover. And Vina Church is good too. I like it. Not Davina, because that's a bit too near "divine" and would be silly with Church.'

'Fine,' said Aidan. 'Hello, Vina Church. We should go home now and pack. Our train leaves at five o'clock. I've asked the waiter to order us a cab.'

'Pack? Pack what? What do you mean?'

'For our honeymoon.'

'What honeymoon?'

'Didn't I tell you? Oh, gosh! It must have slipped my mind.' He grinned. 'We're off to Torquay for three nights. I've booked us a room at the Grand Hotel. Thought we might go and visit Greenway.'

It was at this point, when she was happier than she'd ever been in her life, that Vina burst into tears. She said, 'You're an angel. You're the most thoughtful man I've ever met and I'm just so lucky . . . so lucky. I can't get over it! You've thought of everything I've always wanted to do. I *love* Agatha Christie. I've been longing to visit Greenway. And the Grand Hotel – that's *her* hotel. How did you know?'

'You told me. You've got every one of her books on your shelves, and you mentioned Greenway when we were in Paris. I remember these things. I just listened.'

'Most people don't. Most husbands don't. Last husband I had *never* did. It's . . . I can't get over it.'

The waiter came to their table to tell them the cab was waiting outside. He was carrying a small bouquet of white roses. 'You are married today, yes?' he asked Vina, and she nodded. 'With the compliments of the management, Madame,' he said, and bowed as he presented them to her.

'Oh, my goodness,' she said, 'that's really lovely of you. I shall treasure this. Thank you.'

As the train drew away from the platform at Paddington, Vina took out her phone. She found the photo of herself and Aidan, the one that showed off the rings to such good effect and sent it to Iris with a one-word message. *Married.*

Winter

ROBINSON & TYLER

Wish their customers the compliments of the season and a very happy New Year.

Bruce, Iris, Dominic and Holly

Always ready to help you find the house of your dreams . . .

IRIS

'Champers, everyone. Right now,' said Bruce, as Iris, Dominic and Holly gathered round his desk. 'Well, it's a special occasion. I can't think of when we've had such a good autumn. Mostly, I have to say, thanks to you, Iris.'

Iris blushed, and the others raised the fancy paper cups Holly had gone to buy in her lunch hour.

'And,' Bruce continued, 'I've got a bit of news for you. Head Office says we've done so well that we can become somewhat bigger and grander. They're giving us a complete refurb after Christmas, and when we get back into this office – I'm not breaking any confidences here, I've already spoken to Iris – Iris will officially be the branch manager. The new Bruce, in other words.'

'Hey! How cool is that?' said Holly, taking a sip of champagne. 'But what about you, Bruce?'

'Oh, I'll still be around, don't worry. I'm going to be rebranded as executive officer. Head Office is rejigging everything but basically we'll all be moving up a step on the ladder. With pay rises all round, it goes without saying. More champagne, Iris?'

'Yes, please,' she said. Patrick was picking her up after work in his car, so she could take a few more sips. Branch manager sounded good, and the extra money was great, but Iris foresaw things going on exactly as before, which she found she didn't object to at all.

'It's had its ups and downs, but they've done it at last,' Iris to Patrick. ' Finances arranged, lawyers dealt with, surveys done. They'll be exchanging contracts on the fifth and moving on the sixth.'

They were in Vina's house, working out what Patrick needed to do before moving in. They'd also brought the painting Vina had chosen as a wedding present for Aidan. She'd looked at Patrick's website, and chosen it from there, but he'd agreed that if she turned out to be disappointed with the real thing, she could choose something else. Iris and Patrick were taking advantage of Vina's absence on her honeymoon to visit the house and leave the picture in a cupboard Vina had pointed out to them. Many of the things she no longer wanted had already been taken away, but Patrick had agreed to buy quite a lot from her, including the big fridge-freezer, and the oak table and chairs. The lovely Welsh dresser in the kitchen had become a straight swap for his painting. He'd also bought most of the curtains, which were lovely and in good condition. The walls would need painting and Iris was a bit surprised that Patrick was intending to do this himself. 'Wouldn't it be easier to get someone in for that?' she'd asked.

'Absolutely not. I love decorating. You can help if you like, at weekends. Are you any good at it? Wallpapering maybe? Won't take more than three or four days, I don't think.'

'I've never tried. I'm good at choosing paint colours and buying cushions and things like that.'

'I bet you are. As for the painting, I'll teach you and we'll do some of it together. But tell me how it's going to go, this moving-day dance.'

'Well, Vina will move out of here at ten and her van will go to the flat. Josie will hand over the keys to Vina, and then Josie and Will's van, already packed up, will go from the flat to Mansfield Cottage at twelve, getting there at about one. Aidan will give them his keys, and then he'll be in a van leaving at about three. By teatime on the sixth, they'll all be in their new homes with their things, and I'll be dead chuffed.'

'Great. Come and have a look at the picture Vina liked. I've brought bubble wrap and tape with me so that she can wrap it when she's seen it, if she likes it.'

When Patrick took it out of the big carrier-bag and leaned it against Vina's sofa, Iris gasped. 'Oh, that is so beautiful . . .'

'D'you really like it?'

'It's just . . .' Iris didn't have the words to describe what she felt. It was something to do with how her heart lifted when she looked at it. She tried to list the colours on the canvas in front of her: she could see apricot and bronze and white, and there was a streak of pale green and a shadow that was blue, or maybe mauve, a line of pink . . .

'It reminds me of a garden,' she said at last. 'I love it. I can see why Vina chose it. It'll remind her of the garden she's leaving, I guess.'

'I didn't think she'd choose one of the abstracts but she did. She said it reminded her of Monet and she reckoned Aidan would like it too. I was very flattered.'

Iris leaned closer to the picture to see the details of the brushwork, delicate and luscious at the same time. Patrick touched her shoulder. 'Iris?'

'Hmm? I'm looking more carefully at your picture.'

'Well, you can stop looking for a bit. I want to ask you something.'

Iris straightened up and turned to smile at him. 'Okay, go ahead.'

'Let's sit here,' he said, and took her by the hand to the sofa. They sat very close together and Patrick's arm was around her shoulders. He said, 'I wondered if . . .' He hesitated.

'If what?'

'If you'd move in here with me. We could live together. Couldn't we? I'd really like that. This house is much too big for someone on his own. Actually, it's a bit too big for two people living on their own. But two's better than one, right?'

'You'd like us to live together? Honestly?'

'Yes, I would. Nothing strange about that. I've been with you every possible moment for about three weeks . . . What d'you reckon?'

Iris found that her head was swimming and she felt a little dizzy. Living together. Getting up in the morning together. Sharing a bed every night. Eating and cooking and cleaning and just . . . living together. 'Yes, please,' she said. 'Thank you. We'll have to work out the money side of things.'

'We'll worry about that later. Main thing is, I want to be with you, Iris. Okay?'

'Okay,' said Iris. Patrick began to kiss her then, and everything became fuzzy. Iris lost track of what was in her head – it all seemed to be floating out of her, except for two thoughts, which seemed to be there, together, in her consciousness at one and the same time: *He wants us to live together* and *He's never said he loves me. I haven't said it either but I do. I love him. Maybe he loves me too. He wants us to live together. That means he must love me. Does it mean that? He's never said it.*

Round and round they went, these two warring and almost contradictory thoughts, until Patrick reached up under her skirt and she stopped thinking about everything except the sensations that were rising through her body, overwhelming her.

JOSIE

'Mum, you know why!' Josie flopped down on the sofa and got ready for a long conversation with Phyllis. When it came to arrangements for Christmas, her family was bonkers. Discussions, negotiations, back-and-forth sessions about presents began in early September and increased in ferocity and frequency as the actual day approached.

This year things were more complicated. Josie and Will (and later Zak, too) had got into the habit of going to Sussex to spend the day, and most of Boxing Day, with Josie's whole family. Will's family Christmas was a Skype session with his mother in Australia. From Josie's point of view, it was worth putting up with some annoyance, mostly from Stuart, Matty and the twins, to have a proper family Christmas, and everything done in the traditional way, for Zak's sake. He loved playing with Mike, his grandfather, and Bobby the dog was a big attraction. Josie had never cooked a Christmas dinner in her life.

'It'll have to be a bit different this year, though, won't it?' she said. 'Because of the puppy. We're picking him up from Marjorie on the twenty-third . . . What ? . . . Oh, yes, okay, lunch beforehand with you would be nice but . . .'

'So what are your Christmas plans, then?' Phyllis came straight to the point. 'Are you considering doing it at your new house, so soon after moving in? For all of us?'

Josie did a quick calculation. Her parents could sleep in the spare room, but there wasn't room for four more. 'I'm sure we can put you and Dad up. Stuart and his lot will have to go home . . .'

'Well, I'll mention it to him and see. Not sure he'll be keen on that. He does like a drink at Christmas . . . Maybe Matty would be willing to drive . . .' Phyllis's voice faded away as she pondered the prospect. Josie secretly thought that perhaps Matty's parents might host her brother, his wife and their children. Having the whole family in Mansfield Cottage, plus a new puppy, might be a bit much.

'I really do want to do Christmas in the new house, Mum,' she said, and realized it was true. From the very first time she'd stepped into the lovely square hall at Mansfield Cottage, she'd been imagining how a beautifully decorated and lit tree would look there. She wanted to make a Christmas cake and get Zak to help her ice it.

'Well, I'm happy to come down early and help,' said Phyllis, and Josie rushed in to prevent that happening.

'No, that's okay. I do want to keep things as quiet as possible for as long as I can. I'll have the new puppy to settle in and so on. Lunchtime on Christmas Day is fine. And it's a late lunch. Two o'clock.'

Josie was making it up as she went along, but the more she thought about it, the more she began to relish the prospect of Christmas and the new puppy.

She, Will and Zak had driven down to see the litter shortly after the puppies were born in October. Zak had been so excited he'd hardly spoken on the way to Sussex, but sat staring out of the window as if the puppy would suddenly materialize outside in the road.

When they were shown into the warm shed where the puppies were squirming about with Florrie, Josie took Zak's hand and whispered, 'Remember what I told you, Zak. They're very little. They can't leave their mum for a few weeks. They won't be ready till Christmas time.'

Zak nodded, silenced by the sight of so many tiny creatures. 'I want that one,' he whispered at last, pointing to a tiny, mostly black dog with white patches on his face and tail. 'I like him best. He's called Alfie.'

That was that. Zak had fallen in love, and Josie and Will had to agree that Alfie really was the star of the litter. Between that day in October and where they were now, at the very beginning of December, Alfie's picture had been sent to Josie's phone more times than she cared to count. Every night at bedtime, they had a session of looking through the photos and seeing how the puppy had grown. Josie didn't admit it to anyone, but she was almost as excited as her son at the prospect of Alfie's arrival in Mansfield Cottage. She was pretty sure that Zak's presents this year would have a doggy theme. She'd already spent far too long on the internet looking at suitable beds for Alfie.

Christmas Day

AIDAN

'How about some more roast potatoes, Rob?' Vina said, and Aidan watched the small drama playing out at the other end of the table: Vina tempting, Rob refusing at first, even though they both knew he'd succumb in the end and have another two or three of his mother's matchless spuds. Christmas dinner was something he and Grace had never done very well: certainly another consequence of having no children. Aidan, since boyhood, had loved the carols, the decorations, the food and celebration, but over the time he was married to Grace, Christmas had shrunk and changed, and during the last two years they were together, it had all but disappeared and 25th December had become a day like any other, but with less to watch on TV.

Vina, thankfully, reacted quite differently to the festival. She wanted everything to be done to the utmost, and the table was lit with candles, and decorated with a centrepiece, which she'd made from red velvet ribbons, ivy, holly and pine cones twisted together into a sort of elongated wreath. The flat smelt wonderful too: glass bowls in jewel colours were filled with pot-pourri, which Aidan had known nothing about before he met Vina. The food was better than any Christmas dinner he'd ever eaten.

There was no tinsel to be seen anywhere. Vina disliked it, and instead used ribbons and candles and greenery. A few cards stood on the mantelpiece and Aidan was particularly touched by one from Iris. She'd signed the official one from R & T, along with the others in the office, but for her own personal message, she'd chosen a Monet, and both he and Vina smiled at the kindness of that thought. The message read: *I hope you will both be very happy together in your beautiful flat. It was lovely getting to know you. Love, Iris*

He and Vina had debated about what to buy Iris for Christmas, and whether it was even appropriate to do so. Were you supposed to give your estate agent a Christmas present?

'I don't care,' Vina had said, 'whether it's appropriate or not. I feel like giving her a present and I think she'd like a scarf. A knitted scarf. I've got a lovely one I've been working on in a colour that would suit her perfectly. I started it last month. In any case, I don't think of her as our estate agent, but more our fairy godmother.'

Everyone was talking about websites. This was because Vina had enrolled on a course that would, apparently, teach her all she needed to know about setting one up, maintaining it and dealing with the technical stuff that frightened Aidan a bit.

'You could share it,' Vina was saying to Libby, when Aidan turned his attention back to the conversation. 'You could sell your jewellery on my website, if you like. I wouldn't mind sharing with you. I think you could do a lot of business that way.'

'I sell on Etsy,' said Libby. 'It's always been okay for me.'

'Well, the offer's open. You could sell on both, surely?'

Libby nodded. 'I guess,' she said at last. 'Thanks, Mum, I'll think about it.'

'What's your website going to be called?' Janice asked. She was leaning forward and looked pretty in the candlelight.

'I'm not quite sure,' said Vina. 'Possibly Vina Church Designs.'

'Is it going to be just knitwear? The kind of thing you used to do for Georgiana?'

'To start with, I suppose,' Vina said. 'I may branch out, if it goes well. And if Libby sells jewellery, there'll be that, of course.'

'What about baby clothes?' said Janice, and Vina began to answer, explaining how they'd need to find other knitters and how, indeed, she was looking for people now because some of the older knitters had stopped work since hearing about George's retirement. Aidan studied Janice as she listened to the answer. She looked much prettier than usual, not as skinny in the face. She hadn't been drinking. Now she was asking about baby clothes. He was beginning to wonder whether . . . Could it be? Could he possibly ask? Then Janice herself spoke. 'Vina, sorry to interrupt but I do want to tell you all something.'

'Oh, God,' said Vina. 'I'm *so* sorry – I was rabbiting on. Go ahead, Janice.'

'Rob and I are expecting a baby in June. I didn't want to say anything before because . . . well, just to be safe. But we've had the twelve-week scan and . . .'

Vina made a sound between a squeak and a yell and jumped up from the table to embrace her. 'Oh, Janice, Rob! That is the *best* news, the very best news I could wish for. Like a specially wonderful present. Oh, it's marvellous! Isn't it marvellous, Aidan?'

Aidan agreed that it was. Vina looked radiant with joy. A grandchild. A child who would be a part of his life, too. He was smiling as everyone (except Janice) raised their glasses in a toast to the forthcoming baby. I'll have to make sure that balcony's safe, he thought. He glanced out of the window and what he saw reflected in the glass was the beautiful table: candles, ribbons, happy faces and, behind the reflection, the lights of the city, the riverside and the illuminated dome of St Paul's, a benevolent presence that was now part of their personal horizon: his and Vina's.

VINA

Libby had gone up to the little bedroom, up the flight of stairs near the kitchen. Janice and Rob had left to drive home. It was nearly midnight, and Vina and Aidan were sitting together on the luxurious sofa that had been (as Aidan put it, when Vina complained about the price) their wedding present to one another and also their Christmas present.

'I've still got my wedding present to you to give you. I've left it till now because I wanted us to be alone when you saw it,' she said.

'Wedding present? We're sitting on it, I thought. Wasn't that the agreement?'

'I've broken the agreement. . . you'll see.'

Aidan sat up. 'I'm curious now. Where is it? I don't see any prettily wrapped boxes.'

'It's at the back of my cupboard. I'll go and get it.'

She went into their bedroom, pausing in the doorway as she went into the room to marvel yet again at their luck. At how things had come together in this precise way when they could have been different. She shivered, went to the cupboard and took out Patrick's painting.

'Here you go,' she said to Aidan, giving him the rather bulky package. He sat up on the sofa and began to remove the paper, then the corrugated cardboard and, finally, the bubble wrap.

'What can this be?' he wondered aloud. 'It's a picture . . . Oh, my word, it's beautiful. *Most* beautiful. How very, very clever of you to find this. Where *did* you find it?'

'It's by Patrick Taylor, Iris's boyfriend. The chap who bought my house. Isn't it lovely? A bit of a selfish present because I wanted it. I wanted to look at it every day. It reminds me—'

'Of a garden,' Aidan said. 'It really *is* wonderful. I didn't know your buyer was this good. I'll look him up on the internet tomorrow. I hope it didn't set you back too much, or I'll feel guilty.'

'I swapped it for my Welsh dresser. Patrick was thrilled and Iris even more so.'

'Iris? What's she got to do with it?'

'She and Patrick are in love. I live in hope . . .'

'What of?'

'Marriage. But even if they don't marry, they'll live together for sure, and Iris loved my dresser. So I'm glad they've got it.'

'Me too. I reckon we did best out of that swap.'

Aidan leaned forward to kiss her and Vina closed her eyes. 'I love you,' he said. 'Hasn't this been a good Christmas?'

She kissed him back, and leaned against the dark red velvety cushions of the sofa. 'It has,' she said. 'And I love you too. Merry Christmas, my darling.'

JOSIE

Alfie was busily chewing a beautiful Christmas card from Iris, and Josie sighed. It was going to be difficult at first, she could see, but since the puppy had been in the house, Zak had been so happy that she was willing to be in clearing-up mode for the foreseeable future. They were all watching carefully too, to prevent Alfie from eating everything he managed to get between his teeth. She, Zak and Will had gone round the house very carefully before collecting the dog, picking up pieces of Lego and small toys of every kind, finding a cupboard and a couple of plastic storage boxes where Zak could keep them safely.

Now, he was so preoccupied with Alfie that he hardly took any of his toys out, but was glad to sit and watch the puppy, play with him, stroke him and throw small soft balls around the sitting room for him to chase. They'd gone to the local garden centre and bought Alfie some dog toys: rope to chew, a floppy pig to nibble and a selection of balls.

Alfie's first night at home set the pattern. Marjorie, a brisk and unsentimental soul, had warned Josie to lock the dog into the kitchen at night 'unless you want him on your beds for ever and ever, amen.'

On his bed for ever and ever was exactly what Zak *did* want, so Josie ignored what she had said and put the silver pet bed she'd chosen into Zak's room. Of course, Alfie had other ideas, and spent the night next to Zak, pressed up against his legs, and the silver bed returned to the sitting room.

Josie picked up what was left of the card, and Alfie, thwarted, jumped up onto the sofa and went to sleep.

'When's Granny coming?' Zak wanted to know. He had learned that when Alfie was asleep he wasn't to be woken, and however much he longed to pat the puppy's head, or stroke his tummy, that was not allowed.

'You wouldn't come and stroke me or Daddy when we were asleep, would you? Alfie needs his rest just like us.'

Zak looked doubtful but agreed after only a very short argument.

Josie was rather dreading the arrival of the guests. She'd been up late getting everything ready in the kitchen. This year, there had been a great deal of what Phyllis would, doubtless, call *cheating*. Bought pudding, cake and mince pies for a start, and the turkey (for which, Will said, they would have to get a bank loan) was ready-stuffed for putting into the oven at the right time. All they'd had to do was the vegetables and the decoration.

Everyone arrived together and, of course (why hadn't she foreseen this?), the first thing everyone wanted to do was look around the new house and garden. Luckily, lunch wouldn't be ready for ages, so Will was charged with taking care of the kitchen, Zak and Alfie, while Josie did 'The Tour', feeling like a National Trust guide.

'This,' she announced in the loft, 'used to be Mr Church's study, so I've made it into my room.' Some of her paints and pencils were neatly laid out on the huge worktable she'd bought with the money she'd already made from the pet portraits.

'And I'm going to invest in a good laptop as soon as the website is up and running. I'll get going on that in the New Year. I'm lucky Will can help me.'

'What about Will's job?' said Phyllis. 'Is he going to enjoy being a builder?'

There wasn't really a visible wrinkling of her mother's nose but Josie could almost hear it in her voice. Having a high-powered son-in-law in the City was one thing; someone who managed business for a local builder was quite another. 'He's loving it,' Josie said. 'He likes being hands-on and he's busy setting up the shed out there as an office. He's also,' she added, 'quite well paid. Not on the level of his last job, of course, but he can do lots of work from home and he likes being his own boss.'

'Isn't he working for John, though, so not his own boss?'

Josie thought about this. 'He's his own boss in his part of the business,' she told her. 'He doesn't make building decisions but he's in charge of money and contracts, that sort of thing. Also, he's going to make sure they have a much better internet presence.'

Everyone trooped downstairs to walk round the garden and exclaim about the shed and the fruit trees. Once they were all safely indoors again and the opening of presents had begun, Phyllis had actually said, 'It's a really lovely house, darling, and I think you're very clever to have found it. We must drink a toast to you all!' She raised her glass.

'Alfie too!' Zak insisted. 'Drink to Alfie, too.'

'Of course,' said Phyllis, who was being more affectionate to Alfie than to anyone else. 'And to absent friends, which is our Bobby.'

'Why didn't Bobby come for Christmas?' Zak asked.

'Because,' his grandfather chipped in, 'he's an old dog, and he doesn't like going in the car very much. He'll spend the day with Marjorie and Florrie. He'll like that.'

Josie was standing by the mantelpiece on wrappings duty. Every present that anyone opened had to be immediately put out of reach of Alfie and her job was to swoop down and gather up the paper, ribbon and tangles of Sellotape and stuff everything into the bin bag. At the end of the process, she took the rubbish to the recycling bin. As she came back into the hall of Mansfield Cottage, Josie stood quite still, looking at the Christmas tree shining in the darkness: their tree in their new house. Lights and ribbons and small decorations chosen by Zak hung on its branches, and it filled the space with a fragrance that brought with it a memory of forests. Josie smiled and made her way back to join the others.

IRIS

'That went okay,' Iris said, 'don't you think?'

'Perfect,' said Patrick. 'In every detail.'

'But a bit of a cheat, right?'

'Why? We catered Christmas, that's all. My treat. I'm too busy getting settled in, with the pictures to hang and my studio to organize, to worry about one meal. That's all Christmas dinner is, if you think about it. One meal. I'd have been happy with lasagne. Or fish and chips.'

It was one of the things Iris loved about Patrick: his total lack of interest in food. He liked eating in restaurants, but he wasn't obsessed with the right wine, the right ingredient, the right kind of utensil, and whenever she cooked for him (which she'd done more and more often since moving into the house), he appreciated whatever she put in front of him.

Patrick had fallen asleep on the sofa. Iris closed her eyes and wondered if she, too, could drift off in front of the fire for a bit but felt, oddly, more wide awake than she had done when she'd woken up that morning.

Christmas dinner with June, Patrick's parents, Cynthia and Giles, and his sister Tatty had been, for Iris, like going on stage in a play where she wasn't exactly sure of her lines. Paul and Melodie had flown to New York to spend the Christmas vacation with their mother. The others had been cheerful, very enthusiastic

about the house, and, kindly, gave Iris most of the credit for finding it. She'd been the one to show them around when they'd first
arrived while Patrick stayed downstairs, putting the final touches
to the food and getting the drinks ready. No one was in any doubt
that this was where she, too, was living. There were her cosmetics
in the bathroom, a very obvious difference in what was on each
of the bedside tables, and the king-size bed made it very difficult,
Iris thought, for anyone to ignore the fact that sex was part of
what was going on. No one said a word and, fortunately, Cynthia
and Giles hit it off very well with June. Both of Patrick's parents
had his easy charm, and Tatty was open-mouthed with admir-
ation for the house. They wanted to look at the garden too, and
Iris picked up her present from Vina, which was hanging over
her coat in the hall, even though the day was quite mild.

'Fab scarf,' said Tatty. 'Did you make it yourself?'

'No, Vina did – we bought the house from her. It was an early
Christmas present. She's a professional knitter. '

She fingered the length of soft lace in a gorgeous rust colour
(burnt sienna, Vina called it) that she would never have chosen
for herself, but which made her eyes look very blue.

'Gosh!' Tatty said. 'Would she consider making one for me?
D'you mind asking her? I'd love one like that.'

'I'll email her, if you like.'

'Brilliant!' Tatty had gone off into the garden looking very
happy.

Now she and Patrick had to talk about money. I can't live
here without contributing, Iris told herself. She'd raised the
matter with him before but he'd always waved it away, saying,
'We can talk about it another time,' and changing the subject.
She said it aloud now, testing to see if the sleeping man beside
her was properly asleep or just dozing.

'Patrick, we really do have to talk about money . . .'

'Really?'

So he *was* awake, just as she'd suspected. 'Yes. Otherwise I'll feel as if I'm not properly living here.'

'Right.' He straightened up and was immediately alert, ready for action. It was one of his gifts. 'Okay. Hang on a mo, though. I have to fetch something.'

He was gone and back in less than three seconds, carrying nothing, as far as Iris could see. 'You haven't fetched anything.'

'Yes, I have. It's in my pocket. I got it from the kitchen.'

'Okay, what is it?'

Patrick sat down on the sofa again, put his arm around her and hugged her to him. 'You're too nosy. Wait and see. I thought we were going to talk about money. Weren't we? I don't really want to talk about money one little bit.'

'What do you want to do?' Iris was becoming distracted by his breath on her neck.

'I want to tell you something,' he murmured.

'Go on, then.'

'I want to tell you I love you. I really, really love you. I love you all there is and I simply wanted you to know it.'

Iris felt as though her entire body had suddenly been flooded with light. Had any man ever said it to her before? Had Neil? In those words? In any words that might have been interpreted as those words? Did it matter? Actions spoke louder than words, didn't they? No, she thought. Not completely. Words, *these* words, spoke louder than most actions, which, when you came right down to it, were often prompted either by lust or simple kindness. Love . . . That was something else. Patrick went on, 'I think the words matter and I wanted you to be in no doubt. Because . . .'

He'd done it again. He'd read Iris's mind. She said, 'I think the words matter, too. I can't remember ever saying them to anyone before. I love you too, Patrick, so much. I have for ages but I never dared say anything.'

'I've held off because . . . well, I'm not sure why but anyway, I've said it now because it would have been odd asking you to marry me if I hadn't mentioned how much I love you. I want to be with you for ever. And, if you agree, we won't have to have the conversation about money, and your contribution to the household.'

Iris turned to face him. 'You want to marry me?'

'I want to marry you. I want you to marry me. I want us to be married. That's it.'

'Why?' Even as she said it, she knew it was a mad thing to say. 'I mean, I have to think about that. I'm not sure I want to get married.'

'You've just said you love me.'

'Oh, I do! I really, really do. And I love living together. I'm just not sure about marriage, that's all. Why is it necessary?'

'Because . . .' Patrick thought about this for a moment. 'Because I want it to be for ever. I don't want to call you my partner or my girlfriend or even my lover. I want you to be my wife. To have and to hold, all that.'

'For better, for worse,' Iris added.

'Exactly.' Patrick beamed at her. 'Will you think about it?'

'Okay. . . I will, I promise. But . . .'

'What objections are you going to raise now?'

'I ought to tell you that I don't want to have any children,' Iris said. 'I never have wanted any and I still don't.'

'I've got Paul and Melodie. And so, I'm afraid, have you, if you're going to be living with me.'

'That's okay. They're grown-up, almost, and I'm sure I'll like them.' A thought struck her. 'Maybe they won't like me.'

'Of course they'll like you. Why wouldn't they?'

'They might resent me. For living with you when their mother doesn't.'

'They're quite used to the divorce, I promise you. They'll be fine.' He smiled. 'So, now it's all sorted out, I can give you your present.'

He took an envelope out of his pocket and put it into Iris's hand. 'Go on, open it,' he said.

She tore into the paper. Inside the envelope was a photograph of a ring, lying in an open box lined with red velvet.

'Oh!' Iris said. 'That is so, so beautiful!' And it was: a large sapphire, square cut and set in gold.

'It's Victorian,' said Patrick. 'It belonged to my grandmother and my mother's been keeping it for my fiancée, hidden in the depths of her jewel box. I wanted to ask you before I said anything to her . . . I'd have had to get her permission to bring the actual ring. So I photographed it. D'you like it? You don't have to like it. We can choose something else if you'd rather have something more modern.'

'Stop, Patrick. I love it. But can it just be a ring for now, and not an engagement ring? And what if it doesn't fit?'

He laughed. 'It almost certainly won't. We'll get it altered. And, yes, you can call it a ring and wear it on the wrong hand, whatever you like. Just so long as you go on living with me.'

'I will. Of course I will . . .'

Iris got up and propped the photo on the mantelpiece. 'Can I leave it here? I want to look at it.'

'That's why I printed it out,' Patrick said. 'I could have shown you the photo on my Mac.'

She went to sit down on the sofa again. The curtains were drawn across the window. Outside, the garden lay quietly in the dark.

'Let's go to bed,' Patrick whispered in her ear.

'It's only seven o'clock,' she murmured.

'Been a bit of a tiring day,' he said.

'I guess.'

He stood up, took her hand and they went upstairs together. Exactly like, it occurred to Iris, a proper married couple.

ACKNOWLEDGEMENTS

I would like to thank the following people, who have helped me while I was writing this novel.

Sophie Hannah gave me the title and a great deal of help with many other aspects of the story.

Sue Meredith told me about knitting for money.

Dr Rupert Beale was very helpful about reasons for taking a child to A and E.

Austin Rawcliffe explained the business matters.

Michelle Lovric lives in a property I've wanted to write about ever since I saw it. She's a wonderful hostess and going there is always a treat.

Finally, I have based Aidan's historical research on a project that Helena Pielichaty is working on.

I've set my story in London and High Barnet. Some aspects of both places are factually accurate and others are not. This is a work of fiction. All properties mentioned by Bruce in his Bulletins are entirely the product of my imagination and I've left out house prices for the most part because these change.

As ever, thanks to Jane Wood and all at Quercus, especially Hazel Orme for her sensitive and sensible copyediting.